Frankie McGowan is a journalist and former magazine editor. She has written short stories for a variety of magazines, including *Women's Own* and *The Lady*, as well as longer novels for Endeavour Media.

PRAISE FOR FRANKIE MCGOWAN:

'A really good read' – *Women's Weekly*

'Will surely please everyone' – *Sunday Times*

'One of those indispensable sand sagas or towel tales, a good beach book in which to immerse yourself while relaxing' – *Daily Mail*

A SINGLE JOURNEY

FRANKIE MCGOWAN

ENDEAVOURQUILL

AN ENDEAVOUR QUILL PAPERBACK

First published by Endeavour Quill in 2018

This paperback edition published in 2018
by Endeavour Quill
Endeavour Quill is an imprint of Endeavour Media Ltd
Endeavour Media, 85-87 Borough High Street,
London, SE1 1NH

ISBN 978-1-911445-53-1

Typeset in Garamond by Palimpsest Book Production Limited,
Falkirk, Stirlingshire

Printed and bound in Great Britain by
Clays Ltd, St Ives plc

www.endeavourmedia.co.uk

For Peter.
Also for Amy and Beno and Tom and Karina.

Acknowledgements

It's a well known fact that the writer is only one part of the lengthy process of producing a book. *A Single Journey* has been no exception.

I am therefore very grateful to all those who helped me get it all together. In particular, I want to thank the group of remarkable women I met in Berlin – who for legal reasons prefer not to be named – who talked to me about their work helping abused women and their children to find safety from domestic violence.

The many people who were prepared to share their personal – and often painful – experiences in disputes over inheritance and those who patiently helped me navigate the minefield that is the law surrounding challenging a will, really do deserve my special thanks.

I am also fortunate indeed to have been able to benefit from the very talented team at Endeavour Media, and am most appreciative of their input. My grateful thanks therefore goes to them and – most especially – to the very hard work of Alice Rees who, along with Jasmin Kirkbride and Imogen Streater, got this book over the finishing line.

Huge thanks also goes to my son, Tom Glossop, owner of OrlyArt, who understands the colourful world of artisan market traders, which was invaluable to me. Rob Ellison of the British Guild of Travel Writers kindly pointed me in the direction of those who know Berlin far better than I – no more than an occasional visitor – ever could. My thanks also goes to Ingo Müller

Wodarg, Chair of Friends of Douglas House in Richmond, and the generous response from its members who found time in their busy lives to talk to me about their home town of Berlin.

In particular, I'd like to thank Wieland Jubelt, former volunteer with Berlin's social services for his help, and also Greer Decker, who so kindly shared with me, her view of that amazing city where she has worked and raised her family for many years.

I must, however, stress, that where it suited the plot of *A Single Journey*, I absolutely take full responsibility for my interpretation of the views of all these generous people.

On a very personal note, my special thanks must go to four very important people, Maeva, Ivy, Orla and Aoife, who when I'm faced with a blank screen, provide a never-ending source of displacement activity, and during the writing of this book, never failed me.

Finally, I am indebted to two people, who have undeniably been responsible for getting me through writing this book, and without whom . . .

I am – as ever – most grateful to Lisa Moylett for her truly generous support, clear thinking and endless encouragement and, of course, for making it all happen in the first place. And Peter, for – well – for hanging on in there when, on many occasions, it might have looked like I was losing the plot. Note, *might*.

www.frankiemcgowan.com
2018

Table of Contents

Prologue

Berlin, 1933

Elena slid down in her chair, her eyes darting from her mother to the woman sitting in front of her. One long, slender, heavily-ringed finger, the nail a vivid scarlet, silently sifted the contents of the black velvet-lined leather box which lay open, like a book, on the table between them. Elena caught her mother's eye.

'Up,' her mother mouthed, tilting her own chin upwards for Elena to copy. Elena sat upright, folding her hands neatly in the lap of her pale blue skirt.

The baroness – of uncertain age, and with an even more uncertain title since the new regime had abolished all such social distinctions – fluttered hesitantly between an intricate pearl-and-peridot bracelet and a delicately woven sapphire-and-diamond necklace, that sparkled sharply as the light caught it.

'The peridot,' Elena's mother, Valentina, began to explain politely, 'is still rare. This,' she pointed to the gleaming green gem, 'came from a small volcanic island, Aswan—'

The baroness stopped her in mid-sentence with a bored and impatient wave of her hand. 'No. I don't think you have anything of interest—' She began returning the trinket to the case, when a small, breathless voice burst in.

'It's known to bring good luck. The peridot, I mean. It's famous for it.'

For a moment there was a surprised silence. Valentina looked quickly between her daughter and her client, alarm written on her face.

'I mean,' Elena ploughed on, her face scarlet, a little breathless. 'It's in some of the shrines in the Cathedral in Cologne. And people pray there because peridot also attracts love and – and they say that it calms anger.'

The baroness looked Elena up and down.

'But only,' Elena trailed off, almost on a whisper. 'If the bracelet is worn on the right arm. But the necklace is also special. Its value also lies in its provenance. That means its history,' she added, when the baroness looked blank.

'Of course,' the baroness said, adding, 'I know that,' which she clearly didn't. 'I meant tell me its – history?'

'It was a present to the – the favourite mistress of the Prince Regent. Who became the English king, George the Fourth.'

For a moment the baroness was silent, carefully surveying her. Elena could not bring herself to look at her mother. The fear she knew would be there would make her lose her nerve. She should not have spoken. Not have interrupted. She'd been told to remain totally silent. Give no clues, arouse no interest. What had come over her? But if she hadn't spoken, she knew the sale would have gone. Their last chance to get some much-needed cash so they could leave everything behind, would have vanished, all for the failure of her mother to see that the woman was stupid, shallow, and that only something as ludicrous as mythical nonsense would appeal to her.

Instead she studied the floor, her brown flat shoes with the double straps across her instep that she had begged her mother to buy, and her bare legs. She fiddled with the hem of her skirt and unconsciously pulled it over her knees. Finally an amused voice asked, 'How old are you?'

'Fifteen,' Elena replied politely, adding as an afterthought, 'Baroness,' but she knew her voice was shaking.

'Not at school?'

Elena swallowed hard. She could see her mother's nails were dug deeply into the palm of each hand. She knew how much she hated being asked to make these personal visits to the homes of bored but wealthy women; women who had been installed here by their lovers or husbands, who served the new regime with blind devotion – men in impressive uniforms disguising inhuman souls. But if these smart women felt they were too grand to go to her mother's fashionable little shop, then in these desperate days, she was obliged to go to them.

'Not today,' Elena replied. 'There's a holiday. Herr Goebbels is visiting us tomorrow and the choir is practising. I'm not in the choir,' she said. 'I can't sing,' she added helpfully.

'Your school is very fortunate,' the baroness remarked. 'A busy man like Herr Goebbels finding time to visit. He has many demands on his time.' She turned to Elena's mother. Her tone was mild. 'Your daughter is an entertaining storyteller, even if she can't sing. And a born saleswoman. And I will buy the bracelet because I have been entertained on a very dull day.'

She turned to Elena, holding the bracelet. 'The right arm? Is that correct?' She slipped it on. 'And of course, I must have the necklace. Owned by the prince's mistress, you say?'

Elena nodded. Her throat was dry. Her palms were sweating. The baroness merely pressed a button to the side of her chair. Almost immediately a man appeared dressed in a very correct black suit, over a white shirt with a stiff white collar. The baroness rose.

'See to Frau Guseva,' she ordered and without a word swept from the room.

The clock – on the mantelpiece, crowded with silver-framed photographs and candlesticks in crystal holders, stretching several feet over the fireplace on the far side of the room – chimed eleven. A mere twenty minutes, or less, since they had been ushered into this vast, majestic salon, with its glass chandeliers, suspended in a perfect line along the length of the room, catching the sunlight that streamed through several sets of floor-length casement windows.

Elena couldn't wait to get outside, to walk through the Tiergarten on the far side of the elegant boulevard, away from all of this. But this meeting was so important to her mother, indeed to both of them, if their future was to be secured. What use was it now that Uncle Max was rich? It was what you believed in that now decided your fate. He couldn't turn what he owned into money just like that. In time maybe, but they didn't have time. Her mother's jewellery stock was easier. Not all of it, though. There were some pieces,

pieces Elena's father had designed so lovingly and carefully for her, that she would never part with, and that was that.

It seemed like an age before the door opened and the man reappeared. In silence, he handed a roll of notes to her mother and showed them out. It was only as they moved into the wide corridor, lined on all sides with mirrors and paintings, that Elena looked back to see him staring after her. His face was blank.

*

'I know you meant well,' her mother said, an arm protectively around Elena's shoulders. They crossed the broad boulevard in between cars and the occasional bus and hurried to be out of sight of the spying eyes of the baroness's manservant. Her mother's voice was almost a whisper. She spoke in Russian, they both did. 'But my darling. Do not do that again. Promise me? You don't know what these people will do.'

'She was stupid,' Elena protested. She stared fixedly ahead as they crossed the street. 'But she bought both.'

'I know,' her mother said. 'I'm glad of the sale. But in return, that servant will have noted that you were not at school. He could make much of it.'

'I'm not a child,' Elena whispered back fiercely. 'I know what they can do. I'm – I'm scared, Mama. We've done nothing. We're not even Jewish and Uncle Max isn't either, and he's not even German, he's Swiss, he just tried to help—'

'Elena,' Valentina whispered urgently. She glanced quickly around. 'Not another word. I mean it, Elena. Silence.'

They turned into the Siegesallee, with its rows of white marble statues of Prussian royalty. No matter how mediocre or forgettable their contribution to German life had ever been, they stretched as far as the eye could see, before rounding the corner to the Adlon Hotel. Here, their next appointment, a man the size of a tank, pulling on a fat cigar, clamped in his chubby fingers, was awaiting them. It took much longer than they had expected, but they couldn't run to get home in time. It would be noticed. They even stopped for a moment to pretend interest in a dress shop, just in case. In her mother's pocket was another roll of Reichsmarks, and in return, in the fat man's pocket now nestled a pair of cabochon-and-diamond earrings for someone who was not his wife.

In a while, Berlin would be history. They would take nothing. Start again. They'd done it before, they could do it again.

Nine years old when she had left Russia with her young widowed mother. A warrior, that's what Valentina was. But after years of quiet rebellion under the terrifying eye of the vicious regime in St Petersburg – Petrograd now of course – her mother had helped one dissident too many escape the marauding Bolsheviks who had killed Elena's father when she was only weeks old. So they had fled, she and her mother, to Berlin on a freezing train with their breath turning to icicles, starving, exhausted, but alive, and tried not to notice as the years went by that they were still outcasts in the city they had thought was to be their haven.

One day, her mother would say, one day we will go back. And Elena would nod fiercely, in spite of everything. At nine, she had been happy there. Fitted in. Belonged.

Alone, in her room above the shop, she would dream of that life, sometimes wondering if she had imagined her happiness in the midst of such misery and would look at the only photograph she had of her father. One that she kept in her special box. It was a box her mother had entrusted to her, kept under her bed. There used to be just a few things in it. A leather pouch which held her cherished christening present from her father – a photograph frame, encrusted with pearls, her name etched on the side, and a few family photographs. One taken just a year before, with her little cousin Natasha, or Sasha as Elena called her, who could be very annoying the way she followed her around. She had done ever since she and her parents, Papa's brother Georg and his wife Irina, had arrived from Russia a few years later, starving and penniless. Mama had felt it her duty to care for them, sharing the very little money she earned from her job helping restore jewellery in Mr Hauffman's workshop in a backstreet in Berlin. That was before she had found enough money to buy the lease on this shop, helped by Uncle Max who Mama had met at some meeting or other.

'One day,' her mother had said, as they inspected the dusty little shop with its narrow staircase that led to two bedrooms on the next floor and a small parlour at the back, 'a day will come when women can start businesses without being sponsored by a man. But for the moment I am grateful to him.'

'Who is he?' Elena had asked, wondering if the little room was really to be hers, all hers and not shared with anyone.

'Max,' Valentina had said warmly. 'You will like him, Elena. He is a brilliant architect. He trained here, in Berlin. At the Bauhaus. A fine mind. You can learn from him.'

And she did. It would have been a pleasure, of course, to have spent every Sunday with Uncle Max, who made her laugh and think and believe one day all would be well. But Mama – who in an unguarded moment had agreed with her that a whole day with Uncle Max was the best way to spend it – was a great deal stricter than most about what was owed to family. So, once a month, they trailed out to Potsdam to see Irina, now widowed, and Sasha, taking them food and money. Elena tried not to be bored.

But the photograph she gazed at the most, in the pretty little frame with its engraved bow on the top, was now fading, and not of Max, indeed no. How she wished she had known this father of hers. A man in a white, shapeless jacket, his tie loosened, thick floppy blond hair, a generous mouth, the laughing eyes, who had created such fine pieces of jewellery in the workshops of Carl Fabergé, a matter of great pride to her mother. She wished that at this moment he was there to protect them from these awful people who had, just days before, demanded that her mother drape a sign across the front of the shop saying, '*German owned*', to make sure they were not confused with the Jewish-owned shops, now fast disappearing.

But Mama would not agree to something so wicked and had said so, and he was not there to support them. So Elena would carefully place the photograph back in the box, pushing it underneath the narrow buff-coloured packages, tied with brown thin string, that her mother and Uncle Max wanted to keep in there, and often wished she could climb in beside it and feel safe.

*

'Here,' her mother said. 'Take this. Put it in your box. No. Leave your books. Leave everything. Be quick.'

Elena barely glanced at the hard package wrapped in greased paper. She pushed it into her satchel next to her box and slung it across her chest, when a sudden loud crash on the outer door stopped them both. Her mother flattened herself against the bedroom wall and stared carefully down onto the street. Outside, a black open-topped Mercedes was parked by the kerb. Two men, with peaked caps, shiny boots and uniforms with so much gold braiding they looked like something out of a comic opera. But laughter was not an option. Elena froze. Clutching her hand, her mother pulled her into the tiny bedroom at the back, slung open the window and pushed Elena onto the wide ledge.

'Don't look down,' she whispered urgently. 'Just crawl. *Crawl*. It's wide enough. I'm right behind you. I'll keep you safe. Go, go, *go*.'

Elena crawled, her satchel swinging wildly, gasping with terror until she reached the safety of the roof on the next building.

'Quick, I'll catch you,' a voice hissed. She looked down. Below she glimpsed two men. The taller of them, wearing worn trousers held up by a thick belt and a workman's jacket over a faded collarless shirt, was looking up at her. His accent was English; he was holding his arms up to her.

'Jump,' her mother, reaching the safety of the roof, urged her.

'In your own time,' the man sighed.

Elena closed her eyes, her breath halted and jumped. The young man stumbled, catching her as they crashed in a heap on the fence. The second man, with a cap pulled well down and wearing glasses, leapt forward, dragged her through a wooden gate into a side alley and bundled her roughly into the back of a cart. Within seconds, her mother stumbled into view, being held up by the other man. Half-lifting, half-pushing, they threw her mother on top of her. A canvas cover blotted out the light. They clung together as the two men began to pull the cart over the rough road. They heard shouting, someone angrily barking at them to pull their cart out of their way. They heard the second man protest, grumbling in German. Her mother squeezed her hard against her. A sound like a gunshot reached them, but still the cart kept moving, slowly, until a few minutes later, a sharp lurching movement suggested they'd turned off the main road and into a side one.

'Out,' one of the men ordered quietly. He pulled back the cover. Elena gasped. He put his hand across her mouth. 'Don't make a sound. Promise? Into the car. Valentina?' he ordered her mother scrambling after her. 'Lie on the floor, next to Elena.'

The second, younger man jumped into the driving seat and as casually as if they were going for a drive on a Sunday afternoon, silently took a package from Max, slid it into the inside pocket of his jacket, lit a cigarette and headed south out of the city towards Potsdam, and the little hamlet past the great lake where Irina and Sasha lived, and where Valentina planned to leave their possessions somewhere safe. If they were stopped, they would have nothing on them to suggest they were fleeing the country, and – even then Elena knew that more importantly – nothing could be taken away.

'Sorry,' the young man turned slightly as they drove. 'Should introduce myself. Max here, being Swiss and stinking rich as they all are, also has hope-less manners.'

Elena twisted her head to look up from her position on the floor at the man who had caught her. 'Arthur,' he announced himself carelessly. 'Arthur Banbury. Glad to know you. Now Potsdam first and then I'll drop you off in Paris on my way.'

'Your way to where?' Elena asked fearfully.

He threw back his head, the cigarette clamped between his teeth and laughed. 'Well, nowhere so boring as Paris. We,' he patted his pocket where he'd placed the envelope Max had given him, 'we're going to Monte Carlo. Where else?'

Chapter One

Pimlico

In the distance, the faint boom of Big Ben could be heard striking nine as Harriet Flynn opened up her stall and began the same routine she'd followed most days of the week for the last two years.

Denim jacket slung over the back of the chair, along with a canvas tote bag, weighed down with the spoils of a weekend trawling auctions and salesrooms. The chair was wedged up against the back of a narrow glass casement that served both as a counter and display cabinet, protected by a thick cotton cover which she stuffed under the counter. After that, she carefully balanced a carton of coffee, picked up from the café just outside the arcade, on the edge, while she fished in the pocket of her jeans for the keys to this little kingdom of hers. She began to pull out the velvet-covered trays, lined with mirrors to give the illusion there was at least twice the amount of the carefully orchestrated jumble of bracelets, stick pins, cameos and glittering brooches she had on display than there actually was.

It was a sight that had long ceased to cheer her as it once had. These days, even the alluring sight of a small mountain of jewellery, just begging to be picked up and worn by a new owner, was stubbornly refusing to attract the number of buyers she needed to justify having raided auctions and salesrooms all weekend for stock to feed her stall at Raglan Parade in Pimlico.

'If you,' she spoke aloud as she prodded a pearl-studded Edwardian stick pin, 'are still here at the end of the day, then you are going to be sold to someone who wouldn't know a pearl from a peanut and then you'll be sorry.'

'And they can take this with them,' a mournful voice said beside her.

Mimi Stewart, already at her stall next to Harriet's, was staring dismally at a trail of sequins and seed pearls coming adrift from the neckline of a dress she was examining, scattering across the floor.

'Torn,' she sighed in dismay to Harriet. She held it out. A narrow tear in a jet-black silk frock, so expertly cut in a time when French designers ruled the world, even Harriet – not given to wearing anything so frivolous at the best of times – briefly pictured herself in it.

'It wasn't there when I bought it,' Mimi insisted. 'Someone's tried to undo it and just *dragged* it open when it wouldn't give. Why do they *do* that?'

'Oh no,' Harriet sympathised, stooping to help Mimi gather up the fragile trimming. 'What a bummer.'

Mimi, tiny and thin, sat behind the small, round table she had squashed between two rails of vintage cocktail dresses. Dresses that failed spectacularly to sell on the kind of scale she needed to keep the wolf from her door. A fan at her feet, turned to 'cold' in summer, and in winter, a warm blast that Harriet could feel four feet away. She had never remarried after her husband had left her for a life with a Polish girl he'd met on the internet. Her grey curls – once russet – battened firmly in place with several tortoiseshell combs, she flapped a helpless hand at Harriet. Harriet knew that as the day progressed, and if recent weeks were anything to go by, Mimi would sell even less than she would, but – like her – giving up was not an option either could even contemplate. At least not yet.

She handed the last of the pearls to Mimi and returned to her own stall to begin checking her daily inventory of stock, leaving Mimi to wander off to find a sympathetic ear in Colin Milton, whose stall had been directly opposite hers for as long as anyone could remember. Certainly before Harriet's time.

Tall and thin, always immaculately dressed, gentle Colin, with receding hair and a manner so cowed it was a miracle he ever sold anything, pulled out a chair for Mimi and bent an attentive ear to listen to her gentle complaints about the shocking ways of those who inhabited the world of vintage dresses.

Maps were what Colin lived for. Antique maps of countries now long disappeared or sucked into others, their borders lost in the wars and ambitions of despotic rulers Some delicately painted, others with so much detail their value soared well above the price Colin would eventually have to settle for. He also lived for Mimi, if only she would have him.

Snatches of conversation reached Harriet as she worked, the stalls beginning to fill with yawning owners getting ready to be up and running when the doors opened at ten; but she'd heard it all before. Too many times. The misery of poor sales jostled with the duplicity of auction houses now employing checkers who no longer cared what old tat got through to the salesrooms, followed by the ridiculous hours they were obliged to invest in struggling businesses, not to mention the poor quality of the buyers who wandered in, treating Raglan Parade as though it were only a small step up from a dodgy souk, or somewhere to shelter from the rain.

Harriet yawned, letting it all drift past her, sifting through the post she had collected from the porter's office on her way in.

'Morning,' she said absently to James Hagan, who rented the space on the other side of her. She glanced sideways and peered at him. Hunched in a denim jacket as though it was winter rather than a town in the grip of an unseasonal heatwave, James looked like a man who hadn't got to bed until dawn, if at all. Harriet rolled her eyes.

'You can't,' she protested mildly, 'be cold.'

'Hangovers have no respect for feelings,' he sniffed. 'And on that subject neither do those who should know better and want to call at four in the morning, having thrown me out at two, to make sure I understood we are through.'

'Oh blimey,' she groaned. 'You mean—?'

He nodded.

'It's—?'

'Over.'

'And if he hasn't rung by—?'

'Midday.'

'You're—?'

'Finished.' James said. 'And don't look like that. This time I really mean it. Enough is enough. Midday or he'll be history. Toast. Kaput. Are you going to drink that coffee?'

'Not now,' she said, handing him the carton, 'no,' she shook her head. 'That's fine. I'll get another in a minute. Just got to read this.'

James's complicated love life was an exhaustingly familiar one to her. The shouting, the rows, the making up. These days – although occasionally envious on one level, she had to admit – she was mostly grateful that it aroused nothing more than a flicker of regret that since Dermot, she had no-one in her life to row with or not. Tempers flaring, things being thrown. She'd been there. She was embarrassed to recall such behaviour. But, she told herself, it was a long time ago. Everyone moved on. At the same time, honesty compelled her to acknowledge that two years – well it would be in another couple of months – was not really that long, though it seemed it to her. It had been a painful lesson. A lesson in what, she was still undecided. She glanced at James.

'And don't fall asleep,' she added, sliding the letter out of its official-looking envelope. 'It's not a good—' She paused.

'What?' James asked. He pushed his glasses further up his nose and wriggled onto the stool in front of her counter, peering over her shoulder at the letter she was scanning.

'James?' she didn't look up. 'Have you got one of these?'

'Let's see?' He began to read over her shoulder. 'Bloody hell,' he muttered, looking at the letter from their landlord. 'What does it mean? They're going ahead? I thought the protestors had stopped it?'

'Apparently not.' Harriet reread the letter. 'Surely that's – I don't know – illegal or something? Only twenty-eight days to get out.'

'No, to appeal,' James corrected pointing to the relevant line. He pushed his glasses onto his head and blew out his cheeks. 'Harriet, my love, it was coming. Once they sold, we were all on borrowed time. Eugh,' he grimaced at the carton of coffee. 'No sugar.'

'Get another,' she tried to take it, but he held it out of her reach. 'What a bloody start to the day.'

'And hours and hours ahead to get worse.' James sighed. He walked away sipping her coffee. Harriet turned back and gazed dispiritedly down at the two small carpets of unsold stock sitting on the counter.

'Now what?' she sighed. The day before, she had made less than half a dozen sales and two of those had made no profit at all. A ring to an American tourist, and only then because she had agreed to knock twenty pounds off the price, which had meant her profit on the exquisite diamond-and-sapphire confection that she could date back to at least 1880 was too pathetic to dwell on. The other, a silver bracelet with two miniscule diamonds embedded in the clasp, had fared slightly better. Only ten pounds off. But really, still utterly hopeless.

'You know what,' she frowned looking up as James returned, 'I've got to think of another way. Maybe vamp up the website. Maybe find somewhere else in London—'

'And where would that be?' he asked. 'The rents are ruinous—'

'Hang on.' She stopped. 'What about that market? The one Trevor mentioned? The one that's just opened? Great location, not London, I know, but near enough. And great salesrooms. Wait a minute.'

She crouched down to rummage through a pile of leaflets stuffed randomly under the counter, her white t-shirt riding up above narrow jeans to show a few inches of tanned back, the legacy of a week in Spain at her parent's home in the mountains outside Madrid. 'Here,' she said, straightening up. She extracted a slim, glossy brochure from the bundle, and ran her eye over the double pages.

'Let's see. Next one is – in – ah, here it is. Four weeks.' She looked up at James. 'If I get a move on, I might get a stall for a week. See what it's like. At least Trevor would appreciate a lift.'

James snorted. 'Trevor always wants a lift. You're like a bloody taxi service for him. You must have saved him hundreds on fares and transport, and God knows what it saves him on carrier fees. I notice he never suggests taking *his* car.'

'Don't be so mean,' she chided. 'You'd be trying to cut costs if you had two kids and another one on the way. And listen, why don't you come too – what? Why are you looking like that?'

James laughed. 'God, you never give up, do you?' he said shaking his head. 'We're all facing shutdown and you're talking about expansion.'

'Hardly expansion,' she said grimly. 'Try survival. Why not try as well?'

James shrugged. 'Not much call for watches or clocks anywhere on this or any other planet at the moment. Everyone's cutting back, and when I last looked, the middle of Surrey wasn't bucking the trend either – oh God,' he turned quickly, leaning both hands heavily on the counter so that only the back of his closely-shaved head and lean frame could be seen by the man approaching them. A man shouting and pushing his way across the arcade in a state of barely suppressed fury.

'If I go under,' James muttered, 'the upside is that I won't have to meet Vince bloody Channing ever again.'

'Have you seen this?' the man shrieked, reaching them. A trickle of passers-by – already beginning to browse the rows of stalls that were lined round three sides of the cavernous room, with a single column of stalls down the middle, occupied by those tenants prepared to pay a premium rent for the dubious pleasure of selling no more than anyone else in the arcade but a lot more visibly – turned curiously to watch the plump figure of Vincent Channing storming over to Harriet. His thin, straggling, greying hair, pulled back into a bunch at the nape of his neck, fanned out against the collar of his shirt as he pushed his way through the small crowd. The sleeves of his emerald-green silk shirt flapped frantically.

'Cool it, Vince,' James advised. 'Bad for sales, shrieking like a banshee.'

But Vincent was on a mission to unload. 'I'm *so* shocked. Where are all those fanatics that went on and on about saving buildings? Isn't this listed? How can they close us down? Redeveloped? And for what? An office block? I ask you. Oh God, oh God. Why I'm not curled up in the foetal position behind my counter, weeping, positively sobbing, is a mystery.'

'Oh Vince, come on,' Harriet objected, trying to cheer him. 'It's not that bad, I mean there are other places—'

'Not that bad?' Vince burst in, leaving large gaps between each word. 'Well, let me tell you my girl, it's the end for me. *Finito. Fini. Finalizado.*' He waved his arms heavenwards. 'How,' he asked, halting in mid-wave, seeing her apparently unfazed by the desperate picture of his future that he had summoned up, 'how can you be so calm? What are you on for God's sake?'

'I'm up against it as well.' Harriet eased herself off the stool and walked round to the other side of the casement, hoping if she looked busy he'd go away.

'You?' he stared at Harriet in amazement. She was already pulling a tray out to examine the contents, ignoring him. Her hair, short at the back, long at the front, fell over one eye; she tucked the thick blonde strands back behind her ear. '*You?*' Vince repeated to the top of her head, with a disbelieving shriek. 'Having to rethink? You always pull something out of the bag. It's like a – a social hub for every jewellery fanatic in London. It's a nightmare trying to get past the crowd round your stall. You don't see the rest of us being so inconsiderate.'

'Vince?' she took a deep breath. He was impossible. And hideously lazy. 'If that were the case,' she went on, not looking at him, checking her stock, 'I'd be loaded. But it's not. I have regular clients who swing by to say hi, and sometimes they buy. Usually they just look. I am nice to them because why wouldn't I be? It's called trading. That's all.'

'Oooh. *Tray-ding,*' he mimicked her. 'Is that what it's called? And what about the Tsarina? Surely she's got something else tucked away you can sell? A cameo? A bracelet?' He leaned forward and whispered mischievously. 'The secret of the Amber Room? Oh my word.'

He broke off and stared over Harriet's head to the big double doors on the far side of the run-down arcade. Once an army stores depot, over the last couple of hundred years it had morphed through several incarnations. For as long as anyone could remember, it had been an antiques market. It was cold in winter and far too hot in summer.

Each night, whatever the weather, dead on the dot of seven, the huge wooden doors were pulled shut and locked, leaving stallholders rushing to close up before the stern and humourless porter came along muttering and threatening with talk of permits being revoked if they weren't out in ten minutes.

'Talk of providence,' Vince announced in a loud voice. 'Here comes Her Imperialness herself. What do you suggest? Shall I bow backwards or just clear a path?'

Harriet ignored him. She glanced in the same direction as Vince, to where she could see the fragile but unbent figure of the white-haired Mrs Elena Banbury. On her head, a straw confection with black, beaded ribbons tied firmly round the brim, she threaded her way slowly towards her, leaning lightly on a black ebony stick. This, Harriet knew, could take anything up to ten minutes and not just because Mrs Banbury was hampered by a painful hip. Her progress was always impeded by her frequent pauses to examine the stock on other stalls, or to exchange a word with one or two people she seemed to favour above all the others. Mimi always got a word. Advice Mrs Banbury called it. Instructions was more like it, Mimi had once muttered. Colin, too, could be found carefully and respectfully listening to her suggestions for improving his sales.

But today no-one could halt her, not even comfortably jovial Big Jake. A man who had abandoned a career in the navy – before, it had to be said, it abandoned him – to slog around the country in his caravan, buying up Georgian glassware. He was now convinced he had Russian ancestry, on the spurious grounds that he had discovered, through an online website, that one of his great-grandfathers had been christened Georg rather than George. He refused to accept that back in the day, a lazy clerk in a register office in Newcastle might simply have left off the final 'e'.

This morning, Mrs Banbury's list of those who wanted her opinion was lengthened, not just by an Italian woman who spoke loudly and volubly at the iniquitous prices everyone charged these days for crystal vases, oblivious to the glaring looks from those whose living depended on their sale; but also a new person, a tall blonde woman, as quietly reserved as Mrs Banbury was flamboyant, who had told Harriet she was a collector of cameo brooches. According to Mrs Banbury, the woman had no knowledge of such things, she herself possessing a sizeable collection.

Sometimes they talked quietly for a while, Mrs Banbury carefully examining the woman's latest acquisition, but today as she saw Harriet peering over everyone's head to where she was talking, she simply touched the woman's arm and moved on, lifting her free hand to acknowledge Harriet, and the cameo lady turned away to inspect a coat stand Mimi was now fretting over, strewn with vintage bags.

'She shouldn't be out,' Harriet muttered to James. 'When I collected her prescription, the doctor said to keep her out of the heat. Me? What can I do? She ignores everything anyone says to her. James? Can you keep an eye? I'd better get her—'

'A lemon tea, for Mrs B,' he finished. 'Stay there. I'll get it. Got to buy some aspirin anyway. Out of the way, Vince,' he told the hovering man. 'Visitors to entertain here.'

'Visitors?' Vince sniffed. 'Anyone would think she's hiding half a dozen Fabergé eggs under that preposterous hat she wears, the way you two behave. Pardon me,' he mocked, raising an eyebrow as they both glared at him. 'No intention to offend—'

'Vince?' Harriet cut across him. Her voice was polite, almost gentle, but there was no mistaking the firmness. 'Your only offence is that you're blocking whatever little business I might attract. And by the way, Elena's hat is one that Mimi would give her right arm for and I think you've got a customer.'

She nodded past him to his stand, awash with china plates of which less than half, she correctly guessed, were as genuinely Victorian as he claimed. Alongside them was a stack of cups being passed off as Georgian, when it was obvious to anyone with the smallest knowledge of such things that they had left the factory at least a century after the Georgian period had ended. There was a whole raft of extravagantly decorated porcelain cake stands anyone could buy more cheaply on eBay.

'Oh, goodness me,' she whispered behind her hand. 'Is she putting something in her bag?'

'What? Oh my God,' Vince whirled round. 'Hey, you!' He charged back to his stand to accost a couple of middle-aged women holding up a pair of cut-glass wine goblets, with no greater malicious intent for them than to establish if they were as fake as they looked. 'What do you think you're doing?'

Harriet turned away trying not to laugh, to find Mrs Banbury already heaving herself onto the high stool.

'She picks my brains,' the elderly woman sniffed, allowing Harriet to steady her as she settled on the stool. She waved a vague hand at the cameo woman. 'No idea. Simply has *no* idea at all. She'd buy anything if you're convincing enough. I need to save her from herself. And Mimi? No. Don't tell me. The Mainbocher?' She pronounced the name correctly, *manbocker*, which had endeared her to such a stickler as Mimi.

'I told her. When she showed me the catalogue. I said I saw his work on half the aristocracy of Europe. Stitching, cut, the finish. Unmistakable. But she wouldn't listen. Now look what happens?'

'Elena?' Harriet chided steadying her. 'Why are you out so early? You know what the doc—'

Elena Banbury waved a hand at her. 'Because the world doesn't come to me,' she retorted. 'And it is not early. Half the day is gone. I rise at six. You know that. And stop fussing. I'm not dead yet.'

Her accent, a mixture of Russian from her childhood and German from the years she had lived in Berlin, was still evident, but sometimes she would lapse into French from her decades of wandering from casino to casino with her late husband, Arthur. Whatever its origin, softened from the last thirty years living in England, there was not a tinge of self-pity in her voice about her fragility. And fragile she clearly was. Of late, there'd been a noticeable shift in her frailness, and not in the right direction.

'What,' she said, without turning her head but indicating with a slight wave of her stick to where Vince was now stationed in front of his stand, his arms folded, guarding the inferior stock from further invasion, 'is that dreadful man up to now?'

'Oh nothing,' Harriet dismissed him. 'Just his usual need to shriek and shout. James has gone to get you some tea.'

'And you?' Elena looked carefully at her. 'You look very fierce.'

Harriet smiled. 'Sorry. Just a letter from the landlord. We've got to get out. All of us. Office redevelopment, apparently. And the wretched Vince being a drama queen isn't helping. Anyone would think he's the only one affected.'

'I've told you before,' Elena sighed, peering through the glass top of Harriet's stand to study a pretty stick pin, one of several that Harriet had bought a week before and were, along with the Edwardian pearl number, proving a nightmare to shift, 'you should expand. Now's the chance. Is that a Murrle-Bennet?' she asked, moving her eye to a brooch shaped like a swallow.

Harriet peered over her shoulder. 'Yep,' she said, returning to the landlord's letter, 'and expand to where?'

'An address where you will be taken seriously – Kensington, maybe Notting Hill – one of those arcades in Kings Road, plenty of places – and you could add fifty per cent to these prices. Where did you find it?'

Harriet glanced to where Elena was pointing. 'The swallow bird? A client. She said it belonged to her great-grandmother. Lived in Pforzheim. You've been there. I remember you told me.'

'Of course,' Elena agreed. 'I remember it well. It took a whole day from Berlin to get there. I had never been on a train before.'

'Really?' Harriet said. What was the point of reminding her that last time Elena had told her this story, she and her mother had gone by car with her mother's friend, Max, and it had taken two days because they had got lost. No point at all. Next time, she would probably tell her she had gone by bus, changed eight times and arrived in three days.

'I was bored. I wore,' Elena leaned forward, as though imparting a state secret, 'a grey dress. New. I was very proud of it. It had pockets and I wore black shoes with a little bar, just here,' she arched her foot in its serviceable heavily-strapped sandal and pointed at her instep. 'We were going to Baden Baden. With Max – I mean of course my *Uncle* Max. He was not a real uncle, but – at the time – he was like one to me. We were going to stay in a hotel for one night. Or maybe two. I forget.'

Suddenly Elena stopped, staring into the distance. Harriet threw her a quick glance and then followed the old lady's gaze down the centre of the hall. Nothing. Just an increasing gaggle of visitors clogging the aisles, not sure what they were looking for, and certainly not buying.

It had happened before with Elena. This abrupt pause. More recently, Harriet had noticed these pauses were accompanied by a look of not quite panic, but certainly anxiety. A moment that suddenly claimed the elderly woman's memory. Harriet understood memories. Crashing around you when you least expected it. Catching you up in a moment that could render you motionless.

She waited, quietly arranging a tray of brooches, until Elena was ready to let go of a time when she was young, in a world that had long passed. Sometimes, Harriet could see that whatever it was, was too painful for her to deal with. Once she had asked about her family, or Arthur's, but had been met by a shrug and a curtain had come down, sharply but not rudely, though enough to make Harriet tread carefully. Now was such a moment.

'All right?' Harriet eventually gently touched Elena's arm.

'What?' For a moment, Elena looked blankly at her and then gave her head a tiny shake. 'Yes of course. Now. Where was I?' She blinked. 'Oh yes. Pforzheim. I don't know why James doesn't go. It's still the only place to buy watches and clocks.'

'It's the money—' Harriet began.

'Pah.' Elena interrupted with a wave of her heavily ringed hand. 'What is money? He could go on one of those planes that charge almost nothing. I might,' she looked defiantly at Harriet, 'even go myself.'

Harriet said nothing. Elena did not take easily to being told what to do or, in this case, not to attempt.

'I don't think it's that hard,' Elena looked keenly at her. Actually, now that Harriet came to study the older woman's face, she thought it was more a hopeful expression as though she wanted reassurance.

'No,' Harriet teased. 'Not for someone as adventurous as you. But it isn't just the fare, is it? The trip has to pay for itself. What if you don't find anything worth buying?'

'In *Pforzheim*?' Elena sounded incredulous. 'You find *everything*.'

'Even so.'

Harriet didn't used to be so cautious. But struggling to pay for her space in this less-than-profitable place, an uneasy feeling had started to creep up on her, that she was no longer the star player in her own life, what with having to give way to banks and creditors and – oh God, it wasn't worth thinking about. It had all conspired to make her tread carefully. So she simply smiled and said, 'Finding time of course. It isn't easy,' which sounded better than *I haven't got the energy, the will or the dosh.*

'Time,' Elena said with a vigorous shake of her head. 'Always people finding time. It goes,' she snapped her fingers, 'just like that. If I were thirty again,' she declared stoutly, 'I would go *everywhere*. Pforzheim would be like going to the shops.'

Harriet wasn't sure if that was a question or a statement but she was spared the need to answer. It was due to age, Harriet had decided, that a certain restlessness had seemed, in the last few days, to have settled on Elena. It was a sad but inescapable fact of life that even on such a sharp mind, a recent illness, that had for several days confined her to her flat next door to Harriet's own, had taken its toll.

'James,' Elena shifted more comfortably on the stool, 'is a clever boy, but lacks drive.'

Years, Harriet suspected, of ricocheting around the world had been the root cause of Elena's carelessness in all matters of finance and personal risk. It alarmed and intrigued her in equal measure. Money, to the seemingly frail but steely old woman, seemed to fall into the category of 'Why wait? We could be dead tomorrow!' or 'Something will turn up'. Clearly for Elena, somehow, somewhere, it always had.

Living next door to her in the rather fading block that was Denbigh Mansions in Pimlico – Elena in a much larger and almost grand apartment compared to the one-bedroom rabbit hutch next door that she rented to her – Harriet had learned that an appearance of charming vulnerability hid a vice-like grasp on survival.

To her shame, Harriet was aware that she often – and especially when she knew that the day ahead involved driving in different directions to auctions or salesrooms and was unlikely to end before midnight – would carefully open and close her own front door, holding her breath for fear that Elena would hear and collar her with instructions to fetch this or bring that, inevitably and frustratingly delaying the start of her own day.

Once or twice, when Harriet had been truly torn between Elena asking her to bring back bread or milk from the corner shop, and a buyer waiting to meet her at her stall, she had – fruitlessly as it turned out – braved the Sheltons, the couple in the only other flat on their floor, to see if they were able to help.

'My dear,' had said Mrs Shelton at barely nine in the morning, 'I would, of course I would, but I'm expecting guests for lunch. And besides, I know she prefers you to help. We all do.'

'Sorry?' Harriet blinked. 'Who's *we*?'

'*We*? My dear girl. *Everyone* in the block!' Mrs Shelton gave a titter and waved an expansive hand embracing all three floors of the building. 'I mean you do seem to have a way with dealing with her. She simply barks at me.'

At that point in her acquaintance with Elena, Harriet knew nothing of having any special way with anyone or indeed anyone believing that to be the case. But it was only a matter of days after moving in for realisation to dawn that, while Elena needed a bit of support here and there (but would have sold her soul rather than admit it), few people seemed to be prepared to get involved with keeping her afloat. So, after the second pointless appeal for help to neighbours above and below Elena – including the plump Mrs Shelton in her floral housecoat, her dyed blonde hair clamped on top with a chiffon scarf – Harriet had given up. She even managed to resist the temptation to point out that a quick run to the shops might help Mrs Shelton's well-being just as much as Elena's.

Of course, she had no idea when she had first met Elena, who had heard she was looking for a flat and had taken to stopping by her stall in Raglan Parade. No idea that Elena's flat would come with a few strings. The address was exactly where she had begun to despair of finding anything, and she had started to look further afield. Then she heard about the flat and that, astonishingly, it was at a price she could just about afford.

'I have just,' Elena had told her, 'informed that appalling estate agent, but then they all are, that if he can't find me a good tenant, then I will acquire another agent. My current tenant has moved out. Hopeless with the rent. Such a bother. It would suit you. Come tonight. If you like it, then tomorrow I will have great pleasure in telling that pompous little man what he can do with his "in need of updating".'

'James,' Harriet now loyally defended him to Elena, who, as far as Harriet was aware, had in the two years she had lived next to her, travelled no further than a bus ride to the Russian church two miles away, 'would go anywhere in a heartbeat. Even Pforzheim. It's not just the fare, it's finding somewhere to stay, to eat and all that. Soon adds up, you know. And it's hard times for all of us. Now don't wander off. He'll be back in a minute.'

'Not wandering,' Elena protested. 'I'll just take a look at those watches on his stand. Really? How can he expect to sell anything arranged like that? Look!' She nudged Harriet's arm as she helped her down. 'I think you have a customer. It was the first lesson my mother taught me,' she allowed Harriet to steady her for a moment. 'When I minded our shop. In Berlin. *Looking idle loses sales*, she would say. Now, let go of my arm. I'm fine. I'll be back in a moment. And they haven't any idea at all about jewellery,' she murmured giving a slight inclination of her head at the couple pausing at Harriet's stand, as she walked slowly away. 'I can always tell.'

*

'It's late Victorian,' Harriet explained pleasantly, a good five minutes later, to the man and young woman studying her stock and finally focusing on a gold-link bracelet, plain but pretty. 'Around eighteen ninety,' she added helpfully.

'You don't say,' the girl breathed. 'Fancy that. The price tag says much more than that.'

'Ah,' Harriet smiled gently. 'No the date is eighteen ninety. This is the price.' She pointed to the small white tab.

'Eighteen ninety?' The man laughed. 'Knock it off. No way. I know what you lot get up to. No way of proving that, is there? So must be worth a bit off. Take it off your hands. Know what I mean?'

'She most certainly does not,' came Elena's voice at Harriet's elbow before she could reply. 'It comes,' she said, heaving herself back onto her stool, 'from the estate of a woman called Agatha Wallis. She was very famous for her jewellery collection. I'm surprised, Harriet,' she admonished her, 'that you didn't mention it. But I suppose you assumed that someone as,' she paused appearing to deliberately choose her words with care, 'au *fait* with the jewellery world as this gentleman, wouldn't need to be told.'

'Never heard of her,' the man sniffed.

'Never? Never heard of *Agatha*?' Elena's eyes rounded in disbelief as though he had confessed to never having heard of the entire House of Windsor. 'Then let me remind you,' she said crisply. She settled herself more comfortably on the stool.

'She was, of course, very old when I met her. I was only young. Working in Paris. Just after the war. I had been dresser to the Comtesse Delacroix on Avenue Foch. I chose all her jewellery. Monsieur Le Comte – a most generous husband to such a spoilt little hussy – never bought her anything without consulting me. And I knew everyone who mattered in the jewellery world. My father worked for Fabergé. I am going,' she paused and peered haughtily over her glasses at the young man, 'to assume you've heard of him?'

The man simply laughed. 'Who are you then?' he jeered, 'Anastasia?'

'If I were, then you'd be looking at a ghost,' Elena retorted.

The sprinkling of people who had paused to listen chuckled. For a moment, Harriet almost stepped in to bring an end to the exchange that was rapidly turning into one of Elena's shows, but one look at Elena's face stopped her. She was in her element. And also clearly in the land of fantasy. She couldn't have stopped her if she'd tried.

Last week, Elena had told the same story but in that version, this incident with the Comte had taken place in Geneva. Another time, it had been in Madrid where, for some bewildering reason, dining with General Franco had been involved. All that Harriet knew for certain was that in Elena's muddled history, which she had long ago abandoned trying to figure out, Mrs Arthur Banbury had an unrivalled knowledge of jewellery.

'Send her over to me,' James whispered gleefully having deposited Elena's lemon tea by her elbow. 'Someone's just bought that double hunter watch. Been staring at everyone for weeks.'

'No it hasn't,' Harriet whispered back. 'It's been sitting under a pile of other stuff. She says you're crap at presentation.'

'It has not,' James protested, 'been sitting under *anything*. It was *grouped*. Carefully grouped at that. With like pieces. Quite different. Oh, all right,' he conceded. 'She made it look like a one-off. Point taken.'

Suddenly he chuckled, the greater pleasure of having pocketed enough to put a smile on his face outweighing a slight to his sales technique. 'But I bet she didn't say *crap*.'

'Hey, James?' Harriet stopped him as he moved away. 'Should we all have a drink later? We need to discuss this.' She nodded towards the landlord's letter. 'Maybe we could get a stay of execution. Give us all a chance to find other places.'

'Why not?' he agreed. 'Got to meet William for dinner – and take that look off your face, it's just dinner – but let me know if anyone else wants to come. I suspect, though, we're too late.

'She's on form today,' he nodded to where Elena, sat stiffly upright, on Harriet's stool. 'She could be straight out of central casting. You know,' he dramatically slung the back of his hand against his forehead, 'aristo Russian émigré.'

Harriet grinned, but she could only agree. Elena did not look like an impoverished widow eking out her pension in a second floor, grand-but-fading apartment in a worn-out mansion block. James was right. There was an air about her that had nothing to do with struggling and more to do with – Harriet frowned trying to find the right words – a warrior. That was it. A woman used to fighting for what she wanted. Meek, helpless, frail – all words you could easily apply to a woman of her age and circumstances, were simply not ones that sat easily on this fiercely determined old lady. A lady who habitually wore jewel-coloured scarves over neat black dresses, long dangling earrings, her white hair in a perfect chignon whatever the time of day, and always the same black cavernous patent bag hanging off her free arm.

'What *has* she got in there,' Vince sniffed to no-one in particular. He was ignored anyway. 'The spoils,' he tittered undeterred, 'from a bank heist or a shotgun for a raid on Tiffany's?'

'Now, where was I?' Elena was saying. She frowned, delicately replacing her carton of tea on the counter as though it were bone china, and handed her bag to Harriet, to hang off the back of the chair. 'Ah yes. The Comte.' she gave a resigned sigh, the kind usually reserved by weary parents for the poor decisions of ungrateful children. 'Suddenly he wanted to move to live in their villa in

Amalfi. She was not behaving well with one of his friends. But *Amalfi?*' Elena shook her head. 'At that time, it was too trashy for me. Now Rome. Ah yes. That might have suited me even if they were all still pretending not to be fascist. So, the manager of the Hotel Mercure, when he heard I had refused to go, persuaded me to work in the jewellery store in the arcade. It needed a touch of élan, you see, which he knew I would bring to it. Now where was I?'

'Agatha,' Harriet whispered her head turned away.

'Ooo we're the prompt now, are we?' Vince tittered. Harriet ignored him. She would not see Elena publicly confused.

'Oh yes,' Elena beamed. 'Thank you my dear. That's right. Agatha. She used to stay at the hotel. Looking for another rich husband of course. But when she ran out of money – or rather suitors – she tried to get out of the Hotel Mercure through a kitchen window to avoid the manager. So many guests did that, in the end, he had more guards on the back of the hotel than the front. What's the matter?'

She raised an imperious eyebrow at the man who had triggered her speech, nudging his companion and laughing. 'You're making it all up,' he jeered.

'Go on, then.' Elena commanded him. 'Look her up. You can google, can't you?'

'What do you know about Google?' the man sniggered.

'Clearly more than you do about jewellery,' she retorted.

For a moment he looked at her in astonishment and then laughed. 'Oh, go on then,' the man turned to Harriet. 'What a card. Give us another look at the bracelet.'

Behind Elena, Vince's jaw dropped in fury.

*

At mid-morning, a grateful James escorted Elena to the door, from where she said she would walk the short distance to her solicitor's office in the next street, where she had an appointment; all the way telling him crossly, but to no avail, that she did not like being treated like a relic.

'Tough old bird,' he announced cheerfully on his return. 'Said she was going to meet a friend and didn't need my escort, thank you very much.'

'Bet she didn't,' Harriet glanced at the thinning crowd. 'Meet a friend, I mean.'

'Not unless you count that woman who buys brooches or something – or was it cameos? You know, dull looking, wears weird hats? That's the one. Or the one with the big hair – buys all those Clarice Cliff jugs, husband was that actor? God. What was his name? Played villains?'

'No idea,' Harriet shook her head.

'You know something though?' said James sliding onto the stool that Elena had vacated. 'Hope I've got my wits about me like her when I'm her age.'

'All that Russian blood I expect,' Harriet said. 'By the way, all set for later? I think we've got about a dozen interested.'

'And all expecting you to come up with a solution,' he pointed out. 'All right, all right,' he held up his hands. 'But you have to admit, you take no prisoners when you get a bee in your bonnet. Most of them won't bother to turn up. You do know that, don't you?'

'Maybe. But still better than doing nothing.'

Chapter Two

It was almost six. After an afternoon that was financially so dismal that Harriet thought she might be reduced to selling everything at half price, she shut down her stall and emerged with relief into the warm evening sunshine.

It hadn't always been like that. Two years before, desperate to find something more permanent than open-air markets that almost froze her brain in winter and in summer left her feeling murderous, trying to compete with banked up ranks of stalls selling tourist t-shirts and cheap kaftans that swamped her narrow stall, Raglan Parade had been Utopia. A chance to move on in all kinds of ways. She went from stick pins and brooches to a broader range of bracelets, necklaces and pendants, which cost more, but led to that rarest of rarities in her world: a small, but decent profit.

The new austerity measures had, of course, put paid to that particular dream. Instead of a permanent stall she had hoped would bring in proper buyers, she had found herself in the same desolate trench of sales with the other stallholders. All reining in, waiting for better times. Instead of serious buyers – or even, God help us, she thought grimly, the occasional visitor who knew about jewellery – she had simply acquired tourists.

An endless, aimless stream who, having dealt with the Abbey, Big Ben, and Downing Street, ambled vaguely around the forty or fifty stalls that had crowded into the empty space, deluding themselves from watching gameshows on television and the internet, or a Dickensian or Austenesque view of England fostered by travel agents, that in this particular patch of London, a treasure was to be found. Two things Harriet was sure of, and she finally faced these facts as she rounded the corner and made for the wine bar: to the best of her knowledge there had never been such a find, and that it was painfully clear that the flat would have to be replaced with something cheaper and miles away in a more affordable area.

'Oh God,' she muttered to herself, and not for the first time. 'What possessed me to even think I could afford the rent? Talk about delusional. And this,' she sighed, pushing open the door to the bar, glimpsing the small group of stallholders who had bothered to turn up, 'was a pointless waste of time.' She knew that. 'All clinging to each other before the ship hits the rocks. And bloody Vince.'

'Oh there you are,' Vince simpered as Harriet pulled out a chair on the other side of the wooden-topped table. As James had predicted, only a handful had bothered to turn up. And one of them, she thought viciously, would have to be the ghastly Mr Channing.

'I thought you said the Tsarina was unwell?' He arched an eyebrow. 'But there she is, as ever, working the floor for you. *Tsk Tsk*. What a slave-driver you are. I'm surprised you haven't tried to sell tickets for her performance. You'd clean up.'

'Never thought of that,' Harriet forced cheerfulness. 'Thanks Vince. Always up for new ideas. Isn't that why we're all here? Now who wants what? Or shall I just get a bottle each of red and white? House do?'

The bar was not crowded, but would provide just enough of a wait, she hoped, to switch Vince's attention to someone else. She half-sat on a barstool, tall enough to allow one bare foot, temporarily loosened from its thonged sandal, to skim the ground, and idly drummed her fingers on the marble-topped bar, waiting for the bargirl's attention. It was a few seconds before she realised the blonde girl she had been staring unthinkingly at in the long mirror behind the bar was herself.

What, she thought, had she seen that she had not recognised? A nose that was a bit too straight, a wide mouth, pointed chin and blue eyes, familiar enough but nothing to particularly notice. But it was a tired face that looked back at her. Once there had been hope in that face. Where had that girl gone? So changed. Harriet was used to change, but this new, grave, tired look was beginning to take root. It was, she decided and yawned, what life did to you.

No matter how much cream you slapped on your face – and she'd tried a few, all thanks to Lizzie, who liked nothing better than to trawl through Selfridges on Saturday afternoons searching for the answer to incipient crows' feet or promises of luminous skin – the fallout from crazy mistakes, skewered judgment, unwise lovers, always won. Something to do with the eyes, her mother had once said. And possibly, Harriet reflected, and more likely, having a life that at times rivalled a car crash. If making mistakes on the emotional front had been an Olympic sport, Harriet had to admit she could have played for England. There was Dermot for a start.

Looking back over the year they had spent together, a time when her blonde hair had fallen in a straight curtain down her back, she had been desperate to make sense of her life. All around her, friends marrying, moving in together, careers taking off or, when they didn't find the answers in the boardroom, dropping out to drift round the world. All that left her unsure what she wanted to do with her own future, and honesty compelled her to admit that she'd had choices and had just made the wrong ones. After two – or, she wrinkled her nose trying to recall, was it three? – weeks of intense flirtation, there had come the reckless plunge into something deeper, in the curtained seclusion of his apartment. She was meant to be earning her living as a receptionist in an auction house, not stoking up her future with a blindingly handsome antiques dealer with a string of clients that were as glittering as the jewellery he sold them.

The outcome was entirely her own fault. The legacy – apart from a heart that turned out not to be totally broken but in the more recoverable state of just being badly bruised – was that he had at least made her focus on doing something with her life, rather than living it through his. Selling jewellery was at least more interesting than searching for – what? Something meaningful to do? Something that had *purpose*.

In the aftermath, Harriet had listened to Lizzie urging her to move on, vaguely knew she was right, and later that day had rallied, dumped the wine glasses in the sink and gone and got her hair cut.

Her fists clenched, she had watched as the long straight hair – once described by that perfidious rat as a silken curtain – fell softly to the floor around her feet. She bit her lip as she gazed at herself in the hairdresser's mirror, still wrapped in the black gown they had pulled round her, ruffled the new short cut, forked out a ruinous amount to the artist wielding the scissors and did the only thing she could do. Got on with her life, vowing never again to be so easily charmed by such a practised seducer. And there was, of course, the promise of a flat owned by that odd Russian woman. A way forward, a way from being made to feel so small, so unimportant. So pathetic.

'House red and white, Chloe please,' she turned as the bar girl reached her. 'And – hang on, let me see—' she turned back and counted the group at her table. 'Eight glasses. I'll wait if you don't mind.'

Chloe glanced in the same direction. 'Vince?'

Harriet grimaced. 'Vince indeed,' she agreed.

'Bloody man,' James said joining her. 'Winding everyone up. He's already said this is a waste of time and they should all go for bankruptcy.'

'Then why is he here?' Harriet growled. 'Don't tell me. Just wants to say he told us so. God, he really is the pits. Drinks on their way. Sadly, Chloe wouldn't give me anything to knock Vince out with, but hey – you can't have everything. Won't be a sec.'

'Now,' she said brightly, a couple of minutes later, rejoining the group, who had pushed two tables together in the corner of the wine bar. James dragged another chair round from an adjoining table. 'Can someone move those glasses?' Harriet asked, placing the tray in the centre of the table, into which the assembled group dropped their contribution to the cost. 'So? How are we all going to make our fortunes?'

*

She just missed the lift, watching with a groan as it took its usual eternity to rumble its way to the floor it wanted and then –usually because the outer door had not been closed – take what felt like a week to get back down again to the ground floor. One more minute, she decided, and then she'd have to walk up, dragging a plastic bag full of shopping and a tote bag that felt like it had rocks in it, not just the leather cases full of stock she had lugged home to check for damage before she put them on her stall. A series of flyers on the table in the marble hallway stared back at her. A local shop looking for second-hand clothes, another for window replacing services, a third a petition that someone from Raglan Parade had left, trying to raise local opposition to the closure.

'Too late,' she addressed it, turning back to the lift. 'Way too late. All of you.'

Sleep was what was needed. Tomorrow afternoon she faced a drive to Hertfordshire to a sale and earlier that day, she had sworn on her life, she would get her accounts to Adrian, the sober-suited man who had for the past five years shaken his head, tut tutted and predicted the worst over her once slender profit margin and now, no margin at all.

If she could find her, she still had to call Kerry, her occasional help, to make sure she'd remembered she'd promised to man the stall at the Parade until Harriet got back. Better to have Kerry – with her spiky red hair, earrings dangling to her skinny shoulders, leggings in all weathers and a denim jacket, sitting there scrolling through websites for cheap knockoffs of everything from handbags to shoes by way of scarves and jumpers – than to close for the day. She also had to see if she could get a stall at the market Trevor had mentioned. It didn't look promising but what did she have to lose?

Finally the lift shuddered to a halt; she stepped back to let a woman rush out, so busy adjusting a beret over her head, Harriet had to step hurriedly back to avoid being hit.

'Hope the world doesn't end before you get there,' she muttered after her and slumped against the back wall, as the lift cranked its way to the second floor. Out of habit, as she stepped out, she paused and listened for a moment outside Elena's door to see if she was still up, but there was silence. Relieved, she began to put her key in her lock, too tired to gossip and needing sleep, when the sound of Elena's door opening a fraction put paid to any such hope.

'Oh it's you,' Elena said swinging the door wide open. She was still fully dressed, an embroidered black jacket over a scarlet silk blouse, an ornate gold chain around her neck, holding a scarf as though she had just come in. 'I was just leaving some goods for the charity. They said they would collect first thing. Just a bag of nonsense but it helps. Just by the lift if you wouldn't mind. That's it.'

'You're up late.' Harriet took the bag from her and placed it by the lift. Elena's face looked fragile, tired.

'I was out. A little earlier,' Elena said. 'A fundraising event. I help out a little here and there and I shared a taxi home. A nuisance of a woman. You must know her. She is always bothering me at the market. She's just left.'

'Wearing a yellow beanie hat?'

'I'm sorry?' Elena sounded blank. 'What is this?'

'Rather loose crochet beret thing.'

'Is that what they're called? I learn something new every day even at my age. I recall when I worked in Geneva – nineteen fifty something, a very stupid English woman – some duchess of somewhere or other, or was it a countess? I forget, but she begged me to help her find the right dressmaker, because even then it was important to know what to wear; and the dreadful war just over and so much poverty, you'd think she would have had something more worthy to occupy her. But me? Me? I rise above such things. Where was I? Oh that's right. Hats. She was very keen on hats.'

Harriet's heart sank. She could hear a litany of this long-ago woman's penchant for headgear limbering up for an airing and she was tired. So tired. How Elena wasn't on her knees amazed her.

'You should write a book,' she interrupted as firmly as she could. 'I'd read it. God,' she yawned pushing her door open, hoping it would stop Elena, 'I'm shattered. You must be tired as well.'

'In this heat it is just impossible to sleep. I've tried everything. Now, tell me? How was the meeting? How many are staying in business?'

'No idea,' Harriet pushed the bags at her feet into the narrow little hallway. 'I think Mimi will probably struggle on for a bit. I know she makes mistakes, but you have to admit, most of the time she knows what she's doing. Big Jake might just go back home to Newcastle, and Colin, I suspect will do whatever Mimi does.' Harriet stifled another yawn. 'He struggles at the best of times.'

'I've told him a thousand times,' Elena shook her head. 'He needs to stop daydreaming about writing an absurd book on cartology in the Byzantine age and drag himself into the present one. He should go and work for someone. Take a salary. Write in his spare time. And the one who treats you like a taxi service? Terence?'

'Trevor,' Harriet corrected. 'And you sound like James,' she added. 'I actually don't mind giving him a lift. It's not putting me out. No idea what he'll do. He wasn't there.'

'And Vince?'

'Vince?' Harriet laughed. 'No point in hoping he'll do the decent thing and support himself. Bet your life he'll find someone to bankroll him somewhere else. His poor father I expect. *Again*. I'm worried about James. But—' she shrugged.

'But you?' Elena regarded her with her head on one side. 'What did you decide?'

'Me?' Harriet bent to scoop up the post, spread out on the mat. This was not the moment to tell Elena that she would seriously have to think of giving up the flat. 'I'll think of something.'

'Think of a shop,' Elena said turning back into her own flat. 'Take the risk. Staying still isn't the answer. Get to bed. I am long past mine. I have an appointment at nine.'

Elena closed her door. Honestly, Harriet grumbled to herself closing her own behind her, sometimes Elena was so irritatingly unrealistic. How did she think she would get the money for a shop? Rob a bank? She threw the post in a basket on a small console table just inside the door, all circulars anyway, a couple of bills. She slipped out of her sandals and pushed open the door to the one room, apart from her bedroom, that made up the flat.

It could not be said that Harriet was a domesticated creature on any level if it involved time away from her business. Not like Lizzie, with whom she had once shared a flat, until she had decided she needed somewhere less constricted than a two-bed flat overlooking the Holloway Road, to house her burgeoning pottery business, and had gone off to live in a large flat in Hackney with a garden. Well, a yard at least. There was no arguing with the fact that Lizzie could put the average interior designer to shame. And at half the price.

Harriet loved Lizzie, but in her heart she was secretly relieved that a woman who could have written a government white paper on domesticity, was going to practise it a good two miles away.

Cupcakes poured from Lizzie's oven, everything was cooked from scratch, a woman who believed you could never have enough silk shades or cashmere throws to turn anything, from the most broken down lamp to an ugly sofa, into a piece of artistry fit for the pages of a glossy magazine. Lizzie despaired, not just of Harriet with her insistence on a pared down look in her new home, but also of Elena's encouragement. In Lizzie's mind, Harriet had lost an opportunity to show flair and imagination. What she actually meant was that when Harriet had moved into this flat, she should have listened to her and not Elena.

'It needs big mirrors,' Elena had instructed, echoing Harriet's thoughts when she'd first shown her the flat. 'A Kilim in here,' she tapped the wooden parquet floor with her cane. 'No fitted carpets,' she turned and gave her a sharp look. 'Such things are very déclassé and this room does not deserve it. Keep it simple. So much more effective. You may,' she said over her shoulder, 'keep the sofa. It is old but it has style.'

Startled, at the imperiousness of the more confident figure than her regular appearances at Raglan Parade had suggested, Harriet had glanced around at the faded three seater sofa in its birch frame and looked quickly back at Elena. It was not Harriet's area of expertise, but even a novice dealer would immediately see past the torn and tattered upholstery to a once beautiful Biedermeier sofa. Done up, re-covered in maybe dark blue stripe cotton, it would fetch a sizeable sum. She said nothing, just let Mrs Banbury talk up the apartment to the point where Harriet fully expected to hear there was a queue of alpha celebrities circling the block to get their hands on it. Not to mention the sofa.

'Look, Mrs Banbury,' she had said at last. It was one thing to spot a bargain in an auction house and say nothing, but she couldn't do such a thing to an elderly woman. 'I can't be sure, but I think – restored of course – the sofa could be quite valuable. I think it might be a Biedermeier.'

Elena looked sharply at her. 'Of course it is. If you want to keep it, you're welcome. Now through there is the bedroom. Come.'

And now two years later, having decided that this lanky girl with the blonde hair, serious expression and her stall in a market, was to live next door along with the sofa, now immaculate in shades of blue and grey cotton, and a Kilim rug spread across the highly polished floor that had taken Harriet two weeks to sand and varnish – (with just a shrug from Elena when she asked if she might do it) – Elena was satisfied with the look that made up Harriet's home.

By now, of course, it was too late to mention the more brutal truth that the flat Elena had rented to her was in a far worse shape than Harriet had expected and anyone else would have walked away. There were, increasingly, times when high, peeling ceilings, and ill-fitting windows seemed determined to overwhelm her and she had to steel herself to ignore the noises from the boiler in the kitchen. But she could not bring herself to push Elena to pay for the repairs. And anyway, with what? No-one lived as stringently as Elena unless they had to.

In the end, Harriet settled for the location making her life easier, and cut back on the idea of ever having enough money to get a mortgage to buy her own apartment. In time, she told herself. In time. But as the months wore on, even Harriet could not ignore the lurching stomach, as she slowly realised that trying to stay ahead of the flaws this place daily challenged her with, her life was rapidly becoming like one of those old movies, where the heroine was being pursued downhill by a runaway piano, with nothing but a broken umbrella to protect her. And the faster she ran, the more it picked up speed.

Night after anxious night she had begun to sift through her accounts to find ways of saving, while at the same time she trawled her way through catalogues to monitor if prices were changing in her favour, watched, as she was obliged to let pieces she would once have certainly picked up at auctions, go to higher bidders.

And at the end of such a day as this, she had gratefully crawled under a cool sheet and tried to sleep. The bank had been getting heavy; the latest builder called in to give an estimate, this time on window frames, and had said they would all need replacing and in keeping with the conditions of residency which, too late, Harriet had bitterly observed, were enforceable. They were the most expensive you could buy, but the idea of Elena finding the money to have her own repaired, let alone Harriet's, was laughable.

It was getting light before anything remotely approaching the blessed oblivion of sleep claimed her. The past – she punched her pillow, turned it over, tried to find a cooler spot to help blot it out – was a very tiresome, unwelcome ghost. Just like Dermot. It wasn't as though she had ever really loved him, she knew that now – obsessed? Probably. Blinded by his pursuit of her. Obviously. But love? Of a kind, she supposed, but not the enduring kind that she had seen with her brother and his Kate, or her parents' quiet but undoubted devotion to each other – just something that felt perilously like it. Even so, she lay there staring at the ceiling, wondering what would have happened, had Dermot figured in her life less cataclysmically. Would she have become a jeweller? Certainly money would not have been an issue. His infidelity of course, might.

It had all, quite abruptly one afternoon, unravelled painfully and humiliatingly, when, on her way to his apartment to surprise him, she caught sight of a woman who she thought might have been called Caroline – or was it Christine? She couldn't remember, but she did recall the elfin creature with sleek black hair and a cotton dress that she was *almost* wearing, trying to pass herself off as a secretary. Harriet had left, stumbling wildly away to find a cave to hide in. An encounter that had had the dual effect of launching her as a jeweller, since she had picked up so much expertise from him, while effectively ending her happiness for a considerable time.

If she regretted anything, it was the unimaginable stupidity of not hanging onto the several really good pieces of jewellery that Dermot had given her. She felt ashamed to think how shallow that made her sound, to admit that her unhappiness had more to do with pride than a lost relationship. Traded in, those pieces would have been a couple of month's worth of rent sorted. But on the whole, she preferred to remember them hitting him one by one as she slung them back.

And when she did finally drift off to sleep, it was only to have a very muddled dream and nothing to do with him at all, in which she was wandering around the streets with Elena, not being able to find where she was supposed to be living and all the while trying to tell Elena that it would help her to sleep if she at least took off her jacket, put on a nightgown and put everything she valued out of sight.

Chapter Three

Without the dubious pleasure of having drunk more than two glasses of wine the night before, Harriet woke with a mild hangover, to discover that a new day was not necessarily an easier day after all. Her carefully laid plans were abruptly derailed when she found she was out of not just milk but coffee as well. Facing Adrian, her accountant, even if it was by phone, was a matter she dreaded at the best of times, but without coffee it was impossible.

There was also a text from her mother, from the house in the mountains outside Madrid where she lived with Harriet's father and from where she painted distant hills, flamenco dancers in village squares, white washed houses and contented cats lying on sun-drenched balconies, while her father sat in his study writing well-received thrillers with marginally greater success than her mother's spirited, if over-romantic, take on Spanish life.

I am your mother, the text said. *Remember me? What are you going to do? Is closure inevitable? New York flight booked. Come with us. Ring tonight?* x

Harriet gave a guilty wince, rapidly texting back. *Will do. Promise. Just busy. Love you.*

She pulled a cotton blazer over her t-shirt, pushed her feet into a pair of battered white plimsolls and pressed the buzzer for the lift, relieved that while the bag of jumble was still there, there was no sign of Elena to halt her progress. She scooped it up and dropped the bag by the front door, only to find, as she jogged round the corner into the main road, the elderly woman standing on the edge of the kerb, stick firmly in hand, glancing impatiently up and down the road.

'Okay?' Harriet said, half tempted to just call a greeting and carry on. But there was something about Elena, normally so impervious to noise and bustle around her, always rising haughtily above such inconveniences, that made Harriet go back. 'I've left your stuff for the jumble sale at the door. Elena? Are you all right?'

'I am perfectly all right,' Elena said, clearly nothing of the sort. 'But the car is unforgivably late. Eight thirty they said. And it's now nine and I've missed the post. And milk. I need milk but I'm afraid the car will come when I am in the shop and—'

'Give me those,' Harriet took the bundle of letters. All utilities, she noticed. She stuffed them into the letter box. 'I'll get you the milk later. Not a problem.'

But Elena's agitation only seemed to grow. Her head turned like a spectator at a tennis match, searching the traffic this way and that.

'What car?' Harriet took her arm.

'The one that silly woman on the phone said they would send to take me to the hospital. I am to be X-rayed. My stupid hip. I have an appointment in – well – now it is in half an hour. And I will be late. And they will blame me. They always do.'

'Shouldn't you have someone with you?' Harriet unthinkingly put her arm around Elena's shaking shoulders. Through the thin fabric of Elena's jacket, Harriet felt little more than a set of bones. She frowned. This was so unlike the elderly woman who would generally be composing a strong complaint to those responsible rather than sounding so helpless.

'It was arranged. That ridiculous woman who insisted on seeing me home last night.'

Harriet said nothing. The woman didn't sound ridiculous, rather kind in fact. But then she had long learned that Elena would see any attempt at help as a comment on her ability to cope.

'I think she forgot,' Elena shook her head impatiently. 'Or maybe didn't quite understand, but this morning, she phoned and she had to go somewhere, urgently and I should never have believed her but she was insistent and wasted my time. So – I telephoned the hospital and they said they would send a car but—'

'Hang on,' Harriet said, pulling out her mobile and taking the card from the hospital that Elena was holding. What on earth was going on here? 'Let me call them. Let's see that number?'

Ten minutes later, having been cut off three times and redialled four, Harriet found herself in the grip of a hopelessly pointless discussion with a receptionist at the hospital, who simply repeated that Mrs Branford – sorry Banbury – certainly had an appointment but she wasn't down for a lift in their minibus, let alone a car. It said on her notes that she would be accompanied and most certainly, as her treatment involved mild sedation, she had to have someone with her at all times. Was she Mrs Banbury's carer? Then she must know that if Mrs Banbury was late she would lose her slot.

The only thing that was lost was Harriet's temper.

'I'm her neighbour,' she shouted, above the noise of a passing lorry. 'That's all. I'm nothing to do with this. The friend who was bringing her has been—' The line went dead. Harriet silently swore.

Behind her, Elena was looking uncertain. Almost vulnerable. Harriet hesitated. Oh God. What now? Briefly she closed her eyes.

'Wait,' she ordered Elena. 'Wait. I'll take you. No. Fine,' she said, taking Elena's arm. 'Really. It's fine.'

Ten minutes later, by risking the wrath of a couple of buses, she managed to run to the island in the centre of the street and flag down a cab. For Elena to have managed such a thing without courting disaster, would have required divine intervention. All the way to the hospital, Elena hung grimly onto the strap, while Harriet frantically rang everyone, from the buyers who were scheduled to pitch up at Raglan Parade, to Adrian to swear on her life that the accounts would be there by the end of the day, to James, not answering, meaning there was no point in leaving a voicemail.

'I have made your day difficult,' Elena said as they swung into the entrance of the hospital.

'Not a bit,' Harriet lied and switched off her phone. 'Now, let's see where we have to go.'

Any plans that she would simply make sure that Elena got safely to the right department, then leave to get on with her day, unravelled when it dawned on her that the outpatient receptionist's interest in how Elena had got there was no longer of any importance – if indeed it had been of interest in the first place – and now lay in how Elena would be returned home.

'I can take a bus,' Elena insisted. 'I'm not in my dotage. In fact I could have taken one here if you had given me more time. Quite, quite irresponsible. I can't believe—'

Both Harriet and the receptionist ignored her.

'Your name?' the receptionist demanded of Harriet. Harriet could hardly hear the receptionist, already harassed by the demands of the day and still only a quarter past nine, huddled as she was behind a computer screen in the stuffy waiting area. The whole experience was alarmingly revealing. A hospital that, on first inspection, looked modern enough and fit for purpose was, Harriet realised within minutes of arriving at the reception desk, nowhere near capable of dealing with everything an overpopulated part of the city could throw at them. It was hopeless.

'Flynn,' Harriet said. 'Harriet Flynn. But look, this is nothing to do with me. I'm simply – oh for God's sake – no, no "e" on the end. You don't need my address – oh for crying out loud, Flat four, Denbigh Mansions – no not the same address, it's next door to Mrs Banbury. She's at Five. I told you, I'm her neighbour.'

'Take a seat,' the receptionist said, without even looking up. 'She'll be called when it's her turn.'

'How long will she be?' Harriet asked in alarm. She had only bought herself an hour to get her own day back on track. The rows of people crammed into the waiting area argued heavily against her getting anywhere useful anytime soon.

The receptionist looked at her screen. 'Not long,' she said vaguely. 'About an hour. Once the procedure starts. Now please, would you just sit down? Yes?' She had already turned to the next person in the line behind Harriet. 'Your name?'

All Harriet could hope for was that by some minor miracle, she could drop Elena off and still get down to Guildford by two o'clock. The crowd behind her, which was increasing, now appeared to be at the point where there was standing room only, and evidence, if evidence were needed, that wishful thinking was a waste of time.

'Okay,' she said, as cheerfully as a murderous heart would allow, sitting in a vacant chair next to Elena. 'All sorted.'

Elena turned and for a long moment just stared at her.

'What is it?' Harriet asked. 'Are you okay?'

'I need,' Elena said finally, looking vaguely round. 'To use the facilities.'

*

By the time Harriet had deposited Elena onto her bed, still rather sleepy from the quite mild Valium shot Harriet had been assured it was, which had been administered to keep her still during a scan on her hip, it was too late to go anywhere, let alone the middle of Hertfordshire. There had been several moments on the journey home, when she had wondered if she'd even get her out of the taxi, let alone up to her flat. Only Elena's sense of dignity and iron will, she was sure of that, had stopped her falling asleep.

'Elena,' she said as Elena finally closed her eyes. 'I'll take your keys. All right? Elena? Can you hear me? I have to let myself in later. After I've locked up at the stall. I promised I'd check you. Elena?'

'Of course,' the old lady replied sleepily. 'But there is no need.' She half-raised her hand in a gesture of dismissal but the valium had done its work rather too well and it fell back on the brightly patterned silk cover, which in spite of the sultry afternoon, Harriet had pulled over Elena's thin frame, since her skin was surprisingly cold to the touch.

She had removed the old woman's leather sandals and, with some effort, the black taffeta fitted jacket Elena had been wearing, revealing thin spidery arms hanging limply from a thermal vest. And in this weather? Dear God. Eventually she managed to extract her from her skirt and was shocked at how thin Elena was, her cream silk petticoat almost swamping her. Harriet looked worriedly at the narrow face, the mouth slightly open and her breathing emitting a rasping snore. This wasn't right. Someone must be responsible for her. But who?

Harriet laid Elena's clothes on a scarlet-cushioned chair next to her bed and glanced around. It was the first time she had ever been further than Elena's drawing room with its ornate, uncompromising furniture, deeply draped silk curtains, every corner struggling to contain shelves of books, the walls lined with photographs from a time, she supposed, when Elena's daily life did not involve struggling with the lunacy of complicated hospital appointments or the ferocious challenge of remaining independent.

Somewhere, Harriet reflected – in the midst of this tribute to a life that had accumulated too much in memories but now so little in usefulness to an elderly woman with a bad hip, to a lady with only a sharp intellect and stubbornness standing between her and a life in an institution – somewhere there must be the practical evidence of a local doctor, social services, anyone who could take over. The friend, even if she could find her, who had been scheduled to take Elena to the hospital had been taken ill, so really, she sighed, what was the point in bothering her, even if she knew how?

The idea of anyone in the Banbury family – Elena's late husband's estranged tribe – being prepared to help such an elderly relative, was laughable. For reasons that shifted whenever Elena talked of him, they appeared to have cut him off when he married her and Harriet was pretty certain that anyone in the present generation of Banburys would have trouble recalling Elena, let alone feel obliged to help.

Once, Elena had told her, their opposition to her marriage to Arthur was because they had him lined up to marry a considerable heiress, who had eventually married the duke of somewhere or other. Another version had Elena being pursued across Europe by the lovesick Arthur who had lost his entire fortune to the casinos in Monte Carlo or Paris, where Elena had once worked as a croupier, and the family were united in blaming her for encouraging his dissolute life.

Besides, how would she find them? In the early days, when Harriet barely knew her, she had felt uneasy at the number of brooches, cameos and bracelets that Elena had begun to ask her to sell on her behalf, so she had checked out Arthur's family in Debrett's in case they came looking for their property. There was no trace of him. In the end, Harriet had decided that Arthur had talked up his family in the grandest of terms, in the same way that Elena only talked of hers in the vaguest.

Meanwhile, Harriet had to urgently organise her own life. Softly closing the bedroom door on the grand bed with its carved bed head that occupied most of the room, Harriet bit her lip. What now? She sighed and flicked on her phone.

'James? Look, could you be a dear and help Kerry close up? I'll be back later. I've just got to find someone to stay with Elena for the night. Shouldn't take long.'

'Stay with her?' he exclaimed. 'Blimey. What's the matter with her?'

'Nothing. Well, no more than usual. She had a test this morning. I went with her and they gave her a shot of valium. Just hasn't worn off yet.'

'Ring one of those social services people,' he advised. 'And why were you with her anyway?'

'Long story. Tell you later. Sorting Kerry would be brill. Thanks James, you're a dear.'

Then she called Lizzie and ducked out of dinner with her and her latest boyfriend.

'You're hopeless,' Lizzie said severely. 'I've got the most amazing friend of Clive's coming – oh all right. *All right.* But Clive will be cross, he went to so much trouble to fix this up and you'll be sorry when Carstair—'

'*Carstair?*' Harriet shrieked. 'Don't tell me that's a proper name. He sounds like a butler.'

'Carstair,' Lizzie repeated heavily, 'is French and charming. And when he takes his bank balance and apartment overlooking the Seine elsewhere and marries someone else, you'll be sorry.'

'You mean you'll be,' Harriet laughed. 'Tell Clive I'm sorry.'

Lizzie sniffed, said she might and she would have to square it with Clive because he'd gone to a lot of trouble over this one.

Harriet thanked her, tried not to laugh and knew like most of the men in Lizzie's life, Clive was not permanent. Just another man with first-class looks but half-rate brains who Lizzie thought would be the one and never understood why they bored her in a week.

'If I can find someone to take over here, I'll dash over in time for coffee. With – seriously? – Carstair. Honestly, Liz, I can't leave her. Big kiss.'

'Now,' she said switching off her phone, and to no-one in particular, 'let's see if we can get this show on the road.'

*

'Could you just verify your address?' asked the GP's office when she finally got through.

'You mean Mrs Banbury's?' Harriet corrected.

'No. Yours. You are Miss Flynn? Her next of kin?'

'Her *what*?' Harriet exclaimed. 'No, no. That's not right. I'm no relation at all to her. I'm just a neighbour. I rent my flat from her.'

'Oh dear. Mrs Banbury must have given your name. We need one if anything happens. Oh don't worry, happens a lot. Old people – well the ones on their own – often give a neighbour's name. Doesn't she have any relatives?'

'Not that I know of. I hardly – well, I do know her – but she never talks about her family. Well, her late husband occasionally – look isn't there anyone who can—?'

'It says here,' the voice ignored her, 'she was due to have a scan this morning. Did she go?'

'Yes. I took her. But I wasn't meant to. A friend – no I don't know who she is – let her down at the last minute. I just happened to see her and went to help. That's all. But the hospital said she needed someone to stay with her. A nurse or someone. Surely—?'

'It says here,' the voice broke in, 'that she's on the social services list. Try them. Have you got the number? Here you are.'

Almost five. Harriet rang the number. While she stabbed a finger at what seemed like a million options to get to the right person, she made a very strong mental note that when Elena woke and was feeling better, she would have a word with her about all of this.

'You do know who she is?' she asked the voice on the other end of the phone. 'Mrs Banbury?'

'Oh yes,' said an uninterested voice, after taking several minutes to locate

Elena's name. 'She's on our list. I see we've offered everything in the way of help, but she's refused.'

'Of course she has,' Harriet snapped. It was hot. She was tired. A feeling closely akin to panic was creeping over her. 'She's very stubborn about her independence, but surely someone must have checked on her?'

'Unless she's ill and bedridden – and she's not is she? – we can't make anyone, no matter what their age, accept help they don't want. I'm sorry, we're stretched to breaking point here. The best I can do is to get someone to come in first thing. But,' she paused for a moment as though checking something. 'I'm sorry, but it says here, she does seem to do very well with the help of a neighbour. Is that you? Flyte, is it? Oh, sorry, Flynn. Next of kin it says here.'

'It may well say that,' Harriet tried to stay calm. 'But I'm no such thing. Is no-one listening to—? Oh forget it.'

She slumped back in the chair. This was hopeless. Relations, she told herself firmly. That's who she needed to find. Elena's own relations, not Arthur's. Failing that, maybe a friend or two. Yes, that was it. Much more likely. Very occasionally, early on Sunday mornings, when Harriet had decided a jog in the park was well overdue, she would see Elena waiting for a bus to take her to the Russian Orthodox Church two miles away, and she would think how eccentrically elegant she was. Always one of her silk blouses in a myriad of patterns, tucked into severe linen skirts, and in winter the usual pillbox, which in summer was replaced by a plain straw hat, alternating with one with a brim so wide it could shade her from Mars if required.

Once, she told Harriet that what drew her to church was not so much a sense of identity, of spiritual need, but the carvings, the rich gold tapestries, the candles, which reminded her of her childhood and her mother's strong undentable faith.

It was, though, perfectly possible that among that community at the church, someone would know more. Tomorrow she would ask.

What she needed now was to find someone sensible to bring order to Elena's untidy life, since she had abandoned all hope that anyone could be found that night to stay. In which case, she thought with a groan, it would have to be her, spending the night in this cavernous, dark and unbearably hot apartment.

Air, she decided. Get some air in here. The double casement windows with their little Juliet balconies would be a start. Harriet pushed both doors, but they refused to budge. Finally, and by now her temper not in a good place, she pushed her shoulder against the centre and they swung open with a lurch, propelling her forward onto the rails of the balcony. A lump of plaster promptly showered down, spraying grit onto her face.

'Bloody hell,' she yelped, jumping back inside the room. Cautiously she peered up at the crumbling window frame, wiping her face. Across the top, she could see bare brick exposed and down one side, what looked like lengths of screwed-up paper that someone, probably Elena, had wedged into the crack to keep the draught out and the window in place.

This, she thought furiously, is ridiculous. Elena was not, surely to God, so poor that she had to put up with this? But she was old and probably not listened to. And as Harriet knew all too well, it was hard to help the old woman unless she wanted you to. Tomorrow, she told herself grimly, carefully easing the paper wedge from its moorings, the management company was in for a tirade. For heaven's sake, they all paid enough for the farce known as the upkeep. And she would be firm with Elena. Insist she listened to her advice. Refuse to be daunted by her familiar imperious wave of her hand.

The screwed-up paper came away in a rush, bringing with it more plaster. Harriet pushed it onto the side table behind the window and went in search of something to clear up the mess.

Eventually, having failed to find anything that looked remotely serviceable, she found a disused plastic bag and a tea cloth and swept the evidence of disrepair into it, fully intending to show the social worker when she arrived what Elena was reduced to to keep warm: wedges of paper in cracks, although, she was uneasily aware that arguing such a case in a heatwave was not going to be convincing. Surely, though, they would be able to get someone to help? On closer inspection, the paper wedge appeared to be a couple of cards, rolled into tubes to stop the window sash from crashing down. Maybe tomorrow Elena could tell her if there was someone who would like to be kept up to speed with her health.

To one side of the windows, where she could feel the odd rustle of wind from the street outside, there was an oak table, stacked with books and folders – and not any old folders. Elegantly patterned ones bound in cloth with embroidered peacocks or embossed flowers – well-worn manila envelopes, dog-eared and stuffed with letters and cards, hard to say for what occasions, a musky smell floating out as she rifled through them. She pulled a chair out and sat down, squashing a flash of unease that this was an awful invasion of Elena's private life, but what else could she do?

Since everything seemed to have been written decades before and nothing at all in English, she wasn't sure it mattered. Faded black-and-white photographs and cards written in Russian – no hope of gleaning anything from them since she couldn't speak it let alone read it. A lot in German, but since her grasp of the language, which had been flimsy in the first place, and from lack of use since A-levels was now reduced to figuring out only the simplest of terms, she abandoned them. The ones in French were easier. Demands from creditors, long dead and long given up it appeared, on any hope of ever finding Arthur Banbury, who seemed to slide easily from their radar when they attempted to get him to honour his debts. What kind of man had Elena married? No wonder she struggled with money. There couldn't have been a penny left when he died.

'Bugger,' she muttered. 'A cleaner. That's what Elena needs.' She wiped the top layer of dust away with the edge of the curtain. This couldn't go on. Independence was one thing, but apart from the whole place being in a state of advanced neglect, the apartment was a death trap.

'I'm staying,' she told James when he rang. 'It's awful. Absolutely no-one else can do it. And by the way, she's got me down as next of kin.'

'She's what?' James exclaimed. 'You never told me.'

'Because,' she said crossly, 'no-one told me either. Listen, better go. Got to ring my mother.'

'She's done what?' Jane Flynn gasped down the phone. 'Darling, for heaven's sake. Doesn't she have any relatives? Friends?'

'You'd think,' Harriet agreed. 'But as far as I can make out, not a soul,' and immediately regretted telling her mother so much as the date.

For someone who lived hundreds of miles from both her children, Harriet in London and Seb, Harriet's older brother, happily ensconced by his company in Brooklyn for the next five years, with his American wife – the totally unflappable Kate – and their three, about to be four, children, Jane still remained a close chronicler of both her children's lives. But the air in the mountains just outside Madrid which had turned out to suit Harriet's father, Daniel, and more importantly his fragile chest – even if it did not entirely suit her mother – had been the deciding factor. Harriet and Seb had agreed and had told their mother – who was torn between her adult children and a husband who could not endure another winter in the north of England – that she was mad not to put their father first. And so Jane had compromised with a sprawling house in a village near Miraflores, just off the road that led to the airport, so that a trip to either of her children was no more complicated than getting to Barajas airport in less than half an hour. To Jane Flynn it was comfort of a sort.

This location however, did nothing to improve the fact – and to both her children's cost – that the smallest suggestion of a blip on their personal radar could easily result in a rush of alarming maternal protectiveness, involving her turning up unannounced on the next plane. This could be both a brilliant surprise or so unrelenting in its purpose, it could leave even the unflappable Kate reaching for the gin after she'd left.

'I'll come,' her mother said decidedly. 'You can put me up. No, I can stay with Keith and Hil. In fact I can be there on—'

'No, honestly, no.' Harriet interrupted hastily. Even the possibility that her mother would stay with her oldest friends, living a safe distance away in Potten End, an hour's drive out of town, didn't allay her alarm. 'No need to come. And they're miles away. No point. Truly Ma. Some social worker or other is coming in the morning. I'm fine. It's only next door. Now, how's Dad? How's the book coming on? All ready for Brooklyn?'

A good half an hour later, having discussed her sister-in-law's parenting skills – or in her mother's view, lack of them – which would be addressed during her forthcoming trip to view the latest arrival to the Flynn dynasty, followed by a discreet enquiry into Harriet's ongoing single status and then a trawl through the vicissitudes of trying to make Spanish plumbers – worse than the English apparently – understand that Monday at eleven did not mean the following Friday at four, Harriet promised to find a week in her diary to visit, and hung up the call.

Around ten, when she had emailed a copy of her accounts to Adrian, which he would get, not as she had promised by the end of the day, but at least first thing, and her eyes were sore from staring at her laptop, she began to worry that Elena was showing no sign of fully waking from a restless sleep. The hospital, when she got through, eventually passed her to someone who said to call her out-of-hours GP if she was concerned.

'Me concerned? Why aren't you?' Harriet demanded. 'You doped her up. Look,' she said, past caring who she upset after a day of being shuttled from one uninterested voice to another. 'If I don't get some sensible information, then I'm calling an ambulance and having her brought back.'

'I expect the Valium has worn off and she's slipped into her regular sleep,' said the next person who came on the line. 'She's very old,' the male voice pointed out. 'It could take longer than someone half her age to get it out of her system. Keep her hydrated and call the out-of-hours doctor if you're worried. I know,' he raised his voice over Harriet's concerned one, 'but they'll be able to assess her more quickly than us. We're very busy.'

Busy, busy, everyone bloody busy. Like she wasn't? Harriet threw the phone into an armchair and closed her eyes with frustration. An hour later Elena stirred briefly as Harriet tried to get her to drink some water.

'Why are you here?' Elena asked as Harriet bent over her. Her face was puzzled. She allowed Harriet to lift her head from the pillow to sip the iced water she'd brought with her, but even in the last hour, Harriet thought, her cheeks seemed to have shrunk.

'Don't want you to have a hangover,' Harriet said as cheerfully as she could. 'You had a valium earlier. Remember? When you had your scan? Knocked you out a bit. Some water will help.'

Elena stared at her. 'Yes. Yes,' she said finally, taking another sip of water. 'Of course. You must go home now.'

'No chance,' Harriet said firmly, only wishing that she could. She placed the glass on the bedside cabinet. 'I'm staying until the morning. Come on now. Back to sleep.'

She began to adjust the pillows under Elena's head, decided for the moment against anything more than a sheet to cover her, moved the water to where Elena could reach it if she woke again.

'A shop,' Elena said in a half-whisper, but her eyes closing. 'My mother always said so. Knew it was the only way.'

'And I'm going to make you find it for me,' Harriet said. 'When you're better. Now sleep.'

Elena turned her head so she could see Harriet's face. 'You're here,' she said distantly, almost wonderingly, the thin lips barely moving. 'I knew you would. Thank you.'

'Now you're really worrying me,' Harriet said only half-joking. 'I'll check on you again in a minute.'

'Yes. I want to talk to you.'

Harriet waited, Elena's eyes closed, her body still. She was about to creep away when Elena's eyelids fluttered.

'I want to tell you my plan,' her voice was much stronger. 'Always, always, you must have a plan. We go to Berlin—'

'Absolutely,' Harriet, relieved, soothed her. Frankly, she would have agreed to going to a small banana republic if it meant Elena would rest more easily. But Elena had already fallen back to sleep. Leaving the door half open, Harriet tiptoed away into the drawing room.

'Now what?' she grumbled to herself removing a pile of books and throws from a sofa, and flopping down. 'Can't see this rivalling a night at the Ritz.'

For want of anything to while away the hours, and too frustrated to sleep, Harriet shook the last drops of the wine she had brought from her flat into her glass, and started to wander around Elena's chaotic drawing room, gazing at photographs of long-dead people standing in stiff little groups in grand salons with exotic palms framing them; another of a small girl, probably no more than five years old, with short blonde hair and a thick fringe, leaning against the door of a wooden-framed house, half hidden behind a spreading leafy tree. Next to the child, with her hand on her shoulder, a woman, shading her eyes with her free hand, thin and wearing what appeared to be a scarf wrapped around her head. The inscription was in Russian.

She wondered if the child was Elena, but the image was too distant, taken so far away it was hard to tell. Next to it, a black-framed study of a lazy-eyed man, with a flop of hair over one eye and a cigarette between his fingers, taken, judging by the wide lapels of his jacket, probably in the years between the wars. Harriet peered more closely for clues, but there were none. More than likely, she yawned, the famous – and profligate it seemed – Arthur.

More interesting to Harriet, brought up in a house where books and paintings tended to be prized above the next meal, were the rows of leather-bound books, mostly Russian, packed tightly together on tiers of shelves in the oak-framed bookcases that rose to the ceiling on either side of the fireplace. The strange Russian Cyrillic print meant nothing to her. Squeezed up against them was an English version of the poems of Anna Akhmatova.

Intrigued by this glimpse into Elena's other world, one that had clearly shaped the elderly woman's beliefs and was probably the source of her rebellious character, Harriet ran her finger along the shelf and reached up to take one down. It helpfully had an imprint of the author's face, who she thought might be Pushkin with his black curly hair, high forehead and pointed nose.

'Could just as easily be Beethoven,' she muttered, having no great knowledge of either, but was then obliged to spend ten minutes trying to restore the avalanche of paperwork cascading from the pages of the books. Elena had clearly used them as a random repository for things that had no real home elsewhere in the cluttered flat.

More Russian than German, she sighed, and that was a fact. She was still clutching a bundle of letters when a sound from Elena's room sent her running in, stuffing the loose papers into the pocket of her jeans.

'I'm just next door,' Harriet said quietly. She lifted the old woman's head and gave her a sip of water. Elena seemed quieter, more peaceful. She squeezed her hand and instinctively, gently moved the long strand of grey hair out of her face. Elena stirred briefly, and gave her a vague, puzzled look. 'In the sitting room,' Harriet said.

A small sigh escaped Elena. Not anxious, more a contented one. 'You're near. That's – good,' her voice fluttered away.

'That's right,' Harriet squeezed her hand, relieved she seemed to have rallied. 'Not far away. Promise.'

*

The sound of metal banging sharply against the window woke Harriet from a fitful sleep on one of the sofas of which its size, rather than comfort, was its only saving grace. She sat up with a start, pushing a cushion, that she appeared to have been hugging, from her chest, stifling an oath as a pain at the back of her neck made her wince. For a moment she had to recall where she was, blinking at the sturdy furniture seeming to fill the room, the paintings on the wall in their heavy frames that swam into focus as she groped for her phone. Five, it said.

A pale, watery light was already making itself felt through a gap in the curtains. With a groan, she pushed herself to her feet and rescued the banging casement window, hooking it back on its moorings, before deciding to make Elena some tea and wake her before the social services person appeared. She always rose at six, she knew that.

Dead on the dot of six she went to her. The door was still propped open. Gently, she placed the tea on the bedside table, pulled the heavy curtains partially aside and looked carefully back to Elena to see if she was stirring. There was no movement from the bed. Harriet let the tassel on the curtain fall.

'Elena?' she said almost sharply. She crouched by the bed. 'Elena? What is it? Elena? Answer me? Oh my God,' she breathed. She scrabbled for her phone, wresting it from the pocket of her jeans. Long afterwards, she could not remember giving an address or a name as she hung up the phone and threw it on the bed.

'Oh God.' She fell to her knees by the bed and clutched the old woman's hand in both of hers. Elena's eyes moved slowly, almost unseeingly to hers. Harriet's heart pounded, her hands were shaking. Elena's breathing was shallow, laboured. Hearing, someone had once told her – God alone knew who it had been – but they'd said it was the last sense to go.

'I'm here,' she told Elena gently putting her mouth close to her ear. 'Elena? It's Harriet. I'm here. I won't leave you. I promise. What is it?'

The thin mouth moved soundlessly, but Harriet knew, absolutely knew, she was struggling to say, 'Mama.'

Chapter Four

It was a jovial man, sitting in his spartan office above a row of shops on Fenton Street, tucked behind Victoria Station, just three days after Elena's death, who broke the news to Harriet that she had inherited Mrs Arthur Banbury's entire estate.

'Her what?' Harriet looked blank. 'What estate?' she asked. 'What are you talking about?'

'Well, there's a little way to go yet,' cautioned the plump little man in front of her, peering over the tips of his fingers, confusing her bewilderment at the news with not understanding what it all meant. He had introduced himself on the phone as Derek Pottinger, senior partner in Pottinger and Pottinger Associates, Elena Banbury's solicitor. Social services had found the fat package from him stuffed in a drawer next to Elena's bed, after she had died, and in the circumstances, opened it.

'Rather careless,' he said reprovingly. 'These elderly people. Very forgetful. I mean she'd made an appointment to see me, just a day or two before she died, but she didn't keep it. She rang and said she would come when she was feeling better. She would like some advice, but there you are. She never came back.'

Harriet was only surprised the will was so easily located and wasn't stuffed into the back of a book somewhere in her flat, but she refrained from saying so.

'I expect she wanted to keep it somewhere close to her,' she suggested. 'But at least it was found.'

'I mean, we have to go through probate and the executors are me – or rather this company,' he corrected himself not bothering to point out the company was now, due to a downturn in business and having had to lay off two more junior solicitors, only him and Christopher, his rather reluctant son. 'And her bank manager, of course. So sudden. But at her age, there we are.'

He shook his head at the vagaries of life. 'Quite a few months ago now she came in about it. Well, she said it was her first will, but I have my doubts. Someone would have advised her when her husband died to make one – when was that now?' He rustled the pages backwards and forwards. 'Ah, my goodness thirty-four – no I lie – thirty-five years ago. But she said no-one had mentioned it, so no matter. My secretary witnessed it. And our accountant who happened to be here. All nicely tied up. She hated a fuss, just read it through, made no changes. Her wishes to the letter. We posted her a copy the very next day.'

He gave a hearty laugh. 'And,' he beamed at her. 'As you probably know, she made you,' he leaned forward with a broad smile, 'her sole beneficiary.'

Harriet stared at him. 'She's done *what*? What for? I thought this was about helping you find relatives or something. I thought that's what you wanted to see me for.'

'But she named you her next of kin.' He sat back astonished. 'I thought you would be expecting—'

'Look,' Harriet stopped him. 'Can you start again? I'm not her family. I'm most certainly not her next of kin. Dear God, will everyone stop thinking that. Surely she named someone else?'

He glanced through the beige, very stiff paper document that was unfolded in front of him. He shook his head. 'No. Not a mention. She must have been very fond of you.'

He bent his head sideways to look at her. Harriet had dropped her head in her hands. 'Miss Flynn? Are you all right? Surely you were expecting to be named?'

'No,' Harriet almost shouted. 'No. Not in a million years. Why would she do that? Surely someone else is entitled to her – you know – her stuff?'

'As to that,' he shook his head sorrowfully. 'Rather sad. She said it would make no difference, her will I mean. The way she'd set things up. It would seem that those that are alive, if indeed there are any left – well, her late husband's family she long ago lost touch with and hardly knew. And all her relatives seemed to have died in the war, or disappeared. We tried a while back; a cousin, here look.'

He turned a long piece of buff paper around, to show her the record of their rather pointless exercise.

'The address,' Mr Pottinger said pulling the sheet back round to himself, 'was long gone. Bombed I suppose, and no trace of the family, so it was just returned. I believe she also tried privately every now and then, but so many people were lost, the Berlin Wall didn't help, all rather hopeless. We did our best,' he spread his hands in a small helpless gesture. 'But there you go. Maybe when you're going through her apartment you might find some address or name if you feel you want to contact them. Let them know. Courtesy, really, that's all. I mean, you're named and perfectly entitled not to. It's all yours now.'

'She might have been elderly,' Harriet protested. 'But she had her wits about her. And she would take her will very seriously. If she said there wasn't one before this, or anyone to tell, I would tend to believe her.'

He looked doubtful. 'If you say so. You knew her, of course. I didn't. Actually,' he turned the pages in front of him. 'Ah yes, here we are. She's made one or two small bequests that she wants us to honour. A small sum to the church where she worshipped. The Russian number up the road, and a charity she supported which we've dealt with. Ah yes, and a watch for someone called James Hagan. We'll let him know. We might need a new address of course.'

'James? Yes, that's his address,' she read where he was pointing on the document. 'How very kind of her,' Harriet exclaimed. 'He'll be so touched.'

'Well, she says here her late husband won it gambling and it belonged to—' he ran his eye down the page. 'Ah here we are. The Grand Duke of Selzburg. Somewhere in Switzerland, I think that is. It doesn't say what date. She's even left instructions about her burial and a sum of money to cover the expense.'

'You're kidding?'

'No. Absolutely not. You'll find it all here.'

Harriet took the file he offered her.

'What do I do now?' she asked.

'Well, don't start spending just yet,' he advised. 'I know, I know,' he held up a hand as she began to protest she had no intention of doing anything of the sort. 'Wait for probate. Could take a few weeks. Meanwhile, you might want to make sure she's buried in the way she requested.'

Harriet was not given to tears, but as she made her way down the narrow stairs, past the framed certificates to tell her that Derek Pottinger was a member of the Law Society and that they specialised in wills and probate, and then out onto the sun-filled street, she felt her throat constrict.

Oh, trust Elena. Wilful, annoying, clever, valiantly independent Elena, even now still in charge of her own life. And indeed death.

*

Later, after the funeral, which was attended by an odd mixture of women in headscarves, who stood in a group towards the back of the church, and a crowd of people from Raglan Parade, regular customers among them, milled around in the centre, drawn either by curiosity – Vince – or affection – James, William, Big Jake, Mimi and Colin, she walked home. Not before she had drunk enough wine in their usual wine bar, with the soon-to-be-disbanded crowd from Raglan Parade, where they honoured Elena's memory and exclaimed at Harriet's good fortune.

It was odd how she had become the – well – the chief mourner, she supposed, and she did her best, but at times she'd struggled to make those who approached her understand the odd nature of her relationship with Eleanor, and because she hardly understood herself how she had found herself in this position, she gave up and accepted their condolences.

'Such a dignified woman,' said one removing her headscarf as they left the church. 'I'm sure you will miss her greatly.'

'Yes,' Harriet nodded, shaking her extended hand. 'We all will.'

Others, like the blonde woman who had irritated Elena with her constant nagging for advice, but had at least offered her some help, even if she had been sent packing, simply bowed her head briefly and smiled uncertainly. Harriet smiled back, expecting her to approach her, but she didn't, just turned away. The woman who collected Clarice Cliff jugs on the other hand, pressed her card into Harriet's hands and said she'd be happy to hear if she heard of anything she might be interested in.

'Out with the old,' James muttered as the woman sailed on.

The remainder – half a dozen or so from the local community – had simply touched her arm as they filed past and out of her life.

For a long while she stood in the window of her own apartment looking down onto the empty street, the black linen jacket she'd worn to the funeral thrown over a chair. She'd already kicked off her heels, but exhausted though she was, she felt restless, and for the first time since she'd moved into the flat next to Elena's, she felt irrationally uneasy.

It was not in her nature to be illogical but there was something about being next to the empty flat, yet still so full of Elena, that troubled her. She half expected to open her own door and see Elena suddenly open hers just a fraction until she'd made sure it was Harriet, her white hair – whatever the hour – in its perfect chignon, beckoning to her to look at a piece of jewellery, a book she'd discovered, fetch something from the shop on the corner, instructing her where to leave her latest black bin liner destined for a charity collector or lecturing her in her fractured accent on how to run her life.

She could hear her now: '*Always have a plan*,' or, '*Always look busy*.' And sometimes, when Harriet was a bit stressed, Elena would notice and she would reach out and tuck her finger under Harriet's chin and say, '*You are clever. You will always think of a way.*'

And instead of smiling at the memory, all Harriet could do was feel a sense of shame and regret that while she had found Elena in turns fascinating and frustrating, charming and bullying, she had also often found her a nuisance, not enquired too closely about her comings and goings for fear of being delayed for too long. And so for the first time since Elena had died, she sat on the edge of her bed and wept.

Chapter Five

'Hell's bells,' Lizzie called from the bedroom. 'Look at this will you?'

Harriet glanced into the room at the open doors of one of the cumbersome wardrobes crammed into Elena's bedroom.

'Grief,' she whistled, walking round the bed. 'Who knew?'

A line of evening dresses stared back at them. Colourful dresses, glamorous dresses that spoke of a life so far removed from this leaden flat, and an elderly proud old woman wearing serviceable sandals because her hips were worn out and her feet were swollen, it was terribly hard to imagine it might once have even existed. But there they were.

Fine lace, sumptuous rich velvet, smooth silk and layers of chiffon that wafted slightly in the draught of the door suddenly being pulled open. Jewel-encrusted collars and cuffs, with labels a little yellower than they might once have been, labels that Mimi could only dream about having on her stall. Mainbocher, Schiaparelli, Jean Patou.

Harriet looked thoughtfully at the collection that Elena had built up, a snapshot of her life with Arthur. A world of casinos and low life in high places, mistresses and rogues. Exquisitely tailored jackets and, movingly, a black short-waisted tuxedo with satin lapels that had clearly been Arthur's. Extraordinary, Harriet thought, to equate this life with the Elena she had known, all this evidence of a life that could never be repeated, and not just because the players were no longer there. The excess, the extravagance belonged to another age. Harriet knew a part of her thought it was faintly obscene. No wonder Elena and Arthur had ended up practically penniless. What would such a woman want her to do with it all?

'So what's the answer?' Lizzie called. She sashayed across the room clutching a blue emerald-encrusted satin cocktail dress against herself. 'A museum? Sell them? Wear them?'

'Oh that's definitely it. Honestly, Lizzie, can you see me at the wine bar wearing one of those? Nope. Going to give them to Mimi. Let her decide. No. Seriously. That's exactly what Elena would have wanted me to do. Give them to someone who would actually love them and let them sell them on to someone who would as well. Someone like Elena.'

'You're not serious?' Lizzie's eyes were round with amazement.

'Deadly,' Harriet said firmly. 'Lizzie? I was never that good to her. Not enough to have been given all this. I don't think I could justify it.'

'But you're happy to give some of it away? Even though she wanted you to have it all?'

'Why not?'

'You don't think that's not what she intended?'

Harriet shook her head. 'I'll have enough from the sale of both flats to try and get a small shop somewhere. Probably have enough as well to get somewhere to live. That's plenty.'

'Why not stay here?' Lizzie looked around.

'No,' Harriet said quickly. 'I don't think so. I could easily end up spending that much again putting it all right.'

'That bad?' Lizzie asked glancing around. 'Doesn't look awful.'

'Well it is,' Harriet said. 'The windows alone are an arm and a leg. No, let someone else do it, and – well – I've got a plan. Always have a plan. That's what she used to tell me. A shop is what she wanted me to have, but – I can't, simply *can't* justify the rest. And to be honest, this lot,' she waved an arm around the cluttered room, 'is not worth that much. I know it isn't. She could have paid a few bills, but the sum it would have raised meat it was not worth parting with them. Maybe in the end she would have done, but I don't think so.'

'You have been thinking,' Lizzie raised her eyebrows. 'But not even just a few dresses—?'

Harriet laughed. 'Elizabeth McCoy,' she said, watching Lizzie looking wistfully at an aquamarine silk number, heavily beaded and so sumptuous it deserved to be framed. 'Not even one. Mimi is the right person to have them. And she liked Mimi. It's not like I'm giving them to someone she didn't get on with.'

'And all the bags and shoes in these boxes?' Lizzie pulled back the first of six boxes crammed into the second wardrobe. A faint musty smell rose as she did so. 'Blimey. Looks like our Elena led quite a life. Look at these.'

She hooked a pair of evening sandals from a cardboard box, silver straps, high heels with diamante buckles. 'Stunning. And this,' Lizzie plucked a scarlet beaded bag from a pile. 'All going to Mimi?'

'The lot,' Harriet said firmly. 'But if you ask her nicely, I bet she'd give you that bag. And just look at all those glasses and goblets.'

'I don't want any glasses,' Lizzie objected. Reluctantly she replaced the bag in its box.

'I know that. Come here. Look.'

Harriet pushed open the door into the living room, now swamped with boxes, bubble wrap and evidence of the efforts they had made to extract order from the chaos. Books piled into groups, Elena's letters, old bills and anything that had been stuffed behind books and pictures; in boxes. Lampshades stacked, waiting to be wrapped, glass cabinets; groaning with exquisite china, wine glasses, brandy balloons, goblets that Harriet was sorely tempted to keep for herself, had been emptied and the contents stored in cartons.

'Beautiful,' she agreed.

'All of it. And probably worth a bit. But I've got enough to do with all that lot,' she pointed at the books and Elena's personal effects. She had to sell the flats and find somewhere to live. 'I think Big Jake is the rightful owner, don't you? Not me. And Elena really liked him too and even after she said he couldn't possibly have Russian blood in him, he still liked her as well. Which helps.'

Lizzie plonked herself down on a pile of books. 'Oh I suppose so,' she grumbled. 'I'd like to see Vince's face when he finds out. Oh go on, let me be there.'

'I don't care if he does go berserk. In the first place I can't stand him, and in the second I can't stand him because he is such a cheat and malicious, and never had a good word to say about Elena. Every time I looked round, he was gossiping to even perfect strangers about her. Even the ones just asking her advice. In fact,' she fumed, 'anyone who might be doing better than him. Obnoxious creep.'

'If you don't like him, just say so,' Lizzie said solemnly. 'But hey who cares? Especially as I know you're just waiting to tell me that one of those paintings propped up over there has my name all over it. Isn't that right?'

*

'There? See? Just look at her,' Vince whispered to a girl on the next stall. He nodded towards Mimi almost in meltdown over her good fortune. 'That's the result of crawling all over weird old ladies. Palming off a load of old tat on that unsuspecting idiot.'

'To be honest,' ventured Avril, who specialised in art deco lamps and did quite well, 'some of those dresses look amazing—'

'Oh for heaven's sake,' Vince shuddered. 'Flea market rubbish. Mimi's just another of Harriet Almighty Flynn's wretched fans. Pitiful. Personally, and I speak only as someone who thought the whole Mrs Banbury shenanigans was dreadful exploitation, Miss Flynn over there, should be very careful. But then she's so up herself, who would she listen to?'

'Careful of what?' Avril asked. She rather liked Harriet but she also liked gossip and Harriet had triggered enough for the whole market to be divided between being pleased for her, which – as life generally proves – turned out to be a great deal fewer than those who, out of earshot and her view, were just plain envious, not to say irritated by her good fortune.

Whatever else Vince might have had to say on the subject was drowned out by Mimi suddenly bursting into tears and telling everyone, that she was so stunned by Harriet's generosity, she was going to insist, positively *insist* that she took a commission.

'And Jake's going to make sure she does as well,' Mimi mopped her eyes. 'Aren't you Jake?'

Harriet began to protest but James stopped her.

'For God's sake,' he muttered, 'just agree will you? I think Mimi's on the brink of cardiac arrest. And I'm fed up with you being deified like this. And *I'm* the one, just to stop her bawling, who's agreed to take this lot to her spare room until she can go through it. Not *you*, please note. Or Colin. His back apparently.' He patted his own, grimacing exaggeratedly. 'But *me*.'

Harriet shifted uncomfortably. 'I'm really sorry,' she whispered back. 'I had no idea they'd react like this. I feel ridiculous. C'mon I'm late. Got to meet the estate agent at a shop I'm going to lease.'

'Eh? What shop?' James caught up with her, struggling into his jacket. 'Where? When?'

The wind nearly flattened them as they turned into the Kings Road and began picking their way through the crowds thronging the pavement, heading towards the far end where it would eventually curve round towards Parsons Green and Putney and – she had gleefully told herself – her new kingdom.

'A couple of days ago,' she grinned back at him. 'I didn't say anything because I didn't want to tempt fate. Got to get probate first. Just want to know what you think.'

It wasn't the biggest shop in the world, quite small in fact, but James was duly impressed. The arcade was short and narrow, a mere dozen shops ranged on either side, but while it was not the most fashionable in the world, it benefitted from passing trade as Raglan Parade had not. Harriet's was squeezed between two similar sized shops; on the left one that sold satin jackets in shades she wasn't sure she even knew existed, and velvet coats that she knew for certain would require a superhuman effort not to even hanker after, and on the other, a little emporium dedicated to artificial flowers, so exquisitely made, so easy to see how any of the palest pastels, sharp reds and pure whites crowding the shelves would turn a dull corner into an oasis of light. It was, James remarked, hard to tell the difference from the real thing.

'Harriet my old love,' he waved an arm around the dreary space. 'It's perfect.'

While the estate agent hovered discreetly in the doorway, James marvelled at the grown-upness of it all, and was so gratifyingly lost in admiration, as Harriet told Lizzie later, she had to keep reminding herself it was going to be hers and not his.

'And so many people have asked me about Elena, I'm going to call it Guseva and Flynn,' she told James. 'I have to pay her back somehow and I thought that was the proper thing to do. What do you think?'

'Good name,' he nodded. 'The Russian connection won't harm either. Sounds very established, not new. I am *so* jealous.'

'Don't be,' she advised. 'Elena might have given me the starting point, but I'm not that daft. This is going to mean very long hours for the next couple of years.'

'In which case,' James said, 'supper later, if I won't be seeing much of you. Your treat.'

She only half heard him. Mentally she was ratcheting up what would be needed before she could even open. Repainting of course, and the legacy of the previous tenant – strewn around the room in the shape of old boxes and piles of newspapers – removed. She itched to get started, and get a better sense of space and style; she could tell the place suited her.

More than that, it was just where Elena would have liked to have seen her; she would have approved of her choice. Harriet glanced around at the satisfactory future that lay ahead. It had all gone from zero to this in such a short time, it seemed, in an odd, cosmic way, as though Elena were guiding her. Which of course she knew was nonsense, but at the same time found the idea oddly energising. Who'd have thought it?

*

The rain that had started as a bossy, noisy downpour at dawn, had settled into a drizzle that looked set to last all day. Harriet's impatience to get things done, even by her own standards was almost manic. She still had to earn a living, but for the first time in over six weeks, well, since Derek Pottinger had given her the startling news of her good fortune, the prospect of poor sales and half-hearted buyers left her simply relieved it was now all part of her past.

She found James, already at his stall, signing for a thick white package that had been sent by special delivery.

'Hand delivered just now,' James said, handing it to her. 'For you.'

She'd never heard of Coates and Rawlings Solicitors. Then she read it, slowly sitting down, unable to grasp what was being said. Without looking, she laid her bag aside and shrugged off her coat. Accused of *what*?

With increasing bewilderment, she stared at the letter heading of a company of solicitors in London who, she read on the accompanying helpful leaflet for new clients, were specialists in wills, probate and under a special heading – coercion.

Most of the letter was couched in such complex legal terms she barely understood what was written. All she knew was that her heart was thumping probably an extra beat than was healthy; her face felt flushed.

But four things stuck. The first, was that they were acting on behalf of the late Elena Banbury's family, Arcadia Property Developers, with offices in Berlin, Zurich and Paris. The second, was that she was being accused of coercing an elderly, frail and sick woman to leave her estate to her, when it was the rightful estate of the Weber family in general, the major shareholders in Arcadia, and Natasha Weber in particular. A woman who was now physically very frail and relied almost totally on her grandson, the CEO of the company, to fight her battles for her. The third thing was that they wanted her to give the whole lot back, and this was her only opportunity to do so before they started court proceedings. Lastly, that they had not given her permission to use their elderly relative's name to promote her business.

'What is it?' James leaned around to look at her face. 'Why are you looking like that?'

Without a word, Harriet passed the letter to him.

'*Jeezus*,' James said, blankly reading it. 'I don't get it. Who are these people? What does this mean?' He glanced back at the letter, *Compensation for the distress Miss Flynn has inflicted on the remaining family.* 'What distress? What family?'

'No idea,' Harriet looked with bewilderment at the letter. 'It says that I – look at this bit – *the defendant in this case has taken steps to ensure the late Mrs Banbury was isolated from all those who loved her.* And dear God, look,' she pointed to the amount the complainant felt would assuage their suffering. Harriet sat down with a thump.

James's eyes widened. 'They have to be kidding. Right?'

Harriet glanced back at the top of the letter. Their client, it said, was one Kurt Weber, his grandmother being the first cousin of the late Elena Banbury, née Guseva. 'I hope to God they are,' she said. 'Kidding I mean. Short of selling my soul, where in God's name would I get a sum like that?

Chapter Six

Harriet paced up and down Christopher Pottinger's office, not at all thrilled with his reaction to the letter she'd put in front of him. She had not expected indignation from him, on the level that she herself was experiencing, but at the very least, she had assumed she would hear a robust rejection of the contents and all it implied.

Instead, he had simply shaken his head and said, 'Most worrying.' Followed by, 'Dear, dear. We will of course start by contesting their claim and refusing to accept their demands.'

'What do you mean, start?' Harriet demanded. 'Surely you just write to them, tell them to get lost and demand an apology for even suggesting such a thing?'

Christopher – with his fortieth birthday looming, balding and wearing a grey-striped suit over a pink shirt that made him at least look confident when he left his home each morning, to stride purposefully to Chislehurst Station to catch the same train to Victoria at the same time every morning, five days a week, changing at Charing Cross on the way, and if asked would have been hard-pressed to describe his journey on any given morning, so familiar was his routine –was seated behind the leather-scrolled desk, which until very recently had been occupied by his father. He eyed Harriet nervously. In the whole of his rather dull career with the family firm, he'd never seen anyone quite so angry.

'And you know who these people are?' he asked cautiously, looking up from the letter she'd thrust at him. 'This,' he peered at the letter. 'This Weber family?'

'Of course not. Well, once or twice she mentioned a cousin, Natasha, I never knew her surname. But your father said Elena had lost touch with her years ago. And even if she is still alive somewhere, what does it matter? Elena didn't die intestate. She left a will. Christopher? This is madness. I've never heard of the Webers or Arcadia. Ever.'

Christopher thought it probably not the moment to tell her that until half an hour before, he hadn't heard of them either, anywhere in England, let alone Berlin or Paris or, come to that, a prestigious company of architects of any size. Google had been his strongest source and ally in the short time it had taken between Harriet demanding to see him and her arrival. Christopher, who had relied on conveyancing of ordinary houses and commercial properties to keep the family business going, and had himself never bought anything more than a modest flat in Bromley, followed eight years later – after he'd married and the first of his two children were on the way – by a more ambitious house in Chislehurst, had felt a decided lurch of unease at the scale of Arcadia's reputation across Europe.

Harriet was made of sterner stuff, but even so she'd had to swallow hard to keep her nerve when she'd googled Kurt Weber to get the low-down on this man, living in another country and clearly, in her view, deranged. Head of a company founded by his grandfather in the aftermath of the second world war, a company that had gradually and successfully expanded from designing to developing property, her accuser was, according to the Arcadia website she'd hastily consulted, well known in Berlin for his good works, social conscience and his ex-wife, an American heiress, whose privacy he fiercely protected. No children, she noted.

Being wealthy, a patron of the arts and in his prime, his name, unsurprisingly, had become seamlessly linked with a number of attractive German women, the vast majority of whom seemed to be the mainstay of at least half a dozen European celebrity magazines and social columns in newspapers. Some were even known to be able to push up sales just by arriving at a restaurant without saying a single word.

His photograph showed a man in his forties – greying, urbane, with a wide, even smile – who clearly walked the halls of power with ease. Small wonder his track record with women was successful. She was only surprised, when she'd read his details twice over, that the list wasn't twice as long.

Glancing furtively from under his hand, and noting the rage gripping Harriet's expression, Christopher thought it wise, considering the weighty London firm they had called in to act for them, to resist the urge to tell anyone, least of all her, that the letter Harriet had emailed to him, a mere half hour before her arrival, had left him with an overwhelming desire for a darkened room until he'd got a grip on the situation.

It was, he knew miserably, going to be one of those days. In fact, until Harriet had phoned him dead on the dot of nine o'clock, just as he had arrived, struggling through the narrow door and up the stairs with a cappuccino from the coffee shop next door, and furious that once again his secretary – or rather the one he'd inherited from his father just a few weeks before and who showed him even less respect than she had to Pollinger senior – was nowhere to be seen, he hadn't planned to do much that day at all. His in-laws were descending for dinner, which meant his children would be spoilt rotten and refuse to go to bed, and that was quite enough to blight his day.

Faced with Harriet's frenzied arrival, and her clear belief that he was obliged to do something right then and there, he decided to adopt an expression that was meant to convey a greater depth of understanding of the matter than he actually had. With one finger on his forehead, his elbow resting on the desk top, he reread the letter. It was, and if his father had been there he would have recognised it instantly, not a gesture designed to gain a greater grasp of the accusations it contained, but a device to give him time to think what on earth he was to do next.

'What's he talking about?' Harriet demanded when he finally placed the letter squarely and carefully on his desk. 'What "undue influence"? And what is that anyway?'

'Undue influence,' Christopher began, visibly relieved he was on safer ground for the first time since she'd marched into his office. 'Is power over someone else which is used to push the weaker person into making a decision which they would not otherwise have made.'

Harriet simply stared at him. In front of her lay evidence of Elena's wishes. Wishes that had been prepared by Derek Pottinger, this young man's own father, who now, it turned out, had almost immediately after her first and only visit to his office, departed and was now living in retirement in Southern Spain with his second wife, when it seemed to Harriet he should be here. Now. This minute. Sorting out this ludicrous claim. Or at the very least he could have mentioned to her that he was retiring hot on the heels of Elena's death, leaving her in the hands of his son, who was very red in the face and not much else.

Even by the time she *did* find out about his retirement, the fact that Pottinger Senior had never in any way been obliged to tell her of his own plans simply didn't show up on her radar. In truth, since neither party had ever believed there would be any reason to see each other again, there had been no need. Nevertheless – and she knew she was being totally irrational – she was furious that he wasn't there. And scared.

'And that's what I'm meant to have done to Elena?' she cried. 'Made her do something she didn't want to? But how? When? Elena was so bloody minded most of the time, you couldn't even get her to take her medicine, let alone agree to anything as – as dreadful as – as what they're suggesting. How can they? On what grounds?'

'Well, they appear to be citing a classic example of a situation in which undue influence might be used in the drafting of a will. Someone could pressure the testator – that's the late Mrs Banbury,' he added quite unnecessarily. He noticed Harriet's hands grip the arms of her chair. 'I mean,' he went on hastily. 'To force her to include a legacy or gift which she had no intention of including originally, using a variety of manipulative tactics—'

'What? Such as?'

'Well for example, trickery, flattery, or even suggestion.'

'This,' Harriet grated, 'is pure fantasy. Listen, Christopher,' she pronounced his name very deliberately in an attempt to let him see how deeply underwhelmed she was with his reaction so far. 'Your father saw her. He drafted the will. I wasn't even with her. I knew nothing about her wishes. Or these relatives. She never mentioned them. Ever. It came as a shock—'

'Yes, but that's not a defence, just saying you didn't know.'

'Defence?' She looked puzzled. 'You mean a rebuttal?'

'Yes, yes. Well, I mean. No. I do mean a defence, they've accused you of something; you are responding. That's a defence,' he insisted, annoyed that for some reason Harriet Flynn was not at all like his father had said. Rather charming, self-effacing, he'd said. She was, in his view, quite difficult. Opinionated. She didn't seem at all glad that he was at least going to help. 'Simply claiming you didn't know,' he finished, 'is not recognised in law. Unless you can prove it. Indisputably,' he added to drive the point home.

Harriet pushed her chair back and began pacing around. She was trying to think, but to Christopher Pottinger she looked like a walking storm.

'Hang on,' she suddenly wheeled round. 'Your father?'

At the mention of his father, Christopher looked uneasy. 'Dad? What about him?'

'I remember now. He said she was the most argumentative client he'd had. Couldn't advise her on any level. Does that sound like a weak woman, someone you – or me – could push around? We just need him to point that out. And where in her will does it say she was related to the Webers? Eh? Or even mention them? And I would have known if she were. And what about your father writing to them?'

Christopher's head went up and then immediately down to flick frantically back through the thin file.

'He couldn't find them,' she said. 'So there it is. The evidence that he'd tried and the address or the family – oh God one or the other – were no longer to be found. And if they were in touch with her, surely they would have visited or phoned her or – or anything and they bloody well didn't.

'And another thing,' Harriet's scattergun approach, bouncing from one aspect of the case to another, was hard for Christopher, with his orderly approach to life, to follow.

'The people who witnessed the will? The accountant or someone? Your father's secretary – oh all right, *your* secretary? They would remember. I mean how many elderly clients' wills do they witness?'

'Oh, a fair amount,' he started to say. Anything to recover some ground, but he thought if pressed, he'd be obliged to admit to a mere handful. And very few in recent months.

'They witnessed her signature,' Harriet reminded him. 'For heaven's sake Christopher, ring him. Your father. Tell him what's happening. Go on.'

'I've done it.' Christopher Pottinger glared at her. Fleetingly he wondered if his father had not made a mistake and this blonde, lanky young woman, striding around was actually related to Elena after all. Both quite barmy in his opinion. 'What do you think I did while you were on your way?'

'And?'

'He said, I was to handle it. Look,' Christopher argued, 'in Dad's defence, he only met Elena Banbury three times at most. The first – ages ago, a year at least – when she came in to ask if there was any way her family could be traced, Dad said he'd try. Then a couple of months ago she came in to ask him to draw up her will, and the third time when she came in to sign it.'

'Did he try to trace her family?'

'Of course, but it didn't get anywhere. He rang her to tell her and he recorded her reaction. It's all in here,' he tapped the file in front of him. 'She simply said, "I'm sure you did your best. It's of no matter." Harriet? Believe me. He really is in no position to say if her manner was unduly cowed or that she had changed a previous will. As far as we were concerned – looking at this – she hadn't made one at all. And besides, read this,' he pointed to a line in the document in front of him. *Revoking all previous* . . . see? That covers that point anyway. And I will. Handle it. But,' he took advantage of Harriet's silence to recover his position, 'I'm telling you now, that this isn't just something you can brush aside. They believe they have a case – I know, I know – and you – I mean of course, *we* – don't think – I mean, yes, yes of course, we know they haven't got one. But at the very least, I will take advice from counsel – a barrister – to see what chance we have to get all this dismissed before they try and go to court. Do you understand?'

Harriet sat down heavily on the side of the desk with her back to him.

She didn't know where to start. It had never occurred to her that there would be a case to answer, or at least anyone believing there even might be.

*

Harriet silently listened to the young barrister Christopher had employed, as he outlined her chances of rescuing her life from this absurd accusation. His name was Timothy Carlisle-Brotherton; short, stocky with floppy, blond hair and a nervous habit of clicking his pen on and off on the pad in front of him while he read what appeared to her to be enough legal notes to wallpaper the Grand Canyon. Nor did he have the longest track record at the bar, but Christopher had assured her, Tim was making a name for himself.

As what, she asked herself.

'What is going to be difficult for us,' Tim said gravely, 'if you don't agree to their demands and they insist on going to court, is how to overturn his case by changing the court's perception of your past behaviour *vis à vis*, Mrs Banbury.'

'What behaviour?'

'Their submission,' he tapped a document in front of him, 'is that before Mrs Banbury died, suddenly – and in your care—'

'She was not in my care,' she protested. 'I just happened to be there.'

'But it can be seen that you were involved. You were more than just a neighbour, weren't you? You helped her and,' he held up a hand to stop her interrupting, 'at the time, you had severe financial problems. Your bank account from that time, shows someone who was overdrawn and had been refused a loan. Your business was about to shut down. It was no secret that you were trying to find the money to repair your flat. We – or rather they – have copies of the estimates from at least one company, a window company who you called in to repair and replace the sashes at a cost you could not afford, but you suggested they look at Elena's in the hope she would pay the bill for both—'

'What? What are you talking about?' Harriet stared in horror at them. 'It was just to get her permission to do them. She owned the place. It would have been her responsibility – the upkeep. Not mine. And she'd have known anyway, even if I hadn't mentioned it, which I hadn't. My door was less than a metre from hers. She'd have wondered what was going on, not to mention the noise. God. How could anyone believe such a thing? And everyone in my business struggles at times. Everyone at the Parade is closing, not just me.'

'I would not be doing my job,' Tim said almost soothingly, 'if I didn't demonstrate to you the force of their case. We haven't said we can't demolish it, but it will be hard. You have to understand that. They are clearly not in this for money, which makes their case a little stronger than someone say – challenging the will for money alone. This is about the return of their property which is of sentimental value, nothing else. His grandmother cared very much about her cousin's welfare. According to Weber,' he peered over his glasses, rimless and half-moon at the letter in front of him, 'this woman is now elderly and infirm and resides in a nursing home near to his home, here,' he pointed to the address. 'But the shock of telling her about this case would be very great. They are still trying to break it to her about Mrs Banbury's death and not entirely sure she'll understand even if they do.'

'So close, were they? So close he didn't know Elena had died until five weeks later?' Harriet exclaimed. 'Go on? Tell me why?'

'Well, yes it might seem like that. But that is not what is at issue here, and whether he was in touch or not is not a factor. We've asked – as a matter of routine – for evidence of his concern and her number does appear, infrequently I grant you, but over the last year there were about half a dozen calls, of very short duration, which lends weight to their argument that she didn't respond. Harriet, I'd rather leave that alone because, oddly, it only adds weight to their argument that you took advantage of such poor contact. Believing her to be utterly alone and therefore unprotected. Easy target. Do you see? They've thought of everything. Do you recall Elena making phone calls?'

Harriet shook her head.

Tim Brotherton shook his.

'Why would you?' he agreed. 'The records show her phone was used but only to call her doctor or the hospital. A few showed random numbers which have proved to be utility companies. Nothing else. Certainly none to Berlin.'

'But her cousin? Natasha? What about her phone records?'

Tim Brotherton shook his head. 'His statement says she is very fragile and easily exhausted and early dementia is kicking in. He does everything for her. Her memory is not what it was, Harriet. One has to remember she is in her late eighties now, and how many women of that age are not dependent on some help? Even Elena. You claim she often sought your assistance.'

'Claim?' she looked up sharply. 'It's true.'

'I'm sure it was,' he said soothingly, 'but there is very little independent evidence for that, Harriet. This all comes down to what, in law, is provable.'

'So, justice,' she said dryly, 'apparently has very little to do with the law?'

'Well,' he cleared his throat. 'On occasion it must seem like that.'

Harriet was silent. What, she thought, was she doing here, on a weekday morning when she should have been at the stall or dashing off to an auction looking for stock for her new shop, anywhere but this overstuffed office in the middle of the city. Bundles of legal documents were stacked carefully on roll-topped, brown walnut desks, walls groaning with leather-bound books. In front of her, on a round coffee table, lay a silver tray and on it an untouched cup of tea. A delicate, china, gold-rimmed flower-patterned cup and saucer. The real thing, she decided idly. No cutting corners in this office. Not for the first time, the bill for all this nagged away at her.

She could hear the gold carriage clock on the ornate fireplace ticking. So calm, so tranquil, and outside this room her life was being sifted through as though she were a common thief. The fury, that had initially risen to the roof of her mouth when she had heard from Kurt Weber's lawyers, had now settled into an uncomfortable knot somewhere between her chest and her throat.

By the time they had talked through enough legal niceties in a language that made Harriet long for a darkened room – or at the very least the privacy of her own flat to check online what half these Latin phrases meant (why couldn't they just use English?) – it was already dusk and she no longer had the energy to try to justify why she had helped Elena so much. Even to her ears it no longer made sense.

The vision of herself as a heartless opportunist began to keep her from functioning. At night, she couldn't sleep. Not least because, try as she might, she could not stop herself from straying into a dark world where the horror of what had happened engulfed her. A growing belief that if she had given more thought to what, to the casual observer, it could look like, instead of being absorbed in keeping the business going, she might not be sitting night after night in the shadow of her window, watching the street grow silent, a dark and hostile street at that, down below.

'Why didn't he just get in touch with me without all – all of this?' She waved an arm around the room. 'Why go in all guns blazing before hearing my side of things?'

'They were advised, I suppose, that you were unlikely to back down. You had already made enquiries about registering the shop in both your names. They think you are calculating and had probably prepared yourself for this possibility, Harriet. They mean business.'

'Look,' she said. 'He's a big deal and he'll ruin me unless I defend myself. He's made a *massive* mistake. Why doesn't he just admit it?'

Christopher studied his nails. Tim rearranged the files in front of him so they were neat, square, equidistant from each corner of his desk.

'No,' Harriet broke the silence. Her voice held a tremor but she steadied it. 'I can't say I've done something I haven't. I'd have to plead guilty for them to settle and I won't do that. And listen,' her voice was growing stronger, more determined. 'I am so mad about all this that I may well sue for defamation.'

There was a small silence. Tim and Christopher exchanged a quick glance. 'Well,' Tim finally said. He looked gravely across at her. 'We will do everything possible, but you must prepare yourself for the possibility that you might lose. Please, I urge you to consider carefully all that I've said.'

*

'I think the world's gone mad,' she clicked off her phone. 'With Christopher and Timothy Carlisle-Brotherton leading the way,' Harriet added almost bitterly. She dragged her hand through her hair. 'I know they have to prepare me for a bumpy ride, but I wish they sounded more on my side. Believed me. At least that.'

'C'mon,' James said. 'Leave all this. Let's go and have a pizza and a glass of red. Cheer ourselves up. You're so not guilty, it will be fine.'

She nodded, not finding the energy to tell him that in the last day or two, a creeping fear had been steadily gripping her, that Elena's relatives weren't going to go away. Doubts about Tim being the man to see them off had begun to take root in her poor aching head. Every day, since she had turned down Kurt Weber's initial offer not to proceed and simply give everything back, fresh evidence arrived from his solicitors that seemed to effortlessly twist her involvement with an old woman into something quite warped and unrecognisable.

'Over here,' William called from a table in the corner. James waved back and pushed Harriet ahead of him. He was glad to be out of the wind and even more glad there was a brief respite from Harriet's litany of bad news.

'Now what'll you have, Harriet?' William asked, pushing a menu in front of her. The waitress had uncorked a bottle of red and left it on the table. He filled Harriet's glass to the brim.

'Oh anything,' she said. 'Not hungry.'

'She'll share mine,' James said, staring pointedly at William.

'Every time he calls, he says they've got another statement.' Harriet plucked a bread stick from a canister and bit savagely into it.

'Statement?' James looked up. 'What statement?'

'Oh God,' she began to count off on her fingers. 'Her GP, who, let me remind you, she hardly knew because on the very rare occasions she went, she never saw the same person twice. Listen to this. They said that Elena had insisted I was her next of kin and that I – me, mark you – always made decisions for her.'

'I remember,' James exclaimed. 'The night she died. They all kept saying it.' He paused. 'Harriet?'

'What?'

'I'm not doubting your memory for a second, but are you absolutely certain she never said anything—'

'Dear God, no!' Harriet stared aghast. 'Of course not. You surely don't believe—?'

Hurriedly he placed a hand over hers. 'No. For heaven's sake, no. Just getting it clear that's all. I didn't always listen to her and maybe when you were busy – I mean you know how she would talk about the things she got up to – Harriet? Are you listening?'

She hardly noticed the nervous glance he exchanged with William.

'Then there's the hospital,' she said wearily as though he hadn't spoken. 'The one who gave her the test who said I always accompanied her to hospital visits. *Always?* Once. They're adamant that she was never there on her own. Is there any more red left?'

James silently leaned over and refilled her glass.

'She was very independent,' he offered cautiously. 'Unless she was having treatment, I bet she tottered off on her own and—'

'And even the wretched Sheltons,' Harriet ploughed on ignoring him. She took a gulp of wine and then leaned back, so the waitress could deposit two large pizzas in front of them. 'They said I more or less stopped anyone else from helping. Total baloney. And that duplicitous toad, Vince—'

'*Vince?* James gasped. 'What's he got to do with it?'

'I thought I'd told you? They actually asked him, and he said,' she began to recite from memory, 'while he didn't know me that well, mere colleagues, and was not accusing me of anything, he'd always been concerned at the way I used Elena as a kind of – wait for this – "performing monkey to drum up business".'

'He didn't? You're kidding? Why?'

'Because Elena came to the stall and liked to tell tall stories and garnered, quite unfairly in his view, a lot of business. And – I can hardly believe this bit – I wondered how they knew I was planning to use Elena's name. I never did anything officially, but I told a few people at Raglan. He must have heard and told them. How else would they know? They've done their homework with a vengeance. How have they got all this stuff? So quickly?'

'It's called money,' William sighed. Must have hired private detectives and paid them a fortune. He must be loaded.'

'He is,' Harriet said bitterly. 'Oh God, James. I can't believe all this is happening.'

'Look,' he said carefully. 'Why don't you just do what they say. Give them all Elena's personal stuff. Mimi would willingly return all the dresses and Big

Jake's already said he'll do anything you want. Harriet, get this over with. Just give it *back*.'

'Never,' she said, so angrily he slid along the bench seat to be nearer William. 'I would have willingly returned everything,' she said fiercely, 'if they'd asked me. Told me they thought there had been a mistake, instead of going in all heavy duty and pretending they cared about Elena. I would have been sympathetic. Given them the lot. But they didn't. They said my motives were criminal. How appalling is that? You seem to forget, even if the Webers agree to settle by withdrawing the case, I will have to agree I'm not entitled to it all. According to Tim Bloody-Brotherton, they've got more going for them than I have, and if I lose, where the hell am I going to get the money to pay their fees? Legal aid only applies to innocent people. And God knows why but the Webers think I've unjustly got stashes of her jewels tucked away. It's insane. So what else can I do but fight them? Right?'

No-one said anything. Harriet glanced from one to the other of the two men sitting opposite her. 'Right?' she said again.

Their faces looked stricken. Helpless. She knew she had argued herself into her decision without their help. She went very still. Finally she leaned forward.

'William?' she asked in a calm voice that surprised even herself. 'Is that bottle empty?'

*

'Good decision,' Tim said gently. 'We'll insist on a privacy agreement in case the press get hold of it.'

'They already have,' she pointed out.

And even if no reporting of the actual facts had been printed, no-one could stop them reporting, gleefully, that a war had begun between a market trader – according to the tabloids – or antique dealer – the broadsheets – and a family in Europe. Never slow to see the sales impact of a story involving a shop girl, a wealthy businessman and a fight over a legacy, the story had drifted through their pages for the last few weeks.

She knew if she had gone to court, that quiet story would have leapt onto the front page and she tried not to imagine the creativity of the subs writing the caption. *Shop Girl Accused of Fraud* was the least frightening she could think of. Oddly, a headline declaring her triumph over a family trying to besmirch her good name, didn't seem to form in her head. Largely because she knew it was hopeless.

'Well, yes,' Tim Brotherton agreed. 'But what I meant is that he's a very private man, so I imagine that asking for privacy won't be a problem. After that, you can get on with your life.'

'What life?' She lifted her head as though a ton of bricks were holding it in place. Across the desk in his office, Tim held her gaze. 'You think this won't go round like wildfire? I have to ask Big Jake and Mimi to give all the stuff back I gave them? And Lizzie? It was just a painting, but even so. *They* won't say anything, I know they won't, but others will. And the amount I have to pay in legal fees alone—' She trailed off.

Tim Brotherton seemed to have already lost interest in her. 'There is no law to say people mustn't even speculate, but they can never prove it. Now—'

'Now?' she broke in. 'Now you might as well stamp "guilty" across my forehead. Oh God, oh God. What have I done?'

Chapter Seven

Harriet left it as late as she could to walk, as calmly as a stomach doing an imitation of a Ferris wheel on speed would allow, into the quiet buzz of voices filling Raglan Parade.

She had expected – or at the very least had prepared herself – for being ignored, but she wasn't. But normality was immediately and evidently not on the agenda either. One or two people, who at another time would almost certainly have waylaid her, simply threw an awkward smile in her direction. Others offered poorly disguised excuses not to detain her.

'Oh hi,' Trevor, who dealt in framed art deco posters, who had more times than anyone could count hitched a lift from Harriet to fairs around the country and saved him a useful sum in fares, caught her eye. 'Busy,' he claimed brandishing a roll of bubble wrap. 'Catch you later.'

She knew he wouldn't. Nor too would Melissa, the size of a rake with her tangle of red curls caught up in a silk printed scarf, who sold imported ethnic scarves and jewellery and had often, for days on end – and at great inconvenience to Harriet – stored her stock in Harriet's flat, so that she wouldn't have to lug it back to the house in Lewisham that she shared with her boyfriend.

Brief panic now spread across Melissa's face. She reached for her phone and began to punch in a number, just rolling her eyes at Harriet in a fake display of exhaustion.

'Up to here,' she mouthed holding her hand above her head, as Harriet paused. 'So late with all of this. Oh hi, sweetie.' She turned away to talk to the boyfriend.

It could have been worse. Harriet knew that. She gave a careless wave and began picking her way through the chaos that was Raglan Parade closing down.

Packing cases were strewn everywhere, upended stalls about to be loaded onto trolleys, stock being carried shoulder high to cars parked as near as they could on the road outside, double doors at either end wide open. The only people filling the vast hall were the stallholders. That morning, Raglan Parade had finally ceased trading.

No-one had put up a fight, the stallholders too busy trying to find alternative trading venues – or in some cases any job to pay the rent – to care about somewhere that had made none of them rich but had charged a huge amount for the privilege of keeping them struggling to stay afloat. Once, Harriet would have willingly led a protest to keep it open, there were so few options out there, but now she was glad to see it go.

On Monday, the construction people would be in to remove all traces of its colourful heritage and start the process of turning the inside into a soulless, shiny, chrome-and-steel office development, leaving behind just a small plaque on the wall outside; the only thing they were not allowed to pull down, recording that it had once housed supplies for the army serving Queen Victoria and that more recently it had been the site of an artisans' market.

And much else, Harriet thought as she gritted her teeth. She wanted no reminders, no looking back, the image of a white-haired elderly woman raising a bony, heavily ringed hand to acknowledge her was one she had to blot out. *Had* to. Otherwise she could not move on. The echoes of a husky, accented voice, describing with a great deal of wit but light on accuracy, a world long gone, the ripples of laughter that followed from the inevitable crowd that had been lured to her stall, had started to haunt her. She should have stopped it. *Should* have.

'Give me those,' she heard James call, making her turn her head. He was threading his way towards her. 'I've almost finished. I'll grab a coffee for you. Just sit down and—'

Harriet did none of those things. 'I'm fine,' she said evenly. 'I can manage.

And I'll get the coffee myself. You're just as busy, James,' she repeated firmly but quietly when he started to protest. 'I'm okay. I'm fine. Seriously. Golly,' she said more loudly, 'you *have* made progress. You're nearly done. I'd better get a move on or I'll be late. Dinner,' she added seeing his expression; uncomfortable, anxious. 'Meeting Lizzie.'

James knew she was doing no such thing. Lizzie wasn't due back from the pottery fair in Manchester until the weekend. It had been three weeks since Harriet had agreed to settle out of court, and the ghastliness of Mimi and Big Jake insisting they totally understood, no, absolutely didn't mind handing everything back and assuring her over and over they didn't believe a word that was being said. And then there they were on the last day at Raglan when they all had to finally be out, and as lunch came and went and there was no sign of her, he had pretty much despaired that she'd come at all.

'Of course,' he said a bit too heartily. 'Ah. Now. What was I doing?' he suddenly felt nervous, awkward. Damn the woman. If only she'd open up a bit, accept help. 'Oh yes,' he beamed at her. 'That's right. Coffee. No. No. Coming right up.'

Out of the corner of her eye, Harriet saw Vince, elaborately and pointedly turning his back on her. A mountain of boxes filled the aisle that separated their stalls. A flutter of rage welled up at the sight of him. His monstrous intervention had hammered another nail in her coffin. She hadn't killed anyone for God's sake. Actually, she'd done nothing. This was going to be tough.

The few papers who'd reported the whole settled-out-of-court scenario, had not been untruthful, but the spin suggested another story lay unreported behind it, a story implying she was a bit of chancer with financial problems who'd got caught out.

A mixture of triumph that she had been so brought down, allied to an irrational jealously of her, explained Vince's stance very easily. As for the rest, common sense persuaded her that probably no-one actually believed she was anything but innocent or at the very worst misled, but – and in a world where reputations mattered – no-one was taking any chances. What if?

For a moment, she considered kicking Vince's cardboard barrier out of her way to get to her stand. It would have done much for her feelings but was unlikely to have furthered her cause. She stared at the boxes. Almost laughed out loud. What cause? Totally lost in her case. Or almost.

'Don't worry, Vince,' she called instead, with a studied cheerfulness she was far from feeling. 'No, no you leave them where they are, I'll wriggle through. Unless,' and she couldn't help herself, 'you think I'm going to exploit them in some way.'

Without a word, Vince deliberately and slowly piled two more boxes on top of the row already there, making it impossible for her to go anywhere but back in the direction she'd come. She shrugged and turned away, but a voice booming from behind stopped her.

'These in your way, Harriet?' Big Jake was already lifting the extra boxes back onto Vince's stand and pushing others out of the way with his foot. 'There you go,' he said standing back to let her pass. 'On your way. Want a hand?'

'*What*,' Vince almost shrieked trying to pull his wretched boxes back again, 'do you think you're doing? This area is mine—'

'*Yours?*' Big Jake growled. 'Never was. Not yours or mine, or anyone's come to that. None of us owned a square inch of it. That's why we've been chucked out. So we're all equal here—'

'What a pity,' Vince addressed the nearest stallholders, 'that some of us, I mention no names,' he gave an exaggerated roll of his eyes in Harriet's direction, 'didn't bear that in mind before they exploited—'

He got no further. His feet were suddenly dangling a few inches from the ground, his body rammed against a pillar, held in place by Big Jake's clenched fists, his terrified eyes a blink away from the very annoyed Geordie.

'No . . . please,' Harriet was horrified. She grabbed Jake's arms. 'He's not worth it. Jake? Please.'

'Are you sure now, pet?' Big Jake asked without taking his eyes or his hands off Vince's collar. 'Because sometimes, this is the only way you can make someone with a brain the size of a grape understand about being civilized—'

A crowd had begun to gather. Harriet shook her head. 'No. It's fine. I'll get my things and go. Please. I don't care what he says. Just stop.'

Over her head, Big Jake's eyes met James'. 'Sorry,' Jake said. 'I only meant—'

'I know,' Harriet's throat felt tight. 'I know. I don't need any help. Don't interfere, please.'

'Right then,' Big Jake released his fists. He gave a shrug and walked away. Vince felt his feet meet the floor. His shirt was ruffled. His hair was coming loose in grey, wispy strips from the black band holding it in place.

'Here,' James thrust a carton of coffee at her. He walked away after Jake, his expression thunderous. Harriet briefly closed her eyes. What a mess.

'*Outrageous*,' behind her, Harriet heard Vince shriek. 'Just look at my shirt. Ruined. But at least,' he gave a slightly hysterical giggle as he whispered to a fuming Mimi, 'unlike reputations, at least I can replace my – *ouch*,' he yelped, beginning to hop on one foot. 'Mimi? Are you mad? Have you all gone insane? That was my shin!'

*

Harriet crossed the street, and from the other side of a snarling, traffic-clogged road in Brixton, gazed up at the first floor of the four-storey terraced house she'd just left. Grey brick, a steep flight of stone steps leading to a door with peeling black paint. Net curtains, once white, now grey, hung limply across the three front windows of the building that was to be her new home. The lease was signed. A copy was in her bag. She couldn't bring herself to even say that word, 'home', the one that had once made her feel safe. It's just somewhere to regroup, she preferred to tell herself. That's all.

William had offered her a room in his house, so too had Lizzie but she'd turned them down. And glad to have done so when she detected the obvious relief on William's face and the milder one on Lizzie's. No-one had to tell her the last few months had taken their toll.

She stepped hastily back as a bus rocked past, a horn blared from a car that had been forced to swerve by a motorbike. Both drivers waved a pointless two fingers at each other as they disappeared into the trail of traffic rumbling past.

'Hmm.' She took a deep breath. 'Could be worse. Could be a tent. And this is what you get for the money you've got, so get on with it. C'mon.'

She started to walk towards the tube, which would take her straight to

Pimlico, ten minutes away but it felt like another world, and for her, a fast disappearing one. One that she had understood, felt comfortable in. 'Get your stuff,' she ordered herself. 'Give the keys back, shut the bloody door and start living again.'

At two o'clock the following day, a man with a van hired by Harriet would come and take what little furniture she had. At the same time, William and James were coming to help her shift the rest of her things to this new address. They were glad to be finally allowed to help, relieved they hadn't been treated to another glimpse of the new Harriet when they'd offered. Although they'd been forced to agree she'd pay for the petrol. Pitiful, was William's view.

This new Harriet, an irritated, impatient one, had become brutal in her refusal to be helped. They were beginning to feel more than a bit irritated by her new view of the world.

'You know I adore her, don't you?' James said to William as they prepared to drive from William's Victorian terraced house in Clapham to Harriet's now former flat in Pimlico.

'As do we all,' William lied. He held a new sweater up against himself for inspection.

'And I'd do anything—'

'For her,' William finished like a man who had heard this declaration one time too many. He threw the sweater onto a chair. He leaned both hands on the back. 'But?'

James ran a distracted hand through his hair. 'I feel awful saying this,' he finally said. 'But you're right – you always are, so don't look so smug – but trying to help her is ludicrous. She won't even *try* to be grateful – and that colour is brilliant on you – no, not grateful, I don't want gratitude. But – at least *appreciate* this is bloody difficult for the rest of us and being snapped at isn't helping. Look at Big Jake. I know, I know, she apologised but all he'd done was put that little shit Vince in his place and she told him she could deal with Vince. Let me tell you, right at that moment she had no idea what to do. I was watching. And what about Lizzie? They're barely speaking now.'

Privately, William thought they should all just stand back and let Harriet work things out for herself. It wasn't as though he hadn't tried to help, or that he disliked her. As a matter of fact, she was one of the few women he knew who could make him laugh. But even though he knew he had Harriet to thank for James so often being the first one to phone after a row, he was now fed up with her and her problems.

Not an evening went by without James providing almost exhaustive, irrefutable evidence that she was having a nervous breakdown or, like the night before, asking again if he, William, thought they ought to insist she had therapy or tell her parents? And, oh God, the incessant, pointless trawling through of what James thought he could do to help, when it was patently obvious there was nothing. Not anymore.

Weeks of it, this same old discussion. And, William recalled, not at all sure he understood why, James had even given back the watch, although he hadn't been asked to.

'Solidarity,' James had explained. 'Show of support. I couldn't bear to wear it after all that's happened.'

William had clucked sympathetically but most insincerely. And what of Lizzie, poor cow? A friend of hers, who did PR for a rather nice spa, had said she could have a massive discount for a weekend, so she'd paid for her and Harriet to go, just for a treat. That's all. And what did she get for her pains? A tirade. That's what she got. A refusal that could have quite easily been couched differently, instead of Harriet almost screeching that she was sick of being treated as though she was ill. *If* she went to a spa – *if* she ever had time – *she'd* pay her share. She didn't want *pity*. How, she had asked them, how could they not understand that?

'If we don't go now, we'll be late,' William began to usher James down the stairs. 'And I for one am not risking doing a single thing today to upset her Harriet-ness. So move.'

Meanwhile, Harriet, whether she suspected she might be wearing them all down or not, wasn't ready to acknowledge anyone else's point of view or their feelings in any of this. No room in her exhausted brain. Not yet. If ever.

'It's fine,' she assured her mother, sitting on the window ledge of her now old flat, waiting for William and James. Strewn around the room lay boxes crammed with her belongings, clothes in garment bags, bin liners packed with bed linen, duvets and pillows. Her furniture had gone. She had hesitated over the Biedermeier sofa, but a practical voice had told her to discard it. To do otherwise would be an expensive gesture which right now she could ill afford. Where would she have space to put that, in the one-bedroom flat, waiting twenty minutes away for her to move into, with a sitting room the size of a garden shed? Her phone was pressed to her ear more tightly than she cared. It stopped her screaming – as she was wanting to do these days. Even trying to buy a jar of coffee at the checkout seemed an impossible task. *I'm drowning here.*

'I'll tart it up a bit,' she said to her mother. 'Shouldn't take long. And I definitely won't need my car because the bus is right outside. So I might as well sell it. When I get settled. Couldn't be better actually.'

'Love?' Jane Flynn said carefully, not believing a word of it. She was still feeling shattered after the three weeks she'd spent in London, supporting a daughter who was either not listening or refusing to listen. A daughter who had become almost unrecognisable. 'Listen to me. You've forbidden me to come back – and God knows I really want to – so all I want is for you to come here – no, no, not for good, I know that's not the way forward, but just till you feel better about everything, get back on—'

'No,' Harriet interrupted sharply. 'Mum, please. You only got back there two days ago and I can handle it. Want to. I just need some time on my own. And I swear I'll be in Madrid by the end of March. Promise. Listen, I'll call tomorrow. James will be here in a minute and I have to check stuff. Oh you know, keys and things. Call you in a day or two. Love you.'

Chapter Eight

After a half-hearted attempt to unpack her clothes and no attempt at all to unpack even one of the boxes, crammed with what had made up her life next to Elena for two long years, Harriet simply found herself staring down into the unfamiliar street watching buses crawling past. A sharp wind was forcing passers-by to duck their heads down into protectively pulled-up scarves and collars.

Across the street, the chippie, which also sold Chinese takeaways, was already trying to handle a full shop. The hairdresser, with its 'No Appointment Necessary' neon sign flashing in the window, was not doing anywhere near as well. All Harriet could do was hope if she stared at them all long enough and hard enough, she could blot out the small voice with its persistent question that now taxed her most of the night and long before it was even light: What in God's name did she think she'd been doing?

*

'Okay,' James said. Lizzie stood next to him. Harriet could see she was trying not to stare too pointedly at the untidy room and certainly not through the door into the bedroom and her unmade bed. 'We think it's time to have a very blunt talk with you.'

Harriet looked from one to the other. It was mid-morning on Saturday. Two weeks since she'd moved in. Over her pyjamas she'd pulled a grey hoodie

– the nearest thing she could find when she heard the buzzer go. And go again insistently, until she stumbled out of bed and asked crossly for whoever it was to go away.

'Why?' She handed Lizzie a mug of coffee. 'A blunt talk about what?'

The room wasn't freezing but it was certainly chilly, too cold for Lizzie to discard her scarf. She sat on the edge of the sofa, cradling the hot cup. Harriet turned the thermostat up on the wall.

'You know why,' Lizzie said as gently as she could. 'Harriet, honestly. I hate doing this—'

'Hate what?' Harriet stared at her. 'What do you hate? Lizzie you're talking in riddles. Look, it was very nice of you to trail all the way over here but it would have been easier if you'd just phoned. I've got so much to do.'

'We tried,' James said. 'But you don't pick up.'

Harriet glanced uninterestedly at her phone. 'I just forgot to fire it up,' she said. 'That's hardly a reason for you to charge—'

'If we'd phoned, we'd have been fobbed off again,' Lizzie said. 'And we're worried about you.'

James put his hand on Lizzie's arm but he spoke to Harriet. 'You know we are. You're not moving forward, you're not even trying to.'

'To do what? What are you both talking about?'

'Harriet, please,' Lizzie appealed to her. 'If there's anything we can do, you know you only—'

Harriet placed her cup on the nearest surface.

'I'm not working,' she said carefully. 'True. But that, I would have thought, is up to me.'

'Of course it is,' James said almost angrily. 'But that's the point. It's not like you. You never just sit around.'

'Well,' Harriet said lightly. 'More reason for me to try it for once. Besides—'

'Besides nothing,' he retorted. 'I'm not listening to you anymore. Get your act together or I'm going to do something about it.'

'Like what?' Harriet shouted back. 'I'll do exactly as I please. I don't inter-fere in your life, so please don't do it in mine. I'm not thick—'

'Even more reason for us to be worried,' he shouted back. 'Look, if you don't start making an effort, put this behind you, then I'll – I'll – I'll call your mother.'

Harriet gaped at him. 'You'll do *what?* For God's sake. What do you think this is? A childish rebellion? I'm not twelve! I'm over twenty-one. *Well* over it, now I come to think of it. And did you say – oh please stop it – *you'll tell my Mum?*'

'Harriet, of course not,' Lizzie wailed. 'James stop. This is childish, it's a mistake.'

'I'll say it is,' Harriet said furiously. 'Apart from the fact that Mum doesn't need any more worry, what with Dad and all of this, as well as—' she stopped. 'Look, I'm sorry if I've been a pain and I'm sorry if I'm not rocking up to parties and dinners and all that other stuff that you think will be evidence that I've,' she hooked her fingers round the words, 'moved on. But I don't want to and I want to be left alone.'

There was a silence. Lizzie looked as though she might cry.

Harriet walked over to her and put her arms round her. 'It's okay Liz. Please. I'm not nuts. I just want to figure all this out in my own way. You understand? I swear, when my head is clearer, I'll call you straight away. And I'm not lonely or any of those things. I just want to be left alone for a while.'

What she had wanted to say was, *I'm just so bloody angry, so furious, so beyond rational thinking, that if you both don't go now, I'm going to say something I'll totally regret.* But she didn't. It was hard to tell, when she carefully closed the door behind them, which of them was the most angry. Or shocked at the shouting. And then, as though a cruel alignment of particularly malevolent stars were colluding to make her life a complete misery, she received an email from Dermot. Oh the humiliation of it all. The one man she had vowed would never see her in such misery again, and here he was, offering a drink and sympathy. She deleted it.

*

After they'd gone, she leaned with her back against the door until she heard the buzz of the outer door and instantly remorse began to crash over her. She ran to the window, but she was too late, there was no sign of them.

To her horror, she realised that her hands were shaking. Lizzie? She'd said that to her most trusted and close friend? Oh God, and James? James who had never deserted her? Stuck up for her?

In the oddest way, the dreadful exchange, the anger, the fury, had left her wanting to do something. Anything, to stop herself becoming this horrible person she had started to turn into. No-one had to tell her that.

Finally, she made herself look in the mirror and stare long and hard at her reflection. A mess, she decided. An unholy mess. That's what she was. She was also cold.

A shower, a pair of trackie bottoms and a thick woollen sweater helped. Later, when the knot in her chest had calmed down, when she was less furious with herself, she would ring Lizzie, apologise. And James. Ask for time to get back on track.

She carried a mug of coffee into the bedroom and placed it on her dressing table, a very tight squeeze, but she'd managed to wedge it under the window. Then she stripped the bed, pushing sheets and pillow cases into a bin liner. On top, she began to pile clothes that could do with making contact with a dry cleaner and finally tackled a bag that had lain, to her shame, untouched for weeks, packed with her summer clothes.

Something would have to be done. Across the street, between an Indian takeaway and the hairdresser still underwhelmed by clients, she'd noticed Krystal Klene, a dry cleaners with a red sign stuck to the window announcing a special offer; one that was hard to resist. In a minute she'd drag it all over there and fork out for someone to introduce a happier – and long overdue – fresh note to her wardrobe.

'Come on, you lot,' she grunted at a black bin liner that she knew housed, among much else, a cotton jacket and two or three pairs of jeans. She upended the bag on the floor. 'At Krystal's prices I can afford to do you lot as well.'

The jacket went into the 'to be cleaned' pile, she gave the jeans a shake and consigned them to the washing pile, fishing in the pockets for anything that might not survive the rinse cycle let alone the spin.

'Lunch,' she said, with satisfaction, as she unearthed a five-pound note and waved it in the air. 'And possibly supper.'

A handful of change and a folded piece of card followed a now totally out-of-date one-day travel card, as well as the business card of someone who had pressed it into her hand at an auction and suggested dinner, loaded with much eye contact. He had all but cut her dead the last time she'd seen him.

All of it was placed on the bedside table. She sat back on her heels, sipped her coffee and began to feel that there might after all be a brain between her ears, a brain that had been set to 'halt' these last few weeks.

Much later, she couldn't explain why, she suddenly leaned forward and pushed the small pile of unearthed items apart and picked up the folded card. It was very creased but she remembered it. She'd stuffed it into the pocket of her jeans the night Elena had died. She had placed it where Elena would see it and tell her where to return it, in the mess that had tumbled down when she was scanning the books on the shelves. Something else kept coming back to her.

A date? Not any old date, but one on the envelope which she no longer had. She remembered the date. It had been posted a few days before Elena had died. But from where?

For a while, she sat on the thin carpet just staring at the crumpled card, the strange, mysterious Cyrillic Russian script under a printed message which might or might not be about Christmas, or a birthday or even Easter. Did Russian people send Easter cards? It was, after all, a greeting card. Whoever had signed it might still be located, she wasn't sure why it would help, but it was a link. But where, in the name of all that was Russian and on a Saturday morning, could she find anyone who spoke the language?

*

'I think it says, *Dear Elena, I think of you.*' The young man in front of her, stocky, earnest, she guessed probably older than he looked, with his rimless glasses and a shock of pale red hair, who had introduced himself as Craig Bingley, frowned at the flattened card in front of him. 'Well,' he went on. 'Not *dear* exactly but it's the nearest equivalent in Russian I can think of. Don't hold me to it, will you?'

Harriet shook her head. 'No, no. Honestly, I'm just grateful to you for doing this. Just the general sense will be fine.'

'Oh my goodness. What does that say?' He pointed a finger to the next line. 'I'm so sorry. I can speak Russian quite well. Well, I say quite well, what I mean is I can get around Moscow and St Petersburg without getting arrested and I read it well, but not fluently. This is such a scrawl and it's been so creased, some of the writing has faded. I'm much better with French,' he apologised. 'Actually I did French and decided to throw in Russian when I went to uni. So it wasn't my major subject, I spent my placement year in Paris . . . Should have been Moscow or somewhere but it wasn't an option. Well not then. These days they can opt to go to the South Pole if they fancy.' He stopped.

'Sorry,' he said. He looked embarrassed. 'Listen to me. Rambling on. Look, sit down, just give me a moment.'

'Please,' she assured him. 'Anything is better than I could manage.

She didn't want to make him rush. This was – *might* be, she conceded – one last throw of the dice.

'Nice shop,' she said as easily as she could.

He glanced around at the near-empty shop. 'It's not always like this. A bit of a hub sometimes,' he said.

'Hub? For what?'

'Usual stuff,' he replied. 'Students doing Russian literature, a few expats wanting the comfort of their own language, tourists, oh yes – and if it's raining, somewhere to hang out. But on Saturdays it calms down. Students are sleeping off hangovers,' he explained, and grinned when she laughed. 'On the upside, I do get invited out a lot.'

'You do? You mean on dates?'

He half laughed. 'I wish. No, to fund raisers. And sometimes,' he sighed, 'I get bullied into letting them sell tickets for them. Music festivals, dinners, all that. Very sociable lot, the Russians. Sorry,' he blushed. 'I'm rambling on. Your card, of course.'

While she waited, she sat on a stool just behind a counter, littered with pamphlets and circulars that seemed to have been dumped there by anyone and everyone, advertising courses from cookery to carpentry, fundraisers and where to donate clothes and furniture for those in need, as well as where to start a social life in London with fellow countrymen. Largely, it seemed, the places in which to do so were down-at-heel pubs and church halls, which she could not imagine would be the kinds of places any spirited young traveller would have made the journey from their homeland to see. But who knew?

It had been a stroke of luck that this place was open. While there were other bookshops, museums and even churches that might have helped, on Saturday most of them were closed or too busy to help. But Bing had said to come over, not promising anything, but happy to help. All the way from Brixton to Goodge Street on the tube she'd clutched the piece of card, just in case, only relinquishing it to this kind young man when she'd found his bookshop, which specialised in Russian literature, travel and history, at the back of Tottenham Court Road. On closer inspection, it seemed to also embrace most Slavic countries, judging by the packed bookshelves.

It was neatly kept, the walls lined with clearly marked sections from art to politics, stands of postcards showing tasteful churches and icons from Eastern Europe, orderly rows of the most recent publications arranged on a square glass-topped table in the centre of the room.

'Oh hang on,' he said finally. 'Yes. I see. There was a crease across the card, so very difficult to read. I *think* it says: *All the time*. And this bit,' he moved the card round so she could see.

Harriet peered over his shoulder. 'It's very hard to read,' Craig Bingley said. 'But I think it just repeats *always*. I suppose whoever it is means something significant. It's not a special card, I don't think. Just greetings. Then it's signed with someone's name.'

'What name?' she craned forward. 'Where is it?'

He held the card at eye level, squinting at it. 'Sometimes you can read it this way. Makes the symbols clearer. It certainly begins with T,' he finally decided, 'but it could be a nickname. I'm so sorry,' he looked up regretfully. 'I can't work it – what's the matter?'

'Could it,' Harriet asked in a careful voice, it was only later she realised her fingers were clenched round his arm. 'Could it be short for something? Like, for example, a name? Natasha maybe? That could be Tash. Maybe? Or Tashie?'

'I suppose so,' he frowned and gave it another inspection. 'Certainly someone who knows her enough to use her first name. If it's short for Natasha then Tash would make sense – hey what are you doing?'

It was enough. Harriet decided that an acquaintance of a mere half hour was long enough into a relationship to hug him. Well his arm at least. He blushed.

'That's brilliant,' she told him. 'I don't suppose it's got a date on it has it?'

He shook his head. 'Sorry. I'm afraid not.'

He turned the card over and handed it back to her. 'You haven't got the envelope it came in?'

She shook her head. 'It was on top of a copy of Pushkin's poems. Well, I think it might have been Pushkin. Sort of looked like him. Sorry, digressing. I mean there was a pile of brown envelopes banded together and it was with them, and I'm pretty sure they were all postmarked from Germany. Berlin I think. I just assumed that's where the card came from as well. Anyway, I haven't got them anymore.'

'Guseva,' he said. 'That's the name you said?'

She nodded.

'One of my favourite stories,' he said. 'Well not favourite, but it was inter-esting. It was actually called *Gusev*. Masculine rather than Guseva with an "a" on the end. Chekhov,' he added helpfully.

Harriet waited as patiently as she could. He'd been so kind. 'Not my field, I'm afraid,' she said. She slipped her bag onto her shoulder, longing to get away to phone Christopher. Not wanting to offend this lovely man with a hasty exit.

'Not mine either,' he said. He pulled open the door to the street. 'Gloomy bloke, Chekhov. I know he was said to be comic as well, but mostly Russian black humour. Just thought of it when you said your friend's name. Except Chekhov's Gusev was a Russian sailor. Not an old lady. Sad story.'

'Was it?' As subtly as she could, she glanced at her phone. It was almost five. She had Christopher's home number, it wasn't late, but it was the weekend and she had a strong suspicion that in the Pottinger household, the entire legal profession in the UK halted at five on Friday, so the chances were slim he'd pick up. But even so.

'Very ill on a ship,' he said, frowning. 'Trying to get home to Russia before he died. No-one seemed able to cure him or help him, but he remained totally positive that it would be all be all right in the end.'

'And was it?' Harriet owed him her interest – he had thrown her a lifeline. Not a strong one. But something. She edged towards the door.

'Sadly not. When he died, his body was chucked overboard and he was eaten by fish.'

Harriet grimaced. 'Ugh. Promise me you won't stock it. Far too gloomy.'

Five minutes later, she'd admired his shop, discovered no-one ever called him Craig, that all his friends called him Bing, and he was just back from a year tutoring what he called some ghastly American children in Boston. Now here he was, helping out a friend who owned the shop, and looking for a job.

'Actually,' he said, leaning against the door and peering up at the sky, now heavy with clouds, morphing into night, 'I've wondered of late if I shouldn't have gone for Mandarin. Keep getting asked for Chinese publications rather than Slavic. I mean, that's the way it's going,' he explained. 'But I do a nice sideline in Russian. Interpreting. The trouble is, although interpreting does pay shedloads, it's utterly tediously mind-bendingly boring. Politicians rarely say anything interesting publicly, so I don't really push it. Now I come to think of it, I wonder why I'm bothering at all with any of this. I'd earn a better living rushing round with a plate of blinis at a rich Oligarch's party than as an interpreter. Fabulous tips I'm told. Too old now. And possibly too lazy. Well, that's what my girl – former, I mean – girlfriend thinks.'

'I think,' Harriet assured him, 'that today, on any level, you've been brilliant. You don't know how much you've helped.'

'Anytime,' he blushed again. 'Look. Take my number. If you need anything else translated, well – well anyway, I hope you find whoever it is. Shame there isn't a date. You wanted that didn't you?'

'It would have helped,' she admitted. 'But this is so much better than I'd hoped.'

'Well, at least you know the card was printed less than two years ago. Probably last year.'

She stopped. 'What? How do you know?' she came back slowly to the doorway.

'There,' he pointed to the back. 'It says printed in Germany and a couple of years ago,' he did a quick calculation. 'That's right, always get my Xs and Vs muddled up.'

She looked blankly at the card.

Fancy that. There it was, in front of her all the time. And this time she did hug him.

Chapter Nine

'Look, Harriet.' Christopher Pottinger's voice sounded weary and not a little impatient. 'Yes, yes. I'm sure it was printed less than two years ago, and it might say "Tash". But that isn't enough to open this all up again.

'And,' he went on over her protests. 'Remember why we settled? Because we knew the evidence they could produce would be compelling and the court would have agreed that it was. But this is not compelling—'

'Stop saying that,' she cried. 'I hate the word. And this *is* – that – that word,' Harriet argued. 'Compelling. Don't you see? Kurt Weber said his grandmother been completely out of it for years and if she had been, how could she have sent that card, let alone written it? He's not telling the truth and—'

'And so what? How does that prove that you didn't – er – I mean of course – and I say this only in the face of all the evidence they produced – that you didn't influence Elena's will? Exactly,' he said into the silence. 'You need so much more than that. This might not have come from her. Elena knew lots of Russian people. Have you thought of that? Harriet?'

'What?' she asked dully.

'You know I totally believe in your innocence. We did everything we could, but if you'd gone to court—'

'I get it,' she stopped him. 'But if he lied about this, what else did he lie about?'

There was a long pause at Christopher's end of the phone. He had noticed

Harriet's number on his mobile late on Saturday afternoon, the pleasant request to call if he got a moment, but pitching that against his wife's insistence that they watched *The Parent Trap* with the children – as a family, she'd emphasised – Harriet didn't stand a chance.

It was now Monday morning, and the memory, still fresh in his mind, of the humiliation he had suffered at the hands of the patronizing 'other side' when he had to strongly advise Harriet that she should back down, had left him in no mood to reopen any negotiations, let alone one based on such flimsy evidence as an old greetings card, that may or may not have been sent by an old lady in Germany. And flimsier still, evidence that proved that Kurt had lied in any way. Quite possibly he had. But that didn't alter the central point. She had been accused of coercion. Why couldn't she get that into her head; that was the basis of the case? But he knew that introducing that reminder into the proceedings would, with Harriet, likely go down like lead.

'God knows,' he conceded instead.

Christopher had once thought a few more exciting cases in this company than he'd been forced – in his view by the united efforts of his wife and mother, for once on the same side – to take over from his philandering father, might have suited him instead of the conveyancing disputes on boundaries and retrospective planning permission for walls being knocked down and garages erected, which rolled across his desk daily in a tide of familiarity and contained few, if any, surprises.

Now he looked longingly at the several folders stacked on his desk and his screen filled with those same once-tedious tasks and longed for the solid, predictable safety of that world. Harriet really was beginning to annoy the pants off him.

'Christopher,' she said carefully. 'I know all this has taxed you quite considerably, but I am entitled to get help from my lawyer. No matter what you think, I want you to email his lawyers and—'

'God. No.'

'Christopher,' she repeated firmly. 'It can't harm.'

'It can,' he moaned.

'Well, just say as your client, I insisted you did so and against your advice, even though you didn't think I had a case.'

'I can't do that.'

'Okay,' she squashed a need to shriek. 'Don't say I said it *definitely* is from Natasha. Just, you know, *wondering* if it is. What's wrong with that?'

There was another long pause. She thought she heard the sound of someone banging their head against a wooden surface.

'Christopher?' she called down the phone. 'Are you still there?'

'I think I know better than to say any such thing,' he said rather stiffly. 'I'm your lawyer. Publicly, no matter what, I would support you. I'll copy you into the email.'

'Christopher,' she gave a small crow of delighted laughter. 'You're a star.'

But he was gone.

*

The answer came within a couple of hours and was every bit as scathing and threatening as Christopher had predicted and every bit as puzzling to Harriet.

She read and reread the reply that Christopher had forwarded, a response making it perfectly clear that any further approach from his client would result in their advising *their* client to obtain a prosecution for harassment.

'Harassment?' she said. 'This is the only time I've *ever* contacted them. And one email simply asking them to clarify how his grandmother could have written such a card if she was so out of it, she could barely pronounce her name, is harassment? Oh stop it.'

'Harriet?' Christopher begged her. 'My advice is to let it go. Unless, of course, you have anything concrete, anything that shows without a shadow of a doubt that you have been wrongly accused, BUT—' he stopped her. 'It would have to form the basis of an entirely new claim. And I would not be doing my duty as your solicitor if I didn't suggest that, unless that happens, would it not be a good idea to try and move on? This is not good for you. Not that I expect you to take a blind bit of notice of me,' he ended bitterly.

'It's all right,' she told him. 'I know you did your best. That's all I asked.

Don't worry. I won't try and contact them again. Even I'm not that stupid. And Christopher? I will pay you in full.'

Christopher clicked his phone off and stared out of the window. It wasn't for some time that he realised he hadn't timed the call, and he doubted that god-awful woman, who wouldn't leave his employ as his secretary, would have been so thoughtful as to have stepped in. What did it matter, he sighed, punching in his home number? He knew, although she claimed otherwise, that Harriet didn't have any money to pay him, without wrecking what little life she had left, or the chance to restart it, so why try and pursue her for it? Besides, he didn't want to. He felt he owed her that much. He'd done nothing wrong, of course he hadn't, he told himself fiercely, but deep inside, apart from Noreen, whose wifely loyalty to him was exemplary, he suspected there were those – especially on Harriet's side, friends and family – who agreed, he had been no match for Kurt Weber's lot. Christopher was in need of comfort.

'Noreen? Leaving early,' he said as his wife answered.

'Oh lovely,' he heard her say. 'Now would you like the fish pie or shall I defrost the casserole?'

'Fish pie,' he said, not really caring.

'And, dear?' Mrs Pottinger junior went on. 'I've told the garage you'll talk to them about the knocking noise? I didn't understand a word but you would, you're so much better than me, so I said I'd get you to talk to them. Is that okay?'

For once, such unswerving belief in his cleverness did nothing for him.

*

A long crack ran from the light in the centre of the room to the edge of the skirting board. She'd noticed it when she first saw the room, but now it was creeping slowly down the cream wall. Or was it a dirt mark? She pushed herself up and went to inspect it, switching on a lamp as she did so.

'Hard to tell,' she spoke aloud, as she knew she had worryingly started to do when she was alone, peering at the mark. She ran a finger experimentally down it, a thin film of dust seeping through the crack onto her hands. 'From a distance of course. But close up, a right mess.

'So,' she patted the wall and turned away. 'If you think I'm going to do anything about you, you are seriously mistaken. Meanwhile,' she pushed a pile of boxes out of the way with her booted foot, 'as I'm clearly now not even going slowly round the bend, but already safely on the other side, and I've been sitting here all day – doing what? Waiting for inspiration to strike? The clock to rewind? Talking to myself, deciding whether Christopher bloody Pottinger needs a new spine or a new career? Perhaps I should just,' she peered through the window at the street lamps, just beginning to flicker into life, 'try and find something to eat? In which case my options are narrowed to Amir's, and fighting my way through all that exotic bread and lentils, or splashing out on the chippie? Decisions, decisions, but at least I can make that one for myself.'

Out on the street, head down against the biting wind, she wrapped a long wool scarf several times around her neck, buried her chin in its comforting folds and dodged between the traffic to the grocers. Not that there was anything wrong with the chippie, apart from joining the usual ten-deep queue – she just couldn't be bothered.

All the way back on the tube from Goodge Street on Saturday, and then through Sunday, shifting between pacing up and down and staring pointlessly down onto a street that she was becoming to know in a way she had hoped she never would, she knew she had allowed her hopes to be raised beyond what was realistic. Even her expectations for Christopher to call had been allowed to advance from 'he might', to 'he probably will', and the disappointment when he hadn't had still taken her by surprise.

'And here you are,' she muttered to herself. 'Even more depressed than if you'd never found the wretched thing.'

Amir's was shut. A note on the door explained that they would be open the next day. Please do come back then. Her eyes swivelled to the large wooden board now covering one of the smashed windows, which told a different story.

Harriet slumped against the wall, her arms wrapped round herself. In one direction lay a long straggling road, filled on both sides with a motley collection of small shops and in the other, just out of sight, the dreary flat she now called home.

For a good ten minutes, while she made up her mind what to do, she watched a stream of people go by, hardly noticing any of them, what they wore or looked like. With only mild interest she noticed a misfit of a man with a rasping cough, shuffling noisily along in a shabby coat, pushing a shopping trolley filled with torn-up cardboard and, mystifyingly, an old aluminium sink. His interest in her was no deeper than a brief glance, but seeing no profit in asking a slightly unkempt woman with damp hair and no apparent home to go to for anything to ease his journey, he shambled on.

'Hi,' a voice made her look up. In front of her, a young woman wearing large glasses with a woolly hat ending in two woollen plaits, pulled well down over her ears, was staring at her. She was clutching some leaflets.

'Here. Take one of these,' the young woman said kindly. 'No-one's making you do anything you don't want to, but we're here to help. Somewhere to stay tonight? Or just someone to talk to? Often helps you know.'

Harriet gazed blankly back at her. Then she glanced quickly around to see who she might be talking to. It took a few seconds for her to realise she was the object of this stranger's concern. Her first thought was that this was an elaborate joke, followed swiftly, when she registered more fully the earnest smiling face standing a foot away, by the realisation that it clearly was not.

'Oh for heaven's sake,' she muttered. Hastily she moved away. 'I'm fine. I'm going home. Yes. That's right. Home. Up there.' She waved almost wildly along the length of the street. She knew she was rambling, but embarrassment drove her on. Several passers-by glanced curiously in her direction. 'Just deciding where to go to – no, no. I'm fine. I honestly don't need that kind of help.'

'Up to you,' the girl agreed, following her, wearing a determined bright smile that looked, to Harriet, more borderline menacing than sympathetic. And more worryingly, ever so slightly manic. 'I'm going there now. Come with me? Nothing to be afraid of.'

Harriet shoved the leaflet the woman was brandishing at her into her pocket. 'I'm not afraid,' Harriet said almost curtly. She just wanted to get away. 'You've made a mistake.'

'Of course,' the woman said, in a tone generally used for humouring someone with a fragile grip on reality. 'Our address is on the back,' she called after Harriet who was hurrying away. 'Any time.'

It wasn't until she was well inside her flat, her back flat against the door, that Harriet glanced at the leaflet. *Crossroads House*, it said. *Nothing is so bad, that a quiet talk with the Lord, can't resolve.*

'God in heaven,' she muttered. What had she come to? She felt her face go hot with the whole stupid mess she'd got herself into.

She turned the pamphlet over. A whole host of messages told her of all the things Crossroads House needed to keep going. Cash donations, of course, bed linen – sadly no duvets for health reasons – but old clothes, bags, shoes. All would be welcome. Just to leave them bagged up in the doorway.

Harriet read it again. And then again. Slowly she sat down and wriggled out of her parka, letting it drop onto the sofa behind her. She felt her face grow warm. Careful, she warned herself. Stay calm. But. Of course. *Of course.* She could have kicked herself. How many times had she seen bagged up clothes waiting outside the door to be collected from Elena? Even taking them down in the lift to leave them at the entrance so that Elena would not have to struggle with them?

What kind of bubble had she been living in not to have asked who they were for? She pushed aside the more truthful answer, which was that she had not wanted to get inveigled into carting the whole lot somewhere other than the entrance to Denbigh Mansions, and had found it quite easy to ignore.

She scrabbled in her bag to find Bing's card, punched in his number and hoped he hadn't gone home for the night.

'Bing?' she asked anxiously. 'I hope you remember me, Harriet? Harriet Fl – oh that's great. Yes I'm fine. Bing?'

Chapter Ten

At the offices of the refugee centre on a road at the back of Victoria Station, the one that Bing had directed her to, not far from Christopher Pottinger's office, Harriet found Roots. Not run-down exactly, but certainly a place that preferred to spend the money they raised on more important things, like housing and food, than comfort for those who worked there.

But then it was not a social club, rather a destination for the displaced and weary, those who had escaped from war-torn countries and oppressive regimes, searching for shelter in a kinder country and needing help to navigate a new life. From Eritrea to Sudan, Iraq or Syria, Elena, who had never forgotten what it was like to have for so long been one herself, had cared not a jot where refugees came from. They needed help. That was all she heard.

Bing had thought Roots worth a shot.

'Peter Tamworth,' he'd said when she had raced off to meet him last Saturday. 'That's the man we need.'

Harriet knew she'd been right to call Bing. He'd said '*we* need.' Not distancing himself, on her side . . .

'Known him forever,' Bing had said, putting two large glasses of red wine down in front of them in a pub round the back of his shop. Harriet had got there to find him waiting on the pavement, the shop locked, a long red scarf wound round his neck and delighted to see her. 'And Lorna – his wife.' He squeezed in beside her on a wooden bench. 'Big on helping raise money for refugees.'

For the first time in weeks, Harriet felt she was not being judged. Even when she'd told Bing the whole story, she was beyond grateful that he simply dismissed Kurt and his team as 'prats', and having arranged for her to see Peter Tamworth the following Monday, they settled back and became quite tipsy. Shared histories were aired, including that he was recovering from a failed love affair with a lawyer called Martha who was, he said, wonderful, but they simply didn't suit each other. But they had loved each other. When Harriet finally got back to her dismal room, she fell onto the sofa, almost smiling, and didn't even notice there was a crack in the wall.

And here she was late on Monday afternoon, being greeted by a generously proportioned woman wearing a wool floral shirt over tight black trousers, thick socks pushed into sturdy trainers, clutching a mug of tea. She replaced the remainder of the Danish pastry she'd been eating onto a paper napkin.

'I've come to see Peter Tamworth,' Harriet said. 'Bing – Craig Bingley sent me – I mean, suggested I came,' she amended.

'Bing? Right.' The woman delicately dabbed at the corners of her mouth with a tissue and dusted her fingers. 'And you are?'

'Harriet Flynn. I think he called?'

'Indeed he did,' the woman beamed. 'End of the corridor. Door's open.'

At first, Harriet thought the room at the end of the faded, yellow-walled passage was empty, when suddenly a head appeared behind a wall of boxes.

'Mr Tamworth,' she began. 'I hope I'm not disturbing you. I'm Harriet—'

He frowned. 'I know who you are,' Peter Tamworth stopped her. 'Mrs Banbury's neighbour.'

His face looked unwelcoming, exasperated.

'Please,' she said. 'I know. Don't judge me.'

'Judge you?' he looked startled. 'Why would I do that? Far more important matters driving me up the wall. Now, what do you think?'

As he spoke he held up an unwieldy plaid blanket. 'Would you say this is a small double or a large single?'

'What? Oh,' she looked uncertainly at the cumbersome blanket he was inspecting. 'Well, er . . . let me see? A large single,' she decided.

'Just what I thought,' he said folding it into a box marked *Singles*.

'Be with you in a moment.'

She thought he might be in his sixties, his grey hair thick and wiry but his eyebrows, as shaggy as his hair, were still jet black and added to the ferocity of his expression. He was wearing very comfortable-looking jeans and a pair of quite battered suede boots.

'Forty years teaching,' he went on, reappearing from behind his cardboard fortress. 'The last fifteen in a comprehensive taught me not to judge. When a school fields thirty languages,' he moved several bags to make space to get through, 'other than English as a first language, you learn to keep your powder dry until you know you totally understand. Then, and only then, do you open your mouth. Now—'

She glanced around at the pyramid of boxes, stacked in every direction, marked on the front of each in bold black pentel things like, *Boys aged 4-10, Women's winter clothes, Babies 3 months to a year.*

Behind him in a wire enclosure, like a giant playpen, a mountain of black bin liners holding donated clothes waited to be sorted.

'I admire you,' she said simply. 'Giving up your free time—'

'Don't,' he growled. 'I'm only here because my wife made me. After I retired. She said just wandering round art galleries or going to watch Spurs wasn't good for me. And there was me thinking once I'd stopped being a slave to education, I could become a slave to the beautiful game, but here I am. Two – sometimes three – days a week. She's retired now, both kids grown up, long flown the nest, so this is her baby,' he waved an arm around. 'Fundraising, lending an ear. She's good at it. Says it's because she's got Russian blood in her.'

'Has she?'

'A bit. Hardly any I'd say, but she says it accounts for her energy and determination and she might be right.'

'How far back?' Harriet asked.

'Oh lord. Let me see. Well, her great-grandmother left Russia to settle in

France – to escape the Bolsheviks. There she met an Englishman – that would be Lorna's great-grandfather – in Paris, ended up marrying him and went to live just up the road. Hampstead actually – and since then, the family has been as English as marmalade. But Lorna certainly understands people who are displaced.'

'God, I wouldn't know where to begin,' Harriet said. 'It must be so hard.'

'Sometimes,' he agreed rather ruefully. 'Language, of course. We try and get hold of one of our interpreters – like Bing – or one of the agencies we work with to come down and help them get sorted. All piecemeal stuff though. We're really just a feed for lots of other charities. The ones who deal with homeless families, no matter where they're from. We just do clothes, mostly. Day-to-day stuff to keep them going. Blankets,' he indicated to the pile behind him. 'That kind of thing.'

'What do you do with them, then? When they turn up?'

'Well, we redirect them to the right people, but we do try to reassure them from the start, without giving them false hope, that they're safe. You know what?' he said. He leaned his arms on the top of the box in front of him. 'Here, in this room, for a lot of them, this is the last time they'll feel welcome anywhere for quite a while. It's the prejudice they encounter later. Getting a job, somewhere to live, making friends. We can usually, eventually, find them somewhere to stay, get legal advice if they need it, but being accepted? Huge mountain that one.'

'Elena never really did,' Harriet said. 'Feel accepted, I mean. Never saw her with anyone I'd have said was a friend, English or foreign, and she'd been here for over thirty years when she died. I'm ashamed to say I never even thought about it.'

'But you looked out for her,' he pointed out. 'She regarded you as a friend. Didn't she?'

Harriet flushed. 'Honestly? I'm afraid I never even put a name to it. I rented my flat from her, helped – you know – like you would a neighbour and yes, I did like her. I mean I didn't dislike her, she was just Elena. And look where that got me.'

'Well, in a bit of a pickle,' he agreed. 'Right,' he pulled a chair round and sat down, crossing one ankle over his knee. 'Enough gossiping. Bing said you wanted to find out about Mrs Banbury. Go on then, fire away.'

For the next five minutes, he just sat and sipped his tea, listening carefully to her as she spoke.

'That's it. I wouldn't,' she said into the silence that greeted the end of her story, 'blame you if you didn't want to help.'

'What?' He looked blank. 'No. Sorry. Not that. Quite the reverse. No. The person you need is Lorna. She said as long as I thought you weren't quite mad then to give her a call.'

'Mad?' Harriet gasped. 'Why would I be that?'

'Well for a start, not getting a fat-cat lawyer to deal with that lot, clearly calling the shots,' he smiled.

'No,' she agreed with a rueful grimace. 'Christopher certainly isn't that.'

'More's the pity,' Peter said. 'You might have seen them off. C'mon now. I'll call you later. I'll just show you out.'

'No,' she said taking off her coat and draping it over the back of the chair.

'Sorry,' he said kindly. 'Lorna's phone will be off. She's chairing some fundraising meeting or other. But I do have to get on. These clothes aren't going to pack themselves.'

'I know,' she said rolling up her sleeves and reaching into the pen of black sacks. 'I'm going to help. If you'll let me? So, we sort these clothes? Into one of these boxes? Is that right? And honestly, we'll really get on a lot faster if you don't argue like that.'

*

A ten-minute walk from the tube brought Harriet to the Tamworth's house in Camden. A tall, thin affair, spread over three floors in a once quiet street, but now clearly a rat run to avoid the congestion of the main road. Traffic rattled past the glossy black door, with its tarnished brass knocker, which led straight from the pavement into a narrow hallway.

'No point in polishing it,' Lorna Tamworth announced cheerfully, ushering her into a room overlooking the street. 'Filthy again in less than an hour. Gave up years ago. Peter has a stab now and then. No point though. Make yourself comfortable. I'm just kicking the coffee machine into life. By the way, Peter said you didn't leave until after nine last night. That was very kind of you.'

'God no,' Harriet protested. 'For the first time in ages, I felt I was doing something that actually mattered.'

'And it does. But it was still nice of you. He was able to get back to see the second half of Spurs playing someone or other so he's thrilled with you. Won't be a moment.'

Harriet settled in the corner of the sofa and watched Lorna stride away into an unseen kitchen. It seemed to her that striding was not required in such a small house, but Lorna Tamworth was built like a greyhound, her long limbs swathed in a pair of serviceable baggy flannel trousers and a red check flannel shirt, which flapped in her wake as she walked. Only her solid cap of grey hair, carefully cut into a severe bob, betrayed her age, which Harriet guessed to be, like her husband, in her sixties. In every other way she was an arresting figure. A handsome woman, Harriet's mother would have described her as, rather than beautiful.

It was, Harriet decided, glancing around the living room, a style that Lizzie would have called 'controlled chaos'. Curved button-back dark green velvet chairs, a cavernous cream sofa draped with a multi-coloured Indian silk shawl, walls of books with leather-bound editions pressed against well-worn paper-backs in a way that would have made a librarian swoon. Such blatant disregard for alphabetical order and subject matter, but it all brought a curious kind of jumbled charm to the room.

Family photographs were dotted around, of her now-grown children, clutching their own offspring. In another, she recognised Bing in a morning suit, acting as an usher at the wedding of someone who turned out to be Lorna's son.

'That's how we met him, Lorna said, following her gaze. 'At George's wedding. Five years ago now. To be honest,' Lorna handed her a big mug of coffee, 'I know he's just broken up with Martha, so when I heard about you, I thought at first you might be his new girlfriend—'

'Golly, no,' Harriet hastily took a gulp of scalding coffee. 'I hardly know him. He's a lovely man and he's been very kind. He said straight away,' Harriet, anxious to move things along in a more helpful direction, gently steered the conversation back to the point of sitting in this nice sunny room, 'that you might be able to help me. About Elena.'

'Sorry, not me,' Lorna shook her head. 'Well not directly help. I met her, obviously, but actually it was my late mother who knew her, Not very well, but they used to gossip at fundraisers, that kind of thing. Well, I say gossip, more put the world to rights. Elena simply didn't allow anyone to get near her. I've noticed that with people who've been refugees at some point in their life, they never quite get over being – well, not secretive exactly, but let's say a little distrusting of the world. I sense these things, you see. I've got a lot of Russian blood in me. Did Peter mention that? I expect he said it was no more than a smidgen,' she said cheerfully.

'I don't recall that,' Harriet said loyally.

'No matter,' Lorna smiled. 'It seems my great-grandmother went to school with Elena's mother. In St Petersburg.'

'Elena's *mother*?' Harriet sat up straight. 'Valentina?'

'Oh well done. *Valentina*. That was it. Couldn't remember her name.'

Harriet almost laughed. 'You're kidding? That's amazing.'

'Well,' Lorna warned her, 'let's say she *probably* did. Sometimes Mum was as bad as Elena at getting dates and names wrong. I mean, it was years before Mum discovered her own mother had been married twice. The way they just airbrushed stuff out of families was quite shocking and—'

'But even so,' Harriet brought her carefully back. 'Elena must have been thrilled. Her mother was so important to her. In fact the last word she spoke before she died was *Mama*. I thought at first she was trying to say *Arthur*—'

Lorna stopped, her face shocked. 'My dear. I had *no* idea. You were with her when she died? What a comfort that must have been to her. But – oh my dear – what an ordeal for you.'

'It's fine,' Harriet brushed her concern aside. 'I was glad someone was with her. But what happened to her mother? Did she go back to Russia? Berlin?'

'No. Nothing like that,' Lorna sighed. 'Astonishingly brave though, from what I heard. These days you'd call her a political activist but after the revolution, when Elena must have been still a baby, she risked her life time and time again to help get people out of Russia.'

Harriet's eyes widened. 'Are you sure? I thought she just owned a shop in Berlin. Not that she was trying to save Russia on the side.'

'Oh yes. Apparently Valentina was famed for it. Very active in the protests to stop the people starving while the Tsar dined off gold plate and hoarded jewels worth millions. Went on marches with the women factory workers – the ones that started the Revolution. I hope I would have been that brave, but I doubt it.'

Harriet listened, her coffee growing cold, to a history of Elena's mother, the daughter of a wealthy Russian family, defying authority, fighting for the helpless and starving people, demanding change, marrying a fellow dissenter, Andrea Gusev. *Gusev*, the man Elena had claimed had worked for Fabergé, had been killed by the Bolsheviks on their rampage, going from street to street seeking out anyone who was of the despised Bourgeoisie, leaving Valentina devastated, a widow and a single parent before she was twenty.

'How she managed to escape the city is a miracle,' Lorna finished. 'With a small baby as well – that would be Elena, naturally. But of course, a few years later, it was a case of her helping one dissident too many, and they came after her. But she did it.

'A train to Berlin, faked papers, the lot. Elena must have been about eight or nine. What a life that poor woman had. Anyway, it's all a bit vague after that. She managed to open a jewellery shop but someone must have helped; you couldn't just roll up and open a business in Berlin in those days. Not if you were a woman.

'But can you imagine a natural warrior like Valentina – and she was – being able to ignore all that dreadful business in Berlin? Well, exactly. She never cared what they were, race, faith whatever. If they were being suppressed she waded in. Until of course the SS came after her. Somehow, she and Elena were spirited out of Berlin, which is how she ended up in Paris and, of course, in the end the Gestapo got her and shot her—'

'*No!*' Harriet's jaw dropped. 'How do you know all this?'

'Because my – I have to say,' Lorna gave an embarrassed little laugh, 'distressingly at times – *curious* mother decided, when she could get nothing out of Elena, to ring old friends in Paris who were there in the war, and pieced it together. But please, don't rely on it. Wartime caused great confusion.

'They said at the time it was widely suspected that she was part of the Resistance. I gather lots of British airmen were helped to get out because of her. There's a strong suggestion that Elena was part of it as well. Don't forget, she was a young woman in the war. No longer a child. Elena managed to escape to Geneva when her mother was taken. Poor Elena,' Lorna sighed, 'I doubt she ever recovered. Alone, frightened, in a new country and distraught from her mother's death. How dreadful must that have been? I'm not sure what happened to Valentina's husband,' she frowned. 'He disappeared off the radar after that.'

'He was killed. In St Petersburg,' Harriet pointed out.

'No, not him. She married again. Mark? Martin? No. Max.'

'Max?' Harriet could hear Elena's voice talking of a man she had obviously liked. 'Do you mean her *Uncle* Max? She often mentioned him. He married her mother? How amazing. But what about Arthur? Elena's husband. Where did he come in?'

Lorna shook her head. 'There, I'm afraid, I haven't a clue. At some point they must have married, but who knows when or even where that was. Mind you, Mum said Elena told her once or twice that she wanted to go back. No, not to Russia. Berlin. I suppose she meant to see the shop, but it was just an old lady's dream,' she said sadly, 'of a better time. The shop must be long gone. Her memory played tricks on her, I often suspected that. She got dates wrong, that kind of thing, and there was the small exaggeration here and there. So who knows?

'This I *do* know,' Lorna rose as Harriet glanced at her watch. 'I doubt an event went by at Roots without her contributing something. Which reminds me.'

She reached behind her, and opened a drawer in a mahogany desk, pulling out a white envelope. 'When Peter said you'd turned up, I just thought, ah, that's who must have them.'

Two photographs slid out. Black and white and faded but they were still clear enough to make out the people in them.

A young-ish woman on her wedding day, a bouquet of small flowers in one hand, a plain dress that fell just below her knees, tiny covered buttons running from the neck to the waist, a small flat round straw hat perched like a pancake on the side of her head. It was clearly before the war, a happy time if her face, laughing up at the man whose arm she was clutching, was anything to go by. Young, blonde, his expression was more serious, staring straight into the lens. His suit was rather creased, and he wore what looked like a rose in his buttonhole.

Carefully, she turned the photograph over. On the back were the name of the photographer and the location. Robert Leconte, it seemed, had captured the moment all those years ago, at the Mairie in Montmartre. The couple, on that long-ago day, looked happy. Sure of each other.

The other photograph showed a young girl, a teenager on a country road – where, was hard to tell – holding hands with a very small child, a mere toddler, both blonde, both skinny.

There was something about the eyes of the older girl, the air of defiance, that seemed familiar. Chin up, one hand on a very lean hip scowling into the camera. Harriet almost smiled.

'That's Elena,' she said to Lorna. 'Don't you think? And the child might be the cousin.'

Lorna nodded. 'And I think almost certainly the bride and groom are Valentina and Max.'

Harriet stared at the couple she had heard so much about, but would never know, looking closely at the man who had figured so largely in Elena's childhood; the eyes, the straight nose, holding the arm of the woman Elena had adored.

'If I were her cousin,' Lorna said, twisting round to see the images. 'I know I'd want them back.'

Harriet could only agree.

*

It was as she reached the end of the street, that the stirring of an idea flickered into life. She had listened to Lorna describe the courage of a woman

– now she came to think of it two women – who deserved so much better than this tawdry end. Harriet knew she had a plan.

She could hear Elena's voice, '*Always have a plan,*' and she was right. Now, it was no longer just a shapeless idea, but a firm plan. One she knew was not just probable, but inevitable.

Almost. Give or take a detail here and there. As she walked, it was already sliding into place. Provided she didn't stop to think.

For a while now, Harriet had known that thinking too much only led to sitting down and making another cup of coffee, toying wistfully with all kinds of revenge she could exact on every person – by which she meant Kurt Weber – who had brought her to this point, getting nowhere and finally doing nothing except needing more coffee.

There was, she decided, very little – if anything – left she could do to recover her own reputation, except to hope that in time memories would fade. But maybe she could restore a sense of peace, of closure, if she repaid the woman who had meant so well, been such a warrior, like her mother, and finish the journey that had been Elena's life?

By the time she reached the entrance to the tube, she was running.

Chapter Eleven

An unrelenting rain, driven across the city's endless open squares by an icy wind blowing in from the Baltics, greeted Harriet as she trundled her case behind her, along a street in Friederichshain trying to find her hotel. She halted, resting her bag on the handle of her case while she studied her phone, where the hotel address was listed.

'Vierenstrasse? Vierenstrasse?' she muttered, squinting up through the drizzling rain for the road sign. 'Hell's bells where are you?'

She groaned as realisation dawned that the bus from the airport had delivered her a stop too early. For a moment she considered retracing her steps, but wasn't at all sure she'd get that right either. Instead, she gritted her teeth, swore a bit, hoisted her bag further up her shoulder and marched on, her case rattling behind her. Online, a few days earlier – before she had left her flat for a dawn flight to Berlin – she had a plan. But it wasn't until she actually saw the street for herself, in the eastern part of Berlin, that she knew it wasn't quite what she'd envisaged for the next seven days. However, it was the best match for her slender means. She had no doubt that other parts of Berlin were delightful, filled with desirable buildings, leafy parks and fashionable streets. But this street, in this area – no. She glanced both ways as she finally halted at the small doorway that led into a reception area of Der Starlight Hotel and a stab of misgiving gripped her. Second-rate hotels and cheap bars ran either side of the road, the sight of which was not improved by weather so cold she thought her teeth might freeze.

Her feet felt like blocks of ice, the fur round the hood of her parka was wet and soggy. This, she comforted herself, this ghastly weather was only for a week, less if she was lucky, and she would be able to justify the string of deliberate untruths she had left in her wake, which troubled her far more than a few dodgy bars on her doorstep.

'*Madrid*?' James had approved when she lied about her destination. 'Love,' he leaned over and hugged her. 'It's just what you need. A break. William was only saying yesterday that's what was needed, weren't you Will? Will?'

A brief look of relief swept William's face. No-one had to tell her; if she wanted to still be part of James' life, it was time to start letting William have him back. And she found that, when she considered it, a small lie was not so bad if that's what it took.

Lizzie, of course, was not so easily fooled. Harriet fiddled with her wine glass. They were sitting in a bar, just round the corner from the now defunct Raglan Parade. Nicely crowded, squeezed into a booth and glad to be back on familiar and much missed close terms. 'I just want to be on my own for a while,' she insisted. Later, she realised how brief the hesitation had been before she told her second lie in as many minutes to make sense of the first. 'Mum and Dad aren't going to be there. They're going to friends. In – in El Born. Barcelona.'

'So why go?' Lizzie sounded bewildered. 'You're already on your own. You don't need to go to Spain to do that.'

It was probably then, as Lizzie narrowed her eyes suspiciously, that Harriet had to finally accept that lying was not her forte. She raised her glass to take a gulp of wine.

'Look,' Lizzie's voice softened. 'I'm not buying it.' She leaned forward and gently pushed Harriet's hand down so that she could see her face partially hidden by her glass. 'Look at me,' she ordered. 'Harriet? What's going on? Oh God,' she slumped back in her chair. 'Please tell me it isn't that bloody man again?'

'No. Not him. Well, not directly.'

'*Jeez*,' Lizzie moaned. She let her head fall on her arms. 'I don't believe this. What are you thinking?'

'No, you don't understand,' Harriet said quickly. 'Listen. I'll explain.'

At the end of which, Lizzie didn't look any less anxious.

'So why can't you just call that Brotherton twit and ask him where she is? The name of the home. Send the wretched things to her. It was written down somewhere wasn't it?'

'Because he'd tell Christopher and I don't want him to know. I – um – promised him I wouldn't contact Kurt again, and I'm not, obviously, but he might not see it that way.'

Lizzie peered at her in disbelief. 'And this – what's he called? Oh right. Bing, He's going to put you in touch with a lawyer who'll help you find Natasha? Is he *insane*?'

'No,' Harriet protested. 'Quite the reverse. He's really clever. Speaks Russian, French and a bit of most other languages. Told me a Chekhov story about a man called Gusev—'

'And yet,' Lizzie's voice was filled with sarcasm, 'awestruck that I am at you knowing someone so blindingly clever,' she paused looking thoughtful, 'nope,' she finished cheerfully. 'Still don't get it.'

'Lizzie?' Harriet leaned across the table. 'He was the first stranger I talked to about it all, and he didn't judge me.'

'Why would he?' Lizzie exclaimed.

'He could have done, he could have believed everything he read. But he didn't. He was really nice. I mean, I don't know much about him, except he's just getting over someone and—'

'How on earth do you know?'

'He told me. And Lorna Tamworth did as well.'

Lizzie rolled her eyes. 'And that makes him an okay person?'

'No. Of course not.' Harriet pressed on. 'But the Tamworths like him and *yes*, I did like him. He's put me in touch with his ex – Martha. Martha Dressler. She's German and a lawyer. She was here for a couple of years on a placement apparently, but she's back in Berlin now. Bing didn't want to move there so they split up, although if you ask me—'

'*Enough*,' Lizzie shrieked. She put her hands over her ears. 'I get it, you're new BFs. No, don't say another word. And the dosh for all this?'

'My car.'

'Of course,' Lizzie said wearily.

'Well, I was going to sell it anyway. I don't need one right now. I got enough for it to fund a cheapish hotel and meals without breaking the bank.'

Lizzie sighed and ran her fingers through her hair.

'I think it's ridiculous. You don't speak German, you've never even been there – and for the record, I don't want you to go. Why don't you wait until I can come with you—'

Harriet leaned over and gripped Lizzie's hands. 'And I would, but you haven't got the time. No, you haven't. You have four fairs to exhibit at and you can't afford to lose those sales, and that takes you up to the end of February. I'll be back in a week.'

Lizzie looked past Harriet and shook her head. 'No point in fighting battles you can't win. Okay. You'll text every day? And you are definitely not going near the dreadful Kurt? And once you've delivered the photographs and your letter to this Natasha, you'll turn round and come home?'

Harriet nodded.

Lizzie drummed her fingers on the table. 'Why am I not convinced? Okay. But don't ask me to lie to your mother. And I'll avoid James for one week. Mind you, the mood William's in, that won't be a sacrifice. And give me this Bing's number.'

'Why?' Harriet asked.

'Well not to have lessons in Chekhov, that's for sure. Just in case I decide to kill him for encouraging you.'

*

Harriet dumped her suitcase on a small side table in the room the Starlight Hotel had reserved for her, notable more for the fact that while it seemed clean enough – white duvet, a white towel neatly folded on the flat divan bed – it was an inhospitable place. Not a place for sitting in, that was for sure, since there wasn't even a chair to help in that department. The view from the window with its cheap cream curtains, a rust mark creeping down the edge of the one nearest the wall, was unobliging. A view across the back of the building, brown shutters all closed, with not a sign of life to be had.

Stuck on the wall by the bed, she found a notice of rules and regulations, but beyond the phrases she'd committed to memory, involving greeting complete strangers and enquiring after their health, or how to find the nearest station, it might as well have been written in Swahili. An overwhelming feeling of panic started to rise in her chest. She sat down on the edge of the bed and took several deep breaths.

On the wall facing the bed, suspended from a bracket, was a television, but there wasn't a single channel in any other language listed, unless she counted the porn channels. 'And I bet,' she decided grimly, trying to find a channel that seemed to be the news, 'that would be dubbed in German.' Nevertheless, more out of comfort rather than any hope of finding it useful, she switched it on.

'C'mon,' she ordered herself. 'Get down to it.'

She scrolled down her phone and found the address Bing had given her for Martha Dressler, former lover, now his friend working in this city.

'Frau Dressler? She in Alexanderplatz,' The girl who picked up struggled with her English. At least, Harriet thought with relief, she knew enough to even struggle, but nevertheless it still took a good two strangled minutes, with the aid of her phrase book, to try and make herself understood. It failed spectacularly. For reasons Harriet could not even begin to fathom, the girl seemed to think she needed medical assistance.

'You are hurt? *Ja?*' the girl pressed her. 'You have the blood? *Ja?*'

'Blood? Of course not. *Nein, nein,*' Harriet exclaimed. 'Martha? I just want to find Martha.'

'Okay. You wait, bitte? Ja? I make phone call. You have name?'

After a few minutes the girl came back with fresh instructions.

'You come, I mean,' the girl hastily corrected herself. 'You *go*. You get U-Bahn. You find Alexanderplatz. *Ja?* Martha expect you.'

'Ja,' Harriet said, so relieved her legs felt weak, although she didn't have much of a clue what she was saying yes to.

The room didn't look like it stretched to a safe and the reception didn't look like the sort you'd trust with a tea bag, let alone an official document, so she stuffed her passport into the pocket of her jeans, recovered her boots from the radiator where she'd tried to dry them out, pulled on an extra sweater, managing to get her parka over it, and set off.

Eventually she found the nearest U-Bahn and emerged fifteen minutes later onto Alexanderplatz, in the drizzling mist of the late afternoon, and discovered that it was possible to find herself in an even drearier locality than the one she'd chosen to stay in. A depressing expanse of concrete and glass greeted her. She consulted her phone, pressed in the location she needed and set off, ignoring the fact that the light was fading. Blazing street lamps cast a weird glow across run-down and graffiti-covered buildings. After several false turns, she eventually found the entrance to the office where she had been told Martha Dressler worked.

She wondered, as she craned her head up to double-check the street name, if Martha really was as smart as Bing had insisted. After all, surely no-one with any kind of reputation worked from a crumbling building, accessed through a doorway with only a number on the wall to identify it, but enough entry phones and clunking locks to either keep the world out or the workers in. But then Bing didn't seem taken with appearances either.

'I want,' she said in stilted German into the entry phone, 'to see Martha. *Ich bin ein Freund von Bing. Ja*, friend. No. No – I mean, *Freudin*,' she corrected, holding her book up to the street light. 'I am a friend of Bing,' she added in English, more in hope than belief that it would help clarify matters.

A lot of rattling sounded from the other side of the firmly locked door, until it swung back to reveal a blonde, spiky-haired girl with several rings piercing her ears, baggy trousers, a tight black roll-neck sleeveless sweater and – once they were in the lighted hallway Harriet could see – a tattoo of a sabre-toothed tiger, teeth exposed, crawling up her arm. The door slammed behind them, keys were elaborately turned, and a keypad activated to ensure only those with the code would get in. Or indeed out.

'Martha?' Harriet enquired. She threw an uneasy glance back at the closed door.

'Nein. Ich bin Bebe,' the girl announced peering back at Harriet. 'Stay here.

I get Martha.' She pronounced it 'Marta'. All Harriet was glad about was that she spoke good English and quite guiltily hoped to God that Martha would look a little more reassuring.

The girl left Harriet to gaze around the untidy room; a sign over the door requested visitors to ensure all doors were locked behind them and to double-check the entry system. Harriet knew this largely through the helpful sketch that ran alongside it. She could see immediately the kind of lawyer she was looking for was not to be found in this place. Der Hafen, it was called, with something written under it. Hastily she looked it up. The Haven. Below the title it said in German: *A place to think, to pause, to recover.*

Harriet briefly closed her eyes. Oh God. No wonder they kept asking if she was hurt, bleeding. The entire place was given over to women fleeing from domestic abuse. What on earth was Martha doing here? From an over-lit corridor in an overheated building, the walls badly in need of attention, she could hear the sound of children either crying or arguing. Leaflets plastered every surface with emergency numbers of other agencies who might – but probably in the end would struggle – to find accommodation and employment for those able to move on. A woman doctor's number was amongst them.

She sank down into the nearest chair, a plastic affair with a hard wooden back and a narrow seat. While she waited, she began to compose a speech to explain to Martha Dressler when she arrived, that she had been entirely mistaken in believing she might be able to help her – maybe she could suggest someone who might? She could not face knowing this was a totally wasted journey.

The sound of rapid clicking on the wooden floor made her turn in time to see a tall young woman – severely cut black jacket, pencil-tight skirt skimming her knees, four-inch heels – whirl through the door, followed by Bebe, who closed it carefully behind her. Harriet rose.

'Martha,' the newcomer announced stretching out her hand. Her grip was brief but firm, certainly enough for Harriet to notice the perfectly manicured red nails, that were an exact match for the lipstick.

'All rather rushed today.' Martha's English was impressive, an accent that pronounced 'what' as *vot* or 'think' as *zink*, but grammatically you couldn't fault her. She smiled, sitting opposite Harriet and crossed legs, so slender Harriet simply stared at them. Her skin was flawless, her raven hair sculpted to her head in layered wisps.

'Sorry,' Martha was saying, 'that you had to drag over here, but I'm only here one day a week. An advisory role, legal stuff if anything goes to court. It rarely does. My other office is at Potsdamer Platz, but you said it was urgent so,' she leaned forward, 'we're both in a rush. Fire away. Oh excuse me. Just a moment. Bebe?' she turned away as Harriet began to explain and spoke in rapid German to the tattooed girl.

'I'm sorry,' she turned back, 'I need to be at the Ritz Carlton at five. Traffic will be horrendous, so I've asked Bebe to get my car here in ten instead of fifteen. Now,' she glanced at her phone, 'who is this person you're looking for?'

'Well,' Harriet recovering from the suddenness of it all, became acutely aware of several things all at once. Her parka looked creased and still damp – no wonder everyone kept mistaking her for someone on the wrong end of abuse. Her hair, unlike Martha's, was badly in need of a cut. And this woman, so obviously a hideous mistake on Bing's part to ever have let go, was exactly what she needed. She also realised in the same instant, that if Martha Dressler said ten minutes she meant ten and not a moment longer.

'So let me get this straight,' Martha said when she'd finished. 'You're planning to take on Kurt Weber? Again?'

'God no. Not take on. Look, please try and understand. None of this is what she wanted. Elena I mean. I *know* that. She tried to be so generous to me, and yes, I would like to see justice done, but I wanted to do something she couldn't do herself. Return her family stuff to Natasha. Full circle for her—'

'Okay, okay,' Martha held up her hand. 'And two photographs?'
Harriet nodded.

'And – okay – I've heard of dafter reasons, but I want your assurance this is all it is.'

'Yes. I promise. Elena went through so much, helped so many people, it's the very least—'

It was as far as she got. 'Enough,' Martha insisted. '*Please*. Let's not bring in the violins. Sorry,' she said, taking in Harriet's flushed face. She hesitated and then began to draw a circle on the floor with the toe of her shoe. 'You don't look stupid,' she said. 'And Bing doesn't usually offer help to lunatics. So I'm going to assume you're telling the truth. But I must be blunt with you. I can point you in the right direction, to someone who might know where Natasha Weber is, but my strong advice is to go home. Put it all behind you and start living your life again.'

'Why?' Harriet asked bluntly. 'Because it suits everyone that I just go quietly away?'

Martha shrugged. She began to pile papers into a large leather tote bag.

'Well that's one option. But let me throw some absolute truths into this mix and,' she emphasised her next words, 'I urge you to consider all of them. Okay?'

As she spoke, she began gathering up her bag and coat – black cashmere, sleek as she was. 'You have no money, or any friends in this country. Even if I told you exactly where to find this Natasha Weber, you can't just rock up to see her and expect to be allowed in. To see a fragile old lady? What kind of place would allow that? And finally, have you considered the *very* strong grounds Kurt would be handed to sue you for invasion of privacy? Strong on that in this country, let me tell you. Seriously, that's my best advice, Harriet. If you had more going for you, I'd be advising something else, but legally you don't, and in the end that's what this boils down to. Sorry. It's a fact.'

Harriet rose with her. 'But I do have something going for me,' she said trying to sound dignified in the face of such wounding honesty. 'Something that in the end must mean something.'

'And that would be?'

'The truth.'

Martha blew her cheeks out in disbelief. 'Yes,' she said dryly. 'Very noble but, forgive me, you're not in a soap opera, are you? You don't believe that that means anything, surely?'

'I try to,' Harriet knew she was sounding even more naïve.

'Well, we all do,' Martha said more kindly. 'If truth rather than money did it for the law, you'd have everything going for you. But you haven't. If you want me to help, then take that one on the chin.'

If kicking herself would have helped, Harriet would have aimed at both shins. 'You need to go,' she said stiffly. 'Thanks for your time.'

Martha paused at the door. She let her head drop and then looked back at Harriet. 'Okay. How well do you know Kurt?'

Harriet noticed she used only his first name.

'I've never met him,' she said. 'Just what I've read and through the lawyers.'

Martha glanced at her phone. 'Okay,' she sighed. 'Come with me. I'll drop you somewhere near your hotel. We'll talk on the way.'

*

'Here's the deal,' she said as they both settled into the back of her car. 'Kurt's a very public figure in this city, a patron of the arts, on the A list. His wife decamping to America like that also added tragedy to him. Nothing people like more than reading about someone with a broken heart. But he won't have a word said against her. Blamed himself. Long hours, always away, took her for granted blah blah. You get the picture?'

'Totally,' Harriet agreed.

'I hope you do,' Martha said. 'Because there's more. It's not official yet, but the Minister of Culture is about to make him some kind of special ambassador for the arts, raising money, all that stuff. Perfect choice, with his connections, and it's no secret Kurt is looking for a way into politics. So the chances of anyone willing to help you against someone with that kind of clout, are about this.' She held her thumb a fraction away from her forefinger.

She hesitated before adding with faintly disguised sarcasm in her voice, 'Did I mention women find him irresistible?'

'So I'm told. Do you?' Harriet glanced sideways at her.

'Hmm? Attractive, not irresistible. There's a difference. He's never without some beautiful woman on his arm. The daughter of some count or other at the moment. Must have something going for him.'

'His wallet can't harm.'

Martha laughed. 'Well, there's that too.'

Suddenly she leaned forward, scanning the traffic ahead. 'Sorry,' she turned to Harriet. 'I'm going to have to drop you. I'm so late. This traffic is ridiculous. Franz?' she called to the driver. 'Stop on the next corner. *Danke*. Do you mind?' She turned to Harriet. 'Ten minutes, walk straight up there. Here,' she opened a black leather wallet and took out a card. 'Just in case,' she said. 'I'll see what I can do about locating his grandmother. Sure you don't want to try your barrister again? Much easier. No?'

'No,' Harriet said firmly. She tucked the card into her jeans. 'It might look like it, but I'm not deliberately trying for a hard life, I promise you.'

She climbed out onto the wet pavement. The door slammed behind her. The window wound down.

'By the way,' Martha called with a casualness that didn't sound convincing. 'Bing? Is he okay?'

'I think so,' Harriet called back. 'He's been so kind. Nice man.'

'No need to tell me,' Martha almost snapped. And the car was gone, rejoining the snarling line of traffic, taking Martha to a drinks party at the Ritz for the great and the good of Berlin, leaving Harriet to walk two blocks to the decidedly less glamorous Starlight Hotel to ponder her next move. Mainly where to find something to eat and wonder how two people like Martha – with enough ambition and drive to run a small country – and Bing – so laid back, clearly clever but with no more ambition than to stay doggedly in pursuit of a way of life that seemed to elude him – had ever got together.

A bit like her and Dermot she decided later, as she crawled under the thin sheet and lumpy eiderdown that the Starlight boasted was part of their 'all modern comforts'. No computer would ever have decided she and the man she thought had been the love of her life were a match. She so honest and in love, him so – well, not to be dwelt on. Who knew what went on in any relationship? But it didn't stop her wondering about Bing and Martha.

A long night stretched ahead. Misgivings that Martha might not come up with anything began to increase to the point where, by five o'clock in the morning, she was sitting up, the cover up to her chin, wondering why she had ever bothered with her in the first place.

She knew she was being ridiculous, trusting no-one like this, but then she had never, until now, been given to embark on anything so impetuous as pitching up in a different country on the strength of a crumpled greeting card, in a language of which she spoke or read not one word, to try and sort it out in another.

Half an hour later she rose, made the best of a shower with a decidedly questionable plastic curtain, and finally dressed. Her bag slung across her chest, she used the stairs to make her way down three flights to reception, to find out if there was a way she could check where residential nursing homes were listed in and around Berlin.

The heavily made-up girl in a bright blue jacket and a scarf tucked into the neck of her shirt, preferred, it seemed, not to bother, other than to recommend the Internet. Sitting in the tiny cubicle, facing a computer with a very dodgy connection, the miserable realisation rose, that she hadn't a clue where these places were and that anyone who embarked on such a stupid mission should have done more research before they left England. She was just beginning to check flights home when a text, from someone signing themselves as Martha Dressler's assistant, popped up.

Chapter Twelve

Harriet sat on a high stool in the window of a coffee shop on the main road, drumming her fingers on the plastic counter, looking out on the rain drizzling down the window. A steady trail of workers walked purposefully by before disappearing onto one of the trams that ran down the centre of the road, or to the U-Bahn on the corner.

Martha's assistant had texted three names of residential homes within an hour's drive of the city centre, and try as she might, she could not recall if any of them were the ones mentioned in Kurt Weber's action against her, but all had residents sharing the surname Weber.

The first two, when she phoned, said there were no residents of that name and even if there were, they would not be able to supply that information. At least that's what she thought they said. Overnight, it was not to be expected that her German had improved even fractionally, or that she would find that everyone in the city obligingly spoke English, like Martha. Her phrase book was in serious danger of meltdown.

The final one, Die Linden Baum at a place called Warbellinsee, asked her who she was, why she wanted to see Mrs Weber, followed by a small hesitation before the voice asked her to hold and then came back to say they never revealed information about their residents.

It was enough. Who would care about such things as a reason for visiting if there was no-one there by that name?

She thanked them, agreed she must have made a mistake. And hung up. All she had to do now was find out how to get there. The small matter of what she would say – should she get in at all – was carefully ignored. Plenty of time, she told herself, with a confidence she was far from feeling, to work that out on the train.

*

Having completely misunderstood both the train service and the platform from where the fast train departed that would take her north out of Berlin to Eberswalde, Harriet missed the first train and was obliged to wait half an hour for the next, which stopped everywhere and took twice as long.

Having travelled through small towns, stations with names she had difficulty in pronouncing, deep forests and mists shrouding what little of the country-side she could see, she eventually stepped down at the right station and went in search of a bus for the next part of the journey.

Almost an hour later and over two hours since she had left the city centre, the bus dropped her at the end of the long winding lane where the driver, glancing casually at the address she showed him, stabbed a finger at where Die Linden Baum was to be found. She eyed the lane with misgiving as the bus rumbled away. She had been the only passenger to alight.

At any other time, and in better weather, she would have stopped to explore the picture postcard perfection of the lake, with its yachts and boats, all now – until the weather improved – covered and tucked into the marina. Surrounded by woodland, the air damp, with wisps of mist drifting over the tops of trees, she wondered why she'd never thought to move there. A feeling that lasted only as long as it took to realise the address she needed was a great deal further along the deserted lane than she had thought. Then there had come the necessity of stopping occasionally to give herself a stern talking to, that no-one was lurking in the thick trees to pounce on her.

Once or twice a car drove past, but even the sight of a lone woman walking in such a deserted area was not enough to make them slow down.

After twenty minutes, her feet beginning to freeze in boots that looked fine tripping round Pimlico but were as useful as sling backs in this freezing rain, she found what she was looking for. A small plaque on the gate, discreet and formal, told her it was the Der Linden Baum Klinic. That was as much as she could see. The tall, black gates were filled in, but she could see a CCTV camera recording her arrival as she pressed the bell. Instinctively, she looked down at her feet to check they were not now merely sodden strips of leather, and at least presentable. She needn't have worried, she didn't get past the door.

'*Sprechen Sie Englisch?*' Harriet asked, her fingers crossed.

'*Ja, ja,*' came a disembodied voice. 'Of course.'

Later, Harriet decided that that had to have been the high point of her visit. After that, it was downhill all the way.

'No,' said the voice when she asked to see Natasha Weber. Pleasant enough but firm. 'It's not possible to see a resident unless you are a relative or by prior arrangement. Please telephone for an appointment.'

'But I only want to leave some personal belongings,' Harriet pleaded. 'I knew her late cousin. Elena Banbury. Well, she was Guseva. And I think Weber as well. Please. I've come such a long way.'

There was a silence. Then, 'What name did you say?'

A sixth sense kicked in. 'Bingley,' she lied instantly. 'Um . . . Liz Bingley.'

'One moment,' the voice said. Harriet cringed. She was getting good at lying. So much for the famed 'truth' she had told Martha was all that mattered. Small wonder Martha had practically laughed in her face. The moments turned into minutes. Several passed while she stamped her feet to try and revive the circulation that was threatening to destroy all ability to walk if someone didn't come back soon.

'Please,' the voice suddenly came through the speaker. 'The manager will not be back until two o'clock. Only she can make a decision. If you want to leave a message or – the gift you mention, I can deliver it to her. But if you want to come back, you wait for at least two hours, maybe three.'

It was better than nothing. Harriet could only agree and to trudge away to while away, as best she could, the next few hours. About half a mile further along the lane, in the first hamlet she came to, she found a small café, sank gratefully into a wicker chair and ordered coffee and a slice of cake. If, she told herself – taking a bite into the cake that was high on calories, low on resistance – on her return to London she booked a long spell with a psychiatrist, it might be the best idea she'd had in years.

*

She was led, by a white-uniformed nurse wearing canvas shoes, along a thickly carpeted corridor to what appeared to be a conservatory, but turned out to be a sitting room with views stretching over a garden. Even at this time of year it was possible see how beautiful it would be in a month or two. Urns of flowers filled the entire room, the faint perfume of winter jasmine drifted on the air, aquamarine silk cushions piled high on blue sofas, placed strategically to ensure the occupants were able to enjoy such tranquillity from every vantage point.

This was no average care home. But then she hadn't expected Kurt Weber's grandmother to be scraping together the fees to try and afford one of the heavily criticised, overcrowded, resource-stretched establishments that most of Germany was obliged to offer the elderly. Not when her grandson – and presumably his grandmother, too – could well afford the very best. And this was undoubtedly it. In the window of the sitting room, a woman turned. A slender woman, forty-ish she guessed, dressed in a navy jacket and skirt, a brisk, efficient appearance, her highlighted caramel hair neatly cut into wings around her face.

'Frau Huber? Frau Bingley is here,' announced the nurse and left her.

The woman did not extend a hand, simply indicated Harriet to follow her.

'Frau Weber is very fragile,' Frau Huber said. 'We cannot allow you to disturb her but we are happy to let you leave her belongings and to see for yourself that she is well cared for. Herr Weber is most protective of her.'

She opened one half of a set of double doors to a room off the conservatory. One hand made a small movement indicating to Harriet not to come further into the room.

'My dear,' Frau Huber said gently to the woman. There was no response. An old woman, a birdlike creature, immaculately dressed but with vacant eyes and clearly in another world, rocked gently backwards and forwards in a high-backed chair. The room was uncluttered, elegant almost, facing the garden where a light fall of snow now covered the length of a long narrow wall, enclosing its own small patio garden. A wheelchair was parked in one corner. The occupant didn't look round or even smile.

Frau Huber bent down and gently pressed her hand and spoke quietly to her in German. At one point, she made a gesture to her that suggested eating. The merest, no more than a slight turn of the old woman's face was the only response.

'You see?' Frau Huber rose and rejoined Harriet standing in the doorway. 'Only if she wants to respond. Some days are better than others. Her afternoon snack will be here soon. Her appetite is good.'

Next to the fragile woman, on a glass-topped coffee table were a group of photographs in silver frames. To the side, there was one of Kurt at some function or other and leaning on his arm, a raven-haired young woman, quite beautiful, almost certainly more than just a friend to him. The one in the centre showed a young woman, a thick blonde fringe and straight hair, framing a pretty enough face, her dress short, multi-patterned, floating around slender legs. She was holding a toddler, his hair almost white, serious eyes, clutching a toy car. The woman was pointing at the camera, her head close to the child's.

From the look of her dress, Harriet thought it must have been taken sometime in the early seventies and that the child was almost certainly Kurt Weber.

'Her daughter,' Frau Huber said in a low voice. 'She died many years ago when Kurt was young. He is one of the few people Natasha responds to.'

'And this?' Harriet pointed to one with an elderly man sitting in a large cane chair by a lake. Frau Huber glanced at it. 'Her late husband,' she said of the man sitting in the cane chair. 'Max Weber. Herr Weber's grandfather.'

Harriet hardly heard. The woman was saying something about Kurt's parents both killed in a car accident, how close he was to his grandmother, the beautiful girl in the picture with him the countess something or other, great supporter of their work, but Harriet's eyes were riveted on the photograph of Natasha's husband.

She knew that face. Knew it as well as she knew anyone's. He was Uncle Max and he'd married Valentina. Not Natasha.

She didn't know him, but she *felt* she did. So many times he'd been the star of one of Elena's stories and he was in the picture she had in her bag, Max on his wedding day. To Valentina. Elena's mother. This didn't make sense.

'When were they married?' she asked nodding at the old lady, already lost again in her own world.

'I've no idea.'

'How long has she been like this?'

The woman went on staring fixedly out into the garden. Harriet went very still. A feeling of panic began to rise to the roof of her mouth. The woman wasn't even looking at her. Her stomach gave a painful lurch. This wasn't normal. And then she knew. She should have been shown the door. And she hadn't been. Any moment, the police would come. They were stalling, keeping her here. What in God's name would Christopher say? Martha, who had warned her? Her mouth felt dry.

'Three, maybe four years,' the woman was saying.

'Are you sure?' Harriet located the door just behind her. 'I only ask,' she said, beginning to inch towards it, 'because she managed to write a card to her cousin, just last year. As a matter of fact, I still have it.'

She was about to produce it when a man's voice came from behind.

'May I?'

She looked steadily out over the garden. The rows of flower beds, a dark mass of earth turned over to await the spring, sprinkled with snow. The old woman in her chair didn't even stir. Oh, how stupid, *stupid* she had been. She should have left once she'd seen her. She could have got away and no harm done. She should not have come at all. Harriet turned slowly.

A man, his face grave, but not, she noticed, very surprised to see her, was holding out his hand. She took a step back.

'How do you do?' he said, in faultless, if heavily accented, English. 'I'm Kurt Weber. And you must be Harriet Flynn. Please. No. Don't deny it. It really won't help. No-one else would have such an interest in returning a few – what? Letters? Ah. Photographs is it? In person. The staff were right to be suspicious. An English person and in such weather as this?'

They all turned as one to look silently out at the garden. Flakes of snow were now flurrying gently down. Settling as well, she noticed.

'And just to visit a complete stranger?' Kurt was saying. 'I wonder now? What was wrong with the post?' Or indeed calling my lawyers. Will you,' he asked her quietly into the silence, 'wait for me outside please? I would like to talk to my grandmother alone.'

'I'll just go,' Harriet said when she was safely on the other side of the door.

'It would be better if you stayed,' Frau Huber stared straight ahead. 'Herr Weber expects you to.'

Harriet sat down on the edge of a chair, just as the door opened and Kurt appeared. She swallowed hard and got up, sat down, got up again and simply stared at the man who had ruined her and could now possibly have her deported. Oddly, being escorted from the country suddenly sounded a great deal more preferable to even another hour spent on this insane mission. Why in God's name would she ever want to come back?

'Please?' He indicated a quieter area by the windows. She rose from the sofa. She let him – because it was too embarrassing to push him away – take her elbow and lead her out of earshot of the women standing waiting for more instructions. The nurses were positively simpering. In another minute, she thought savagely, they'll be dusting the carpet before he sets foot on it.

But then, she couldn't help noticing, he was ridiculously good-looking. His height, build, the smile. The whole package, as Lizzie would say. Martha was right. Unconsciously she smoothed her hair, tucked the blonde strands behind her ears.

'You must stop imagining things,' he urged in a quiet voice. They stood, rather than sat. 'By rights I should call the police. Apart from disliking such attention, I'm making allowances for someone who has – let's say, made a mistake, has become irrationally obsessed with me. This is, *must be*, as far as this goes.'

Harriet glanced around. A nurse hovered. 'I am not obsessed with you,' she hissed. 'Trust me, that is not one of my problems, if indeed I have any.'

'Now what new fantasy has gripped you?' he asked. 'There must be something going on in your head to make you behave in this stupid fashion.'

'I would just like to know how,' she said in a rush, knowing her best chance at getting out of there was to answer, 'that frail old woman in there could have written a card to Elena. Almost a year ago. When she's been like this for at least three. Your assistant just told me.'

'Ah,' he sighed. '*That* card. Well, quite obviously, she didn't,' he said it so calmly she thought she'd misheard.

'She didn't? Then who—'

'We did. Or rather Ilse here kindly did it. What is the problem?'

Harriet wasn't sure but her mouth might possibly have opened and shut of its own accord without a sound coming out.

'In spite of not being my favourite person,' Kurt was saying. 'I didn't want Elena to worry – not at her age and with no likelihood of seeing my grandmother again, even though we had asked her so many times to keep in touch. We simply signed it for her.'

Harriet could feel, if not the carpet, a fair chunk of her case, sliding from beneath her. 'What do you mean, *we*?' she managed. '*You* wrote it? You admit it?' She glanced at Ilse Huber. Who in God's name was she?

'I think the word, "admit",' Kurt was saying, 'is a little misplaced. Well of course, as I haven't seen the card in question, I can't be sure. Where is it?'

'I've left it behind. In my luggage,' Harriet said, not able to bring herself to part with the reason she had come all this way.

'Ah. No matter. So you see?' he said. 'A harmless white lie. And, sadly,' he sat down on the edge of one of the sofas, linked his hands in his lap and looked up at her, 'you've made a legal case out of it. What did it say that made you so sure we were all villains?'

'I can't remember. I mean, I don't know. It's in Russian.'

Harriet looked steadily at him. His eyes never left hers. He raised an eyebrow. 'You seem determined to think that it was entirely the other way round, that we ignored Elena. Did it ever occur to you that it was Elena who refused all our attempts to include her in the family, to care for her when you accused us of neglecting her? No. You saw what you believed to be a lonely old woman instead of the wilful, and the little unbalanced one we knew, who having had rich Russian grandparents and hobnobbed with a tribe of European trash with money but no manners, decided to pass herself off as some kind of impoverished duchess.'

Harriet felt behind her and sat on the edge of a sofa. This was indefensible, horrible. She tried to say so, but it came out in an incoherent mess, and her insistence that she was sure he was wrong and Elena wasn't like that got lost in the sheer misery of just being there. She longed for even the mean little hotel room.

'Don't,' he sighed, listening to her stumbling through her defence of Elena, like a man used to unravelling such stories about, at best an eccentric elderly relative, at worst, a fantasist. 'My dear girl,' he said. 'Please just listen. I'm telling you this, to help you get a sense of perspective. Please put Elena into context. Yes, her family lost everything in that terrible time. Elena, in her defence, never knew luxury, except what her and that absurd husband of hers were able to get for nothing. In fact she was a pauper. Well she would have been, if it hadn't been for my grandmother's family. They took them in when she and her mother eventually got to Berlin. And how did they repay them?'

Harriet shook her head. It was unbearable.

'By stealing all my great-grandmother's jewellery when they fled to Paris. Irina she was called. My grandmother was only a child, but she remembers her mother being horrified when they realised it was all gone. And to this day, we have no idea what they did with it all. Spent it, I expect.'

He was looking keenly at her.

'I had no idea,' she whispered. 'Elena was a very private person. She certainly didn't appear to have any money. Quite broke in fact. Look,' she took a deep breath. Last chance, but even before she spoke she knew, just knew, there would be a perfectly rational explanation.

'Your grandfather. He was married to Elena's mother. It doesn't say that on the Arcadia website. Why not?'

'Goodness,' he gave a small laugh. He looked quickly over her head at Ilse Huber. 'You have studied us well. How flattering. Yes. His first wife died. Valentina she was called. Convenience I gather. Not a love match by any means. They had to escape to Paris. Easier as a married couple I'm told. But once they were in Paris, off she went, taking Elena with her and I don't think he saw them again. After the war, he came back, met my grandmother, and in spite of the age gap, they fell in love, married and the result was my mother. I gather he preferred not to mention his first wife, what would be the point?

'We are a private family. We care for each other *in* private. Or have you found something wrong with that as well?'

'Except that Valentina was in the resistance – and Elena – and she was shot. Surely, he must have heard about that? Cared about what happened to them?'

He shrugged. 'Maybe, but he never said. I think he just wanted to forget such an unpleasant time. Only my grandmother tried to keep in touch with Elena when it was all over. Maybe Elena couldn't accept how different their lives were. Her own was certainly a disappointment to her. Who knows?

'Now,' his voice became brisk. 'Anything else before I ask you to stop all this nonsense? You know,' he said when she didn't reply, 'all this could have been avoided. We're not invisible. Not in hiding. When she died, someone could have told us, instead of waiting until I made my routine check on her.'

There was a cat outside. Pawprints delicately traced in the snow, his nose against the window. Harriet would have liked to have swapped places with him.

Instead she said, 'I have to get a plane – maybe even tonight. Can we just wrap this up?'

'Of course.' His manner was patient. Not unfriendly, which made her feel relieved and puzzled in equal measure. She'd had enough of his detailed defence of his actions, every base covered to prove she was an arch villain, that he was the aggrieved party and Elena little more than a spoilt grasping brat who spun tall stories to get attention.

'So,' he got to his feet. 'Why don't you just leave whatever it is you've brought with you and then outside there is a car waiting to take you back to wherever your hotel is.'

'No,' she said. She shook her head. 'No. I want nothing from you. No. *Please*. I don't need any help.'

'Whatever you say.' He didn't try to argue. 'And if anything else turns up, just hand it to my lawyers in London and we'll say no more. By the way, where did you find these?' He took the slim package she handed to him and without a glance at it, passed it straight to Ilse Huber who had simply stood as a silent witness throughout this painful exchange.

Harriet swallowed. The idea of involving Lorna Tamworth was not even up for grabs.

'In the back of a book,' she lied. 'Pushkin I think. They fell out when I was packing up Elena's flat. I put them on one side and forgot about them.'

He stood aside to let her go before him, out of the drawing room and into a long, wide corridor. They began to walk, an arm's length apart, towards the main entrance, followed by the silent Frau Huber.

If someone had asked what was her worst nightmare, Harriet would have been hard-pressed to find something to top this.

A car, a Mercedes, its engine purring, was parked outside the entrance. The driver, a heavily built man wearing a dark suit, alighted as she approached and held a door open. Kurt waved a dismissive hand at him.

Harriet walked past the driver, wishing she could have ditched her dignity and accepted a lift in such a warm, comfortable car. She didn't look back, simply turned and began to walk the good twenty minutes it would take to get to the end of the road. Within seconds the car Kurt had dismissed swept past, its tail lights activating as it swung round the first bend and out of her view. A moment later, in a second car, she glimpsed Kurt, sitting in the back with Frau Huber next to him. She halted and stepped back into the hedge. They didn't even glance at her. Clearly she was no longer part of their day, their life.

'And you're no longer part of mine,' she called loudly after the speeding car. 'And bloody good riddance.'

*

The fury at being so falsely accused and not listened to insulated her from the cold, as flakes of snow whirled into her face. Finally, she boarded the bus to the station and the train that would take her, in just over an hour, back to her seedy hotel. It was only when she was finally on the train that she looked in her bag for her phone, and carefully tucked the card that had started all this into a back pocket and zipped it up. She couldn't think why she had kept it, except to remind her she'd had strong reasons to regard it as significant, and not that she was totally bonkers. Who she was going to prove this to was unclear. Probably, she sighed to herself, just myself. Who else would care anymore?

The train sped towards the city, lights from the occasional town pinpointing through the darkness, but when she looked out of the window, only her reflection stared back at her. She slid down in her seat. It had been unbearable to have to listen to such a shoddy view of Elena, but against the word of a man who could draw on all of those who knew his grandmother to back his version of events, impossible to challenge. She had no-one.

Poor Elena, she groaned, unable to defend herself. Eaten by fish? Gusev had got off lightly, she thought grimly as the train began to slow into the station. This lot clearly wouldn't stop until they brought in the sharks.

*

The day had gone when she walked into the lobby of the hotel and took the lift to her room. As it rumbled to the top floor, she checked her phone and found texts from Lizzie – to call as soon as she got this, her mother having just arrived in Brooklyn. She'd call in a day or two. And one from Big Jake, who was going to be back in London from Newcastle and thought they might have a drink. Familiar, comforting, reliable names. Suddenly, she longed to go home, get back on track, away from this wet and inhospitable city and, no matter how bad, back where she understood not just the language, but where she belonged.

She would, she decided as she inserted the plastic key into the slot on the door, have a shower, find something to eat, check if there was a plane in the morning – too late to get one tonight – and then put all this behind her. She yawned as she closed the door and felt for the light switch. Oddly, the cover of the bed was on the floor, and the television was still on – she could have sworn she'd turned it off.

She took the first blow to her head. Someone standing behind the door pushed her forward onto the floor, leaving her more stunned than hurt. She cried out, but the noise from a game show on the television drowned her out and then a foot to her stomach doubled her over. A searing pain went through her head as she hit the side of the heavy oak sideboard. It was over in less than half a minute. She didn't think she even screamed, just lay stunned and feeling sick, half-fainting. She thought if she moved, her eyes would fall out. Carefully, she tried to raise herself off the ground, but she couldn't. From a long distance she heard a door slam hard. Quite calmly she said to herself, 'He's gone,' and then she fainted again.

When she came round she was alone. Whether it was seconds or minutes later or even an hour, she couldn't tell. Somehow she managed to crawl to the phone.

'I wonder,' she said to reception, 'if you could call the police, and maybe you have such a thing as an aspirin?'

Chapter Thirteen

The journey to the hospital was a blur of strange faces, urgent questions and the terror of thinking about what had happened to her. Even if she could think straight, the pain in the side of her head made speech impossible.

Her head was scanned, and eventually mild concussion was pronounced, along with shock and severe bruising to the ribs. She was told to lie still. A voice in reasonable English kept asking her loudly if she had a friend or a family member they should tell. She shook her head, but they insisted they must tell someone. The only person whose contact details she knew in the whole of Germany was Martha.

The card was still in her pocket. A nurse fished it out and went away. Someone was on their way, they eventually reported back. After which they eased her into a hospital gown, and wheeled her, unprotesting, to a small ward with only two of the four beds occupied. This was where she was found a couple of hours later by Martha, propped up, half asleep, with a face that was almost unrecognisable as the attractive woman Martha had met the day before.

'I'm not,' Martha said after peering closely at her, 'going to add to your woes by telling you it's very unlikely the police will be interested.'

Harriet tried to shake her head but the room swam.

'No,' Martha insisted. 'Don't move. I'll try to organise your hotel and get your passport and any valuables back.'

'Nothing of value,' Harriet assured her. 'But I'll need my credit card to pay for stuff. I think I'd be okay to go back if you'd help me get a taxi.'

'And a night on the town to follow?' Martha said with heavy sarcasm. 'You,' she pushed her gently back on the pillow, 'are going nowhere. Not tonight at least. They won't let you go till tomorrow, so you might as well lie back and relax. I'm due at a dinner, otherwise I'd help, but I'll try and get someone to go to the hotel for you. Now, sleep.'

In spite of every intention of staying awake, her eyes closed.

*

It was still only nine o'clock in the evening when she was woken from a very troubled sleep by a nurse who had a man with her. He was tall – rangy is the word her mother would have used to describe him – with a shock of dark hair, rimless glasses and an expression that did not look like he was thrilled to be there. He gazed cautiously over the nurse's shoulder at her.

'Your friend sent this gentleman to help,' the nurse said. 'This is,' she turned back to him, 'I'm sorry, I forget the name?'

'Neil,' the man said. 'Neil Charlton. A friend of Martha Dressler. She asked me to help. Because I'm English,' he added helpfully.

'Just for a few minutes,' the nurse cautioned him. 'This young woman needs to sleep and not be excited in any way.'

She briefly took Harriet's pulse, pulled her eyelids down and peered at her pupils. She shone a light in her eyes, before saying she would be back later. A doctor, she added before she whirled out of the door, would be doing a round at ten.

Harriet turned her head to try and see the newcomer. 'Would you,' she asked, 'mind turning that lamp on? I can't reach it. This is very kind of you, but I don't understand who you are or why you're here.'

'Neil,' he repeated slowly and carefully as though addressing someone who was slow on the uptake. Which it had to be said, at that moment, she was a front runner. He switched the light on, turning the lamp a little away from her face. 'Is that better?'

She nodded, winced and groaned. 'Oh God, what a mess.'

'No. Not a mess. Just a nuisance,' he said bracingly. 'Martha will organise everything. She simply asked me to go to your hotel and pick up your things. Not something I do that often. Well, never, now I come to think of it.'

'Excuse me,' Harriet stopped him. Her voice sounded hoarse. 'What are you talking about? Why were you packing my clothes? I don't understand.'

'Your room. You know what hotels are like. They wanted to book it out. So I just grabbed everything. I've put it all over there. On that armchair.'

She tried to swivel her head to look at where he was pointing, but a sharp pain seared into her neck and she fell back onto the pillow with a loud groan.

'Look,' he said. 'You must lie still. Do as you're told or you won't—'

'Stop talking,' she begged. 'My head. Look, who are you? Are you Martha's assistant? Who?'

'God no,' he almost shuddered. 'She's one of my oldest friends. At uni together. Nottingham. A lifetime ago. She was doing a year there to get her English up to speed. And I'm very fond of her. But *work* for her? God forbid. She's a nightmare. No. I'm just here for a couple of semesters.'

'Semesters? I'm sorry,' she felt her head, largely to make sure it was still there. 'What has that to do with packing my clothes? Please? I'm going mad here.'

'No, no. You're just concussed. Sorry, I should explain. I'm on a year's sabbatical at Humboldt. The university here? I teach maths.'

'Just tell me,' she interrupted. Her teeth were gritted. 'Why have you brought all my clothes here?'

'Why? You mean you don't know? Didn't you get Martha's message? She rang you.'

'Battery's dead,' she said. 'I forgot to fire it up. What did she say?'

He cleared his throat. 'Um, well. That I would be getting your things from the hotel. I'm afraid they've asked you to leave.'

'They've what?' She stared at him. Was he mad? A lunatic? '*I'm* attacked, but *they* throw *me* out? Please? Where's Martha?'

'I'm sorry,' he said ruffling his hair. 'She's at a dinner thing. She said she'd told you. I'm sure she'll be in touch. Look, I'm really sorry but I have to go. My students are expecting me. Not sure why I bother, they all seem to be in another world. They've organised a reception for someone they've asked to speak at a debate and I gave my word I'd be there. Finishes around now. I've settled your bill—'

'My bill? Why? Oh God. Where's my wallet? I must pay you.' To her horror tears began to well up in her eyes.

'Please,' he looked at her with alarm. 'No. The money isn't important. I'm sorry – here, have a tissue—' he thrust one at her from a box on the table beside her. 'The hospital needs your passport. I've brought your bag.'

'It's in the pocket of my jeans.' She tried to locate them. 'For safety. Pickpockets,' she added.

'Very wise. Here,' he reached behind him and handed her jeans to her.

'Could you?' she asked. Every time she moved her head swam.

'Your bag,' he said, handing her passport to her. 'Do you want to check that as well?'

Painfully she opened her bag. Every movement made her wince.

She felt in the pocket where she kept her money, amazed it was still there.

'So money okay? Anything else? Credit card?'

She breathed a sigh of relief. 'No that's still here —' And then she looked again, tipped the bag out, searching frantically among the few objects she carried in it.

'Natasha's card,' she croaked. 'It's gone.'

'What card?' Neil asked.

'Martha knows about it.' She began to babble, trying to impart the importance and the history of the card, which even to her ears sounded increasingly, utterly incoherent and complete nonsense. 'It was important,' she ended, 'to me.'

'If it was just a crumpled card,' Neil looked bewildered. 'Maybe it was just thrown aside. Seriously, I don't think you should read too much into it or,' he added, clearly without much hope she'd listen, 'get so upset. Look, if it makes you any happier, I'll call the hotel, see if they've found it—'

'No,' Harriet let her bag flop on the bed where it promptly slid to the floor. 'They'll have cleaned the room. Chucked it away.'

Her whole body ached. Crying was not something she did at any time, but tears were a mere blink away and if she was going to sob, she would prefer to do it alone and not in front of this awkward man. He placed her bag more firmly on the cabinet beside the bed, then changed his mind and shoved it into the cupboard underneath.

'Just in case,' he explained.

'Honestly,' she tried to lift her head. 'It was nice of you to pay the bill. If I could just get to a cash machine, I'd pay you back straight away.'

'Don't even think it,' he stopped her. 'Please. I mean it. Martha won't be back for a bit. But I'll make sure she's on the case. Look, is there anyone you'd like me to call? Friends in England, Martha said you're a friend of Bing's—'

'No,' she shook her head quickly. 'No. Not as such. I mean he's been so helpful to me, and really nice. Please? You won't call him will you? There's no point worrying anyone tonight, they can't do anything. You must promise me. *Please*, you won't, will you?'

'No, no,' he promised hastily. 'Now please. Stop getting upset.'

'I'm not upset,' she tried to keep her voice steady. 'I just don't want to cause any more trouble—'

'And you won't, but you really must try to sleep.'

Finally, she nodded and obediently closed her eyes, partly because she needed to, but mostly because it would mean he would go away and she could deal with the sobs currently crowding her chest.

He stood up, appeared briefly as though he was going to say something, thought better of it, scooped up his parka and tiptoed out.

It didn't take her long, left alone in this strange room with a woman she'd never met before in her life, sleeping yards away in another bed, to regret wishing he'd leave. Why hadn't she accepted his help, let him stay? Here she was relying on just Martha, barely known to her, certainly with no obligation whatsoever to help her, to bail her out. At least he spoke English, indeed *was* English. It would have been something.

The misery of it all left her with silent tears running down her face, until even misery exhausted her and she tried to sleep. But the bewildering, unfamiliar nocturnal noises of a busy hospital kept jolting her awake.

As the night wore on, she longed to talk to someone who actually cared about her; Lizzie, her mother, James. Anyone. And as she drifted in and out of a troubled sleep, she just wished she had never known Elena, never left London, never gone near Natasha, and certainly not been so swept away by Lorna's heart-stirring description of the struggles of two women, that she'd so easily taken leave of her senses. What in the name of God had she been thinking? Loneliness swamped her.

It was the longest night of her life. She slept fitfully, each time waking with a start. Once it was a nightmare of a burly, nameless assailant looming over her, kicking her. She opened her eyes to find instead a nurse, calming her and checking her pulse. Someone with a trolley replaced the water by her bed. Another time, a man she thought she recognised hovered briefly by the bed with a nurse. Probably a doctor, but the medication they'd pumped into her to keep her still and relieve the pain in her whole body had, she decided, closing her eyes and drifting back to sleep, made her delusional.

Around four in the morning, forgetting for a moment she had no battery left on her phone, she slid her hand under the pillow to find it. She was about to replace it when she halted and looked at it again. She remembered it had been out of battery, but now it was fully charged. She placed her arm over her eyes. She really was losing the plot.

By the time dawn broke, and the sounds from a busy hospital starting its day shift prevented any further possibility of rest, she was left firmly of the opinion that if there was a psychiatric unit in this place, that's where she should be. She had never felt so shocked, afraid or tearful in her life. Or stupid.

*

'Ah, that was me,' Neil Charlton said. It was shortly before eight o'clock in the morning, and for reasons that were unclear to her, he had persuaded the nurses to let him call in at such an early hour. She'd been half expecting Martha to swing by, but not until at least two o'clock in the afternoon, if at all.

'I had to charge my own phone,' he said. 'So I just took yours as well. You were out cold when I got back. That rather grumpy nurse said she had to accompany me, but that I could just slip it under your pillow.'

Sheer exhaustion prevented her from doing any more than nod gratefully at him.

'Now,' he said, plonking a plastic bag onto the only chair in the room, 'I'll just dump these and be off. A bunch of hungover students waiting for me. And I don't want to give you my cold, which I'm pretty certain is what this dry throat is about.'

As though to demonstrate the point further, he pulled a thick scarf more firmly around his neck, defying anyone to challenge that a substantial black parka, jeans and boots were not enough to armour him against further damage to his health, especially in an overheated hospital room. She couldn't have given a toss. Not right then.

So here she was, with nowhere to stay, her body aching like there was no tomorrow, and concussion. She was grateful for his kindness, but wondered if he had any idea how much these things eclipsed a sore throat – especially only an impending one.

She watched in silence as he took a bottle of mineral water out of the bag, found space on the table for it, and left two oranges there, still in the cardboard carton in which they had been bought.

'I can't stop I'm afraid, but Martha,' he screwed the plastic bag into a ball and failing to find a rubbish bin, stuffed it into his pocket, 'rang me. She told me to bring this lot. She's in court. She said I go past on my way to work, so it was easy. And obviously,' he added hastily before she could speak, 'it was no trouble at all. But I do have a long day ahead – but Martha will be in. I gather she's sorted out somewhere for you to stay.'

Relief flooded through her. 'Oh that's brilliant,' she said. 'Once I'm in a hotel and out of here I can get back on track. Repay you, for a start. Now please. You've done enough. I don't want you to be late. Take care of that cold, won't you?'

'Sorry?' he looked blank. 'What?'

'Your sore throat,' she reminded him. 'You thought it might be the start of a cold.'

'Oh,' he said nodding. 'That. Yes. Of course. Right.'

When he'd gone, Harriet gingerly got out of bed, rummaged through her suitcase for fresh clothes, and by the time Martha arrived, was sitting in a chair next to her bed, waiting to go. Earlier a policewoman had turned up, had asked a few vague questions about why Harriet was in Berlin, reported that a check had been run on her for any criminal convictions in the UK, asked what had been stolen and read out a doctor's report that said she had concussion and had been told not to fly home – unless it was an emergency, but to see the duty doctor even if that were the case, otherwise to report back to him in a week; earlier if the headache got worse. Or the British Consulate, she suggested, giving her the address.

After that, she told Harriet to be careful next time – as if there would ever be a 'next time' – and that they'd contact her if they had any news of her assailant, and left. Harriet didn't need to be told she was unlikely to ever see her again. Martha wasn't surprised.

'Hotel room in an area that's a bit down at heel? It happens a lot. Now. I have a one-hour window and I need to see you settled before I crack on. Ready? Here, I'll take that.'

Martha grabbed the handle of Harriet's case and began pulling it along the tiled corridor. 'Can't find a hotel that will take you, I'm afraid. Well, not looking like that. And the police pitching up wasn't exactly in your favour at Der Starlight. But you'll be fine. It's the best I can do, it's only for a few days after all.'

*

'In here,' Bebe stood aside for Harriet to walk ahead of her into a narrow room with its one window and worn-out shutter, through which she could see onto an alleyway that had a heavily bolted door at the end. Trying to regain her poor wits, she leaned forward and noticed to the left, a solid black iron gate sealing the entrance from the road, preventing anyone entering the alleyway. Just above it was a battery of CCTV cameras, carefully monitoring anyone who tried.

'It might be a bit, you know,' Bebe snapped her fingers. 'You know the word, ah that's it, *oppressive*, but Der Hafen is next door and we cannot take any chances with the women's safety.

'Now. This is my apartment – goes with the job – gives me a bit of privacy. You will stay here. Harriet? Are you okay?'

Harriet looked around fearfully. *Here?* She had to stay here? Was Martha insane? She knew nothing about Bebe, and even less about the area.

She swallowed hard. 'I'm grateful of course,' she began, 'to Martha – and indeed you – but I don't think I should be here. I haven't been abused by anyone.'

'Technically,' Bebe said leaning against the doorframe, 'that is not true. Mugging *is* abuse. And,' she paused staring carefully at Harriet, '*technically* you're not staying in the shelter but Martha would rather you were under her eye.'

'Please,' she held up a hand. 'I am happy to help. Martha said, to find a hotel to take in someone looking – well, a little beaten up – is impossible. And besides, they all cost a fortune. Which Martha doesn't think you have. This is true? *Ja?*'

Harriet could only agree. She was perilously close to her limits with all her bank accounts. She just knew that the soulless voice at the bank call centre, if she tried to negotiate a little more credit, with no income to justify it, would be deeply unimpressed. On the other hand, she also knew that if she asked anyone at home to bail her out, they would do so willingly and, to her shame, without rebuking her. But they'd done enough. They'd had enough. This was all her own doing. Her head ached, in fact her entire body ached. She knew she was fighting tears.

'Look,' Bebe said more kindly, 'it's just for a few days until you're given the all clear by the doctors to fly home. This is not a prison. Martha just—' she paused. Whatever she was going to say was left unsaid.

'Martha, what?' Harriet tried to keep her voice steady.

Bebe tied her scarf more firmly round her neck. 'She wanted you to be – you know, safe. Not on your own.'

Harriet found a tissue and blew her nose hard.

'I'm so sorry, you're being so kind,' she mumbled.

'And I'm sorry, but I have to go. We have two new admissions and I fear one of them has already told her boyfriend where she is. And the police will be very useless. Better not to deal with them anyway. I'll be back as soon as I can. Settle in. The kitchen is through there.'

With that, she closed the door behind her.

Left alone, Harriet switched her gaze between a bright blue velvet armchair with its best years behind it, in spite of the bright turquoise and red cushions that Bebe had propped on it, and a narrow sofa that seemed to double as a bed, with an alarmingly colourful bedspread – which didn't help her headache one bit – thrown across it. In the end she chose the sofa, which is where Bebe, accompanied by Neil, found her a few hours later, propped up on a pillow with her parka pulled over her knees and her face the colour of chalk.

*

'Just thought I'd check on you,' he said.

'It's okay,' Bebe assured her. 'Martha ring. I know he comes here. One hour,' she told him severely. 'She is very tired. And don't leave without telling me. I let you out. This okay?'

He nodded dutifully. It was hard to imagine anyone objecting to so much as the date if Bebe had decreed it otherwise.

'Just passing,' he added, turning back as the door closed behind Bebe. 'Well, all my classes finished for the day. Thank *God*. Have you,' he enquired mildly, 'ever tried to interest a room full of students in David Hilbert's list of unsolved mathematical problems, while they're all checking their text messages? No, thought not.'

Harriet toyed with telling him that she'd never heard of David Hilbert or his problems, but suspected she might then run the very real risk of him explaining it all, in minute detail. Hilbert and his wretched problems, she decided, could not be anywhere near as terrible as hers, especially while her poor head could barely compute the date or how she'd ended up here.

'Well,' he went on, 'I thought you might give me sanctuary for a while. Martha's got a whole bunch of lawyers at her apartment, and lovely people of course, but I said I thought I should check on you, which is the only reason she wouldn't make a fuss about me not staying.'

'Glad to have been of help,' she said drily.

'No,' he protested. 'No. I – we are all concerned, but think of me? I mean when I left just now, someone was banging on about *erga omnes*. What *is* that?'

'It's Latin,' she said almost unthinkingly. She wondered vaguely why he hadn't just gone back to his own apartment. 'It means *toward all*. Wrongful acts, or something, that harm everyone and not simply one injured party.'

'Really?' He looked amazed. 'You know all this stuff? I thought you were a jewellery dealer.'

'I am, I mean was. *Am*. Oh God,' she sighed. 'I don't know anymore. And I have no more idea about legal terms than I have of those – you know, those ones you mentioned.'

He looked blank. '*I* mentioned? I haven't a clue about the law.'

'No,' she said impatiently, 'the maths thingies. You said your students hadn't a clue.'

'Ah. No. Not the same at all. I mean it's all in English. Or rather in German at the moment. Not in Latin. No, trust me. They wouldn't understand a word. Sometimes, I wonder if they understand their own language.'

'Well, whatever.' Her head ached, but courtesy demanded she struggled on, 'My lawyer used those kind of phrases a lot. In the end I dreaded his explanations as well—'

'As well?' he interrupted. 'Are you saying it's possible that my students are bored as well as lazy?'

'Give me a break,' she pleaded. 'You know I didn't mean that. Just at the time, when all that rubbish was going on in my life, I waited till I got home then looked up anything I didn't understand. I just hated sitting in that office. Listening to my life being dismantled and not a bloody thing I could do about it.'

This time, he took his parka off and perched on the edge of the armchair.

'Sorry,' he looked around. 'I had no idea this is what Martha had in mind for you. She's concerned you'll—' he stopped. 'Concerned you don't know this city and might find yourself in the wrong area or – or something.'

'I thought Berlin was safe.' Her voice was tired. She also thought he had meant to say something else. She was too tired to care. 'I checked. I wouldn't have wandered off round that park where all the druggies are. I'm not daft. And I wasn't just wandering round looking at the sky, I was attacked in my own hotel room.'

'No of course not,' he said, a little too heartily. 'And in spite of all this,' he nodded at her bruised face, 'Berlin is a pretty good place, beautiful actually

– well freezing right now. I may,' he looked solemnly over his glasses at her, 'have to take to wearing two pairs of socks.'

She gave a weak smile.

'But the summer,' he went on, 'you'd love it. Well, I think you would. It's like a different city. Hot, too hot sometimes, pavement cafés order of the day, practically lived in the parks when I first came. Shame you didn't come a bit later.'

'It's a shame I came at all,' she retorted bitterly.

'Listen, seriously, you were just unlucky,' he gazed at her with concern. 'Are you sure you don't want to tell anyone at home? See if they can help?'

'I texted Lizzie – a very close friend.' She struggled to sit up. 'I said I was staying on for a few more days. She's the only person apart – well apart from Bing – who knows I'm here. They don't know each other so they won't check. And I didn't lie. Well not directly. I never mentioned this to her. You don't understand. She didn't want me to come. She tried to stop me. She made me promise all sorts of stuff, but I wasn't expecting to be mugged, so I just said Martha was being helpful and a few days more might be useful. Which she is. Being helpful, I mean.'

He glanced around, clearly registering Martha's idea of helpfulness. He didn't seem impressed.

'Sorry,' he turned back to her. 'And if you don't think I'm interfering, none of this is making a great deal of sense to me. And yes, I might not have been paying as much attention as I should have done to Martha—'

'On account of the cold,' she reminded him.

He blinked. 'Oh the cold,' he agreed. She thought he was trying not to laugh. 'Absolutely. Can't be too careful. This is a mess. Not just the room. Which,' he peered around, 'seems to have cornered the market in practically blinding me with colour – I don't like messes. I'm forever telling my students – well the ones I think might still be awake – you must pare back to the basics and not allow the central issue to be clouded in conjecture and guesswork. Just apply logic. Mind you,' he stretched his legs out, crossing his ankles, arms folded on his chest, 'you should see what some of them think is a literate and coherent description of Quine's Set Theory, a trained cockatoo might have made more sense. And I bet the ones who got it right mostly downloaded something from Wikipedia. Can you imagine?'

'Not in a million years,' she agreed. Which was perfectly true. *Quine*? Who in God's name was he?

'So I thought, what if you told me right from the beginning. Please,' he added as she hesitated. 'It's warmer in here than outside, so you've got a captive audience. And it sometimes helps to say it out loud to someone who has no vested interest in the outcome. Obviously,' he added hastily, 'I mean, only if it's in your favour.'

'Obviously,' she agreed politely.

Whatever it was, needing company – which she knew was true but sounded rather pathetic – or that it couldn't do any harm, which was at least better than pathetic – she suddenly found herself telling him.

It didn't help that she kept forgetting bits or that she had developed a habit of questioning her own facts mid-sentence, but finally she stumbled to a close.

'The weird thing,' she said, 'is that Kurt Weber was never angry. Perfectly charming in fact. It's hard to understand how someone that charming could be so duplicitous. I could have understood if he'd been furious, shouted even. But he didn't. Not once.'

'Hmm,' he said. 'It would help though if you stuck to the facts.'

'I did not,' she said indignantly, 'stray from the facts.'

'I'm pleased to hear it,' he said. 'But you've let other people do that. That team of lawyers for start—'

'One,' she corrected. 'Not a team. Oh sorry, you mean his Kurt-ness? Not poor old Christopher? Oh well, money talks, and I expect they were being paid shedloads to get him the result he wanted.'

'Even so,' he conceded, 'if you want to stop driving yourself nuts wondering why you were mugged, then for goodness sake start to rationalise it. Let's see if you really have got something to worry about and if Kurt is behind it all.'

Her eyes flew open. 'I never said that,' she protested. 'I never said it was him who attacked me. Who said it was?'

'Whoa,' his eyes now widened. 'I said behind it all. Not *did* it.'

'Well,' she insisted, 'it definitely wasn't him who attacked me. The guy who did that,' she faltered and stopped. She took a deep breath. Steadied her voice. The thud as she fell, the scuffle as he pushed her to the wall with his foot, it was all there. The volume from the television deliberately turned up to drown her screams. She knew the horror of it would never leave her. Her hand steadied her head.

She sensed Neil lean forward; he closed his hand over hers, clenched in her lap. 'Steady,' he said gently. 'Don't go there. Okay?'

'Yes. Fine.' She tried to smile. 'Thank you. I'm fine now. Just being stupid.'

'I'm prepared to believe you're a bit foolhardy,' he released her hand with a gentle pat. He smiled. 'But I won't believe stupid. Shall we talk about something else?'

'No,' she shook her head, trying to smile. 'I'm not going to cry. Promise. And I'm not being brave. I just prefer to cry about things that matter. Not a total low life and coward. So,' she released his hand. 'There.'

'That's my girl,' he grinned. 'So. Why not Kurt?'

'Because he was a big guy. Twice Kurt's size. At least that's what it felt like. All I said, if you're interested in accuracy, was that Kurt was the only one who would have been interested in that stupid card. And nothing else was taken. Credit card, wallet. All there. And besides, he was perfectly pleasant, not at all threatening in the circumstances, and he could have been. I expected him to be as vile as his lawyers. But even though he was being awful about Elena, I could see why everyone thinks he's charming, actually *very* charming—'

'Oh for goodness sake,' Neil groaned. 'He's as rich as Croesus and with enough charm to make Casanova want to throw the towel in. Most crooks are. Well, Martha, says he is. And I never argue with Martha. But simply being charming doesn't mean he's as clean as a whistle. Try and look at the facts, not how attractive you found him. Would you like some coffee?' he got up. 'I'm sure Bebe won't mind.'

She nodded, grateful. 'But I never said that,' she called after him. 'That he was attractive. Not my type.'

'You mean blond and handsome?'

'No. Millionaires.'

She heard him chuckle. Then she lay back on the cushions.

While she waited for him to return with the coffee, she shifted herself, with great care, to a more comfortable position against the pillow. She tucked her feet under the thin quilt and within minutes – despite her intention to fight the waves of tiredness – she found her eyes closing. She knew he had been right. Just saying it out loud gave it relevance, shape, stopped the questions circling in her poor, tired brain. So, what else could she do but enjoy, just for a moment, the relief of not having to struggle to keep her eyes open, and hope the small hammer, that seemed to be attacking the area behind her eyes, would pack it in. Comforting just to have had her hand held.

She woke several hours later, the light outside having gone, to find Bebe standing over her with a cup of tea.

'You were in a very deep sleep.' She switched on a lamp over Harriet's head. 'Neil said to leave you. Actually, what he said,' Bebe frowned, 'was that he thought you might have overdone it working out some theory or other. Is he speaking English? I never heard of this man. Kline? Krine?'

'Quine,' Harriet said. 'Don't ask. I haven't a clue. Something to do with his job I think. Bebe,' she pulled herself up to a sitting position and took the tea, 'you are fabulous. You're so busy as well. This is so welcome.'

'He say he come back. Maybe tomorrow, maybe the next day. And Martha called. She'll—'

She broke off to peer through the window. Harriet gingerly got out of bed and leaned over to see what the noise was. Across the alley, peering through the window of the adjacent building, were two or three little boys. Bebe flapped her hand at them to go back.

'*Eine minute*,' she called to them. 'Sorry,' she said, over her shoulder to Harriet. 'I sometimes take them when their mothers need a break. *Zuruck*,' she ordered. No-one took a blind bit of notice of her; instead there was a lot of pretend firing of guns, along with some finger gestures that made Harriet wonder where such small children could have learned to be that explicit. Bebe called, in a voice that was a cross between a shriek and a threat, '*Zuruck Ich Sagte*.'

By which, Harriet decided, she was ordering them back across the alley to where their mothers were, in various shades of anguish. She knew then, that this had to stop, her taking up Bebe's time. She had her hands full and clearly didn't need a daft English woman cluttering up the place. Tomorrow, she'd sort something out. Just get today out of the way. By then, she might have heard from Neil, what he thought. Oddly, the prospect lifted her spirits, something she had decided a mere few hours before, was unlikely to ever happen again.

Chapter Fourteen

James phoned the next morning, just as she was gathering up her washing, which was drying on the small radiator in her room. It was almost midday. Eleven in London. After a restless night, filled with images she couldn't shake off, dark shadows looming and a room spinning, she had pulled herself upright, sweating, at around six. She'd been woken by the sound of Bebe in the kitchen. Even if Kurt himself had pitched up to confess to everything, she doubted she would have found the energy to brave an airport, let alone a journey home with such a headache. And the exhaustion. Oh God. Would she ever feel normal again?

'I will be just next door,' Bebe had announced, so cheerfully for such an hour, Harriet wondered if she might be on something. She handed her a cup of strong, black coffee. 'And just go ahead and help yourself to what you need.'

She knew that getting to a state of normality would not happen if she remained huddled under the duvet, sipping coffee. She needed to get moving, try and shift the defeated feeling. A washing machine in Bebe's kitchen – a room so small it made a broom cupboard look spacious – and the feeble radiator in her room to try to launder some essentials, was a start.

'So are you going to stay away forever?' James was demanding.

She took a deep breath. She couldn't bear it. To lie anymore. 'No, of course not. James? I have to tell you something. I'm not in Madrid. I'm in Berlin.'

'I know that,' James didn't pause. 'William said he never bought that business about Madrid. And it wasn't Miss McCoy if that's what you're thinking. She's a worse liar than you. I rang her and she just shouted she wasn't your bloody keeper. Typical. It's her default position when she doesn't want to tell you something. Keep shouting until the other side backs off.'

'I'm so sorry,' Harriet said miserably. 'I just didn't want anyone worrying anymore, or to upset your lives—'

'Stop,' he said. 'Stop right now. I can get past the whole Berlin thing. But not that you thought we would all make a terrible fuss. No, you haven't been easy, and yes, I was – okay – *relieved* – when you said you were going away. We're only human and you wouldn't be helped. Are you okay? Did you get anywhere? And who is Bing?'

Harriet groaned. 'I found him at the back of Tottenham Court Road. He's really nice. He translated some stuff for me, and introduced me to Martha – she was his girlfriend – she's a lawyer here and she's been really helpful. Just a minute – how do you know?'

'Big Jake.'

'*Big Jake?* How in God's name does he know?'

'He told me when Lizzie wouldn't. For some reason, the fact that Big Jake told me means she can say quite truthfully that she didn't. It's a Lizzie thing. Don't ask. She said she'd gone to see Bing just to make sure he wasn't another maniac in your life. She took Big Jake just to be on the safe side and he thought it was only fair to tell me because I was worried.'

Harriet doubled over, one arm clutching her waist. Oh poor Bing. What must he think? Faced with Jake? All those tattoos? Any flickering idea that she might tell James about being mugged, fled.

'I'm so sorry,' she whispered. 'I'll call Lizzie. I'll text Big Jake. Oh God. I'd never make a spy. Or at least, I would if I didn't have such smart friends. James? It's all over now. I promise. Nothing more I can do here. I'm staying with a – a friend of Martha's,' which she silently comforted herself was not exactly a lie. 'I need now to come home, get a job, try and find somewhere proper to live. Give you a hug—'

'Don't try and soft soap me, my girl,' he said sternly. 'You're not in a spy movie. And what you've done is plain daft and dangerous, going off on your own like that. And frankly, I think Lizzie is a nightmare to have let you.'

'She's not,' Harriet protested. 'She didn't want me to go. There were loads of conditions she imposed, you should have heard her—'

'Harriet,' he stopped her. 'You could have got killed, murdered anything, on your own in a town you've never been to. And the Webers? Please. They're not to be messed with anymore. Surely you can see that?'

'I know,' she agreed meekly. In other circumstances she would have told James to back off, it was her life, but for a start she felt too ill, and in the second, perhaps more important place, she knew he was right.

'Sorry,' James said gruffly. 'I don't mean to nag. I was just worried. Look, they've got back the wretched pictures so that's an end to it. Now. Do you need anything? This must be costing you—'

'No, God no,' she lied. 'I'm fine. Seriously. I'll be back soon. I've got a couple of things to do here first. See Martha and thank her. She didn't *have* to do anything, you know. To be honest, she did it for Bing. Can't work that out. Their relationship. She's so high powered and he—'

'Please,' James begged, 'do not get involved in anything else.'

'Well,' she said, 'there's a couple of places I'd like to see.' As she spoke, she caught sight of herself in a mirror over the bed. On her chin, a bruise the size of a plum had started to spread almost to her ear. Was that haggard face hers? The deep shadows under her eyes? 'It's actually,' she said turning quickly away, 'a great city. I mean I haven't seen a lot, but Bebe says I shouldn't judge it by the vile weather. I doubt I'll be coming back here anytime soon so why not? I'll tell you all about everything when I get back. How's William?'

'Do not speak to me of that man. His idea of compromise would floor you. Just listen to this.'

She let him go through the highly complicated, well-documented arguments that had led to the latest break-up, oddly reassured that there was an old familiar life – albeit one with some exhaustingly tiresome elements – waiting for her when she got back. But suddenly she didn't mind a bit. Home. It was the most fabulous word in any language.

'So I've given him till seven to apologise,' James finished. 'And this time I mean it.'

*

Harriet spotted Bebe in her miniscule office, sitting in front of her computer. For almost two days now, Harriet had barely left her narrow room; it was fast becoming a prison rather than a sanctuary. She longed to get away from here, back to familiar surroundings. Surely, the terrible fear of what might have happened would subside? It constantly gripped her, made her feel sick. She had to get home.

'Come over,' Bebe invited when Harriet called her. 'I let you in.'

'My head is so much better,' she lied, stepping into the chaos that passed for Bebe's office. A desk rammed under the window, a sofa along one wall. A box full of assorted toys in a corner. The noise from the day room down the corridor was unsettling. Bebe closed the door and returned to her computer.

'And I know you'll be glad to see the back of me,' Harriet pressed on. 'I just wonder if I could use the computer? I need to book a ticket to go home and my phone is useless.'

'Two things,' Bebe said without taking her eyes off the screen, 'that prevent that. The first is that, no I won't be glad to see the back of you. It's actually a good change to have someone who doesn't need looking after – and cheap, I doubt you've eaten more than a bread roll since you got here – and who doesn't have some madman trying to get in here after her that I have to see off. And second – and the most important – Martha says I am not to let you go until she knows and the doctor says it okay.'

'Well,' Harriet smiled. 'That's kind of Martha and I'm very grateful to her, you know that, but she has no reason to feel responsible for me anymore, and in spite of appearances, honestly I hardly know her. She's just been so kind, but my appointment at the hospital is on Friday morning and I know they're going to say I'm okay.'

'Maybe,' Bebe said, glancing up. 'I wouldn't agree, but I'm not a doctor.'

'Neither am I,' Harriet said firmly. 'But I know myself better than they do, so I would like to book a ticket. Weekend prices are awful, so I thought maybe Monday.'

Bebe looked doubtfully at her. 'You are still – you know,' Bebe nodded at Harriet's face. '*Sehr blass*. You understand?'

'Very pale?' Harriet guessed. 'I know. But I feel fine. Well, apart from a bruise here and there. I'd be better off at home. I'm not silly,' she said feeling grateful for such kindness. 'Even I know if this – this bang on the head was going to get worse by flying, I wouldn't go. But if the doctor says okay, I'll get out of your hair. And Bebe? When I get home, I will send you some money for all this. It's just I'd rather not use my bank at the moment—'

Bebe flapped a hand at her, shushing her, her gaze never leaving the screen. 'I will say okay,' she said, 'because I think you will argue and I don't argue. But still, Martha doesn't like being disobeyed and I don't like Martha in a bad mood, so let me know what she says. Has Neil called?'

Harriet shook her head. 'No. But there is no reason for him to either.'

'Probably trying to placate that wife of his,' Bebe frowned and typed something into her computer.

'Wife?' Harriet was surprised. 'He's married?'

'Tricky business,' Bebe said. She went on typing. 'No idea who's left who or who's trying to get back with who. I just heard Martha say the word one day, "*placate*". Does that mean he's trying to make her happy? His wife, I mean. Not Martha.'

'Kind of,' Harriet said. She leaned her shoulders against the wall. This trying to get home was a tiring business. 'How do you know?'

'I was at Martha's. A couple of weeks ago. She had some questions from the last meeting with the trustees, and he was there. She was very cross with him. I think she wanted him to stay and have dinner. But he wouldn't. Anyway, I sit in another room, but I could hear Martha saying it was no way to reunite. Doing this placate thing. Better to stay for dinner and meet some of her friends and get over it. But,' she spread her hands. 'I might be wrong. Anyway he left. I went over my notes with Martha and then I left too. That is all. Now,' she pressed send and then swivelled round in her chair to face Harriet. 'Have you got a moment? I would like to talk to you.'

'Of course. What about?' Harriet pushed a pile of books towards the end of the rather elderly sofa and lowered herself carefully into it. Her head was not up to sudden movements.

'It pains?' Bebe tapped her own head.

'Nothing I can't handle,' Harriet assured her. 'To be honest I think it's more my shoulders and neck. Shock I expect. I'm fine. Now, what do you want to talk to me about?'

'Kurt Weber.'

Harriet sat very still. She adjusted a cushion behind her back.

'How do you know about Kurt Weber?' she looked up.

'I don't listen at doors,' Bebe retorted. 'If that's what you think. I work it out. Martha said you had been attacked after you came back from seeing him. Or something like that. Why do you think you're here?'

Harriet felt her heart thud. 'You mean—'

'I don't mean anything. Martha says nothing and,' she gave her a warning look, 'you don't either. I think she want you safe.'

'Safe? From Kurt?'

'How would I know?' Bebe said. 'Martha is practical. You know, not waste time. And she know Bing would expect her to take care of you.'

'Bing? Why?'

Bebe sighed. 'I see Martha would rather you did not speak of him either.'

'Either?' Harriet shook her head, and knew straight away that was a mistake. 'Bebe? You're not making sense. Martha hadn't told me to not talk about Bing.'

'But Kurt?'

'Or him. She did tell me he was powerful in this town and to be careful—'

'Ah ha,' Bebe crowed. 'She did say it. And you won't talk because you think I might be – what do you call it? A flake? No it's okay. It wouldn't be the first time I've been accused of that.'

Harriet blew out her cheeks. 'Bebe, I don't think you're any of those things. Not in a million years. You're clearly strong, smart and capable.'

Bebe laughed at her. 'Not true, but I am smart enough to know when I have met someone who might be able to help me. In fact, I think we could help each other. I find you interesting. You ask for nothing. You accuse no-one. I see a lot of life here,' she waved an arm to embrace the entire building. 'I learn a thing or two. I know the women who genuinely want to escape, and the ones who will go back and the beating start again because they want to believe this monster who assaults them will change. You are just upfront. You would like to bring whoever did this to you to – what's the word? Justice. That's it. You would not be afraid.'

'Oddly,' Harriet said drily, 'justice is the only word I fear. As you can see, hasn't done much for me so far.'

She studied her clasped hands. She was grateful to both sides. Martha and Neil on the one, Bebe on the other. Soon she would be history for them all. Even if Neil did get back in touch, it was likely to be after she'd gone home. Martha had no obligation to her at all. To Bing, obviously. It was what friends did for each other. With no-one else to turn to, Harriet struggled to stop her loneliness and panic sinking irrationally into expecting more of them. That being the case, the less said the better, best leave them in peace.

But she owed more to Bebe. It was Bebe who'd checked on her, made sure she was not getting worse, heard her having a nightmare and had come from her adjoining room to wake and reassure her. And the small lamp she had unexpectedly brought in so that she didn't have to sleep in the dark. Harriet almost wept at the kindness of it all.

In the end she said, 'Look. Why don't you tell me what's going on. Why did Martha want me here? Let's go from there.'

Their eyes locked. 'And we then say,' Bebe said studying her nails, 'that this conversation never happened?'

'What conversation?' Harriet held her gaze. She raised an eyebrow.

Bebe smiled. 'Okay. Martha has never said, but I think she knows Kurt is not a good man. She isn't stupid. But she isn't going to call him out. I know her, and she clearly wanted you kept hidden so he could not come near you.'

A rush of fear filled Harriet's chest. 'Am I in danger?'

'Not here,' Bebe assured her. 'But wandering round on your own—' her voice trailed off. She raised her hands questioningly.

'Now, I tell you something which Martha knows but chooses not to acknowledge. Someone who was here. A woman. She came to be protected. Twice she came. She was called Gisela and she was obsessed with him. Kurt I mean. She was involved with him for a long time, even through the time he was married. Ignore the papers. The devoted husband was a – what you call? A pretend?'

'Fake?' Harriet suggested.

'Yes, that is it. Thank you. But Gisela. She won't listen. Twice she returned to him and twice she came back. Once it was a broken arm. She told the hospital she fell downstairs. But I knew.'

'What are you saying?' Harriet's eyes were round with horror, 'That Kurt beat her?'

Bebe laughed and shook her head. 'No. Not Kurt himself. God no. But he arranged it. Of that she is sure. When I was mopping her up, she said it. Denied it later, of course. But I know what I hear. I keep it all up here,' she tapped the side of her head. 'And his wife. Gisela said he beat her too, but she had money, she got away.'

'Why didn't the wife say something?' Harriet asked, horrified. 'If she had money?'

'The scandal,' Bebe shrugged. 'Besides, she has married again now, lives in New York. Rich man, east coast banker. So, you tell me honestly. What's in it for her? Or, more importantly, her husband. Does he need the taint – you know, the association?'

Harriet's throat felt dry. 'What,' she asked carefully, 'has any of this to do with me?'

'Because you also think he was something to do with you being mugged, ja?'

'I never said that,' Harriet warned quickly.

'Of course not. You didn't need to. Martha told me where you'd been and then you come here like this. And then I hear Neil telling you just because you found him attractive—' she stopped. Harriet was holding her ribs, her face almost contorted. 'What I say?' Bebe demanded. 'Why you laugh?'

'Stop,' Harriet begged. 'My ribs are still sore. I mustn't laugh. Yes, I thought he was attractive, and who wouldn't? He's the full deal. Looks, charm, perfectly nice to me. Even for a while, made me feel I might have got the whole thing wrong, but until the other day, I'd never actually laid eyes on him.

'And,' she went on, 'I do bear in mind, no matter what it looks like, what I suspect, that Neil said to look at this rationally. And I have. So the answer is, while my instincts say it's possible he had all this done to me, my head says I have no way of proving that he had me mugged.'

'But *I* would like,' Bebe said almost savagely, 'very much for him to be exposed for what he is.'

'Then why,' Harriet said, puzzled, 'doesn't someone say something? Make a complaint? Nail him?'

'And who's going to do that then?' Bebe asked. 'He's so powerful. Money talks in this town. He owns so many properties, a yacht and his own plane. It's an attractive package. Power's pretty potent too. Hard to challenge his behaviour, especially when you're trying to argue from a women's shelter. I arranged for her to speak to a lawyer—'

'Martha?' Harriet exclaimed.

'I wish,' Bebe said gloomily.

'He had lawyers send me a letter, warning me not to repeat what this – his words – *mad woman* – claimed, that I was going to pursue him in the courts on her behalf.'

She laughed. 'And what with, I'd like to know? I'd lose my job,' she snapped her fingers, 'just like that. And now,' she sighed, 'I don't know where she is. Not with him. I would have heard. And why would she be? Too flaky, too unstable. He doesn't need her. So she disappears and until you came along, the well dried up, but now—?'

'This Gisela,' Harriet said after a silence. 'What if I tried to talk to her?'

'How? You know where to find her?'

Harriet glanced sideways at her. Bebe's face was a mask, but she sensed there was something else going on here. Why, among all the men who inflicted such damage on the women who found their way here, was Kurt in her sights?

'Anything you're not telling me?' she finally ventured. 'Why Kurt? Why not the husband or boyfriend of someone hiding here?'

Bebe fiddled with the chains around her wrist. 'We share?' she finally said. 'Okay?'

Harriet nodded.

'Drugs,' Bebe said flatly. 'I used to do them. No, it's okay, I've been clean for five years. You meet people when you live in that world, who help keep the likes of Kurt from not being found out because they need this,' she rustled her fingers.

'Most of the people he's surrounded by are prepared to do whatever he wants – drugs, hookers, thugs. And then he blackmail them, so they never get away. You get the picture?'

'I won't tell anyone,' Harriet promised. 'But I can't try to help you if I've only got half the picture. Up to you of course.'

'Okay,' Bebe said finally. 'My father. He was like Kurt. He has money. A lot. People do what he say. He beat my mother. She was always running off. Once, someone asked me if I loved or hated him and I said neither. I simply feared him. Still do in a way. Although he can't touch me now.'

'What about your mother—?' Harriet began.

'My mother. Practically invented partying,' Bebe said flatly. 'She was not into children. I am mistake, you see. She could find me anytime she want. But she doesn't. I was eight when she sent me away to school. Switzerland. In the holidays, I was mostly looked after by the housekeeper. I mean, whichever one they had at the time. And when they finally left each other, I was shunted between them. They were free but I was still trapped.'

Harriet pretended not to notice the fists clenching and unclenching, the flush in Bebe's cheeks that betrayed the dreadful hurt under the studied indifference at such appalling neglect.

'You're sure?' she eventually asked. 'About your mother? Knowing where to find you?'

'One hundred per cent,' Bebe insisted.

'And the drugs?' Harriet asked.

'I was sixteen, back from school, living in my father's house in Frankfurt, and I couldn't stand it anymore, so I left. The housekeeper didn't even know I was missing for two days. They didn't come looking for me.

'A few years later, in my twenties – one night, it all caught up with me. Deep down, I knew it would. Living like that, no job, getting high, stealing to stay high. I was with the wrong people in the wrong club – but I knew enough to demand a lawyer.'

'Oddly,' she gave a wry smile. 'At least I learned that from my dad. First sign of trouble, bring in the suits. This woman came to court. She was the first person who asked me what I wanted out of life, and even then it was only because I was a project for her. But I was in someone's sights. A novelty for me.'

'So,' she got up and plugged in the kettle. 'Prison or freedom? No contest. Coffee?'

Harriet nodded. 'Please.'

Bebe spooned coffee into two mugs. 'They got me off the drugs, got me some voluntary work and then found me a paid job; a carer. All sorts of clients – the longest was a woman with dementia. She would wander off. But I see I make a difference to her family.

'She could stay in a home she loved, it was familiar, it helped, until even that was not enough and she had to be taken into care. It turns out I'm good at dealing with the world, and when, a couple of years ago, this job came up, I applied. And here I am. Do you want one of these disgusting biscuits?'

Harriet peered into the tin, in which lay a pile of biscuits, dotted with jam and shook her head. 'Bebe?' she said carefully, 'I want to help. Honestly. No-one deserves my gratitude more than you—'

'Please,' Bebe looked appalled. 'I don't ask for your gratitude. I just wanted you to understand that it's not personal for me with Kurt. It's what he stands for. Day after day, I witness the results of such men's behaviour.'

'I know that,' Harriet said. 'And if I had a scrap of evidence, I would be first in court to say so, but I haven't. I'm more sorry than I can say.'

Bebe's face remained impassive, but Harriet guessed at the disappointment she must be feeling. Hoping for so much more. As she herself had done with Martha and Neil.

She laid her hand on Bebe's arm. 'I'm not saying I won't help, it's not wanting to let you down until I know what I can genuinely do. But,' she looked around, 'at least let me help a bit here while I'm doing that. Or until I can go home.'

'You mean you sweep the place?' Bebe laughed mimicking a Hoover. She handed a cup of coffee to Harriet and walked next door to her room. 'Or maybe you station yourself at the door and shake your fist at those awful men?'

Harriet grinned. 'No not a great idea. Even I can see that.'

She stopped. Two women, their expressions bearing all the exhaustion and misery of a life they hadn't planned, were walking along the corridor trying to shush some bored and unhappy children who were never out of their sight. Just in case.

Harriet watched them disappear up the stairs where they slept in one room, shared a kitchen with at least five other women and had no idea what was to become of them, beyond finding something to give their children to eat, so at the very least, it would not be an empty stomach keeping them awake. It was wretched to watch.

'What about,' she repeated turning to Bebe, 'I help with the children? Well, the younger ones. Not sure I could deal with the bigger ones. I know, I know,' she stopped Bebe starting to point out the obvious. 'I don't speak German but I could read to them. How hard could that be?'

'Be my guest,' Bebe gaped at her. 'There's some books somewhere. I'll tell their mothers. Good luck. Let me know when to send in the Valium.'

Chapter Fifteen

Harriet closed the door, leaving behind a babble of children's voices. She leaned against it and closed her eyes. Better than yesterday, when somehow she'd managed to read a book in German about a dragon and a space invader – at least that's what was on the cover – to a handful of four and five-year-olds, jeered at by five older ones. Drawn to the spectacle of an Englishwoman reading a story with such a funny accent, they had abandoned their iPods and filmed on their phones this infinitely more interesting spectacle on their very doorstep.

All she could hope, Harriet muttered to herself, was that she wouldn't end up going viral on YouTube, destroying what little credibility she had back home. Or indeed anywhere else. At least today, the older ones, easily bored, had found other targets to bully and the smaller ones had mostly listened intently, on the grounds that she was a grown up and that was that. They'd even laughed.

'Go and lie down.'

She turned to see Bebe swinging through the doorway. 'You might,' she said, 'have to do a second stint. Two of the mothers managed to take a shower and wash their hair while the kids were with you and two more asked if you could be on duty later so they can do the same. And a counsellor is coming at two, so you might be needed then.'

Harriet tried not to look appalled. Bebe laughed. 'Is okay. I told them you only work part-time. You have a rest. Your head,' she tipped her own to one side, 'it must be exploding. Oh, and Martha called. She said your phone is not going to voicemail. The signal here is pretty dire. You call her please?'

*

'This is so kind of you,' Harriet said warmly. She took in Martha's apartment on the tenth floor of a new building on Potsdamer Platz. All glass and chrome; long, wide, cream sofas piled with cushions, statement artwork on the bare white walls, the lights of Berlin providing a backdrop through the plate glass window. It was, she decided, impressive.

The location, the achingly cutting-edge style, sofas that didn't have duct tape holding them together; she was pretty sure the shower would not have cracked tiles or a plastic curtain that barely stretched across the opening. She found that, while she enjoyed the brief luxury of it all, she didn't covet it. How on earth, she thought to herself as she glanced round, would you feel at home in such a place?'

'Glad you made it,' Martha took her parka. 'Drink?'

'Sorry about the jeans,' Harriet said, taking in Martha's very slim black dress, the heels. 'I travelled light. And just something soft. Still on painkillers.'

'And if I didn't have a really heavy-duty dinner in an hour, then I would be in my pyjamas,' Martha sighed.

They both turned as the sound of a door slammed shut.

'Neil? Oh good. You can drop Harriet back later.'

'Of course,' Neil came in, unwinding a long scarf from around his neck, a very full-looking canvas satchel slung across his chest. 'Nice to see you,' he smiled at Harriet. 'Your calls all go to voicemail. You've saved me a journey. I was going to swing by the refuge this evening to see you but Martha said you were going to be here.'

'My fault,' she said. She felt strangely relieved. 'The phone hasn't been the same since – well. I get texts though.'

'Not if it's not charged,' he grinned. 'Oh never mind, you're here now.'

He glanced at his phone, 'Just got to take this.' He walked to the other end of the room, his face turned away.

'Here,' Martha said. She looked after Neil with a frown, handing Harriet a chunky glass, limes and ice piled into sparkling water, 'How's your head?'

'Surprisingly good,' Harriet lied. 'Obviously tough as old boots,' she grinned.

'You'd make an awful witness,' Martha remarked. 'So transparent. It must ache like hell, but you just want to get home, and I don't blame you. Come and see the view. It's the reason I bought the place.'

Bought? Harriet thought Martha was extraordinary. Smart, clever, good humoured, each day holding down a job unravelling corporate legalities for a string of companies whose names could rattle stock markets on a global scale if they so much as sneezed.

And then, all thanks to Bebe's unflagging ability to know every last detail of the lives of anyone useful to her – and Martha was right up there with the best of them – she had discovered, that since her return from London over a year ago now, Martha had been a fixture on the social scene in this complex city, but still found time to handle cases of women fleeing from dangerous men and violent lives.

'Not my doing,' Martha explained. 'It was Bebe's. I was asked to speak at a conference for women's rights and she was there, and the next thing I know, she is laying siege to my office until I agree to talk to her. Actually, she redefines the meaning of determination that one. Someone was having trouble hanging onto their kids, the husband was getting more sympathy for winning custody because of where the children were living. Der Hafen isn't exactly Balmoral, so she waylaid me as I left the building and told me I had to find ten minutes for her, even if it was just walking to my car. And made me take the case.'

'Did you win?' Harriet asked, knowing immediately it was a daft question. And nor did she believe that Martha had ever been made to do anything in her life that didn't suit her.

Martha grimaced. 'Just. I guessed he didn't really want the children back at all, but it was another way to get to the mother. So—' she glanced at her watch, 'I decided to test the case in court. Very brave woman, she was. Didn't back down as I half expected her to, but Bebe said she wouldn't – and he skulked off once the courts were involved. It wasn't such a gamble as you might think. Rule of thumb. Never fight battles you can't win.'

'So do you look after all of them?'

'Wish I could, but no. The cost, you see. I can't always underwrite them, or rather my company won't always stump up. Bebe is pretty good at sussing who'll stay the course if we go to court and who will eventually go back to the man who gave her a split lip. She should have been a lawyer.'

'And the children? What about them?'

'Injunctions mostly. Stopping their father taking them without consent, out of the country, or to live with someone unsuitable. Not perfect, because desperate people are unpredictable, but usually it's enough to keep them at bay. Better than nothing.'

'How's the head?' Neil said, returning.

'Good,' Harriet nodded. 'Thank you. Hoping to get home at the weekend.'

'Don't rush it,' he advised. 'You had a nasty knock there.'

'And you?' she asked politely. 'When I last saw you, you thought you might be unwell.'

Martha rolled her eyes skywards. 'Tell me you didn't say that?' she pleaded.

'I never said I was *unwell*,' Neil corrected. 'Merely that it was a *possibility*. And my suspicions were unfounded. Thank you Martha. Always delighted to get your vote. Harriet? Another drink?'

'I'm fine,' she said, waving her glass, trying not to laugh, 'but dizzy from admiring this extraordinary space.' She glanced around.

'I hardly ever see it,' Martha admitted. 'If I'm not in New York or Geneva, my days in Berlin tend to be the twenty-four hour kind.'

'And that's on a good day,' Neil interrupted. 'And she's getting worse. She's a workaholic so don't get too sympathetic. And I bet you, she's off on some charity do tonight.'

'Can't get out of it,' Martha agreed. 'I just wanted to catch up with Harriet and this was the only slot I have before Sunday – by then she may well be back in London. Hang on, my earrings. Won't be a minute.'

'You will?' he raised his eyebrows at Harriet, as Martha whirled out of the room.

'Seeing the doctor on Friday. Can't think of a single reason why they won't let me fly. Bebe thinks Martha should give the okay though.'

'Martha? Good God, why?'

'Because she asked Bebe to care for me, and for Bebe that means Martha is in charge. And besides, Bebe said it's mandatory to be in awe of Martha.'

'Tragic, isn't it?' he sighed. 'You wouldn't take a blind bit of notice if *she* said not to go, would you? Oh nonsense,' he said as she began to protest. He sat on the edge of the sofa. 'You look to me like someone who wouldn't take much notice of anyone. Thing about Martha,' he raised his voice so that Martha could hear, 'is just because she wears those jackets and four-inch heels, she thinks everyone will stand to attention. When we met,' he confided, 'at some student party or other a hundred years ago, she was flirting with some geek who was smitten by her accent – much better now – and all the while she was dressed like a peace warrior, you know, Doc Martens, dungarees—'

'It was a *peace* march,' Martha interrupted coming back. 'I recall your girl-friend at the time – Sarah, nice girl, no judgement – said you might be going down with double pneumonia and might not make it.'

'But I did,' he said mildly. 'At great risk to my well-being.'

Martha turned to Harriet. 'Take no notice. He made a very good speech. He should have been a lawyer.'

'What?' he exclaimed. 'And end up like you, in a job where they throw shedloads of money at you, so you can afford an apartment the size of the Grand Canyon and be forced to go to fabulously chic parties every night?'

'It is not huge,' Martha pointed out. 'It is, by most standards, quite small. Just one bedroom, but perfect for me. Talking of which—' Martha glanced at her watch, 'I have to go and sparkle. Can't move in this town for someone raising money for something. The arts, usually. Matter of fact, Bebe mentioned earlier that your new friend might be there.'

Harriet jumped. 'Gisela?'

'Who? No. Kurt. Sorry? Who's Gisela?'

Harriet could have kicked herself. 'No-one. Sorry, I mean no-one you'd know,' she stumbled. 'Someone at the refuge. Wanted to know something or other.'

Martha gave her a sharp look and then turned to the mirror on the wall behind her. She fiddled with her earrings; small diamond hoops. Exquisite. Cartier. Harriet recognised the style. She caught Martha's eye in the mirror.

'Nice,' Harriet enthused. 'Um – how does Bebe know about Kurt being there?'

'If there were such a thing, Bebe would be a magazine stalker,' Martha said dryly. 'She follows his progress in those ghastly gossip magazines. She's got a fixation about him. Well, men like him.

'Now,' she picked up a box-shaped evening bag, encrusted with rhinestones, lying on the console table under the mirror, checked the contents and snapped it shut. 'Is there anything I can do? I'd like to help. *And* you haven't mentioned it, but Bebe said you've been great with the kids.'

Harriet felt embarrassed. 'Oh please,' she protested. 'You've done enough. And I *will* pay you.'

Martha flapped a hand at her.

'Well, I will,' Harriet said stubbornly. 'And honestly, the kids thing was nothing. I had to find some way of keeping the noise down, so I was very nice to them and in the end got what I wanted. Works every time.'

Martha flicked a startled look at her. Neil looked down at his drink. Too late, Harriet realised what that had sounded like.

'We might as well go too,' Neil said into the silence. 'I have to meet my – someone in less than an hour. Got to get changed.'

'No,' she insisted. What in God's name had possessed her? 'No. I can get back on my own. It's not late. The walk will do—'

'It's on my way,' he stopped her. 'And I bet you don't know the way yet. Martha, I'll go straight on. See you whenever.'

'Fine, but don't get talked into—' Martha began and then stopped, clearly remembering Harriet was there. 'Fine,' she repeated. She sounded resigned to something. 'Whatever.'

Harriet stood by silently while this exchange took place. On another occasion, she might have felt curious about what Neil might or might not get talked into, but she simply felt stupid, furious with herself. Wishing she had insisted she found her own way home, so as not to be obliged to these two perfectly nice but unknown people. Not wanting to lie, but what else could she do? Bebe had trusted her. And such a stupid, stupid remark.

They drove in silence until Neil suddenly pulled over as they neared a U-Bahn and stopped the car.

'Are you dropping me here?' she asked. All she hoped was that he wasn't going to insist she walked the rest of the way just because of a thoughtless remark. It was damp, it was cold, she'd been mugged, she was fed up and annoyed with herself for saying such a stupid thing. But he said in a matter-of-fact voice, more a statement, not a question:

'So Gisela.'

'What about her?' Her heart sank.

'Who is she?'

'No idea.' She shook her head.

'Nonsense.' He sounded calm. Not aggressive. Weirdly normal. 'You didn't just pluck the name out of the air, did you? You looked startled when you thought Martha knew her.'

Harriet sat in silence.

'Bebe?' he pressed her. Almost cheerfully, she thought. 'And I expect she told you not to say anything? Especially to Martha.'

'Something like that.' It seemed ridiculous to pretend otherwise. Also a little childish. 'I promised.'

'And so far you've kept your word. But I don't think it counts if you tell someone who isn't German. At least, I'm pretty certain it doesn't.'

'But you might tell Martha,' she pointed out.

'I might.' He reached forward and wiped the inside of the windscreen with a glove. It wasn't his. It was a woman's glove. Cream leather, soft, trimmed at the wrist with fur like an ostrich feather, a small pearl button on the cuff. 'But it's unlikely,' he said cheerfully. 'Especially if I were told not to. And besides, you're bursting to tell someone aren't you? So it might as well be me.'

'You'll ruin that glove,' she said.

He glanced at it, and stuffed it into his pocket. 'You are dramatic. It's leather, it will dry. Now. This Gisela?'

*

'None of it makes sense,' she said when she'd reached the end. 'And she might be my last hope of finding out what all this is about.'

'He may not have confided in her,' he pointed out. 'She might not know very much about Elena.'

177

'For goodness sake, she slept with him,' Harriet exclaimed. 'Not just casually. They were lovers. For *ten* years. She must know *something*.'

'Sleeping with someone is a million miles away from confiding in them.' He made it sound like an indisputable fact of life. 'Even with a lover. I doubt love came into it.'

'You believe that?' she stared curiously at him.

In the year she'd been with Dermot, she'd been – and she squirmed at the memory – desperate to share everything with him, who he liked, what kind of day he'd had, was he happy? Sad? Feverishly trawling food markets to make him his favourite dishes, and for days on end, little room for anything in her head other than how she could make him happier and love her more.

And for what? A man who, as it turned out, had only a fragile relationship with fidelity, but was in a class of his own when it came to breaking hearts and shattering dreams. Instinctively, she pressed her fingers against her face at the memory of the sheer stupidity of it. Likewise, it might have been love for Gisela, but clearly it was one way.

'What?' Neil asked. 'Are you okay? Your face is sort of – um – flushed. Is it your head? Do you want a doctor or—'

'I'm fine,' she stopped him, feeling her face go even redder. 'I was just thinking that someone like Gisela must have got to know him really well. I mean if Bebe's got it right, Kurt has been a fixture in her life for almost ten years. Trust me. That is very different to a casual relationship. Even if he didn't care about her, she cared about him.'

'And that gave you a rush of blood to the head?' He looked doubtfully at her.

'No of course not,' she said crossly. 'I think it's just the heat after the cold outside.'

'Ah, that must be it,' he agreed, not sounding at all convinced.

'Look,' she moved hurriedly on. 'Even if he hadn't confided in her, she was around him enough to pick stuff up, and she'd have been interested in anything *he* was interested in. Maybe they talked about Elena. Who knows? Remember this was before Natasha became so frail. He adores his grandmother.

I'll say that for him. You've only got to look at that place to see only the best is good enough for her.

'Oh I know he can afford it, but she wants for nothing. Oh God,' she stopped. 'What's the point? Bebe doesn't know where Gisela is, except she thinks she's still in Berlin somewhere. And I barely know where I live in this city, I don't understand the districts, the tube, let alone any other part of it, so it's a pretty bleak outlook.'

'Unless,' he said, 'she's living on the streets – this Gisela I mean – then she must be somewhere. If Bebe is right, then at least we know one thing, that she's not back with him. Someone has taken her in. Someone always succumbs to hard-luck stories.'

Harriet stared at her hands. 'That was a stupid remark I made back there. I was just embarrassed that Martha was thanking me when I will never be able to repay her kindness.'

'Except you came here through Bing, and that would have counted for a lot. Can I ask – I mean, I obviously don't want to intrude here – but are you and Bing – you know?'

'No,' she said, startled. 'Heavens no. Just a lovely man who helped me. Anyway, Martha would be a hard act to follow.'

'Maybe,' he said. 'Some people are harder to get over than others. Not impossible, but tougher.'

'Look,' she said into the silence that followed. 'I don't expect you to believe me, but in spite of that stupid remark, anyone who knows me knows I didn't con Elena or anyone else. *Ever.*'

'I know that.' He sounded matter of fact.

'You *do*? Why? No-one else does?'

'You are tiresome. Don't exaggerate. Stick to the facts. You told me *all* your friends believed you, and Bebe certainly does. Even your twit of a lawyer. That's hardly "no-one", is it?'

He didn't look at her. 'What I think you mean,' he said, leaning his head back on the headrest, 'is that Herr Weber doesn't believe you. Or rather he does believe you, but he chooses not to. And I'm guessing he's the only one that matters to you in all of this.'

'No,' her voice was sharper than she had intended. 'You're wrong. He doesn't matter that much. Trust me, I know when it matters. He did matter, and he still does in a way, but it's something else now. Something more important. At least to me.'

She hesitated, not sure if she was going to make a fool of herself, but in the same moment realised she was becoming an expert on that front, so why not go for gold?

'This,' she said, treading carefully, 'might sound melodramatic and I don't expect you to understand. But yes. It matters a hell of a lot to me that I've been ruined – or near enough,' she added hastily before he could correct her. 'And I think it monstrous that he's getting away with it. There is also the fact that Elena and her mother were both truly amazing women. I just know that he's got it wrong about Max and Valentina. Maybe he's just repeating what he's heard, I don't know. What I do believe – *know* – is that Elena and her mother went through times so tough you wouldn't believe, and I know, just *know* that if Elena were here – I mean I know she's not, but you know what I mean – she would hate what's happening to her stuff, to her reputation. She trusted me. And that *does* affect me.'

It occurred to her that he was regarding her, patiently but not entirely hopefully, more as one would a particularly difficult student, clawing their way through a definition of some complex mathematical procedure, unsure of how to arrive at the other end, but living in hope that they might.

'Well, even if you don't know what I mean, *I know*,' she went on doggedly. 'She would have fought back. She didn't want her wishes to end up this way. Her possessions just hijacked by people who didn't care about her. I knew her well enough to know that. After the way she tried to help so many people when she was younger, I don't want her epitaph to be that no-one tried for *her*. And I think, for no other reason but a gut feeling, that I am meant to complete their journey. And if you think that's the ramblings of a deranged woman with a brain the size of a pea—'

'Now you're just being silly,' he said calmly. 'There you go again, overstating your case rather than letting the facts speak for themselves. I never even speculated on the size of your brain and yes, you are rambling, but I don't think you're deranged. Although you might have noticed, I've kept the car doors unlocked, just in case. And you really are ridiculously defensive. You have no reason to be.'

'All right,' she said, trying not to snap back at him. Practical though his reasoning was, she was the one who, over the past few weeks and months, had felt like the entire world was pointing fingers at her. 'So why do you believe me? I've only met you three times.'

'And you fell asleep last time, but I won't hold that against you. Why do I believe you? Well, leaving aside the very laudable but entirely irrational belief that you owe Elena or her mother, without wishing to cause offence, you're clearly not smart enough to be that devious. You tend to say the first thing that comes into your head. You haven't got a backstory worked out to defend yourself. Anyone who had deliberately set out to defraud someone would have covered their tracks.'

'Like what?'

'Invented conversations with your – sorry – *their* victim. You didn't. Pathetic when you think about it. And you don't look daft. But appearances can be deceptive.'

'All right, all right,' she said. She was almost laughing. Relief swept over her. 'I get it.'

'Meanwhile your evidence – for what it is – is so slight, you're going to need more than a greetings card you no longer have, which Kurt openly admits he got someone to write anyway, to get anywhere.'

'I know,' she said miserably. 'But what else can I do? At the most I have only two more days to stay here. Three tops. And of course I'd rather go back knowing the truth, to start putting things right at home, but I don't speak the language and I have no idea how Germany works, up to and including those white sausages they all seem to eat—'

'Not all,' he corrected. 'Some, I agree.'

'Fine, fine,' she flapped a hand at him. 'But according to Bebe, no-one in their right mind accuses Kurt of anything. So what are the chances? Well, exactly,' she finished staring out of the side window. 'Unless I can find this Gisela and make her help.'

Little drops of rain were trickling down the pane. She didn't want to walk the rest of the way, but he'd mentioned his apartment was in Kreuzberg – entirely the opposite direction to Alexanderplatz, where the refuge was. She felt oddly secure, but knew she couldn't just sit there any longer, much as she wanted to. For the first time in so long, she just wanted to melt into the sheer safeness of being there.

'And you still think he was behind having you mugged?'

She blinked and sat up straight. 'Oh yes. He may not have thrown the punches, but his weight was behind every one of them.'

He sat back in his seat with a resigned sigh. 'Sorry. If I wasn't meeting someone – and it's important – I'd suggest finding something to eat.'

'No,' she said quickly, feeling mildly disappointed. She could have done with some company. 'You've done enough. I'll find a way. I've got two or three days after all. A lifetime,' she forced a grin.

'No. I meant it's – well, personal stuff. A bit tricky. And I know it will undoubtedly make me very unwell, but I'll only get the blame if you get into any more trouble—'

'But why? Why would you get the blame? I hardly know you or you me—'

'Because,' he said, starting the car and moving away, 'while you were talking, I was giving it some thought.'

'Thank you,' she said politely.

'No. I heard every word. Okay. Here's a plan. I speak German. I know the country better than you. But more importantly, everyone would say I should have stopped you. By everyone, I obviously mean Martha.'

'Obviously,' she agreed, trying not to shriek with relief at what he might be going to say.

'And lastly,' he slowed to allow a bus to overtake them as they pulled out into the traffic, stretching an arm in front of her to push her gently back against her seat to clear his view, 'while I do have to work, I can at least try and point you in the right direction. And I've just got time to drop you.'

Harriet opened her mouth to speak.

'Don't be boring,' he stopped her protests. 'And before you can say anything, you should know I never waste time on anything that is clearly impossible. In this case, trying to make you see sense and go home.'

He sounded just like Lizzie.

*

Neil's brief text later that evening after he'd dropped her back, that said something had cropped up, but that he'd be in touch as soon as he could, was not exactly a note saying she had been abandoned, just re-prioritised in his life. Still, she felt both silly and disappointed that she had placed so much dependence on a man – and one she hardly knew – to leap to her aid, not once but twice now, who had offered her one last slim hope to get her life back, and justice of a sort for Elena.

It was hard to tell what the weather was like outside, sitting as she was in the creaking armchair in her room, facing the window, her feet resting on the windowsill, staring out at – well, nothing when she thought about it, a blank wall was not exactly inspiring, but suited her mood. On her lap lay a copy of a morning newspaper, opened at the page Bebe had pointed out to her. A paean – really that's all it could be called – to Kurt and his sponsorship of some charity or other, mentioning the strong possibility that he would soon be a special advisor to the Minister of Culture.

There he was, smiling at the centre of a group of people at this fundraiser, whatever it was – her German might have improved, but not that much – the countess he was linked with, smiling by his side. Somewhere in the crowd behind him must have been Martha. What a world.

Having nothing lethal to hand to exact revenge on his smiling confidence, the perfectly even white teeth, the immaculate appearance, she stifled an oath, and slapped the paper face down next to her.

Really, she couldn't stay much longer. Neil must know that. She'd told him. And it was unfair on Bebe, who could find a much better use for her room. It was then, staring pointlessly out of the window, that she made one last plan. Not much of one, it had to be said, but better than doing nothing at all. Time was not on her side. Men – all of them – were pointless, and Monday, she decided, tapping her fingers on the window, that had to be it. Cut off point. And then she'd go. Monday was three days away.

She would not, *could* not bring herself to call either Martha or, especially, Neil. Too needy and certainly too pushy is how it would seem.

'I'm taking the children for a walk,' Bebe's voice came from the doorway. Harriet twisted her head to see her with her coat on. 'I could use some help. Just the small ones. They're more manageable with you. They think you're better than a cartoon.'

Harriet mustered a smile. She pushed herself up out of the chair. 'Only because I keep getting *sind Sie* and *haben Sie* muddled up.'

'Even I would laugh if someone asked me, "*Are* you a coat?" instead of, "*Have* you got a coat?"' Bebe chuckled. 'You, my English friend, are wall-to-wall entertainment.'

'Thank you,' Harriet dipped her head graciously, adding casually, 'By the way, Neil hasn't called, has he? My phone's doing weird things.'

Bebe bent down to tie a scarf round a toddler's neck. 'I'd have told you,' she said. 'Do you want to use my phone? The signal here can be not so good. Or I ask Martha. I'm talking to her later. Would you like me to do that?'

'No, no,' Harriet said hastily. 'I just didn't want to appear rude not calling back, that's all. If he had. Bebe? I've got to do a bit of shopping later. Take something back for Lizzie. Would you mind if I slipped off for an hour when we get back? I think you said the Kurfurstendamm was the street to go to? Is it far to walk?'

'The Ku'damm?' Bebe didn't look up. She patted the zip on the child's coat. 'About an hour. Or ten minutes if you take the U-Bahn. In this weather, I know what I'd do.'

*

Apart from feeling sorry for herself, badly missing the comfort of Lizzie or James to moan to, Harriet had never felt so cold. When it wasn't trying to knock her off her feet, the icy wind seemed determined to freeze the muscles of her face into an immoveable mask. Didn't it ever get warm in Berlin? A drizzling rain was rapidly turning into sleet; snow couldn't be far away. Doing something, even if it was just to see where Kurt operated from, was better than sitting in that dreary place with all those dysfunctional people.

As she walked – still a rather stately walk, to stop her ribs and head from taking any more punishment – she thought about how much Bebe had pinned her hopes on her coming up with something. In turn, she had pinned her hopes on Neil. And here she was now, adding to it all by hoping her destination might inspire a thought. Ridiculous and pointless. What a mess.

While she pondered on this mess, she found her way to a street just off Ku'damm in the west of the city. The long, tree-lined boulevard filled with shops and restaurants, cafés and boutiques was, even in this weather, swarming with visitors, undaunted by icy winds and the fading light. For a moment she saw herself, sitting at a pavement café, with someone special – and for once, puzzlingly it didn't appear to be Dermot – enjoying a glass of chilled white wine and the headiness of a summer day in such a glorious setting.

One day, she told herself – turning away to survey from her vantage point on the corner of the Ku'damm, the side road from which she would see where the family who had caused her such grief made their money – one day, I will come back and sit there, right there she told herself, and wonder if all this really happened.

Arcadia, the name etched in gold on the wall, stretched elegantly and impressively halfway along this calmer, but still stylish street. A terrace of square and sturdy planters, holding ice-topped topiary balls, were lined up like sentries either side of the glass doors that led directly from the street into this exclusive establishment. At the kerb, a black Mercedes waited, its engine purring. She was too far away to see if the driver was the same one who had come out to Der Linden Baum. His back was to the street, as he watched for his passenger to emerge through those glass doors.

No wonder, she thought savagely, that Kurt bloody Weber could afford to have a string of mistresses. No wonder no-one challenged him. She huddled against the wall, a woollen hat pulled down to her eyebrows where it met a thick scarf covering her mouth. Shoulders hunched, hands dug deeply into her pockets, she waited. But unsure what for. No-one should get away with what he did. No-one. Rage started to rise in her chest. What if she just went across and—

'Harriet?'

Chapter Sixteen

She stifled a scream, spun round, clutching her arm to her waist, to find Neil standing only feet away.

'What are you doing?' he demanded, ushering her none too gently out of view of Arcadia, around the nearest corner – which also protected them from the biting wind – and out of sight of the man who had chosen that moment to emerge from the building and slide into the back of the limousine.

'Nothing,' she knew she was shivering. 'How did you know I was here?'

'You told Bebe where you were going. Not rocket science. Thought you might do something – you know—'

'Stupid?'

'No,' he said, exasperated. 'Just perhaps – not helpful.'

She dropped her head and leaned against the nearest wall. 'To who?'

'Well, standing here spying on the chairman of a company who's already tried to ruin you, I'd say is certainly not helpful to you.' He glanced at his phone. Locked it. 'C'mon,' he said, touching her arm, 'I'll buy you a coffee.'

'No,' she said quickly. 'No I'm fine. Thank you. Really. You're all busy. I understand. I'm okay. Fresh air will do me good.'

He took her arm with what she thought was a muttered oath. 'You're not fine,' he said. 'Clearly you're not. Oh shut up and do as you're told. If *you're* not frozen, *I* am. And quite likely to get pneumonia standing here, and arrested if Kurt Whatsisname comes back and catches sight of us. For a man with my parlous state of health that's not the healthy option at all.'

He guided her into a nearby bar and ordered coffee for both of them. After that, he peered over his glasses at her, rubbed his chin and asked when she had last properly eaten.

'I'm not hungry,' she insisted.

He then ordered, and made her eat, a bowl of mushroom and pepper risotto. 'I could have suggested sausage and sauerkraut, but it's quite heavy at this time of day and this might be better. You must learn to charge your phone,' he sounded mildly annoyed. 'Two lecturers have gone down with flu and I had to cover and I had to see someone—'

'It's fine,' she assured him, wishing she could say no it bloody well isn't, that she'd wasted two days waiting for someone to turn up who doesn't know what it is to keep their word. But another part of her knew it must be his wife who was the complication. Annoying as is was, there was no getting around the fact that in a mess like that – and it sounded a mess – nothing and no-one else would get a look in. Especially not a stupid woman they all clearly regarded as being on a mission to madness. And her phone needed replacing. That she did concede.

'And I wasn't going to do anything stupid,' she said, leaning back to allow the waitress to place a steaming bowl in front of her. 'I just wanted to get his measure, the scale of his life. That's all.' She peered at the bowl and gave it a cautious stir. 'I'll never eat all this,' she said watching the steam being released as she pushed her fork into it. 'I'm not really hungry.'

'Try,' he advised. 'I've just got to make two calls. Won't be a moment.'

So she tried to eat and found that she was actually quite hungry, forking mouthfuls up, Neil watching all the while as he stood in the doorway of the café, his phone pressed to his ear. Once he closed his eyes and dropped his head on his chest, seemingly in disbelief. After a few – and what appeared to be heated – minutes he checked his watch again and then hung up. She looked away quickly, pushing her empty dish to one side.

'Sorry,' he said sliding back into his seat. 'Longer than I thought. So,' he gestured to the empty bowl. 'Not hungry eh?'

'I think,' she said, 'it's the not having to make it. Delicious. Thank you. I think I needed nagging.'

'My forte,' he agreed. 'I spend my entire day doing it to less worthy causes. Now, what's all this about? Stalking Kurt, I mean.'

'Oh God,' she sighed. 'I know it looks weird, but I have to go home before Bebe throws me out – no, of course she won't – but I can't stay forever and I just needed to do *something*. I know you said you'd help, but when I come to think of it, I don't know what you *could* do. And you have no reason to help at all. Bloody men,' she stopped. 'Sorry,' she grimaced. 'What must that have sounded like? I was just echoing Bebe. When she was talking about Kurt.'

'Don't worry,' he sighed. 'I know someone who would have no trouble agreeing with you. About men, I mean. But since I'm generous to a fault, I'm going to assume whoever it was who broke your heart had a hand in it.'

'What?'

'The one you mentioned the other night. You said, "Trust me," just like you knew what it was like. I'd like to know,' he added when she just stared at him. 'Okay if you'd rather not, but I'm interested.'

'Just an unwise relationship.' She was surprised she could speak so calmly about Dermot and without much prompting. But she knew instinctively people going through heartbreak tended to latch onto anyone else who'd gone through it, to compare notes. Will it get worse? More painful? How to stop the misery? Can you move on? She'd been there. Got the badge. If it helped him, then she owed him that.

'I was a bit, you know,' she rolled her finger at the side of her head, 'daft back then. I was besotted and he was – as it turned out – less besotted. In fact, probably not besotted at all. He managed to dismantle my life for quite a while and it took time to recover. Sorry,' she gave an embarrassed laugh. 'I'm beginning to sound like one of those girl group songs. You know all those victim lyrics like, *You said that and it made me feel like this*, instead of manning up and telling them to get stuffed. Even if saying it means lying through your back teeth.'

He laughed. A nice laugh. One that briefly lifted the rather distant expression he seemed to wear. Fleetingly, she thought it was a shame he didn't smile more, instead of fretting over his health.

'The truth is,' she said, 'I brought the whole house of cards down on myself. You know? Unrealistic expectations. Wanting him to be responsible for my happiness. Huge mistake. Expecting one person to make you feel fabulous all the time. Total fantasy land. I know that now. Actually, I knew that quite quickly. When it was over, I mean. But I'm not great at letting anything go. Or admitting defeat.'

'No,' he said. 'I gathered that.'

'It wasn't all bad,' she said, a wave of honesty prompting her. 'I got a career out of it.'

'You did?'

'Of course. Dermot was – still is – brilliant at being a dealer. I learned a lot from him. I'd been drifting around the edges of it all, selling jewellery, going to auctions, buying without really working out what I wanted to buy or how much I wanted to spend, or where my stuff would find the best market – not all markets have the same vibe, you know. I learned all that from him. He made me focus, take it all more seriously.'

'And you did?'

She looked away frowning. 'I thought I did. I wanted to be like him. Passionate about it rather than just interested. The trouble is, I could never put it all before anything else in my life. The way he did.'

'How?'

'Well,' she frowned, recalling so many instances. 'Once he jetted off to some auction in Paris because a rare Albertina bracelet had come up for sale. Right in the middle of—' she stopped, '—dinner,' she said, seeing no reason to explain that a king size bed, champagne and not much else had been involved.

'If I knew what an Alberwhatsit was,' he said apologetically.

'Albertina,' she said.

'Ah, thank you,' he said. 'As I was saying, to be honest the only Albertina I've ever heard of is the museum in Vienna.'

'It's just a rather intricate watch chain,' she said. 'Like this.' She scrolled down on her phone until she found a photograph and handed it to him. 'Your grandfather might have had one. Named after Prince Albert, but they added the "ina" on the end when it became fashionable for women to wear it as a bracelet. This one had black opals set in it. Really rare. Big bucks,' she added.

'Well obviously.' He handed her phone back. 'Put like that. Did he get it?'

'Of course. That's why he's so bloody successful, and I ended up struggling.'

'Would you have him back?' He studied her carefully, almost leaning forward. 'I know that's intrusive, but it sounds like it was a big deal. You might have got past it. Feeling like you did about him.'

She paused. She remembered too many tearful scenes, no sleep, wanting – in bewilderingly equal measure – to be left alone but longing for him to call. Dermot pleading for her not to overreact. Calling or texting her not to be so silly, just a stupid mistake. He'd said sorry a dozen times, hadn't he? He'd even shouted at her that she was being stupid, it was nothing, a moment of madness. But she couldn't get past it, no matter how much she'd wanted to, tried to. In the end, she gave Neil an answer that wasn't entirely truthful, but not a lie either.

'Very unlikely. We never got to a point where I could factor in forgiveness. The whole thing just exhausted us both until there was nothing left to say, except go over the same ground, and nothing changed.'

'What did you do?'

'Had my hair cut,' she grinned. 'Very therapeutic. I'm sorry. Seriously, I can't really remember when I began to feel normal, it just happened. Life went on and took me with it. Hey, you should have stopped me. Rabbiting on like this. Boring.'

'No,' he shook his head. 'Not boring, definitely not that.'

'Well,' she said, pretty certain he was simply being polite, 'how about you? Have you resolved all your – um – complications?'

He sat back, shook his head. 'Not yet. My wife was here – or rather my ex – actually no, not ex yet. Not quite.'

'You don't know?' She stared at him.

'Sounds ridiculous,' he agreed. He rubbed his hands down his face. 'Sort of in between. For someone who unravels problems all day, I'm being useless at this. In my head, I'm both defence and prosecutor in my own case and getting nowhere.'

His eyes, she suddenly noticed, looked exhausted. Sleep, clearly a stranger to him. A surge of sympathy for him welled up along with a pang of guilt. Where would he have found the time, let alone the energy to help her?

'It's sometimes,' she said carefully, 'easier to tell a complete stranger what the problem is. The advantage in saying it out loud to someone with no vested interest, who you're unlikely to ever run into again, is that it doesn't matter what they think. Someone I met recently told me that. He was right.'

'Is that so?' He gave a small smile. 'What a wise person that must have been. But then this complete stranger would be given a very skewered view of it. Very one-sided. They couldn't possibly be capable of offering unbiased advice.'

'Who said anything about advice?' She smiled. 'Say it out loud and you might find you don't need any from anyone. The answer might be staring you in the face. Or it might, at least, put it in perspective. Try.'

He looked carefully at her.

'I'm not in a rush,' she said. 'I'm going nowhere. I don't know your wife, or your friends. I barely know Martha. I have no agenda other than ordering another cup of coffee. How am I doing?'

He grinned. 'Not bad. Okay. Why not?'

So she listened while he told her about his five-year marriage to Sylvia, a temperamental artist – more temperament he added than was, in his view, necessary to be creative. An opinion that hadn't helped when she'd walked out. That had been three months ago, just as he was about to leave for his year being bored witless by his students at Humboldt.

'How was that going to work?' Harriet asked. 'Sounds like a long time to be apart.'

'I thought she was coming with me, but apparently she'd been considering the opposite, on account of the – er – you know—'

'Yes, yes,' Harriet nodded. 'The um – yes. Sorry? Do we have a name for him?'

'Not one I care to repeat,' he said grimly. 'So I came here, thinking that was it, got drunk a lot, walked at all odd hours, and then she rang. The nameless one hadn't worked out because, she said, he thought she wasn't over me and until she was, there was no point. And I gather she agreed. So here we are. And I don't know where I am.'

He spoke of a woman who was a rising star in the world of portraiture, a woman who knew she'd made a terrible mistake and needed to make him see that's all it was. At the time, when she'd phoned, he'd been blind drunk in Martha's flat, and he might, he grinned ruefully, have passed out in Martha's spare room, so not in the best state to negotiate a reunion.

'And I wasn't entirely blameless,' he admitted. 'There was so much I should have mentioned before we married. What I was like, what I wanted out of life. I gave her space to work, because I thought that was what she wanted, but she saw it as lack of interest. I never saw it like that. I had no idea. Never known anyone apart from the Queen who has such a planned life as Sylvia. Possibly Madonna, of course.'

'Like what?' Harriet asked.

'Oh you know, going out to dinner, weekends away, I tend to leave it all to the last minute, and that was hopeless for her. She knows three months in advance where we're having dinner and who with. I should have been more understanding. The trouble is, in the end I can't decide where the core of this problem is. I'm trying to keep a cartload of emotions, that are skewering both our minds, out of it, and the facts intact. When we try to discuss it, we get bogged down in accusing each other of stuff that I'm not even sure happened. It just seems like it did.'

'And you still love her?' She tilted her head on one side to see his face.

'No, I hate her, but that might be for what she *did* rather than her. How the hell do I know? They feel like the same thing. If I didn't still love her, surely I wouldn't care, I'd be relieved? And I miss what we had. And I don't know if I can get past that. And it hasn't helped that I had agreed to do this year at Humboldt. I couldn't stay in London even if I'd wanted to. Too many people would have been let down, but Sylvia thinks – thought – I should have got out of it. Spent time mending us. Maybe,' he pushed his glasses onto his head, rubbed his eyes. 'Maybe, I should have.'

'Has she gone back? To London?'

He nodded. 'Coming back next weekend. And I think I outdid you rabbiting on. Enough.' He looked round for the waitress.

'What will you do now?' she asked carefully.

'Certainly not,' he shook his head as she began to hand him some cash. 'You've easily earned the price of a risotto. I suppose,' he found his card, 'Martha's right. I need to take my mind off it all, so I suppose we might as well get started.'

'With what?' she asked.

'Try and keep up,' he sighed, handing his card to the waitress. 'To help you find this Gisela, of course. Unless you can think of a better idea?'

'No, but surely, I mean you need time to, well you know, concentrate on your own problems?'

'So no ideas from you?' he sighed. 'Thought not. Buck up. Work to do.'

*

Days of exhaustive calls followed, from Bebe to anyone who might have possibly known Gisela Neumann – although there was nothing to say that was her real name, but what else had they to go on? Any address where she might once have lived was checked out; anyone who might have just heard of her in passing; a job, a companion, even a marriage, anything in fact. All drew disheartening blanks.

A trawl through all the registers recording where every citizen in the country lived or had lived, defeated Neil. Clubs where Gisela might have worked, bars that Bebe knew the missing woman had frequented, the internet, Facebook, proved conclusively that Gisela was determined not to be found.

Neil checked the death records, just to be sure. Harriet had held her breath for a few hours on that one. Even the women Bebe could find who had been at Der Hafen at the same time as Gisela were inclined to suffer from sudden amnesia at the mention of her name. Women who had learned from tough experience that they were largely safer not putting their heads above the parapet. Bebe didn't blame them. Neither did Harriet. Well, not much anyway. The only problem she had was that the lion's share – actually the entire share

– of the task fell to Bebe and Neil. Upping the hours she spent with the children to ease the load was her only way of thanking them – and indeed in Bebe's case – helping. She became adept at making endless cups of coffee and trying not to scream with frustration at the lack of progress.

James and Lizzie were fobbed off with a story for her continuing absence; that there were some antique markets she wanted to see, and maybe even buy stuff from, so that she could have some stock when she got home to restart her life. Bebe and Martha's names were shamelessly hijacked as companions to keep James and Lizzie happy.

Lord, she thought as she closed her eyes; the list of confessions she was going to have to make when she got back was growing longer and longer. Neil was right. Lying was not her natural forte. Her only justification, that might enable her to live with herself in the months to come, was that she had done so in an attempt to understand what it was that had caused the Webers such anguish, and to finally feel at peace with her memory of Elena. At least she could look back and know she had tried. Maybe that's what Neil should do as well. Try, just to be certain. But oddly that didn't, to Harriet, sound like much of a plan.

Might be able to go Pforzheim, she texted both James and Lizzie. *Elena always said I should. Will keep you updated.* Then, to be on the safe side, she hurriedly googled the exact location of this place that Elena had said was the only place to find watches. Just in case.

Chapter Seventeen

Harriet's role of childminder at least justified her staying on for another week. It was a job for which she had neither training or inclination, and was staggered that it wasn't immediately obvious to everyone that, half the time, she hadn't a clue what she was doing, compounded by the fact that she was also not doing it properly in another language. But this seemed a minor flaw to most of the families sheltering there.

'I can sleep,' one young mother told her, her face white with stress, 'because of you.' She carried a small baby on her hip, who reached forward to grab at a chunky wooden necklace Harriet wore. A little boy aged about four, clutched at Harriet's jacket. 'Four whole hours. I say *danke*, *dankeshöen*,' the woman managed, almost tearfully. She tried to wrest the necklace out of the baby's clutch, who promptly began to struggle and wail.

'Here,' Harriet pulled the necklace from round her neck and handed it to the child. Later, she realised that even if she'd been wearing something of Cartier's, she would have done the same, to save her poor head from a setback.

They all watched, wincing as the baby immediately sank her gums into the smooth, wooden beads, dribbling contentedly down her chubby chin. Her mother tried to remove it from her grasp, looking anxiously at Harriet.

'It's okay,' Harriet assured her hastily. The woman looked blank. 'Bebe?' Harriet turned to her. 'Can you explain? It's perfectly safe. It won't break. One of my nephews practically grew a whole set of molars munching on one just like it. And at least,' she muttered under her breath to Bebe, 'she's stopped shrieking.'

'Another fan to add to your list,' Bebe rolled her eyes. 'Her name is Klara. The child driving us nuts is Lilli. Klara said she would make sure you got it back and she is so grateful.'

'No, no,' Harriet insisted, shaking her head at Klara. Mild guilt nagged at her. Compared to them she had very little to worry about. 'Keep it. A present. That's fine.'

Which was just as well, as Lilli, who had now imprinted her mark on Harriet's necklace, showed no sign of letting go.

A small tug on her sweater made Harriet look down at Lilli's little brother. She summoned a smile, ruffling his hair, listening as he struggled with the English phrases she'd taught him – just *hello, goodbye* and *hurray for football* – but he left Harriet laughing with delight.

It was only later it occurred to her that she was actually in good spirits. But exactly why trying to find an unknown woman had left her feeling more optimistic in these last few days than she had in months, when every recent circumstance dictated that she should be on the edge of despair, eluded her. She wrinkled her nose. No, not *happy* exactly. More . . . hopeful. That was it.

Neil was perfectly fit and there wasn't, as far as she could tell, and obviously on such short acquaintance, a single thing about him that suggested otherwise. He was, she decided, a bit of an oddity. A nice one, good company, but no open book.

He made her laugh, and argued with her while they waited, with increasingly fading hope of anyone coming up with anything that could lead them to the elusive Gisela. For the last few days, they had simply wandered for an hour or two, through avenues of faded grandeur that had escaped the ravages of war, and then streets of plain, severe buildings that had replaced those that had not. Each had a habit of morphing, at the turn of a corner, into a chic neighbourhood, where rents were almost as high as any in Mayfair or Manhattan. Or sometimes, they stumbled through street after street of bars and restaurants, with strings of lights threaded through awnings, which came to life as the day progressed into night. Two nights in a row, they had braved the cold and walked back from supper, visiting the small, bustling cafés that now made up the market at Hackeshe Höfe. Once in the grip of a pitiless regime, now heaving with boutiques and bars, it was a favourite of Neil's. As they lingered over coffee, laced with brandy to keep out the cold, in a small bar where they squashed into a booth near an open fire, Harriet agreed that, of course, his was for medicinal purposes. A voice that had been hoarse from two back-to-back lectures had been the culprit, and he insisted they had another to be on the safe side. He made it three. Other customers stared curiously as the couple in the corner clinked their cups and laughed helplessly at God knows what.

Thank God, she decided, as he dropped her at the refuge in a street in Alexanderplatz and drove off to his own flat in Kreuzberg twenty minutes away, that he was the easiest person to be with, and so funny. Sylvia must be off her rocker. But that, she decided, was what happened when you had a common cause. Of course, that's all it was.

Which was why, the next day, she was so looking forward to telling him about the success she was having teaching Lilli's little brother to speak English. Neil, swathed in a bright blue checked scarf, a black parka and glasses pushed on top of his head, was already waiting for her on the corner by the U-Bahn.

'It was so brilliant,' she cried gleefully. 'This little boy. One of the kids I read to. He can say, *hello*, *goodbye*, *Spurs forever* and *Beckham is the greatest*. Go on,' she lightly punched his arm. 'Feel free. Tell me, how great am I?'

'I know you are,' he said, and without warning, laughing, he hugged her, kissing the side of her head. Instinctively, she pulled back. He hesitated and then pulled her woolly hat further down over her face.

'Now,' he said turning away and scanning the small cafés nearby. 'Which one shall it be?'

'Oh, anywhere,' she said more brightly than she had intended, making a big play of tying her scarf more tightly. 'What about that one?' she said, hurrying forward ahead of him.

'I think,' he called after her, 'you'll find that's a supermarket. Easy mistake to make. Of course. Although I'd have thought the trolleys by the door were a bit of a clue. What about the café next door?'

'I meant that one,' she lied. 'Just looking at something in the window. And before you ask, no-one at the refuge has any idea where Gisela is or even if they know her. Bebe suspects some of them do, but I don't blame them for staying quiet. But ten to one,' she grumbled, 'even if they said they did, they'd probably be about as reliable as a sailor on shore leave.'

'And you know a lot of those, do you?' Neil inquired politely.

'I might do,' she said loftily. 'I might not. I couldn't possibly say. Do you want to go in, or shall we just loiter in the doorway?'

He chuckled. 'Listen, if you're not in a rush, do you want to walk for a bit? I've been stuck inside all morning. Don't feel you have to, I'm shamelessly using you for company.'

'What girl could resist when you put it like that,' she agreed, privately relieved that he'd asked. The alternative was wandering round on her own until Bebe reported back from a contact who was so obscure, who said she might know someone who might know someone else who once knew Gisela. The tiny nagging little voice that nudged her into questioning if it had been anyone else suggesting a walk, the invitation might not have been so appealing, was sent packing.

'Is the Tiergarten far?' she suggested. 'I've never been. And it might not snow. And you might not be getting a sore throat.'

*

At the tangled junction of broad boulevards heading towards the entrance to the Tiergarten, Neil took her arm while they waited for the traffic streaming down from the Brandenburg Gate to ease up to allow them to cross.

On the other side of the street, for a while they walked in silence through the wide tree-lined paths of the Tiergarten, dodging around the familiar sight of families found in any big city on Saturday afternoon; babies in buggies, parents calling to children to watch out as they swerved on scooters around unsuspecting strollers, lovers with arms entwined, oblivious to anyone but each other. It could have been any park, in any city, anywhere in the world.

'I should be careful,' she smiled at Neil. His hands were dug into his pockets. He was walking, frowning at the ground.

'What?' he looked blankly at her. 'Sorry, miles away. About what?'

'Falling in love.'

'What?' he looked startled.

'With this city,' she confessed. 'Well, perhaps not the cold,' she added quickly, beginning to remember his slavish devotion to accuracy. 'Or the white sausages, or those nightmare men pounding on the door of the Hafen every night.'

'Even after all you went through?' He gave her a curious look.

She nodded. 'It's weird, isn't it? It was only two – no crikey three – weeks ago. I shake when I think of it. I – I'm not that brave. I have a light by my bed – Bebe found it for me – and the dark isn't great. But I can't seem to associate that with this – all this magnificence. Neil? Are you okay?'

He was staring at her. 'Yes,' he said. 'Just wondering if the market up ahead, has somewhere to grab a coffee.'

They found a stall that sold coffee in the tightly packed aisles of the famed flea market in the centre of the park, ambling companionably through them, stopping only when Harriet inspected the vintage jewellery. So long it seemed, since she had bothered with any of this. Not knowing quite what she was looking for, since she had no business anymore to make it worthwhile, she wondered where the drive for any of this had gone. Temporary, she consoled herself. It was another city, another time. It would come back to her.

On one stall, she turned over what looked like an amber and silver brooch, which she guessed had been copied from a time when more heavy Victorian tastes had melted away to be replaced by Edwardian delicacy.

Neil peered over her shoulder. 'Is it real? The amber?'

'Here?' she glanced around the market. 'Unlikely. Anyway, if you want to invest in amber, you should only ever buy Baltic,' she advised. 'And this is certainly not it.'

'How can you tell? Just in case,' he went on, 'I'm ever asked. Well, you never know,' he objected when she laughed.

'Okay. Well, if you rub it with a soft cloth, then pluck a hair from your head, if it clings to it, it probably is. Or some people recommend washing it with soap and water and then licking it – it should be tasteless by the way – and then there's the nail varnish test—'

'Good God,' he said hastily. 'How do you know all this stuff?'

'Well, a gemmology course helped – and there is all sorts of nonsense talked about tests for genuine stuff, but then I met Dermot and it was mostly through him. He could tell from the other end of the room what it was worth.'

'He taught you?'

'Not exactly. More that, when you're with someone who is a total expert, you kind of *want* to know. A bit like you telling me something about a maths problem and – what's the matter? You *are* impressive, okay, *I* think you are, but then I flunked maths at school so what do I know? Don't look so shocked – I probably wouldn't remember everything you said, but I'd remember enough not to sound ridiculous.'

'Could you—?' he seemed to be about to hold out his hand, but stopped. 'Harriet? What's the matter?'

She was staring through a closed glass case at a bracelet set in silver, the gleaming green gem caught in its clasp, catching the light. For some reason she shivered. It was also, she noticed with surprise, horrendously expensive for these surroundings.

'You wish to try?' The young man behind the stall came forward.

'No,' she said quickly. 'Just a surprise to find it here. I have – had,' she corrected herself. 'A small business in London. In a market. It seems rather expensive for a place like this.'

'Ah,' he said. 'You're right. I come once or twice a year. I miss this now I have a shop. People not afraid to look, to pick up. I bring just one or two really good pieces, to showcase what I do in the shop, and I rarely go home with any of them. And this,' he said encouragingly, 'is a fine piece.' He removed the bracelet from the black velvet cushion where it lay glinting away next to a simple silver charm bracelet.

'It came to us through the great niece of someone who used to live on Unter den Linden – over seventy years ago now, of course. The companion, I believe, of someone who was in those,' he paused adding delicately, 'let's say *unfortunate* days – very high ranking, very wealthy. We know no more.

'If you change your mind, I am just nearby,' he smiled and replaced the bracelet, carefully locked the glass case, pocketed the key and then moved away to another customer who looked more likely to buy.

'Do you like it?' Neil frowned, tilting his head doubtfully from side to side. 'Not sure I do. Weird colour.'

'It's actually beautiful,' Harriet told him severely. 'It's a peridot. Meant to attract love. I was just thinking, I bet Elena would have known all about the mistress and what happened to her and—' she broke off stifling a gasp.

'Hey,' he put his arm around her shoulders. 'What is it? You look like you've seen a ghost.'

Suddenly she faltered. 'For some reason it made me think of Elena. It's nothing,' she tried to sound brisk. 'Nothing I can't deal with.'

'I'm not sure I believe that,' he said. 'Would you like to sit for a minute?'

She shook her head, but didn't move. His arm felt warm, comforting, it had been a while since she'd felt physically close to anyone. Since that awful night, she had, without realising, missed the comfort even that small contact would have given her, and missed it quite badly. James would have hugged her and Lizzie would have, too. That's all this was, loneliness, wanting to go on feeling the warmth of someone's concern. Feeling that she – well – *belonged*.

And then she heard the low buzz as his phone rang. He glanced at the screen of his phone, dropping his arm at the same time. 'Sorry. I didn't realise the time, I don't want to leave you feeling anxious—'

'No problem,' she mustered a smile. 'I'm okay,' but she wasn't. She didn't want him to go, she didn't want to walk away and not know when she was going to see him again, and just like a blinding light coming on, the realisation quite shocked her. This had to stop. 'And anyway,' she said, 'we've pretty much done all we can here, haven't we?'

He glanced at the time on the face of his phone. 'Well, another half hour will be okay—'

'That's not what I meant,' she said. 'Neil?' She caught his arm to make him stop. To listen to her. It was out before she could stop herself. 'Do you mind?' she asked bluntly.

'Mind?' he dropped his empty cup of coffee into a bin. 'Mind what?'

'That you're not back together?'

'I don't discuss it,' he said sharply.

'Okay,' she said. 'I'll take that as a yes. Oh stop it,' she said before she could stop herself. 'You're certainly not behaving like someone who doesn't give a damn. Look how you jump when the phone goes.'

'It's not as easy as you think,' he said. 'Nothing ever is. I try not to talk about it.'

'You talked to me the other day,' she pointed out. 'You said it was helpful.'

'But the other day,' he said staring away from her, 'you were a stranger. Today you're not.' Almost absently he kicked a nearby bench. 'Are you?'

A weird sensation gripped her. One she wouldn't like to put a name to, instinct, self-preservation, avoiding hurt, whatever it was, she knew it was not a feeling she was used to, that it was probably one best avoided. She wished she'd never said anything, but it was too late for that.

'No,' she tried to make her voice sound level, normal. 'No. But nor are you – I mean, I hope – what I'm trying to say—'

'Is that this isn't straightforward anymore is it?' he finished for her.

They both looked in opposite directions. People skirted round them, beginning to bring their days to a close, ushering children home for tea. Couples walked more quickly past them finding the icy wind not so easy to deal with as it grew dark.

'Neil?'

She swallowed hard. She should have seen this coming. 'I *am* grateful to you, for all this – you know – this support,' she began. 'You know that. And you didn't have to.'

'I know.' He sounded surprisingly calm. More resigned. 'But I rarely do anything that I don't want to. You know that.'

'You have your own life to deal with,' she stumbled on, 'and – I hate to admit this – but we both know this is going nowhere.'

'You're referring,' he said, 'to finding Gisela I assume?'

'Of course,' she said. 'Gisela. Of course.'

She felt her face flush. 'Look, your – thing – with Sylvia. That's your affair. Nothing to do with me. Of course it isn't. I had no right to talk like that.'

She tried to smile. 'You once said I don't think things through. And I don't. Big time, this time. And big foot in it to boot,' she tried to joke. 'I'm sorry.'

He shook his head. 'Harriet, it's not easy. None of this is. I wasn't expecting something like this – please, believe me, if I could have done this some other way – but you can't just walk away from something just because you might be distracted—'

'Hey,' she stopped him, deliberately misunderstanding him. 'You teach maths, you don't run MI5. I'm not saying you wouldn't be good at it, but I think you'd want more of a challenge in life, than just finding missing people.'

He watched her in silence. She ploughed on. The urgent need to just clarify that wires weren't being crossed, or the kind of boundaries that new friend-ships, relationships, or whatever this was called, this *closeness* – she could see now – this very rapid and very unwise *so unwise*, closeness, were not confused with something else. 'If,' she clutched her cup, 'she's in Berlin, Germany even – we'll never find her. We both know that. Oddly,' she raced on as he remained silent, 'just like Elena, in a way. Not wanting to be in touch with that family. If that was the case. Which I don't believe, so perhaps not like Gisela. Oh God, sorry. Rambling on. So,' she took a deep breath, 'I think this isn't going to happen. Finding her. She is – I mean was – my last hope and besides, it's time I went home. Got on with my life and let everyone – Bebe, Martha – you – get on with yours. I've intruded on you all for long enough.'

There was a long silence. Harriet made a big fuss of checking what was going on around her. An eerie glow enveloped the walks and paths; the exodus from the park had long started.

'When will you go?' he asked.

'Day after tomorrow. Late night flight. Cheaper,' she explained. 'There isn't a seat until then. I'll text Lizzie or James. Let them know I'm coming back. Golly,' she gave an over-bright smile. She knew she was gabbling but she couldn't stop. 'To be honest, I might go straight to Madrid to see my parents.'

Of course she wouldn't. She knew she wouldn't. She just had to keep talking. Not make it sound like there was no plan to guide her when she got back. No-one to team up with. At all costs she must not sound dependent, pathetic.

'Midweek,' she went on, sounding stronger. 'A cheap ticket.'

Stop it, she inwardly screamed. She'd already said that. Going on about being penniless, like some daft student. What is the matter with you? Aloud she said, 'I might surprise them. They'll be back from the States in the morning. And I have so many pictures of my new niece on my phone, Amelie she's going to be called. Did I tell you—?'

His phone rang again. He glanced blankly at the screen, half-turned away. She didn't have to be told who it was. The way he stiffened like that.

For a moment she waited, trying not to listen to the exchange; the shorthand that only a couple on intimate terms develop.

'There's stuff in the fridge. No. The other kind. I asked. They don't seem to have any here. I'll bring something in. No. I'm going past there.'

Then she did the polite thing, the only thing. Not wanting to know what was in the bloody fridge, or what it was he was going to bring in, she pulled her bag more firmly over her shoulder, waved her phone in front of him, tapped the face and mouthed, 'I'll call.'

He simply nodded. His face looked strained. She blew an airy kiss, as though he were nothing more than a friend, one she might see again tomorrow or in a month, or even longer but not notice how the time had gone when they met up again, and walked steadily away.

Chapter Eighteen

She reached the corner of the park without a moment's awareness of how she'd got there. She pressed through the crowds as she walked towards the bus stop that would take her back to Bebe, and another evening listening to embattled mothers trying to persuade disturbed children to go to sleep. An evening of rows erupting between traumatised women, as they fought for space in a kitchen that had long ago abandoned all pretence that it was fit for purpose, and always, at least one enraged, usually drunken man, swearing at an Olympic level and banging on the door.

The bus dropped Harriet near the corner of her street. She turned to walk back to the top of the dimly lit road that led to the place she'd called home for the last three weeks. *Home*, for God's sake? Was she quite insane? Then she knew that for now, for the next hour, she couldn't face it a moment longer. Not just then.

From the corner, she glanced down the narrow road towards the dismal entrance, the street almost empty, a couple locked in a doorway, a lone woman on her mobile, looking both ways. A car drew level with the woman, paused and then turned into the main road. Abruptly, Harriet turned and walked back the way she'd come.

She longed for James or Lizzie – or indeed anyone really – to be waiting just round the next corner, in a cosy bar, a bustling restaurant, to gossip with, to find comfort with, and even though she'd ramped up her sense of awareness of the perils waiting in such an area for a lone woman, a woman such as herself, she refused to be fearful of going any further than the corner on her own. She strode on, texting first Lizzie and then James as she walked.

Back latest Monday. Dinner?

If not, action will be taken, came Lizzie's instant reply. She must walk round with her phone in her hand, Harriet thought.

As long as it involves a large bottle of red, do your worst, she texted back.

How was Pforzheim? James replied. Harriet winced. *Stay here? Drive you back to yours in the morning?*

Great, she texted back.

She felt better. A text from her mother, just arriving in Madrid, attaching even more images of the wondrous Amelie, made her smile.

Can't wait to see the real thing. Def Seb's eyes and Dad's chin. A real Flynn. Love to Dad, she texted back. Then texted Seb to admire his new daughter. So normal, so part of their lives, such a sham.

When she got back, she decided, she'd tell her family – or even better, as she'd wildly suggested to Neil, why not find the money for a flying trip to Madrid? – and *there* she would tell them the truth. But for now, why alarm them? The arrival of her mother in Berlin within hours was a real, and frankly unnerving, possibility. Lovely in other circumstances but right now – just until she knew she could be relied on not to burst into tears in front of her – to be avoided.

Normality. It beckoned invitingly, reassuringly, only two days away. Away from this lunacy. She started to grow impatient to be gone.

It wasn't quite six o'clock. She'd find, she decided, somewhere to get a pizza or something. Buy an English paper, read while she ate. Stop thinking, put a brake on this tiresome feeling that had been bothering her for a couple of days – she could hardly bring herself to believe she was even now identifying it – as envy. Envy of a woman she'd never met. She had no idea what she was like – well apart from what she'd seen on her website, of course. Even the memory of how casually she had pretended the search for Sylvia Littleton had been almost accidental, now made her feel ridiculous. The red hair, tumbling over one shoulder, had been little short of amazing, and the wide, friendly, engaging smile. But neither of these revelations was anything compared to the catalogue of achievements, that had pushed the artist's standing in the art world from well-thought-of, admired even, to teetering on the brink of celebrity. Harriet had never heard of her.

Quite clearly the rest of the world – or at least the art world – had. Awards, medals seemed to settle upon her with an ease that had to be rooted in talent. That this gifted woman was important to the man Harriet had left behind in the park, was never in doubt. All this envy, she decided, was because she wished she was as important as Sylvia was, to someone as – well – as nice as he was.

'*Singles Bar Neueröffnung?*'

A young man with a stack of leaflets thrust one in her direction and smiled encouragingly at her. His companion danced in front of her, making her dodge round him.

'A what?' She stared at the glossy leaflet. 'Singles bar? Are you deranged? No-one goes to them anymore. Have you never heard of *Tinder?*' She thrust the leaflet back at him. 'And frankly, it sounds like the eighth circle of hell. Out of my way.'

'*Englisch,*' the man stared after her, turning to his astonished companion. '*Thatcher ist schuld.*'

'Blame who you like,' she muttered striding on. 'I'm going home.'

Lonely, she argued, as indeed she had done now for days, that's all she was. A bit depressed, and why not after all she'd been through? But she had taken a dislike to her, this Sylvia, tipped to win Artist of the Year and a prestigious award worth a six-figure sum for something or other, because of this man – this kind, nice man, not particularly good-looking in a conventional way. Tall and probably too thin, but that might be stress, she decided, ignoring the obvious fact that until three weeks before, she had never laid eyes on him, so how could she tell? But with the nicest smile, the gentlest eyes that made you want to be liked by him.

This man, this unnervingly perceptive, clever man, had appeared out of nowhere and somehow made her feel she wasn't a raving lunatic on a mission to madness, had befriended her when she had sod all going for her, her hair a tangled mess, her weight loss leaving her cheeks hollow, never wearing anything more glamorous than jeans and sweaters, a man who didn't deserve to be treated like someone you could just drop when some random – as she decided had most certainly been the case with Sylvia's lover – third party pitched up to distract you.

Dear God. She almost stopped. What was she going on about?

She began to walk, searching for any café that looked crowded enough not to attract unwelcome attention, trying not to notice laughing groups of people compounding her loneliness by piling into bars before the evening really took off elsewhere.

Occasionally she stopped, looked around, frowned, suddenly uneasy and not as brave as she thought, until she was forced to acknowledge that her face was frozen, her feet not far behind and she was tired, *so* tired, and there was nothing on this long, glaringly bright street worth any of this. And she knew, absolutely *knew* that for the last ten minutes she had been followed.

She began to walk quickly, crossing the street, glancing behind, trying to see through a small knot of people behind her if her pursuer had given up. When she reached the other side, she began to run towards a tram station, the now familiar yellow carriages heading down the centre of the road to the narrow platform with the lit-up destination screen, a handful of people waiting to board. But a stream of traffic either side stopped her, and in that second a hand gripped her arm, propelling her backwards.

'Get away from me,' Harriet shrieked. Oh God, her brain whirled frantically, not again? She tried to pull away. At first she thought it was a particularly slender young man, a pickpocket, but in the same breath under the harsh yellow light of the streetlamps, she realised it was a woman. A hollow-eyed woman, her black hair cut severely short, almost like a brush; her face wore the haunted look of someone who lived on their wits, and sparingly at that. Astonishingly her English was, if not good, at least good enough to make herself understood.

'Please, one minute,' the woman said. Her grip tightened. She pushed Harriet back onto the pavement. A few passers-by glanced at them; no-one intervened. In the recesses of her brain, Harriet knew she should scream and go on screaming until someone helped her, but the suddenness of the whole thing silenced her.

'My sister,' the woman said, her grip tightening. 'At Der Hafen. Klara. She tell me to tell you. I follow you from the corner.'

'Klara?' Harriet stopped struggling. 'What about Klara? For Christ's sake let go of my arm.'

The woman let her hand drop.

'You look for Gisela? *Ja*? I can help you. Please just listen.'

*

Standing in the shelter of a doorway, the lights of trams rumbling past, having to shout over the noise to make themselves heard, the deal was struck. At least, Harriet agreed to what Lottie, Klara's sister, suggested, with no idea of whether she could do anything at all to bring it about.

'Her husband,' Lottie said, lighting a cigarette. She exhaled a cloud of smoke out of the corner of her mouth into the street. 'He is madman. Drugs, you understand? He now tries to get custody of the children to force her into coming back. She is very afraid of him but she would suffer anything for her children.'

'Why would she be made to go back?' Harriet shouted in return. 'She was beaten. Her little boy was traumatised. Still is. He saw the whole thing. Surely no-one would take her children away?'

'Because,' Lottie leaned forward, shouting into Harriet's ear. 'Klara does not have the best record. She was – you know—' she gave a little balancing act with her hand. 'A little loose.'

'Loose?'

Lottie looked anxiously around. 'Come,' she beckoned. 'Round the corner. Quieter.'

Harriet looked past Lottie to where she was pointing. The side road was lit well enough, but it was out of the mainstream. She was learning fast. 'No,' she shook her head. 'We're okay here. No-one knows what we're talking about.'

Lottie shrugged. 'She take things,' she began. 'Not big. Food for the children. Clothes. Once it was a jacket for herself. She has twice been cautioned, but for the children's sake let go. Next time,' she twisted her hand around like someone turning a lock. 'She will be taken away.'

'You must understand,' she urged Harriet. She tried to clasp her arm again but Harriet stepped back. 'She was on her own, he had vanished. And then he come back and he said he would change, but the beatings started again. And now she is frightened because she has a record, and he hasn't. He says she got the bruises when she threw herself down the stairs, that she is mad. That his children would be in danger left with her.'

'What about your family?' Harriet asked appalled. 'You? Couldn't you help?'

'What can I do?' Lottie said fiercely. 'I have no money, I get jobs as a waitress, maid in the hotel, you understand, or in the kitchen, but no-one will employ me without a home. So, no money. Klara and I have been in care since we are this big.' She placed her hand low to the ground.

'So last time I tell her, wait till morning, I come when he is out. A friend let me use his car, but I cannot think of anywhere to take them. He knows where I live – he would have come. Then I remember Bebe, I help a friend go there one time. So I take them there. And now he's started court proceedings and she is desperate.'

'Will he get them?'

Lottie shook her head. 'I don't know. But he's managed to rent an apartment with a terrace opposite a park – oh the way these people who control our lives place such things above common sense. A park? But no mother? Is that sane? He works at race tracks on and off, but a couple of months ago, some friend help him get a job, a respectable one, consultant to some company or other. Such a joke. But it is big fraud. If she have no home, and is a known shop lifter,' she shrugged, 'he will win. What hope is there?'

'And what do you want me to do?'

Lottie ground out the cigarette. 'Ask Martha,' she said bluntly. 'To take her case.'

'But surely Bebe is the person to ask?'

'Klara did. But she say no. Martha can only take cases if there is money in the fund. And the fund is empty. Bebe won't have Martha bothered. She said Martha teach her. Only fight battles you can win.'

'So how can me asking her change that?'

'Because you need my help,' she said bluntly. 'Bebe doesn't. You will try harder.'

'Martha owes me nothing,' Harriet said equally bluntly. 'Quite the reverse. And she can't conjure up money where there is none.'

Lottie looked her up and down. Shrugged. 'Then we say goodbye,' she turned and started to walk away, taking with her Harriet's last, very slender, hope of finding Gisela.

Harriet watched her go, looking both ways before she crossed the street. Not once did Lottie turn. She couldn't let her go. She began to run after her, ducking through knots of people, a half-glance as she dodged traffic to cross the street. Horns blared, a tram halted her progress; she willed it to go faster as it rattled past. When it did, she saw Lottie already at the tram stand. She sprinted towards it and grabbed Lottie's arm.

'If I agree to talk to Martha, you will tell me where Gisela is?' she panted.

'Not quite,' Lottie said, as a tram approached. 'When Martha say yes. Then I tell you where to find someone who probably knows where Gisela is.'

'Who?'

'Her mother.'

The tram was shuddering to halt. 'But if your contact turns out not to know where Gisela's mother is, or has never heard of her, then I will call Martha off. Okay?'

Lottie jiggled a pack of cigarettes in her hand. A gentle surge pushed Harriet along with the queue.

'Okay,' Lottie said. 'I meet you tomorrow with her address. I give my number. Put it in your phone. Call when you get Martha's reply.'

Harriet stabbed it in as Lottie recited it, her fingers all over the place.

'Wait a minute,' Harriet called as Lottie began to board. 'Where shall I meet you?'

'That wine bar,' Lottie called back. 'Over there.'

Harriet turned to see where she meant. 'Okay,' she turned back, but the tram had already moved away.

*

It wasn't until much later, when Harriet had almost given up hope of hearing from her, that Martha called. From her car, Martha's voice left no doubt that this conversation was being squeezed into a day that had apparently segued effortlessly from a breakfast meeting at the Adlon, to a day in court, to drinks with a new client and then, if it went as planned, dinner to seal the deal.

'So,' Martha said, and Harriet couldn't tell if she was joking or serious, 'you're on the clock. Ready? Go.'

Harriet felt grateful. Even if she was joking, she knew Martha had made an effort to fit her in. She also knew, even as she spoke, that she was not being at all convincing. She managed to make her encounter with Lottie sound like the ramblings of a woman who'd slept on the streets for longer than was good for her.

Twice, Martha interrupted her to clarify a point; several times Harriet corrected herself, knowing if James or Lizzie could have heard her, they would have flatly refused to believe they were listening to the girl they knew. But then, James and Lizzie had never known her to be this exhausted, confused and struggling in a world that was as alien to her, as a day without a fight with William, was to James.

'Look,' Harriet finished. 'The deal isn't that you *have* to take Klara's case.'

'How generous,' Martha replied with heavy sarcasm.

'No, no. I don't mean it like that,' Harriet protested. 'I meant I haven't promised Lottie anything, truly I haven't, I wouldn't dream of it. Besides, you owe me nothing, so even if I wanted you to help, I wouldn't ask. I'm *so* aware of that. So I said it had to be on the basis that at *most* you might agree just to talk to her—'

'Harriet?' Martha interrupted her. 'Stop. No . . . stop. I know this is important to you, but you do realise that the chances of this leading to anything are pretty much zero? And bloody risky too?'

'I know. Lottie told me. But what would you do? This is the first break I've had. And,' she didn't hesitate to lie, 'don't worry, I won't go alone.'

'Is Neil going? I thought Syl—' Martha stopped. 'Sorry, I mean he never said.'

'Well that's because he doesn't know,' Harriet said quickly. 'He's done enough. You both have. And – and he's got his own problems. Pretty complicated ones too, by the sound of it. I mean I don't know all the ins and outs of it, but fixing a relationship is hard work. I've been there.'

'You must give me lessons sometime,' Martha said dryly. 'He won't listen to me. Just says he can fix it himself, won't give up until the final credits roll and even then, I'm not entirely sure he'd think that was the end.'

'Is it?' she asked, unable to resist.

'Who knows? But this time it seems to be different.'

'In what way?' Even to her ears, the question sounded anxious and not indifferent, as she had wanted.

'They had a life together, a house together, friends, the whole deal. Hard for anyone to walk away from. And you have to remember he was blindsided; he loved her. And even after all she's done, I think no-one can know for sure how he feels. To be honest, I'm quite grateful to you. Taking his mind off it all.'

'Not a problem,' Harriet said politely. 'I hope he hasn't been too bored?'

'Bored? God no. Quite the reverse. He said the other night, that for the last few months, he'd felt he was going round the bend. But then you pitched up and he realised you were too, so at least he had someone to go round it with him.'

'Did he?' Harriet said stonily. 'Glad to be of use.'

'Now,' Martha said briskly. 'Two problems with this. One: for the foreseeable, I have a schedule that makes the UN look idle. Two: I don't think the board will buy it. Oh, because they'd rather the charity I help out is more saleable – wildlife? You betcha. Sport? Now you're talking. Battered women? Ach . . . not so much. And remember, we've used up all the money for this year. The well is dry. Listen, I'll get back to you. Don't get your hopes up. Okay?'

'No wait,' Harriet cried. 'If that's a real issue – the money I mean – I promise I'll try and raise something. I've got some stuff I can sell when I get back and—'

'Well, that's a first,' Martha laughed. 'Let me know how that goes. You might just have to.'

It was some time after she'd hung up, that Harriet realised Martha's concern had been only that she was on a fool's errand, and she didn't seem to have a great deal of interest in Klara. She didn't know whether to be heartened by this or depressed, so by the time Martha finally called, nearly an hour later, Harriet had almost chewed through her fist with anxiety. The fact that Neil thought she was halfway round the twist hadn't helped one bit.

'So,' Martha said, without preamble, when Harriet answered. 'Sorry to have been so long. Not exactly what you want, but better than nothing. Now, what's this Lottie's number?'

*

Lottie was standing outside the wine bar, a curl of smoke rising above her. In daylight, she looked less haunted, but her habit of constantly looking around and hunching her shoulders lent her the air of a fugitive. The sort of slouch that, far from deflecting trouble, invited scrutiny. Harriet wondered why she wouldn't just walk and talk like a normal person, rather than someone out of a low-grade, cheap-budget crime movie.

'By the way,' Lottie said, without sounding in any way worried about it at all. 'Klara is disappointed. I tell her it won't be Martha herself who will handle this, but she send someone who was available. I said you'd explain.'

'Thanks a bunch,' Harriet muttered. Personally, she thought, far from it being a misfortune that she wasn't getting the top player on the case, Klara was bloody lucky to have any help at all.

'And Bebe?'

Lottie grinned. 'I do not have the word in English. But it is not one that means she is happy. But you also explain to her.'

Harriet thought at this rate, she would have no teeth at all if she gritted them any further.

'And the address?' She was anxious to be gone, but Lottie's suspicion of the entire world extended to refusing to text anything that might incriminate her.

'And you go in daylight,' she warned, waiting while Harriet put the address into her phone. Somewhere in Neukölln. 'And come back before dark.'

'That bad?' Harriet felt a tingle of fright go through her.

'It can be. Not such a great area. Not like this.'

Harriet glanced quickly around. Not as good as this? Grief.

'It's a dumping ground,' Lottie said flatly. 'People from everywhere, other countries with nowhere else to live. I moved out a few weeks ago. The guy next door had a gun. Not the only one either. But next door? No thanks. And he wasn't afraid to use it. Not exactly the Hollywood Hills.' She gave a crooked smile. 'I'd offer to come with you, but I have to keep out of trouble. You understand?'

Harriet paused. She wasn't sure she bought into the air of violence that Lottie so luridly painted. She said nothing, pretty sure it was one of the areas that Bebe had told her she would love to live in, awash with musicians, and artists, cafés and galleries as it was. A place where, these days, only those plump in their pockets and after a hip address, could afford. And that was not Bebe.

A wave of uncertainty came over her. 'Lottie?' She tried to read the expression on the other girl's face. 'Gisela *is* living with her mother, isn't she?'

It was already ten o'clock.

'I have no idea,' Lottie ground out her cigarette with her boot.

'Hang on,' Harriet cried, trying to grab her arm. 'You said—'

'I said I knew where her mother is,' Lottie removed her hand. 'I never said Gisela.' With that, she moved swiftly away into the crowd and disappeared. Harriet cursed under her breath. This street life was not for gently reared girls from London, she told herself grimly.

Alone on the pavement, she took a deep breath and headed for the U-Bahn that would take her to the outer suburbs of Berlin where, she hoped, Gisela's mother would be waiting – along with the end of her journey, in more ways than one – and that this woman would have some idea if her daughter was alive or dead. Or living on another planet.

There should be training courses, she muttered to herself, where you learn who to trust, interpret what they're saying and learn to stop and think before you rush headlong into trouble. And this, she thought as she glanced at the address, was probably trouble, and more than likely on a grand scale.

Chapter Nineteen

When the phone went, Harriet was dodging through the crowded pavement, heading towards the station, and was inclined to let it go to voicemail. After all, (she glanced at the screen), he'd thought she was going home, made no effort to stop her and now she knew he thought she was halfway round the bend, which didn't act in his favour. But honesty won. She knew she wanted to hear what he had to say.

'You've done so much,' she turned away and stood in the doorway of a shop selling t-shirts with works of art airbrushed onto them. A sign said they were ten euros each or one hundred for immediate printing. 'I had to act quickly and I didn't mean to make you feel obliged, or upset or—'

'I'm not,' Neil interrupted, 'any of those. Of course, I'd rather have heard from you what was going on than Martha. She called to see what I thought. I just wonder, only a thought of course, if you're now deranged as well as being an expert in shooting from the hip?'

Harriet clutched her phone. 'Well that's what people who are halfway round the twist do, isn't it?' she shot back. 'Neil I appreciate the call, but I have to get the train. I have to be back before—' she almost said 'dark', but she knew that would be an admission that she was scared. Not, she knew, of being alone or lost in unfamiliar streets, but that it would all come to nothing, so she finished lamely, 'Before Bebe locks up.'

Somewhere in the recess of her brain, she knew she sounded ridiculous.

She was thirty-two for God's sake. Not a child. She swallowed. 'Neil? I *have* to do this. I have to go.'

'Where?'

She checked the address again. 'Neukölln,' she said omitting the rest. 'And then a bus. So you see, it's a bit of a hike and I must go now. I don't want to be trudging over there when it's dark, I mean, only because it might make it more difficult to find.'

'And on your own? You know the area?'

'Well, no of course not. But I'm becoming an old hand at Berlin,' she lied. 'Practically a native now. It can't be that hard. Oh and good luck with all the Sylvia stuff. I hope it works out. Must dash. I'll text when I'm back in London.'

She hung up the phone before he could reply.

'Now,' she muttered disappearing into the S-Bahn and the train that would take her to this address. According to her map, it was not that far out of the centre, past a strange parade of names and places, until she got to Neukölln. After that, she needed a bus. A bus? She stuffed her phone in her pocket. She'd sort that out when she got there.

'First,' she muttered, peering at a timetable on the concourse of the station. 'Finding the right platform would be a help. And where to get off for a start.'

As it turned out, it took her two changes and a missed stop, and the realisation when the train pulled into somewhere called Hermannplatz, that she was on the wrong train and needed that one on the pale blue line instead, and leapt off. But she got there.

*

The entrance to the station, when she eventually emerged onto a rumbling, noisy road, seemed, in anyone's language, boring rather than threatening. But she still found comfort in evidence up and down the street, that this was a melting pot of identities and no worse or better than where she lived in London and if so, how bad could it be? Lottie had exaggerated. At least it was dry and light and although it was threatening to snow, it wasn't doing so yet.

'Hey,' a voice called. 'I'm over here.'

She turned, slowly.

Neil was waiting by an iron stand where some passengers had left their bikes. A bus, slowing to stop with a screech of brakes, prevented her from replying.

'Stop being such a hero,' he called. 'Oh God. What now?'

'Nothing,' she said. 'I don't know what you're doing here, I didn't invite you, and surely you should be at work?'

'Even more boring. Please. My car's on the next block and probably without all its wheels by now. And we haven't got all day. Okay,' he stopped, seeing she wasn't moving. 'If you must know, I gave a tutorial at nine this morning and another at ten, so it was a bit of a dash, and I've another at five, but if you think I would just let you waltz off on your own, you really are insane, Harriet.'

She waited.

'I wish things were different.'

A shop on the other side of the concourse, selling electrical sockets, suddenly seemed fascinating.

'You mean that I wasn't this flake you'd got caught up with?'

'Flake? What on earth are you talking about?'

She clutched her bag to her chest. This was loyalty time, to Martha. 'No reason,' she decided was the safest answer. 'I just get that impression.'

Neil shifted his weight from the bicycle stand where he had been leaning and briefly inspected her. 'Ah,' he said. 'And would this have anything to do with Martha?'

'God no,' she forced surprise. 'What on earth makes you say that? What a weird thing to say.'

'So that's a yes?' he said.

She leaned one hand on the iron railings, staring straight ahead.

'It may,' she said, with as much frostiness as she could muster, 'come as a complete shock to you, but sometimes I just figure these things out for myself. I can do that, you know, in spite of not getting a handle on the bloody U-Bahn, or what that man Russell's problem was, the one you were banging on about the other day.

'Paradox?' he supplied helpfully. 'Russell's Paradox.'

'Yes, and that other one you thought your students should have known about and didn't – you know the one?' She clicked her fingers to help her memory. 'To do with prime numbers?'

'Euclid?'

'Exactly.'

'And your point would be?'

'That I don't have to be a maths wizard to get through life or look after myself. And so far I haven't been regarded as someone who is a complete ditz. Crackers, I grant you. At times. But that's all.'

He said nothing, just frowned at his shoes.

'Got it,' he said looking up. 'What I said – to Martha. That's it, isn't it? I think I said you had enough problems to send you round the bend and as I had a fair amount too, we might as well go round the bend together.'

'Ah,' Harriet said. Not quite the same. But even so.

She blew her cheeks out. She must stop overreacting. Use all that energy, that had kept her awake half the night tossing ideas around and quickly discarding them, on how to keep Neil in her life, but at arm's distance while he remained married. 'That,' she smiled, 'would explain it.'

'For a lawyer,' he said mildly, 'Martha doesn't always choose her words as carefully as she might. Actually,' he frowned, 'it never occurred to me that someone as smart and clever as you would put that spin on it.'

Inexplicably, an image of her and Dermot flashed into her head. On their very first date, she in a sliver of a dress that had been bought expensively and hurriedly that morning, her hair tumbling round her shoulders, him telling her across a table –an achingly stylish restaurant in Mayfair, where she knew the idea of a random booking at such short notice was out of the question, unless you could pull a few strings – that she was fun, delightful company but apt to think something had been said when it hadn't. In a matter of days, she'd mistaken his pursuit of her for a man wanting more commitment to this relationship, and not the womaniser he turned out to be, and she had managed, oh how easily she had managed, to mistake a dazzlingly good-looking man's practised flirting, for love.

'Look, make a fresh start. Move. Really get on with it and move,' Lizzie had urged, sitting in Harriet's flat – well, more a room with a loo as she had called it – over a betting shop in Lewisham. Dermot's defection had been picked over, mulled over, shouted over and, in Lizzie's view, gone on for far too long. 'You've been in this dump for a good six months.'

'Eight,' Harriet corrected.

'Even worse,' Lizzie said. 'But for your own sake and,' she muttered, 'mine as well, *do* something. You're making me feel terrible for moving out and leaving you—'

'No,' Harriet had wailed. 'Stop it. I agreed. I'm happy for you. Oh God, I am a total mess.'

Weeks of Harriet staring stonily into the distance had morphed Lizzie's feelings from total solidarity at the sheer callousness of Dermot's behaviour, into impatience that Harriet would not move on. Lizzie sat back helplessly into the only other armchair and watched Harriet stare fixedly into the distance.

But Harriet was too swamped in the misery of pointlessly switching between visions of a sobbing reunion – usually with Dermot begging her to come back – to dreaming of the number of ways she could inflict equal misery on such a man instead. So the chance of finding time to consider doing something that would make, if not her own, but at least Lizzie's life a lot easier – like moving for a start – had, at that moment, been out of the question.

They had been sitting in Harriet's studio flat, where she had moved when Lizzie had decamped to Shoreditch. Its only redeeming feature was that the tops of trees outside framed the windows and hid the ugly block of flats across the street.

'It will help, honestly it will.' Lizzie sloshed some white wine into one of two glasses, and pushed it at Harriet, curled up in an armchair facing the window. 'Go out with someone else. I know, let's do some swiping. Can't harm can it?'

'The only thing that will help,' Harriet took the glass, knocked back a mouthful and said viciously, 'is if he falls over a cliff, taking that airhead with him. And I'm not going online. Don't even suggest it.'

Lizzie opened her mouth and shut it again. Harriet had put up with far worse from her. Indeed she cringed at the fallout from a litany of car-crash relationships she had poured out to Harriet, who'd listened so patiently when no-one else would, the jobs that were all wrong, or never materialised, the endless nights spent setting up her company so that she now had a healthy, if not exactly flourishing, ceramics and pottery business. Even the name, *The Real McCoy,* had been Harriet's idea.

This time it was different. This time, Harriet was on an iffy street in another country and here was this decent man, not trying to complicate her life, not looking for diversion, but not wanting to abandon her either. When it came down to it, it was simple. He was saving his marriage, she was going home. And that was it. For crying out loud, woman, she ordered herself, quelling another voice that said she didn't actually like this conclusion, keep this in perspective.

'Sorry,' she turned to him. 'Not much sleep, and Bebe is not thrilled to bits with me. For going over her head to Martha. So,' she asked. 'How's that going? You know,' she gave a self-conscious smile, 'the whole round the bend thing?'

'You mean Sylvia?'

She nodded. 'I mean, it's none of my business . . .' she began, but he shook his head to stop her.

'Getting there,' he said, and then added: 'I think. Anyway, I'm in Paris at the weekend. Conference. I thought away from work and – well – everything else, it might be easier for me – I mean us – to think clearly.'

'Lucky Sylvia,' Harriet managed.

'Paris isn't her favourite city,' Neil added. 'So we'll see. Listen,' he abruptly changed the subject. He stamped his feet up and down. 'Could we go now? If this address is right, it's at least a twenty minute drive, my feet feel like ice, it's started to snow and I'll probably get frostbite. And then you'll be sorry.'

'Probably,' she agreed.

Paris, she muttered inwardly, following him from the station concourse. Not her favourite? What did it matter what city she liked or hated, if she was with someone she cared about? Was Sylvia completely stupid?

*

This address wasn't, she had long realised as they left the centre, even in Neukölln. That was miles back.

'Displaced,' Neil had said, as she peered fearfully through the windscreen, while he parked the car at the address Lottie had given her. 'People who lived in the centre in social housing, forced out by developers, and their homes rented out to those who can afford the ludicrous rents. Those who can't cut it end up in places like this. Quite scandalous but it's called progress. And when Bebe says she would like to move to Neukölln, she doesn't mean here, that's for sure. Okay,' he leaned round to see her face. 'Let's go. Or,' he added in a hopeful voice, 'shall we go back?'

'No,' she said more stoutly than she felt. 'Of course not.'

He gave a deep sigh. 'That's what I was afraid of.'

*

The corridor on the third floor, that wrapped itself round the inside of the tenement block, was like an arctic tunnel. Icy blasts gusted through the dismal cement blocks of the deserted, soulless building, the destination of those who had once hoped for a better life – and still believed it might be out there somewhere – and those who had never had one in the first place.

Harriet peered nervously along the corridor's length. Ten apartments to each floor, and on the first two, they had drawn not just blanks, but threats and suspicion – at lunchtime, in broad daylight. Abuse on a scale that she was fairly certain would, if compared, elevate the most explicitly rated movie to family entertainment.

'I don't think this is a good idea,' she whispered to Neil, just ahead of her as they rounded the top of the stairwell. The lift, without a word being exchanged, and just one glance between them, had been abandoned. Just in case. She plucked at his arm.

'Of course it isn't,' he muttered. 'It's a terrible one. Got anything better?'

'You know I haven't,' she whispered back. They stood close, their backs to the wall, eyeing the swing doors that led to the next corridor. 'What if Lottie's got it wrong? What if Gisela's mother isn't here? What if that girl was lying? What if we get attacked?'

'What if you try not to be so depressing?' he hissed back.

'Sorry,' she said. 'But that's two whole floors and not a clue. Neil? Do you think your car will be all right?' She tried to see out over the parapet across the bleak landscape of this housing estate, on the farthest edge of Berlin, down to the street level where they'd left his car. Now, through the swirling snow, she could just about make out a string of apartment blocks stretching to the left, a solid block of concrete in front and no sign of anything to relieve it. And she had thought Der Hafen was grim.

'Jeez,' he muttered. 'You are *weird*. *We've* got more chance of being done over, never mind the bloody car.'

'Oh dear God,' Harriet grabbed his arm and instantly made for the stairwell. 'C'mon. Let's get out of here. I can't risk this anymore. You might get hurt—'

'For God's sake,' he said grabbing her back. 'This isn't my idea of how to spend an afternoon off either, but we're here, we might as well try. God knows, I don't think you're going to get much out of this, but at least you'll know you didn't walk away. And I think you know you couldn't live with that if you did. Could you?'

'No, but I didn't realise how awful it would be.' She glanced at the graffiti-strewn walls, the stale smell of God knows what making her pull her scarf over her nose.

'No. Nor me. He removed his glasses and wiped the wet lenses with the corner of her scarf. Their eyes locked. Instinctively she reached for his arm and gripped it.

'Look. The first sign of trouble,' he promised, 'and we'll be out of here. And by that, you do know, don't you, that obviously you let me go first?'

She gave a weak smile.

'C'mon,' he said. 'Cheer up. Only ten apartments to choose from.'

Three doors remained firmly closed, although the sound of a television blared out from one, and a woman's voice raging at some unseen children echoed out from another, but on the fourth attempt, the door opened on a chain.

A woman's thin face peered through. Free of make-up, fading blonde hair with streaks of grey, her expression was one that years of trouble had made naturally suspicious, rather than the specific arrival of two strangers at the door. She pulled the edges of her candlewick dressing gown protectively across her chest.

'Forgive the intrusion,' Neil began in German. 'We're looking for someone. Gisela.'

'Who wants her?' the woman demanded. Harriet leaned forward. At least she hadn't said she wasn't there. Her heart beat against her ribs.

'A friend,' Neil assured her. 'Someone in need of help.'

'What kind of help?'

'To find out why Kurt Weber had her beaten up.'

The door began to close. Harriet had had enough.

'Please,' she said urgently pushing past Neil, sending him staggering backwards. She rammed her bag in the gap so the door couldn't close. She spoke in halting German.

'If she doesn't speak to me, I will – I will – oh God,' she staggered on. 'What's the word?'

'Tell Kurt where she is?' Neil finished for her.

'Please no,' the woman begged. 'She moved. A year ago. I don't know where.' She glanced along the corridor, where a shabbily dressed man was just emerging from the lift. 'Please. Leave her alone. Leave me alone. I can't help.'

'Do you at least want to know if we find her?' Neil asked. 'Because we're going to keep trying. I just thought, being her mother, you must be anxious.'

'No. Don't come here again. I mean,' she amended in a fluster, 'when she wants to get in touch with me she will. Now please go.'

Neil stood aside to let the stranger pass, but instead he stopped.

'*Kann ich ihnen helfen?*' the man asked, standing squarely in front of Gisela's mother. '*Was wünschen Sie?*'

'No,' Neil smiled. 'Fine thank you. No help needed. We've got the wrong address.'

The man glanced at the woman, who was almost paralysed in the doorway.

'Okay, Maria?' His voice was kind, concerned. Nothing more than a nice neighbour.

'Ja, ja,' Gisela's mother sounded panicked. 'Wrong address. Try the next floor.'

The door slammed, the man shuffled on and let himself into the flat next door. Neil began talking loudly in German about how confusing these flats could be.

'It must be the next block,' he said taking her arm. Harriet said nothing and they walked away, trying not to run.

'That's that then,' Harriet said glumly as they emerged onto the street. They pushed against the rising wind, across the wide frozen street, now almost obliterated by swirling snowflakes. Neil wrapped his arm round her to steady her. Not wanting to appear a liability, she said it wasn't necessary to give her such support, but he pointed out that since his glasses were once again defeated by snow, he wasn't actually holding her up, more that she was guiding him.

To Harriet's relief, the car was in one piece, all four wheels where they should be, no loose wires betraying that the engine had been tampered with, still where they'd parked it, behind a clump of trees, but now covered in a light layer of snow.

'Now what?' he shouted against the rising wind, as they reached it.

She looked at him across the roof. 'I go home,' she shouted back. 'What else can I do? Any ideas?'

He looked away down the street and then back at her. 'I'm working on it,' he called back. 'Unless, of course, I get pneumonia first—' Suddenly he stopped, and stared over her head.

'What? Neil? What is it?'

He walked around the car, grabbed her arm and pulled her along behind him, back towards the buildings.

'She's just left the apartment. That woman. C'mon.'

'But why? She doesn't know anything?'

'Possibly,' he agreed. 'But she was going nowhere ten minutes ago, and suddenly she's rushing out. Just wonder why.'

Chapter Twenty

'Where's she going?' Harriet yelled over the noise of the traffic, pushing their way through the swirling white flakes. 'Can you see her?'

'I doubt she's going far,' he called back. 'Otherwise she'd have taken a bus.'

Short as she was, the woman, bundled up in a thick jacket and boots, steadily, and surprisingly swiftly, pushed her way through a small press of people, until she reached what looked like a convenience store in the middle of an arcade of mostly neighbourhood stores. At first they thought she would walk straight past but instead she halted, seemed to look both ways – they shrank against the window of a newsagent, their backs to her – then retraced her steps, and without pause pushed open the door of a dingy bar and quickly went in.

'Stay there,' Neil said. 'Let me see how big the place is. Who she's meeting.'

Harriet nodded. Neil stationed himself in the doorway, pretending to answer his phone, casually glancing into the interior. After a while he put his phone away and came back to where Harriet was sheltering in the doorway of a disused shop.

'She's talking to someone behind the bar. A woman. Come and look. But be careful.'

At first she could see nothing, but as the door opened and a couple walked out into the chill afternoon air, she glimpsed the woman; her back to the street, leaning across the bar, talking to a blonde, who was wearing a red sweater, her hair tucked under a gold, loosely knit beanie.

Harriet took a step back. She blinked. She couldn't recall doing so, but she must have gasped.

'What?' Neil whispered urgently. 'What is it?'

'That woman.' She felt breathless. 'That woman. With the beanie hat on. I know her. What in God's name is she doing here?'

She began to make for the door, but the older woman had turned and was leaving. Harriet shrank back against the wall. She heard, rather than saw, the woman come out and turn back the way she'd come, not looking either left or right. Harriet waited mere seconds before she made for the door.

'Wait!' Neil whispered urgently. He tried to stop her but she was gone. 'Harriet,' he called pointlessly. 'Oh God,' he muttered striding after her. 'What now?'

*

Harriet pushed her way through the few crammed-in tables towards the blonde, who was talking rapidly into her phone. The woman gave an audible gasp and snapped it off.

'Go away,' she hissed in English. Her voice was panicked. 'How did you find me? Leave me alone.'

'*You*? You're Gisela aren't you?' Harriet hissed back at her. 'You were in Raglan Parade? Why? What have you got to do with Elena? With Kurt? Why are you hiding from him?'

'I am not hiding,' Gisela whispered fiercely. 'Go, or I call the police.'

'Excuse me,' Neil cut in. He pulled his phone from his pocket. 'If anyone's going to call the police, it's going to be me—'

A long, thin hand snaked out to grab the phone. Neil held it just out of her reach.

'No,' she panted. 'I beg you.'

'Then tell Harriet what she needs to know. It's really terribly simple.'

Gisela eyed him helplessly.

'Not here,' she finally muttered. She moved away and whispered something to the barman. 'I have a room. Above the bar. It will be easier.'

*

Even from her student days, Harriet could not recall anywhere so cheerless, or depressing as the room Gisela led them to, up a narrow staircase above the bar, but a closer look showed that here and there was evidence of a life that had once had finer moments.

A black coat – a silver fox fur trailing from the collar – was slung over an upright chair. Beside it on the floor, a bag that had once, a few years back, been the essential finishing touch for a league of celebrities. Such an accessory not only revealed that its owner possessed a sheep-like obedience to the fashion industry, but also a bank balance so healthy they wouldn't have had to ask the price. And now this? She glanced around the shabby room. How far had this woman fallen?

Close up, the woman who had haunted Raglan Parade for weeks all last summer – an eternity away, Harriet thought – and had aroused little more than faint curiosity, the way she so constantly waylaid Elena for her advice on her collection of cameos, looked ill. A faded glamour clung to her that had not been evident in London. Her skin like tissue paper, too much rouge, a slash of lipstick; all simply emphasised her age rather than disguise it.

'Please, Gisela,' Harriet began carefully. 'You have to tell me. What's going on?'

'How should I know?' Gisela protested.

'Are you saying that,' Harriet asked more calmly, 'because you're frightened he'll beat you again?'

'He never beat me! *Never*,' Gisela insisted. 'It was someone else. A mistake.'

Gisela began to weep. 'He loves me,' she sobbed. 'No-one understands. It was out of love. He does not want to lose me—'

'Oh for God's sake,' Neil muttered. 'Give me strength.'

'Delusion' sprang to Harriet's mind. Followed closely by 'almost certainly mild derangement'. But in Gisela's hands it was no such thing. The exploitation, she claimed, that she had suffered, had been born out of a grand passion. Never abuse. The beatings, an almost natural by-product of a man who, in Gisela's mind, was fearful of losing the love of his life and wouldn't let her get away. Who tried to make her – in alternation with a slap across the face – jealous, by having affairs with other women.

On and on she rambled, justifying in turns her addiction to such a man, and why he was obsessed by her.

She was, she claimed, discovered by a model agency, while working as a waitress. A poor girl from a tenement block, with just her looks to escape from it all. A place where dubbed English television shows, featuring grand houses in days gone by, had become her tutors, her finishing school. The model agency was an establishment that would have been hard-pressed to have enjoyed a meaningful relationship with a teacup, let alone a glossy magazine, but was unrivalled when it came to matching bored, rich, sleazy men with desperate or ambitious girls. Girls who were prepared to laugh at their jokes, hang off their arms, who knew how to behave in every possible way. Girls like Gisela.

But, Gisela insisted, Kurt had not been a client. It had been love at first sight when they met at a weekend house party several years before.

'I was with someone else, but we became,' she claimed, her hand stroking her throat, 'soulmates. We were inseparable, two people who—'

'That's enough,' Neil stopped her. 'Sorry. Very touching, but it doesn't explain why he wanted to ruin Harriet? He most certainly wasn't in love with her.'

'Because Elena was being manipulated,' Gisela cried. 'He was fearful for her.'

'How?' Harriet asked curtly. 'And be careful what you say. I am this close,' she held up her thumb and first finger with barely a sliver of light between them, 'to not even bothering to give you a hearing. Do we understand each other? Kurt Weber is a psychopath. Do you understand what I'm saying? When he goes down – and he will – surely you don't want to end up in jail as well for helping him? Because with God as my witness, that is where I am sending him.'

Gisela licked her lips. Suddenly she looked fearful. Unsure.

'He told me it upset him and his grandmother when they heard that someone,' she stumbled before continuing, 'was making her cousin – a very vulnerable woman, he said – perform like a monkey just to get more business—'

'Vince?' Harriet's face was like a storm. 'You mean Vince said it.' It was a statement more than a question.

'Vince?' Neil looked at Harriet.

'A nobody,' Harriet said curtly. 'Someone who did nothing for anyone but wanted everything from everyone, and he didn't like me. He was the one who gave a statement to—'

She stopped. She stared at Gisela. 'My God,' she breathed. Her eyes were wide. 'It was you,' she said. '*You* told them about Vince. Kurt's lawyers. Of course it was you. Who else would have bothered? But why? You helped Kurt clinch his case against me. Are you completely mad?'

She felt Neil's hand on her shoulder and shrugged it off. Her rage and disbelief had reached the roof of her mouth. 'Call the police,' she ordered him.

'No,' Gisela cried. 'No. No. Don't call anyone. I tell you. I promise. He said his grandmother had asked him to find someone they could trust to go to London—'

'Don't lie,' Harriet abruptly cut across her. 'She couldn't have done. Natasha has been in a home for over three years. She's out of it, Kurt himself told me.'

'You spoke to him?' Gisela whirled round. 'When?'

'When I tried to see Natasha. At the home. Someone called Ilse Huber was there, she heard everything. If you know her, ask her. She'll tell you.'

'Ilse?' A warm flush began to creep across Gisela's pale face. 'She was there? With him?'

For a moment Harriet hesitated. A sixth sense suddenly made her say, casually, 'I assumed she was his partner. I've no idea really. They seemed close.'

As she spoke, Gisela rose in one agitated movement and leaned against the window.

'Not his partner,' she finally said. 'He is using her. That's all.'

'In what way?' Harriet eyed the door, just in case.

Gisela gave a mirthless laugh. 'That wasn't Natasha you saw. She's well hidden away. *Well* away. Ilse has seen to that. She arranged it.'

Chapter Twenty-One

'You're making it up,' Harriet said flatly. 'I saw her. Natasha. She knew Kurt.'

'No she didn't,' Gisela told her. 'She has the – what you call? Alzheimer's. Anyone who is nice to her gets a smile. I don't care if you believe me or not.'

Gisela suddenly sat down. Her voice was exhausted. 'I tell you only the truth. I don't care. Not anymore. He will kill me anyway if he knows I speak to you, or you will give me to the police. What difference does it make?'

'I'm sorry,' Harriet said, and meant it. 'But what have I got to do with any of this? I did none of the things I was accused of and I gave everything I rightfully owned, back. What could I possibly do to harm them?'

'You make them panic,' Gisela said. 'You kept asking so many questions. He thought he had dealt with you.'

'One,' Harriet corrected her. 'Just one question. Not many. About a card Natasha had sent Elena.'

Gisela shrugged. 'One, two, twenty. What does it matter? He said you were not going to go away, he could tell. They had to make sure you could not find Natasha. So Ilse told him she had a plan. Her grandmother was in a home that was not very nice and she wanted her moved but she couldn't afford it, so she said she would agree to say her grandmother was Natasha if Kurt paid the money for the home until she dies. She's in love with him, you see. But she is also – you know – *gierig*.'

'Greedy,' Neil explained.

'Yes,' Gisela said. 'That's it. She'd do anything—'

'The thing is, Gisela,' Neil pushed Harriet further up the sofa and took Gisela by the hand. Harriet blinked. 'Is that she might well be, but it makes no difference. Let Ilse take care of herself. We care about you. You're no longer safe, whatever you do, unless you listen to me.'

'What can you do?' she asked wearily.

'I swear,' he promised her. 'If you tell us the truth, then the police – or Kurt – will never know from us where we got our information. You won't have to do a thing—'

Harriet opened her mouth to object, but Neil carefully pushed his knee against hers and stopped her. Instead, he kept talking to Gisela, quietly, kindly, no demands, no threats.

'Just think. You might say he loved you, and maybe he did. And you may think you loved him, and I don't blame anyone feeling grateful for a nice home, expensive clothes and cars, yachts and private planes on tap, being taken to nice restaurants—'

'He didn't,' Gisela corrected him. 'Take me anywhere. Privately,' she said almost sadly, 'when he entertained and there were other people, I could be there. But it was never just me and him. Not in public. At first, it was to stop his wife finding out, but she left. And then it was his reputation because he wants public office, so many things. But he loved – loves me. It is what it is. Our relationship. I don't expect you to understand. Love is different for everyone, it doesn't rely on being together all the time. Being conventional. It's about sacrifice—'

'And it's in the past,' Neil urged. 'And I *do* understand. Love isn't straightforward, but beating women isn't love, it's control. Look where it's got you. All this sacrifice. Living here because you've done what he asked, found Elena, checked her out, and now terrified into thinking that if you talk to anyone, you and your mother will suffer. And all the while he's living in total luxury, with Ilse Whatsername waiting hand and foot on him. And she'll be next, you know that. I know it. Once she holds no more use for him, someone else will take her place. Gisela, you must see he's a sick man. He needs help and the only way he's going to get it is if he's stopped, and you could help him by helping us. Love him less, Gisela. Help him more. Do you understand?'

Gisela flicked a glance between them. Harriet looked at her hands clenched in her lap. Gisela gently removed hers from Neil's, rose and stared out of the window onto a dark street, snow flurries obliterating what little there was to see. Very gently, almost as though she was releasing a sob, she cleared her throat and began to tap her head against the pane in a small rhythmic movement.

*

'He asked me to help, he knew I would not refuse. I had no alternative. My mother has nowhere else to live and she was threatened with eviction. *Eviction*? And from such a place. A release is what I think it would be, but where would I take her? I get money from him and I save and I hope.'

'He pays you?' Harriet asked. 'To do what?'

Gisela fiddled with the fringe of her scarf. 'I am – was – nice to certain people he entertained. Don't look like that!' She stopped and glared fiercely at Harriet's frozen expression. 'When you are faced with ruin, then you tell me you would say no. Okay?

'One day, last summer, he phoned me and said I was to go to London. He booked me into an apartment near Victoria Station. I had a credit card from him to pay for everything. I'd never heard of Elena Banbury, and he wasn't even sure what she looked like.'

'So he *wasn't* in touch with her?' Harriet said. 'He *was* lying. All the time. But why?'

'How do I know?' Gisela snapped. 'He said it was important to his grand-mother to find her and they couldn't use a detective because they wanted to keep it very quiet. He said she had things that belonged to Natasha, or knew where they were. Or something. But how was I supposed to get them back? He said if I told anyone, something awful would happen to my mother.'

And this, Harriet silently thought, was Gisela's idea of love? Later, she vowed to herself, when this was over, she would find someone to help this tragically pathetic woman find a life worth living. Even as she vowed it, though, she knew, as Martha always said, she would be fighting a battle she had no hope of winning. Not while this poor creature still held out hope that her future lay with Kurt.

'So that's why you're hiding?' Neil was asking her. 'Because he thinks you've told someone about Elena? Have you?'

'Nothing,' Gisela cried. 'I would never let him down. What do you think I am? Some kind of—'

'No, of course not,' Neil soothed. 'This is hard for you, I can see that. But I know if you help us you will feel better, more in control of your own life. Gisela, you know, you have something very special going for you.'

'What?' Gisela paused.

'Courage,' he said. 'You are far, far braver than you think. And you are clearly a very bright woman, but he must know that, otherwise he wouldn't have trusted you so much, would he? And trust, for someone like Kurt, with his secrets and lies, is more valuable than all the Ilses in the world.'

Gisela sniffed. Briefly Harriet wondered if Neil had ever considered the stage as a career.

'Well, maybe,' Gisela said. 'He did say, it had to be handled discreetly. And he knows I am that. All he wanted was to find out where Elena had put all the stuff that belonged to his grandmother, who was very upset that her family things had been taken. I don't know when. Years before I think. And to find any letters or anything she'd had from anyone here. In Berlin. He said that's all I needed to know. I was surprised. That he was helping her. Natasha I mean. He hardly ever saw her.

'She lives alone in that big apartment near the Tiergarten. Or at least she did. With that maid or whatever she is.'

'What maid?' Harriet asked.

'Toto she's called. Never leaves Natasha's side. She's been with her since before his grandfather died. Kurt said she is hoping for something big when the old lady goes.'

'Like what?'

Gisela rustled her fingers together. 'Money. Natasha is worth a fortune. She owns the biggest share in Arcadia and there is supposed to be a fortune in jewellery somewhere. Kurt will inherit everything. It's why Ilse wants him. She wants power – and money is power isn't it?'

She paused and said almost wistfully, 'He told me not to heed her; she is useful, that's all. That it is me he loves—'

'I'm sure he did,' Harriet agreed, terrified she might wander off again into the past. 'Did Elena tell you anything?'

'Nothing,' Gisela sighed. 'She was very difficult to get to know. Very – you know,' she hugged herself, 'closed.'

For once Harriet readily agreed.

'Everything I ask to do for her, she says, "I will ask Harriet," or, "Harriet will fetch it for me." And I look at you, and wonder what your game is, because no-one does anything for nothing.'

'Was it you who told everyone I was her next of kin?' Harriet chose to ignore the insult.

'Of course not,' Gisela snapped. 'Why would I, when Elena had already done that? She told me. She said that you were like a daughter to her, and she had told everyone you were, and she did not need help from me or anyone.'

'Oh,' Harriet winced. 'Oh God. She never said. Never asked me. And I wasn't anything like that, I was—'

But Gisela wasn't listening, 'So, when I tell Kurt about you, he said we would have to arrange things.'

'Arrange?'

'Yes,' Gisela said impatiently. 'So he could get his way. You know? Fix things. It's what he does. He said we have to start asking people about you, and that man with the absurd ponytail, yes, Vince – he tell me everyone knew you were just using her to attract attention to your stall and that you believed she had some serious jewellery hidden away that you wanted to get hold of, but this puzzles me because I can see she has nothing and think he is mistaken, but he said you never leave off about her father being something to do with Fabergé—'

'I did not,' she gasped. '*Never*, not once. Sometimes Elena did, she was proud of it, and as for inheriting – oh God – and all this was being said? Behind my back? Oh God—'

'Calm down,' Neil whispered. 'One hysterical woman I can deal with, but not two.'

'I am not hysterical,' she whispered back so violently he winced. 'I am perfectly calm—'

'What on earth must you be like in a rage?' he muttered.

She ignored him. How could she begin to explain that the fury erupting inside her chest was directed more at herself for such carelessness, to allow her behaviour to be so mischievously misinterpreted, and so spitefully, as Vince had done? She didn't much care for the answer.

'Then that girl who has the silly boyfriend,' Gisela was saying, oblivious to Harriet's anguish. 'She said she sometimes stayed with you, and that Elena had practically given you the flat, the rent was so low, but you were now indispensable to her.'

Harriet dropped her face into her hands. 'Because it was practically falling down,' she pleaded to no-one in particular. 'No-one else wanted it.'

'And then I am not well,' Gisela wasn't listening. 'So I did not go out but then I go to the market and they all tell me that Elena had died a few days before, and I hear from Vince that you inherit everything, and it was the talk of the place, so I tell Kurt and he goes very angry. And he orders me home but I stay for the funeral because it seems respectful and I am tired of being told what to do. When I get back he is – well—' She waved a dismissive hand. She didn't need to spell it out. 'And then he tells me they have another plan. They would get the courts to return everything she had given to you, everything, including letters and diaries. They would say you were a bad influence and stopped her contacting them. It was all so weird.'

'What about the phone calls?' Neil asked. 'They were listed on his phone records?'

Harriet knew what was coming.

'Even I could do that,' Gisela said scornfully. 'He has people to do these things. Everything. He has people everywhere. Well paid. You just remove a number here and there on the original bill and you put in another to prove you make the call. Or had tried to call. A child could do it.'

Harriet suspected that it was not that easy, but regardless, Christopher and

Tim had not challenged him. What innocents they had all been. She could have screamed.

'And is that when he decided to sue Harriet?' Neil asked.

'He said it was the only way they could overturn Elena's wishes. Ilse was there and I didn't want to be involved, but I had no choice so I tell them everything everyone had said. I just wanted to run away. And it was awful.' Gisela's eyes filled with tears, her voice disjointed; a torrent of anguish that clearly she'd said more than she had planned to spilling from her, almost as though the unloading of such appalling memories was her salvation.

'His grandmother was there, I don't know why. I could hear her telling him to leave you alone. That Elena knew nothing. Nor you. He wouldn't believe her and then she screamed, and I tried to go to her, but Ilse stopped me. I think he was shaking her.'

'*Shaking* her?' Harriet clutched Gisela's arm. 'An old woman? His own grandmother? Did no-one help her?'

Gisela shook Harriet's arm away. 'Who do you suggest? Me? The maid? She certainly wouldn't stand up to him – her past you see. It is not of the Virgin Mary variety. That I do know. Kurt himself told me. And then I tell my mother and she said what they were doing was wrong and if it all went wrong, I would be as much to blame and probably go to jail and then she really would be on her own. She is not well – she has the depression, you understand?

'So I tried to tell them, you could not steal from Elena because she had nothing to steal, and he shook me and said it had nothing to do with her life in London, but something from years and years ago, and it would be the end if I said anything, so I run away and hide here, and that is all I know.'

Oh God, Harriet muttered to herself. Where did the lies end and the truth start, if there was any truth in any of it.

'Where's Natasha? Gisela? Do you know?'

'Not for sure. I know she has a very large house on the lake. Out near Potsdam. She liked going there, away from the city. I think she grew up there.'

It was as far as she got. A loud thump on the door was followed by a torrent of German. Gisela rolled her eyes.

'*Ich komme, ich komme,*' she shrieked, hammering back on her side of the door. They heard footsteps retreat down the wooden stairs. '*Dumm schwein*. He is,' Gisela said defiantly. She jerked her head at the unseen barman outside the door. 'In fact he is more than a stupid pig. But I need the job.'

They watched in silence as she straightened her beanie beret, pulled her shoulders back and examined the ravages of her hysteria in the mirror. She fumbled in her bag for a lipstick and smeared more on, inspected the result and led the way down the stairs.

'You won't tell him – or anyone that you've seen me?' She turned as she reached the bottom of the narrow uncarpeted stairs. Her hand gripped Neil's arm. 'You won't,' she begged staring straight into his eyes, 'will you? You promised. My mother – me. I am not frightened of him, not in the way you think, but I want him to suffer. Not being able to find me will hurt him. You understand?'

'You have my word,' Neil said. He put his hand briefly over hers. 'That I promise you.'

'You are very lucky.' She glanced at Harriet standing just behind him. 'You might think you have a bad time. But at least you have a good man here. Cherish him.'

'No,' Harriet began. 'No. You're mistaken. We're not—'

But Gisela was gone. She didn't look back. The pushy, confident barmaid dispensing drinks and cheeky banter had taken over, and the confused delusional woman with a hopeless future, unless someone or something rescued her, had vanished.

'Not now,' Neil said as Harriet began to explain Gisela's mistake. 'Not now.' He pushed Harriet out of the bar ahead of him and out of Gisela's sight.

*

'He can't go round beating women up,' Harriet seethed, as they reached the pavement. 'He's got to be stopped. What a shit. I don't care what Martha says, I'm going to tell the police.'

Negotiating a small patch of ice slowed her. Neil reached back to take her hand to steady her. A bus rattled past in the gathering dusk, a stream of cars made conversation impossible until they reached his car.

'No you're not,' he said, pulling her along behind him by her sleeve. 'You're not telling anyone. Not yet. We have no evidence and Gisela's not going to say a word against him to anyone. You must see that?'

'Then what do we do?'

'Not sure,' he admitted. 'Unless,' he went on, as they began the drive back to the city, 'we can find out why he's so desperate to find that bloody bag or box or whatever it is. And I doubt it's all for a piece of Fabergé.'

'Fabergé is worth a small fortune,' she protested.

'But he's already got one of those,' he pointed out. 'Hang on,' he said stabbing in a number on his phone. 'Got to ring Martha. I think we might as well know our legal position. Martha? It's me.'

'She said,' he reported, when he'd finished, 'that we both need close psychiatric care.'

'Can't argue with that,' she agreed. 'Neil? What do you suppose she'll do now? Gisela, I mean?'

'Do?' He looked grim. 'I'd say she's probably already done it.'

'Done what?'

'Called Kurt.'

'You're kidding,' she gasped. 'But why?'

'Same reason she helped him get all that rubbish together in London. Anything to make him think she's useful, so he'll take her back. You heard her. She's hiding because she wants him to miss her, not because she thinks he'll kill her. God, does she need help. And badly. And she must know he could find her in five minutes if he wanted to. And when he wants to, he will.'

'Neil?' Harriet stopped him. 'I must try and see Natasha. I must find her before he really harms her. Sod the bag or whatever it is they all want to get their hands on. He might kill her,' she paused. 'To be honest, I don't know why he hasn't.'

'Probably because he doesn't know who else she's confided in, and if she's dead, he'll never know who's coming out of the woodwork. Just like you.'

She glanced at her phone. In less than three hours he was getting a plane. Her flight left tomorrow night. She still had tonight and most of tomorrow to do something.

'You have to go, but I've got almost a day to try and find out. And I know I can't come back to Berlin. Not for a while anyway. I'm practically out of money. I'll have to get a job working for someone till I get on my feet and find the money to— Neil? Are you listening?'

'Of course I am. Something about your plane, not getting back and – what was that last thing? Oh that's right, getting a job? See? I heard everything.'

*

'Right,' he said, pulling the car up at the top of the road that led to Der Hafen. 'Can you walk that bit? I've got to get to a tutorial. They'll be thrilled if I don't make it, but I like to disappoint them.'

'Of course.' She started to scramble out, 'But Neil—?'

'I'll collect you around seven tomorrow morning. Don't sleep in.'

'What?' she shouted. 'Why? Neil? Listen to me. What about Paris? Your flight?' She called through the open window. 'You have to be there—'

'I'll go tomorrow night. It'll be fine. At least you'll go home knowing every last possible thing has been done.'

She couldn't let him do this.

'You mustn't,' she began. 'You need to *think*. You need this time – the two of you. Together. And for God's sake, what will Sylvia say?'

'She won't mind. She hates early starts.'

She held onto the door handle. 'Neil? Where are we going? Tomorrow?'

'To a place just past Wannsee. Martha just texted me the address. Natasha's. He'll have the place ring-fenced if that lunatic has alerted him that we're here. But it's our only hope.'

'Neil?' she said carefully. 'Why are you doing this?'

Their eyes locked. A look of pure uncertainty crossed her face. She released her grip on the door.

He sighed. 'If you don't know, then there's even more reason for me to come with you.'

'I don't know what you mean,' she said, stiffly. She dreaded what was coming next.

'I think you do,' he insisted calmly.

She waited.

'Oh for heaven's sake woman,' he sighed. 'Do I have to spell it out? Okay. I have a car. You don't. I know the way. Do you?'

'You know I don't,' she said.

A short tussle ensued in her head while she decided whether relief or disappointment was the winner.

'In which case,' she said, stepping back onto the pavement, 'I'll get an early night.'

Chapter Twenty-Two

It was still dark when Harriet carefully pushed open the door to the tiny kitchen next to her room, only to find Bebe already there, dressed for the outdoors. For once the house was silent.

'I am coming.' Bebe was struggling into a vast grey coat, a fringe of fake fur trailing down the opening. 'Do not argue.' She rammed a mauve wool helmet over her head as she spoke, leaving only a glimpse of scarlet glass bauble earrings dangling wildly underneath.

'If he's beating old women, then I am the best person to be there.' She held up a hand as Harriet opened her mouth to object, 'Stop. I know how to handle these situations. You don't. With;' she added politely, seeing Harriet's face, 'the greatest respect.'

'Bebe, honestly,' Harriet exclaimed in dismay. 'The whole of Wannsee can't be packed with beaten women—'

'I know that,' Bebe said patiently, 'but the difference is, I don't look like trouble. With *that* look on your face, I'd run a mile.'

'What look?' Harriet demanded.

'A – what you call?' Bebe snapped her fingers. 'Ready to kill. That's it. And you haven't slept. Don't deny it. You look grey.'

'Thank you,' Harriet replied stonily. 'You're much too kind.'

'You're welcome,' Bebe beamed. 'In fact you can sit in the back and doze or something. We can grab some food on the way. There's nothing here. See?'

She pulled open the door to reveal a fridge, empty except for a carton of milk and the remains of the pizza they'd shared the night before.

'But I haven't told Neil you're coming,' Harriet pointed out.

'It's okay. I did,' Bebe beamed. 'After you went to bed last night. I text him. He is very pleased.'

'He is?' Harriet asked doubtfully. 'What did he say?'

'He said, *Oh great. That's all I need.* So I come.'

*

Harriet meekly took her place in the back of the car, found a rug and wrapped herself in it and ignored a red suede jacket lying next to her. In the front, Neil was extracting a promise from Bebe that she wouldn't do anything without consulting him first.

'Of course,' she said loftily. 'Why would I not?'

'I'm working on that,' he told her. She sniffed.

A crowd of early morning commuters were making their way to trams and trains as Neil pulled the car onto the main road that led past shops and cafés, some still in darkness, before heading south towards Wannsee, then Potsdam and beyond, to the house they hoped would lead to Natasha.

'By the way,' Bebe announced as they drove. 'Martha sent someone called Gregor to help Klara. He is an idiot—'

'*Bebe,*' Harriet chided her. 'How can you say that? I'm amazed Martha managed to send anyone. She's up to here in work.'

'And you say I'm not?' Bebe demanded indignantly. 'As though I haven't enough to do? So I talk to him and I can see that I will have to help him. He asked,' she rolled her eyes, 'how much contact the children had with their father since they arrived at Der Hafen. *Contact?* She'd never have got them back. And he calls himself a lawyer?'

Harriet privately had to admit it was a lunatic question. Instead, she said she was sure Gregor would appreciate Bebe's help.

'As indeed, we all do,' Neil said. 'Just as a matter of interest, who's looking after the shop?'

'Shop? What shop?' Bebe stared at his profile.

'Just an English expression,' Harriet explained. 'He means while you're away, who's looking after the refuge.'

'Then why not say what he means?' Bebe said, puzzled.

'He rarely does,' Harriet said, before she could stop herself. 'He's good at it.'

In the driver's mirror, she caught Neil's eye.

*

Through the leafless trees that ran the length of the lake, Harriet glimpsed the deserted expanse of water at Wannsee. A sturdy wind was blowing, bending trees and sending ripples across its surface. It was so hard to imagine a summer's day, when the shore would be packed with sunbathers and those escaping the heat of the city, but Bebe assured her it was so. Maybe one day, she thought, surprised at herself for even considering a return.

It was not as straightforward as they had imagined. Even the sat nav seemed to give up at times, taking them down dead end roads and once to the very edge of a lake.

'It's got,' Neil muttered, reversing back up the lane, 'to be here somewhere. Let's start again from the main road.'

Ten minutes later, and nearer two hours than the one hour they had planned since they set off, Neil swung the car off the main road and they headed inland until the road changed into nothing more than a rough wide track. Ahead of them a village; a scattering of houses – less than half a dozen it would seem – fanned out around what appeared to be an oversized village green. It was covered in a blanket of snow, which stifled the sound of any sign of life.

'Here?' Harriet almost whispered. She wound the window down to be met with a blast of cold icy air. 'Is this where she lives?'

Bebe nodded. 'Somewhere around here.'

'How buried away is this?' Harriet leaned forward to peer between them at the road ahead. She took in the silence, the deserted lane, the empty snow-filled fields. 'How can anyone know where she is? How does she get anywhere?'

'Not everyone wants a coffee shop on every corner,' Neil grunted.

Harriet looked startled. 'Well of course they don't,' she exclaimed. 'I never said that. It's just exceptionally deserted and she's already old and this is very isolated, that's all.'

'Sorry,' he gave a crooked grin. 'Sorry. You're right. She's certainly not easy to find. Or a coffee shop.'

'Good. We agree,' Bebe said, studying a map on her phone. 'I think it very lonely. I expect the house will be well guarded but that should be easy enough to overcome if we—'

'You're not suggesting we break in?' Neil exchanged an alarmed look with Harriet.

'You think I'm stupid?' Bebe glared scornfully at him. 'I just read somewhere that Kurt's house was very guarded, so I assume hers is too. I like to be prepared.'

'Quite right,' Harriet said, as they began to drive slowly through the deserted hamlet. 'As Elena always said: Always have a plan.'

In a few minutes, they reached the edge of the village, and then descended a slight incline into a wooded area, until the only house that matched Martha's description came into view.

Framed at the back by a row of tall spruce trees, there was no sign of anyone living there, not even on such a cold, and now increasingly misty, day. There was no wood smoke from any of the chimneys. Neil pulled over onto a snow-covered verge.

All three surveyed the deserted country lane; rolling fields on either side, a wire fence to their left, more trees to the right. Only a tractor broke the silence, trailing what looked like an oversized sledge piled high with logs, as it rumbled slowly up the lane.

Bebe jumped out and flagged down the driver. He leaned over from his perch and shook his head.

'I don't deliver here,' he called. 'They manage themselves. But I tell you they won't be in anyway. Not at this time. That old woman and her companion. They'll be at the church, lighting candles, praying. Same time every day, they walk a mile up the road and back—'

'In this weather?' Harriet asked.

'It would,' the man chuckled, eyeing the banks of snow, 'take more than this to stop those old women praying. The church is at the top of the hill. The Russian one. You can't miss it.'

*

In a clearing, well back from the lane, the startling sight of a minute, square-shaped Russian Orthodox church came into view. Its sharply pink-washed walls, onion-domed roof, boxed in on all sides by tall black wrought iron railings, were as unexpected as they was extraordinary.

'What on earth is it doing here?' Harriet gazed at it. 'It's in the middle of nowhere.'

'There's an old Russian community here,' Bebe screwed her eyes up, scanning the church. 'I remember now. If we go further we come to their village, then there's a big town about three kilometres beyond that. Very interesting. Big. Lots of tourists. They come to see this church. I have a feeling about this,' she said excitedly, already starting to walk up the lane towards the church.

'Keep your voice down,' Neil advised.

As they neared the church, they saw the small area around it was deserted, except for a heavily coated woman wearing a thick fur hat, pulled well down over her ears, sitting outside on a low wall, smoking and checking her phone. She glanced up as they approached and then turned away.

'Here,' Neil muttered, pulling something from his inside pocket, 'take this.' He handed Bebe a wafer-slim camera, no bigger than a cigarette packet. 'No. Don't use your phone. Try and look serious about this. We're tourists, okay? Just keep taking pictures. If you're stopped, just ask daft questions.'

'What will you do?' Bebe examined the camera.

'Take a look inside, but don't you come in. Not till I tell you or you see Kurt pitching up. I'd quite like to know if that happens. Give us a head start out of here. Okay?' He looked at Harriet.

She nodded.

'Don't be long with those pictures,' Neil called loudly and deliberately to Bebe as he and Harriet moved away. 'Just ten minutes. There's not much to see here. Come on,' he affected a weary voice to Harriet. 'It was you who wanted to see the wretched place. But be quick, I'm starving.'

The smoking woman looked up and then went on with her messaging. Bebe began snapping away, and as Harriet glanced back, she was leaning perilously over the spiked railings, the camera trained on the onion dome, asking the woman if she would mind keeping an eye on her bag while she captured this magnificent piece of architecture. Harriet was amazed that the woman simply stubbed out her cigarette, shrugged and did as she was asked. But then she had never known, in the short time they had been acquainted, anyone to refuse Bebe anything.

The door of the church, wooden and with a heavy iron handle, creaked slightly as they walked carefully inside, their eyes blinking to get used to the half-light of the church. Candles were flickering in small red globes, the walls filled with iconic images of saints and scenes of religious history, that on another occasion Harriet would have been only too happy to examine more closely.

At first it appeared empty, just a few benches seated around the perimeter wall. The middle, as is the custom in Russian churches, remained empty for worshippers to stand and reflect on their own needs.

A sudden small movement made them both turn. They stared into the gloom, straining to see who was there. A figure appeared, a tall elderly woman, her heavy coat touching the top of sturdy black boots, her head bowed, lost in thought. She stopped in the centre of the church, her head covered with a thick woollen scarf, just a small wave of grey hair showing at the front. Although she used a stick, she was not stooped or bowed, but upright. She turned, as though to leave.

Harriet groped behind her for something to lean on, found Neil's arm and just stared.

Neil glanced down at her then turned back to the woman. Harriet let go of his arm and walked towards her. The woman gave a start and began to move backwards, away from her.

'No, don't be frightened,' Harriet said in broken German. She reached out her hand and laid it on the women's arm. 'I'm not going to harm you. My name is Harriet Flynn and—'

For a brief moment, the old woman looked as though she was going to stumble. She gave a slight gasp. Neil shot a hand out to steady her.

'It's okay,' he spoke gently. 'Here, lean on me. I am Harriet's friend.'

He placed an arm around her shoulders, but she was looking at Harriet.

'I knew,' she whispered, her voice was trembling. Her scarf slipped from her head. 'I knew you'd come. I don't deserve it. But, oh thank God. Thank God.'

Chapter Twenty-Three

Harriet stared, transfixed. The tall unbending figure, the grey hair, cut into a close bob around the long narrow face, the determined chin, the piercing blue eyes. And she knew. From the moment she'd watched her emerge from the shadows, she'd known.

'It's you, isn't it?' she said to her. It was a statement, a gentle one, an expression of relief more than a question. 'You're Natasha.'

'You're sure?' Neil looked uncertainly at her.

Harriet nodded. 'They could be twins. Her and Elena.'

Neil turned to speak, but the elderly woman waved a hand at him then held it out to Harriet, shaking, but more, Harriet suspected, from shock than fragility. Her English was poor, but she managed.

'I understand her,' the woman said to Neil. 'Very well. Oh, so very well.'

Harriet helped her sit on a nearby bench. 'You came,' she plucked at Harriet's sleeve. 'I knew – I mean I hoped you would.'

'Natasha?' She took Natasha's shoulders. 'That woman outside. Is she with you?'

Natasha nodded. 'Always. My grandson pay her. She is stupid, but she doesn't let me out of her sight. Except here. She knows I cannot leave without her seeing me. Even if my strength allowed it, I have no escape from her.'

'Natasha,' Harriet took her shoulders. 'Come with us. Please. I swear you will be safe. You're in danger if you stay here.'

'No.' Natasha shook her head. She looked stubborn. She looked so like Elena. 'I cannot leave. And I don't care anymore. But I promise Elena—'

'In a card?' Harriet said eagerly. 'I found it. I *knew* it must be you.'

'You have it?'

'It's long story,' Harriet told her. 'I'll tell you soon. What did you promise her?' Harriet crouched down beside her.

'That I would return her things to her.'

'Things?' Harriet looked round. 'You mean the box? The bag? The one she left? You didn't mention it in the card.'

'I didn't have to,' Natasha whispered. 'She would have known what I meant. I waited but – then I heard she had died. So soon. At first I feared it was the shock of hearing from me. But then I know she is like me, it would take more than that, but my heart,' she pressed it, 'almost break. I can never find forgiveness, but I can be at peace with myself if I make sure no-one touches her things. I can't do anything now, I am too old. All I do is come each day and guard everything. My leg, you see. It is now impossible. I can hardly walk. So wretched I have become.'

Neil crouched down beside them. 'Natasha? How can I help?'

'You go for me?' Natasha asked doubtfully.

'Of course.' He glanced anxiously towards the door. 'But go where?'

'Up there,' Natasha pointed to a narrow staircase hidden behind the altar. 'There's a wooden chest,' Natasha said. 'With a carved back. There is cushion on it, blue, I think. I'm sorry. I don't remember.'

'It doesn't matter,' Neil urged her. 'Is that where this bag is?'

'A satchel. Elena's satchel. It's under the floor. Inside the chest. You pull. Like this,' Natasha gave an upward tug with her hands. 'Under there. That's where Max put it. He told me.'

'Max?' Harriet whispered. 'You mean Valentina's Max?'

'*My* Max,' she reminded her. 'He was my Max for all those years. He knew it would be safe there. So long ago.'

'And you're sure it's still there?' Neil asked. 'It's been a long time—'

'Oh yes,' Natasha said. 'I know as certain as I am sitting here. And I don't want to do any of this, but the time has come, I know that. I pray and I know it has caused so much – misery. It's all been so terrible. I am,' her eyes began to fill up. 'I am to blame. Entirely.'

Harriet squeezed her hand, not knowing what she was seeking to be responsible for, but still she said: 'I doubt that very much.'

'No,' Natasha said sharply. 'I know what I say. I – I tell you – then you will see.'

Over her head Harriet said, 'Neil we can't stay here. Bebe can't take many more pictures. That woman will come.'

He looked quickly around. To one side of the door, a heavy wooden table with sturdy turned legs and a red cloth covering it, was weighed down with pamphlets, a box of votive candles and a donation box.

'Take the other end,' he ordered Harriet. 'Now lift.'

'Oh my God,' Harriet panted, her arms almost collapsing under the weight of the table. 'What's it made of? Lead?'

Together they staggered, just a few inches, not much, but sufficient to ensure the door could not be opened enough to let anyone in.

'Good girl,' he panted. 'That should buy us a few minutes. Now. Take Natasha and go.' He thrust his car keys at her. 'Over there. In the far wall. That small door. There's a key hanging next to it. You won't be seen until you're round the corner. A couple of yards to the car. Put her in and get going.'

He pressed a number on his phone.

'What in God's name are you doing?' she asked.

'Bebe?' she heard him say. 'Just say *Hi there*.' He paused. 'Excellent,' he continued. 'Now listen. Natasha is here. Bebe? Stop. Just listen. We've managed to barricade the main door. Harriet is going to leave by the side door and make for the car. She's taking Natasha with her. She's okay, needs her stick to walk, but she'll do it. We have very little time. Bebe? Please? Just start walking that way to the car. And then go. Yes. Go.' He switched the phone off.

'You?' Harriet said urgently. 'What about you?'

But he had disappeared round the bend in the stone staircase.

She felt Natasha's fingers on her arm. An eerie, almost calm expression had settled on her face, nearly a smile. 'It will be fine,' the old woman said stoutly, with an assurance Harriet was far from feeling.

Given she was nearer ninety than eighty, it didn't take rocket science to work out that for Natasha, even walking was going to be a deadly slow business. Maybe the danger they were in had not entirely pressed home.

'Can you make it to our car?' Harriet asked anxiously. 'I'll hold you.'

'I will be fine,' Natasha said firmly, sounding so like Elena, that in other circumstances Harriet might have laughed. 'I am old but I do my best.'

Harriet pulled open the door, an icy blast of wind rushed in but Natasha seemed impervious to it, merely pausing to drape a long knitted scarf more sturdily around her neck.

With one hand clutching Natasha's arm, the other round her waist to steady her, Harriet cautiously peered around the edge of the church. She could see the top of Neil's car parked in the lane. Near enough, but it felt like a distance the length of a football pitch.

Bebe was already halfway down the path, walking backwards, pretending to snap away at even more interesting angles on a building, which while arguably very beautiful, could not possibly require such attention from even the most dedicated admirer of Russian architecture.

Harriet peered round the edge of the church and saw the woman who had so obligingly kept an eye on Bebe's bag, grind out another cigarette, glance at her watch, give a grunt and start for the door of the church.

Harriet thought her heart would stop. Agonisingly slowly, she willed Natasha on, the only sound to break the silence, the crunch of their feet as they edged across the icy snow, towards safety.

And then there was the very clear sound of an iron handle being banged and pulled, followed by the door of the church being pounded and an enraged torrent of German, which did not require interpreting into any language. A few seconds saw the robust woman round the corner of the church, slipping and cursing as she saw Harriet and Natasha within touching distance of the car parked in the lane by the gate.

Harriet stared wildly around, but at the same moment she heard Bebe shout. 'Go, *go, go*. I get this.'

Harriet only had time to see a flash of red earrings, before Neil's camera flew from Bebe's hand, as she aimed it straight at the woman, who took the force of it on the side of her head. Not hard enough to do any real damage, but enough to make her stumble while she collected her wits. Harriet, who abhorred violence of all kinds, was horrified that she felt only elation.

An exchange of shrill screaming filled the air. Bebe, waving the fallen branch of a tree she had scooped up to protect herself, was clearly challenging the overweight woman, warning her if she came an inch further, of what she planned to do with the branch she was wielding And quite graphically at that. Harriet grimly kept going, not looking back, aware that Natasha was breathing heavily.

They reached the car. Natasha allowed herself to be eased into the back. Gasping, she slumped heavily against the backrest. Harriet clambered behind the wheel and fumbled with the key, cursing loudly until the engine sprang into life. A wild U-turn in the lane followed. She glimpsed Bebe reach the gate to the lane, look swiftly over her shoulder and then begin to run. Harriet slowed enough to allow Bebe to pull open the back door and fall in.

'Go,' Bebe yelled. 'I'm in. Harriet? What's the matter?'

'Neil,' Harriet said, turning to see over her shoulder, as she began to reverse back down the lane. 'I'm not going without him.'

'You must,' Bebe shrieked. 'He said to go. Oh God. Look!'

The roof of a black jeep could be seen above the wall on the opposite lane, slowly making its way to the top of the hill where the church was perched. The stout woman was already in the road frantically waving her arms.

Bebe twisted in her seat. 'It's Kurt.'

'Ring him,' Harriet calmly ordered Bebe. 'Neil. Tell him to cut across the field opposite, away from the church, I'll pick him up where that man was. With the logs. Be quick.'

'You can't,' insisted Bebe. 'We have to pass Kurt,' she screamed wildly. 'He'll kill us. He carries a gun.'

'Oh God,' Harriet felt her stomach lurch. 'How do you know?'

'Gisela told me. Oh this is madness. We must go.'

'We are not,' a stern voice broke in, 'leaving without Harriet's friend. We are allies. We do not leave anyone behind.'

'Oh *Jeez*,' Bebe moaned. Natasha just stared at her. 'That's all I need. A hero. And I bet,' she said stabbing at her phone, 'I can't get a signal.'

But she could. They didn't dare look, as Harriet backed down the lane, made a sharp right turn across a rough track at the bottom, the car bumping angrily over ruts and holes that were impossible to see, covered in snow as they were, and drove around the perimeter of the field until she reached the junction of the road, just as Neil was climbing over a gate. Panting heavily, a very red-faced Neil slung a battered parcel into the footwell of the car and fell in after it.

Without thinking, without taking her eyes off the road, Harriet reached over and squeezed his shoulder. She felt his hand briefly close over hers before she put her foot down and headed back to the city.

'He can't know exactly where we're going,' she said as she narrowly missed a lorry on a bend in the road. 'Just back to Berlin. Call Martha. Bebe says he's got a gun. Ask her to meet us.'

When he hung up the phone, Neil twisted round in his seat and smiled at Bebe. 'Well done,' he grinned. 'Hope you got some good shots.'

'I have no idea,' she said calmly. 'I'm afraid I was forced to use your camera as a missile.'

'Of course,' he said switching to Natasha. 'Natasha? I've got an old leather bag lying at my feet. I had a quick look, it's got some envelopes inside. Other stuff too, smells a bit, but so packed, I didn't dare try and find out if it was the one you said. Would you like to open it?'

He passed the bag over the seat. Bebe helped lower it into Natasha's lap.

'I don't have to open it,' Natasha's voice began to break. 'I know it. Look. There. On the front. Elena's initials. E.G. Elena Guseva.' She began to weep. 'It's been so long.'

Small stifled sobs escaped, tears were running down her lined cheeks. Through the mirror, Harriet saw Bebe place an arm round her, hushing her like a small child.

This was not the moment for explanations, but as she drove, Harriet knew the speed she was going at was in direct proportion to her, now, almost desperate need to know. The speedometer hovered at almost twice the legal limit.

'If,' she eventually heard Neil say quietly, 'you continue to drive like a maniac, our chances of survival might well be greater in Kurt's hands. Just saying.'

She put her foot down.

Chapter Twenty-Four

'I think we should get a doctor,' Harriet whispered. 'She's very pale.'

Bebe started to speak, when a surprisingly firm voice from the armchair told them a doctor was completely unnecessary, but a cup of tea would be welcome.

The noise beyond the doors of Bebe's little apartment could be clearly and head-splittingly heard. Children shouting, mothers beseeching, a television blaring out the results of a heavily watched gameshow promising to find Germany's greatest singing star, all competed with two refuge volunteers pleading for patience from the several women demanding their attention, all needing help to deal with the life they'd left outside.

But they were safe. Harriet briefly wondered when the line had been crossed for her, when such a place had stopped being a nightmare and become a haven of safety. She knew the answer. The first night she had come there, she had known that she had neither the time nor the awareness to deal with what she'd been through. But she had also known that this was not the end of the line, just a pause – and these incredible people who had taken her in, to help her get back on track, had been waiting until she was ready to do that. The refugee motto stared down at her. *To pause, to rest to recover.* It had never been truer.

Martha's plane was due to land in one hour. Neil had promised they'd be at her office, to discover if it was legal to abduct an old lady who was perfectly willing to be abducted, just how many laws they had trampled over to do so, and if an injunction to stop Kurt coming near Natasha could be activated. And quickly at that.

'Natasha.' Harriet crouched down next to her as Bebe sped off to get the tea. 'I think you should let someone check you. I don't know if you take any medication at all—?'

'No,' Natasha insisted. She patted Harriet's hand. 'I am beyond medicine. And I don't mind. My heart,' she explained. 'It can only be a short while more—'

Harriet gripped her arm. 'Then I insist,' she began.

'Thank you,' Natasha shook her head. 'No. I just want to put everything right. I want to take my share of the blame. I wanted to tell Elena. To explain. And I must make sure her wishes are carried out. And the last thing I can do for her is to make sure I help her do that, restore to you—'

'Natasha, I want nothing,' Harriet said more sharply than she intended. 'I'm fine. I only wanted what you want, to return Elena's possessions to you. And now you've got them we—'

Natasha stopped her with an almost angry shake of her head. 'No. I never wanted her possessions. Ever. You have no say in this.' She looked up at Neil. 'I owe you,' she told him. 'Very much.' She spread her hands to show just how substantial she felt that debt was. 'You understand?'

Neil shook his head. 'Nonsense. But if I'm to get Martha to help, then I really should know what this is all about.'

'And I want him arrested, whatever it is,' Bebe came back and placed the tea next to Natasha, no milk, as she had instructed. 'I want him put out of action, I want – what?' she stopped, seeing the warning on Harriet's face. 'Oh,' She shot a quick glance at Natasha. 'I'm so sorry, he's your grandson and—'

Natasha waved a fragile hand at her. She shook her head. 'I am not stupid. The kindest thing would be to say that he is the result of his parents' neglect, of stupid decisions, selfish ones. But it isn't. You will see. I am to blame. Most entirely, I am.'

Suddenly she began to weep again, as though after years of holding her very soul together, she was finding a natural release in these bleak overheated surroundings. Gulping sobs, that shook her body. It was impossible to continue until she had collected herself, Bebe's arm around her, Harriet holding her hand.

Finally, she took several deep breaths which steadied her enough to speak. On her lap she clutched the satchel she had held closely to her on the journey back. Her bony hands stroking the worn leather – like a mother comforting a child. The leather straps, not so much worn as folded into permanent creases from years of lying under a thick heavy plank and, according to Neil, several heavy volumes of leather-bound books and wooden boxes.

She began to open the bag. Slowly, she slid out a sheaf of musty smelling envelopes. Harriet watched, fascinated as the past, wrapped in old newspaper and envelopes, slipped effortlessly into Natasha's lap.

Natasha's breath was now coming in shallow gasps. Harriet tried to stop her.

'Her heart,' she whispered frantically to Bebe. 'Neil?' she appealed to him. But Natasha ignored their efforts to calm her.

'I must know, and make you understand. Here,' she handed Harriet a flat package, wrapped in greaseproof paper, sticky with age. 'Open it. My hands are not as nimble as yours.'

Bit by bit, the paper, disturbed after so long, crumbled into a fine dust as each layer was peeled back. Finally, Harriet lifted away the last of an old newspaper, German of course, now so yellow with age it was unreadable and felt a flat, square, heavy object slide out. Tooled black leather, at first it looked like a book, but then she saw that the front was really two flaps, held together with a narrow black ribbon that fell open to reveal a black velvet-lined case, like a presentation tray, a smaller version of the kind she had on her stall, that she closed up at night and took home with her.

Except she had never traded in anything that could begin to compare with its contents, although clearly needing to be cleaned and polished, as they saw air for the first time in decades, it required no imagination to guess their value which, if sold as a collection, could buy a fair sized chunk of Kent.

'We're talking big bucks, right?' Bebe breathed over her shoulder.

Harriet nodded. She turned to the other package, carefully unfolding similar layers of paper until finally, a miniature photograph frame, but *such* a frame, holding the picture of a man, slid into the palm of her hand. Harriet took a sharp intake of breath.

Oval, translucent pink enamel, a border of gold seed pearls, and on the top of the frame, a carved, almost jaunty, silver ribbon. It was, Harriet thought, if she thought at all, breathtaking.

Cautiously, she turned it over, and on the edge, the unmistakable Fabergé mark stared back at her, and so finely engraved, she could hardly read it. Something in Cyrillic script could be seen along the edge.

'I don't have to look,' Natasha said. 'I know it by heart. It says *Elena*, and the date is nineteen eighteen. Her birth year. Eight years older than me.

The face of the man in the photograph, half-smiling, stared back at her. A man wearing a shapeless white jacket, a tie loosely knotted, a flop of blond hair tumbling lazily over his forehead. A kind face, not just handsome – and he most certainly, by any standards, was – but a thoughtful gaze, intelligent eyes staring at her from almost a century before.

'Elena's father.' Natasha stared at the image. 'Andrea Gusev. He was my uncle. I never knew him. Nor did Elena. He was killed. In the Revolution. He made it for her. He worked for one of Fabergé's work masters. So clever. She was terrified that if she were caught when they were escaping to Paris, it would be taken from her.

'The rest – the jewellery – belonged to Valentina. It was to support them, when they reached safety. Start a business. They had plans, such plans – for what they would do to help people like themselves. My mother – Irina – she told me, that when they got to our house, Valentina sewed so much into the hem of her skirt, mostly the things that Andrea had made, my mother thought she would never walk with the weight of it all. So Max took the rest and hid them in the loft of the church. He told no-one, not even Valentina where. He promised her that one day he would come back and recover them. And he persuaded Elena that this—' she nodded towards the frame, 'would be far safer there than stolen by those – those thugs.'

'Is this what Kurt wants?' Neil asked. 'Is this what all the fuss is about? It all looks priceless.'

'It is,' Harriet stopped him before he could finish. 'But to Elena it must have been beyond a mere price. This was her only real link to her father. And this,' she nodded towards the tray now being pored over by Bebe, 'her last link to her mother.'

She glanced at Natasha, at the visible look of real pain on her face, her thin fingers seeming not to want to touch the rest of the contents of the satchel. 'Dermot would know the value, just like that,' she said almost absently. 'But,' she turned quietly to Natasha. She reached out and pressed her hand. 'But this isn't what Kurt wants. Is it Natasha?'

'No,' Natasha didn't look at them. 'He is terrified – and I don't blame him – that someone will discover that this,' she pulled a folded newspaper towards herself, not opening it or even attempting to, 'was his grandfather. Not Max.'

She held it out to Harriet. They all leaned forward to see what she was staring at, with a look of pure revulsion on her face.

A row of men in uniform, with enough gold braid to trim several sets of curtains, stern, unsmiling faces, arrogant. The face of one at the back of the group was squared off like a frame with what must have been ink; it was hard to tell, it had long faded and was now brown.

It was hard to see what he looked like, this man that had been singled out. Harriet turned the paper over. Over her shoulder, Bebe read out loud the man's name and rank; a highly regarded member of the ruling party of that time, it seemed, a party that had as its leader a man who sported a moustache lampooned so brilliantly by Charlie Chaplin in *The Great Dictator*, and was profoundly insane.

Only it didn't say that. The caption underneath, preferred something more glowing, adoring, a tribute that this man, squared off in the photograph, had paid to a maniac he was happy to serve. Taken at some function or other in Berlin. The date on the paper said it was nineteen forty-three. The man was smiling broadly at his leader.

'My daughter's father,' Natasha said. 'Kurt's grandfather.'

For a moment, the impact of what she had said was lost on them.

And then Harriet heard Neil mutter, 'Christ.'

At the same moment Bebe sat down with a thump. '*Mein Gott*,' her voice was strangled. 'Natasha? How?'

Natasha

I

Berlin, 1947

'How did you find me?' Natasha glanced quickly at the little girl playing with a doll in the corner. Not a doll really, not a proper one, just a piece of coloured cloth, a length of string pulled tightly round the middle to form a narrow waist, another fashioning an oblong head that flopped to one side. The girl wore a coat and a pixie hood, tied under her chin. And yet, if you touched her hands they were frozen.

'I went to the labour office,' Max said. 'You'd registered this address. I've been searching for days. And then I saw your name. Chalked on the wall outside.'

One side of the building had been blown out, but it still had a roof and the remains of one room partially intact, somewhere at least to escape – or to recover – from the attentions of the marauding, savage Soviet Army and their belief that the abuse of women in a vanquished country was their rightful reward for victory.

'Come with me,' he was saying. 'Away from here.'

He bent down and scooped up the child, who instantly curled her face into his neck. 'We'll go to your old house. Away from all this.'

'No. It will be fine.' He hushed her protests that the house had been almost destroyed. He rocked the child gently. 'I can get it mended. And – besides, I promised Valentina, you see. To find Elena. I go to where she might return.'

She hadn't seen him since she was about ten. Barely knew him. That day, when he'd arrived at her home with her aunt and cousin and an Englishman, a careless man who laughed and smoked cigarettes in an amber holder, with a ring of gold at the end that had fascinated her.

They were barely in the house before they were gone. She knew, looking at Max, trying to remember the cousin who was now at the centre of this man's life, that without a shadow of doubt, if it hadn't been for his search for Elena, he would never have left Zurich. Never come looking for her. Why would he? No-one would. But she could not afford to be proud.

'But my mother's house? It's barely standing. Why would she go there?'

'I know it's unlikely, but where else is there? Just before,' his voice faltered. He cleared his throat. 'Just before Valentina was taken, we'd managed to get Elena out of Paris. To Arthur. He was in Geneva. When the war finished and I finally contacted what is left of his family in England, they had no idea where he was. None. And they'd never heard of Elena. Just a letter posted from Madrid, saying he'd married and would be in touch. But he never has. They'd disowned him you see. Feckless, they said. Ran up debts all over the place. And it is true. Reckless, he is. Totally irresponsible.'

'Yet, Elena went to him?' Natasha watched his expression.

'She was passionate about him.' He shook his head, still not understanding. 'I once asked her why someone as clever and beautiful as she is, would simply wait for him to turn up, usually on his way to some casino or other, or yacht, and she said it was because he didn't pretend to be safe; she had no expectations of him, so she couldn't be disappointed. And they understood each other, so that was all that mattered. Living for the moment. She is so headstrong. Almost as bad as him, in a way.'

For a moment, he stared into the distance. 'But how can anyone,' he turned to Natasha, almost in despair, 'find anyone in this world? One that's taken leave of its senses?'

'I have no idea.' She didn't know what else to say. 'I wish I could help. But as you can see . . .' she touched the back of Ingrid's head, now almost asleep on his shoulder.

'Where's her father?' His eyes travelled to a small photograph, tucked into the frame of a mirror. 'Is that him? Where is he?' his voice trailed off.

There was a long silence. Her brain was racing. If she lied, as she had for the last three years, it might work. But somehow she knew that with this man, only the truth would do. He chose that moment to place his free hand on her shoulder.

'For her sake,' he said, gently inclining his head towards the sleeping child.

'I pretend, for her sake that it is him, but I have no idea who he is. No-one does, but he has protected me from so much.'

'Then who?' Max asked sharply. 'A Soviet?'

'No.' Natasha said. 'He used to come to The Kaiserhof Hotel,' she whispered. 'They all did. Those officers. I was a chambermaid. And then, one day, he came and he forced me to go with him. They wanted us to have babies. Their babies, pure children. They wanted her to be adopted, but before they could give her to another family, it all ended. We knew Russian soldiers were coming, and we were abandoned. I just took her, in a blanket, and fled. I lived in the attic of another house with a family for two months until the British came and we were able to come out. I found the photograph,' she nodded at the anonymous young airman, 'in the rubble. And he became my husband. My dead husband. But please. I am not such a girl. Was not—'

'No more,' Max stopped her. His voice was curt, fierce. 'His name? This officer?'

For a moment she just looked at him. He hadn't condemned her, as even her own countrymen had started to do to girls such as her. She let her breath out and crossed to the narrow bed she shared with her daughter, slid her hand under the thin mattress and pulled out an envelope. Silently she handed him a newspaper cutting. 'I recognised him,' she whispered. 'And I kept it – I thought one day—' her voice trailed off.

Max shifted the sleeping child to a more comfortable position on his shoulder. He glanced down at the newspaper, turned it over and read the caption, the man's name, his rank, but he needed neither. Max knew him. Most of Germany did. Then he slowly raised his eyes to look into hers. 'Are you sure?'

'I was given a paper. He was very proud of being her father. Oh, not just her, I know that, many, others. But even without the paper, I can see him in her,' she nodded, stroking the little girl's cheek, as she now lay, breathing evenly into Max's shoulder. 'But I love her,' she whispered. 'So very much. It's not her fault. One day,' she whispered fiercely. 'I find him and I make him pay.'

He looked silently at her. He did not know this girl, not really. This thin, emaciated girl with her child and their desperate life, terrified that she would be exposed as the mother of what that hideous regime called a 'Lebensborn' child.

He looked down at the little girl. She chose that moment to briefly open her eyes and stare up at him. And he remembered Valentina, his adored wife, who had loved him in return, with her fierce, unswerving belief in fighting injustice, who had known Natasha, had felt responsible for her and her mother, even from Paris where at first they'd done so well.

For a while he stared down into the street, careful not to wake the child on his shoulder. So many airmen, soldiers, hidden, so many spirited to safety. So many dead. And now this. Down there, in the street, women, gangs of them, clearing rubble from buildings destroyed by the country he had helped win this war. A line of them, passing buckets of bricks and stones to each other, dragooned into clearing up the mess, to do such back-breaking work, because there were no men now. He knew he had no option. Valentina would have expected him to do it.

'My dear,' he turned back to her. 'Listen to me carefully. This is for your safety. We must get married.'

She stared at him. Marriage? Her brain raced incomprehensibly. He was almost twenty years her senior. He was, she knew instantly, doing this out of the kindness of his heart; he didn't know her or even love her. Oh God. She held her face in her hands. What did it matter? Love had nothing to do with her life.

'Of course,' she said. 'And I can work. I am a good housekeeper, I can pay my way,' she added eagerly. 'We will not be a burden—'

He stopped her. 'No. You will never be that. This is for both our sakes. I will adopt Ingrid just as soon as I can. Then she will have a name she doesn't have to be ashamed of. Meanwhile—'

He slid the envelope into the inside pocket of his jacket.

'Max? What are you doing? Give that to me!'

'No, let me.' His eyes were full of rage. 'I'll hide it somewhere safe. Until the day comes when he will be forced to tell the truth. They all will. I promise you that.'

'How will we live?' she asked anxiously.

'I have a little money of my own,' he said. 'And Valentina made provision for Elena.' He began to walk up and down rocking the child on his shoulder. 'It's better you don't know where it is. But it can be turned into money when we need it. We don't want to arouse suspicion. Don't worry,' he assured her. 'We did it when we got to Paris. We sold a little at a time to rebuild our lives. And we will. And I will make sure that Elena is repaid. Properly, legally, so that if – when – oh God yes, when she returns, I will give her what is rightfully hers. Now,' he said briskly, 'take what you need. We can get there before it's dark.'

For a moment – one that left her feeling briefly ashamed – she hoped Elena would not be found. If she returned, what then? She and Ingrid had suffered enough for this chance to be snatched away, and all because Elena was so adored, so entitled to everything. Don't think, she ordered herself. Deal with now. She would deal with Elena when she had to.

Ten minutes later, her belongings and Ingrid's stuffed into a small suitcase tied with string to keep it together, she was ready.

'Ready?' he said.

She nodded.

II

Berlin, 2016

'How long?' Natasha demanded. 'No flannelling me please. I'm not stupid.'

'Never said you were.' The doctor began replacing evidence of his trade back into a black case. 'The truth? No idea,' he replied bluntly. 'The results are pretty much what the consultant expected. Who knows with heart failure? Five minutes, five months, five years. Keep active, but no stress.'

'The whole world is one long stress,' she pointed out sharply.

'Tash,' Toto warned.

The doctor smiled at the plump little woman standing behind him, who had been, for as long as he could remember, Natasha Weber's companion, had watched over her like a hawk, and fed her a daily cocktail of tablets and capsules that at least helped her move slowly around. The only person, since Max had gone, that Natasha listened to. Over twenty years ago now, he reflected.

'I'll look in tomorrow. I fully expect to find you still with us.'

With a grunting effort, Natasha flapped a hand at him in farewell and then, while Toto showed him out, she slowly crossed the room into the wide, highly polished corridor that led to the dining room, with its tall windows and the late evening sun sending a long ray of light onto the rich Indian rugs. In the middle was a mahogany table; bare, except *for three bowls of flowers placed at intervals down the centre. It used to seat twenty people, and once, at this time of day, the housekeeper and the butler would be busy laying it with crystal and fine china. Not now, of course. The days had long gone, when Max had reluctantly entertained people with deep pockets, who could help shift his vision of low cost housing projects, hospitals, a couple of schools and libraries, from his drawing board to reality. Berlin, then Paris and now Zurich. 'Arcadia', he'd called it.*

'It's what everyone dreams of,' he'd told her all those years ago. 'It means a safe haven.'

And this, she looked round, was her safe haven. Or rather, had been. All of it. Well, most of it. And she'd kept it that way. And until now, there had never been a reason not to.

In Arcadia's wake, of course, and increasingly as his reputation grew, as did the public appetite for every last detail of those who attracted attention, had come those who pursued him for insightful interviews about his success, his philosophy on life, his background. He always refused to answer journalists' questions, disliking, as Natasha did, the alarming intrusiveness of their nature, loathing the modern need for total strangers to know everything about their lives.

'I am a designer, an architect,' he would growl. 'That is all. I am not a celebrity. What I have for breakfast, or the name of my tailor, is no-one's concern but my wife's.'

His wife's anxiety grew and she had become almost breathless when each request arrived and was refused. He was an honourable man and Natasha had to be protected. Her mere expression, eyes wide with fright, her presence, a constant reminder of the long hours she'd worked making sure Arcadia didn't stay just a dream. He had brought Toto into her life. Someone who was, if possible, even more fiercely protective of Natasha's past than him. He was no match for either of them, let alone their united belief in secrecy.

'She's a good girl,' Max had insisted all those years ago.

'You say that about everyone that committee foists on you,' Natasha had grumbled. 'If she is so good, why was she in Stadelheim?'

'A lover on the run, and she hid him. She truly believed he was being framed. She is not a thief or a murderer, but what else could be done? The law is the law. Prison was the only recourse.'

'Oh, all right, all right,' Natasha had sighed. 'Four weeks and then she must go.'

For reasons that no-one could remember, Toto had stayed, moving seamlessly from domestic chores to helping with their charitable work to being indispensable to them. In fact, the rest of the staff grew to fear expressing the mildest grumble about their employers when she was in earshot, so fiercely loyal was she to this rather odd couple who, as far as anyone could tell, slept apart, yet were discreet about the odd and brief liaisons in their separate lives; the only division of opinion between them seeming to be how to deal with the waywardness of their tiresomely spoilt daughter.

And Toto had been there. On the day when the first letter from Elena had arrived for Max. Elena had not been sure the letter would even get to him, but prayed that it would. She wanted him to know that Arthur had died, that she had never regretted her marriage, that she thought of Max, and her mother constantly, and that all her efforts to find him had failed. Toto had simply nodded when Natasha had insisted she was not to mention it to Max.

And then, a few years later, came another letter, passed on by a different solicitor in London from the one Elena had first used, with a change to her address, stating that if they had any information about Max Weber they would be grateful to know of it. And the year after that, the arrival of a private detective at the door, who had not, for which Natasha was thankful, been very good at his job; Toto had easily dispatched him with a convincing display of annoyance that this woman in London should keep pursuing them. They were not the Webers she was looking for.

'Look,' she stabbed at the dates. 'Herr Weber was not even in the country during this time. Check,' she invited, knowing the turmoil of war, and then a wall, for so long, cruelly dividing this city and the country, meant no-one could ever be sure where anyone was. 'I'm surprised you haven't done so. But then,' she regarded him with a haughtiness, which in itself was enough to send any but the most insistent caller heading for the street, 'the chance of foreign travel in such a dull job, on such a slight pretext, must have been irresistible. Now please,' she knew her hands were shaking, 'we will take action for harassment if this happens again.'

And then came the Ingrid episode, but there, even Toto could not protect Natasha. In her grief, after it was over, Natasha had bared her soul to this kind, uncritical young woman about the evening when her now grown-up daughter had appeared unannounced, with Hans, her husband, in her wake.

'Good,' Ingrid had declared. 'No Papa to get cross.'

Natasha's heart sank. Hans avoided her eye. Snobbish, lazy, laden with inherited and meaningless titles, but not a penny to his name, he relied absolutely on Max's bottomless *generosity; although of late, an unwelcome, but resolute toughness, in refusing their endless requests to fund their extravagant lifestyle, had crept in.*

'And Kurt?' Natasha had asked her visitors. Anything to delay the inevitable. Max might be here by then. 'Not with you? I would like to have seen him.'

'Mama,' Ingrid protested. 'We spent the weekend with friends. Kurt would have been bored. Much better he stayed with Kirsty. His Nanny,' she reminded her mother. Natasha shook her head. There had been so many. 'He's only eight. He sends lots of kisses, of course.'

Natasha doubted that very much. He hardly knew her.

'Now Mama,' Ingrid was saying. Her short dress revealed long, tanned legs, a curtain of blonde hair fell past her shoulders, a thick fringe above heavily kohled, startlingly blue eyes. She was quite, quite beautiful. Hard to believe she was the mother of an eight-year-old. 'Please,' she cajoled. 'Can you help? Just a little? We need a small summer home. For Kurt,' she added. 'He can't be cooped up in the city every summer, he needs to swim, fish—'

'Ask Papa yourself,' Natasha said firmly. 'He'll be here soon. But I know he won't agree. Now, have a drink and let's talk of something else.'

Even when Ingrid flounced off, announcing that she wanted to call Kurt to say goodnight, Natasha suspected nothing, and was just rather pleased it was turning into a long call between mother and son. So small to be left so often.

Then, she'd heard raised voices.

Natasha could see her now. Ingrid. Standing by Max's desk. Max still in his jacket, clearly having disturbed her. The door of the small wall safe, behind the leather-topped desk, ajar. The top drawer of his desk open. Ingrid knew that Max – his memory not what it was – had written the combination on the inside of the drawer. She was holding the wall behind her, to steady herself.

'What is this, Mama?' She was ashen. She held out a newspaper cutting in a cardboard folder, a document with a very official-looking stamp on the front clipped to it, with the name of some man recorded. 'Paternity', it said. Underneath was listed Natasha Guseva as the mother, and the child born to her; a girl's name and the date. 'Who is he?'

'Ingrid, no.' Natasha tried to go to her. 'You don't understand—' Ingrid pushed her away.

'Papa?' Ingrid looked past her at Max.

And now, here she was, a widow, still mourning a daughter who had, within weeks of that terrible evening been abandoned by her husband, and in less than a year had taken her grandson to live in Cape Town with a new, extremely rich, lover, away from everything and everyone who might betray her paternity. And she had immediately cut off all contact with her mother.

Natasha sighed. What could she have done? Max so ill, she couldn't have left him to help her only child, when two marriages later and a ruinous life had led Ingrid to her third husband, who refused to take her son. Kurt, at fifteen, should live with them, she wrote, and be raised by two people who could at least give him the chance of a lifestyle that she had been so cruelly robbed of. But, Natasha knew within the first few weeks of his arrival, the damage to Kurt– clever, sharp, furious with the world – with his mother who had put her own happiness before his, had been done.

By the time he had graduated from university, his contact with his mother was pretty much over, as Natasha's was with her daughter.

*

In the distance, Natasha could hear Toto talking to the housekeeper about dinner for Natasha in her room. A number of things began to collect in her mind, until now separate but linked. She had always known in some part of her brain that this day would come, but she had pushed it aside.

Outside, it was a lovely evening, the sun slanting across the terrace, but she no longer wanted to sit out there, listening to the far-away noise of Berlin going home or preparing to go out for the evening. Natasha had no idea where Ingrid was now. And now it was too late. A few more months, the doctor had said. Kurt had just left a message to say he would be dropping in at breakfast on his way to the office. Carefully, she lowered herself into an armchair, just inside the doors, and she knew. It was time.

*

'Special advisor? To who?'

'The Minister of Culture,' Kurt replied, without looking up from his phone. 'Advising them on the arts, charitable stuff. You know the kind of thing. They like having people like me on board; a great track record in business, the right contacts. And no matter how much you disapprove of my social life, Oma, dear, it hasn't harmed the company.'

'I've never disagreed, with that,' Natasha said. 'I doubt even Opa could have done better, but that is very different to public office.'

And it was true. The continued success of Arcadia had been down to this publicly charming, frighteningly clever man. Privately, a complex and difficult one, with his league of acolytes doing his every bidding. Now he was sitting at breakfast with her in one of his expensive, hand-stitched suits, one of the cuffs of his bespoke shirt not quite covering his Breguet watch. Natasha was horrified that she now only felt pity and duty, rather than love, towards the man he had grown into.

'Kurt? Are you listening to me?'

He held up a hand, stopping her, continuing to scroll through endless messages, taking calls. She rarely saw him, even though he could walk here from his apartment just off Friederichstrasse in ten minutes, so this visit at breakfast had made her suspicious.

Finally, he locked his phone and smiled. 'I might need you to help. Just a photograph. A nice wholesome image. The media do rather go overboard on the social scene with me, which isn't,' he chuckled, 'the right look for a rising political figure, is it?'

'Then maybe you should avoid it a little more,' she replied stonily. He couldn't be serious? 'But the answer is no. I am a private person—'

'And it can stay that way,' he interrupted. 'Just a photograph and a few memories of how you and Opa met, started the company—'

'No,' she almost shouted. A wave of fright rose up. 'I will not talk about him – he would hate it.'

'You mean you would,' Kurt retorted. 'Stop hiding behind him. All this reclusiveness, refusing to talk about anything. Mama never telling me why she and Papa split up – and God knows where she is these days. She didn't even go to his funeral. You know she didn't. It doesn't matter. None of it does. Not anymore. If I want to talk about my own grandfather, then I will.'

'Talk to who?' she asked. 'Trashy magazines? Gutter newspapers? Talk shows on TV? Please Kurt – you don't know where it will lead—'

'Sorry.' He pushed his chair back, drained the coffee in front of him. 'It's no longer your business what I do. I was just being courteous. I have to go, they're waiting.'

'Who is waiting?' she tried to take his arm.

'A film company. A documentary director. They begin filming in a week. This is just for background.'

'You can't,' she insisted. 'I can't let you. Listen to me!'

Something in her voice made him stop. And when she was finished, there was a very long silence. He did not take his eyes off her. When he finally spoke, she was bewildered that he made no reference to his true grandfather, only Elena. Instead he said, 'And after all this time you've now decided to get in touch with her?' He studied his nails. 'This Elena? No-one else is there? No other family members I should know about?'

She shook her head. 'No-one. There is no-one. Just Elena, and it was just a card. I hope she's still at the same address. Toto posted it yesterday. I will tell Elena everything when she gets in touch. Kurt, I want to die in peace.' Her eyes filled with tears, 'I am sorry.' She looked up at him, 'So sorry about your mother. I think of her every day – but it never seemed necessary to tell you. And when you came to live with us, she made me swear you would never know. But these days, nothing is private. You attract so much attention, all those dreadful magazines. All those – friends. Someone will start delving into your past. I couldn't let you walk into it.'

Slowly, he pushed his chair back, adjusted the cuffs of his shirt and with one movement, he swept everything on the table in front of him to the floor. A shower of china, glass and silver crashed onto the Aubusson carpet that she had bought when they were no longer poor, but making headway in the world, the light from the morning sun glinting on the shattered pieces that their lives had become.

Chapter Twenty-Five

'Martha called,' Neil said.

Harriet slumped down into the only armchair in the office. Natasha had finally been persuaded to lie down on Bebe's bed. A hot water bottle had been found from somewhere, her boots removed, a cover pulled over her, the lamp by the bed dimmed. A doctor was on her way. In spite of Natasha's protests, Bebe had insisted.

'She'll be in her office in about forty minutes,' Neil went on. He handed Harriet a cup of coffee. 'How is she?'

'God knows.' Harriet took a sip. It was black, strong and tasted like tin. But it was hot. 'That lawyer, Gregor, the one who turned up to see Klara? Bebe turned him straight round and ordered him to find this Toto person. Kurt threw Toto out when he bundled Natasha off to the country. Poor Natasha, she's been frantic. Terrified he'll tell the police that Toto once served a prison sentence. I know, I know,' she stopped him, 'of course it shouldn't matter, and it doesn't, but that generation are still haunted by their pasts. It's why Natasha didn't tell Toto she knew where all this stuff was. Trying to protect her. If she was asked, Toto could then honestly say she didn't know.'

'Don't tell me we've got to find Toto now, as well,' Neil pleaded.

She almost laughed. 'I think Gregor's up to it. Bebe said there is a homeless shelter that Natasha used to donate to. Near where Gisela lived, on that huge estate. Not sure it's any better than here. But she might be there. Neil? What will happen to Kurt?'

'Well, If you're running for advisor to the Minister of Culture or whatever it is, having a grandfather who was up to here in the SS, practically chairman of Hitler's fan club, is not the best PR in the world. Not Kurt's fault, but there would always be doubts around whether he'd inherited some of those genes, those views.'

Harriet stared at the floor. 'I don't care about Kurt. Just Natasha. What will it do to her? People knowing.'

'Who knows? It's still a big deal in this country. C'mon,' he said. 'Martha's waiting. We'll talk on the way.'

She hesitated. 'Neil, you know I haven't got any money. I can't pay Martha and there's no reason for her to do this for nothing. And another thing—'

'Trust me,' he pushed her coat at her. 'Martha won't let a case like this go over something as trivial as money. But she hates to be kept waiting.'

*

A parking ticket had been pasted onto the windscreen of Neil's car, which he'd parked illegally right outside. But it was the sight of Kurt leaning against it that made them halt.

As they approached, a woman jumped out to join him on the pavement. It was unlikely, wearing those heels, that Ilse Huber would be any kind of threat, but the street that ran behind the refuge was not the kind from which you could summon help by merely shouting. Kurt looked ready to kill. When he saw them, he began to lever himself off the bonnet.

Next to her, Harriet heard Neil sigh.

He removed his glasses and put them in his top pocket as Kurt moved towards them, holding what looked suspiciously like an iron bar.

She felt herself being pushed to one side. 'At least it's not a gun,' Neil muttered. 'Now I suspect I'll have a splitting headache for days. Get back.'

In the same moment that Harriet yelled at Neil to run, Kurt tried to grab the satchel from her arms, and she screamed and turned away, hugging the wall, her back to him. He raised the iron bar, warding off any attempt by Neil to protect her. It was over in seconds. As Harriet tried to pull away, gasping for help, she fell into the snow. But instead of the sharp pain of someone hitting her, all she experienced was the sound of Ilse screaming. No heavy blow rained down on her head, no punch to her ribs. She looked swiftly around in time to see Kurt lifted off his feet and hurtled backwards against the wall, where Neil began to systematically crash Kurt's head against the brickwork until he began to sink slowly to the ground. A trickle of blood ran down his face.

She felt herself pulled to her feet. 'Go. Harriet, for Christ's sake, leave him. Are you quite mad?' Neil yelled, grabbing her arm. 'Run, will you? That bar nearly had my eye out.'

'*Liebling*,' was all she could hear an anguished Ilse shriek. Harriet glanced back to see her crouched over Kurt, beginning to pull himself upright.

'Leave me,' he screamed in German at the distraught Ilse. 'Leave me alone. For fuck's sake, you stupid woman.' He pushed her to one side. She fell with an audible gasp against the edge of the pavement.

Harriet's last glimpse of the couple, sprawled, for different reasons, on the wet street, was Kurt scrambling towards the discarded iron bar and Ilse crawling after him, trying to grab his ankle.

*

At the end of the street, when they'd reached the safety of a market square, they stopped running. Neil pulled her into the doorway of a shop that appeared to sell hats. Extravagantly stylish, each perched on a white slender stand, some were hardly hats at all; more works of art. A stream of people, pushing past on the pavement, glanced curiously at them, but no-one appeared to want to arrest or attack them.

At that moment, all Harriet cared about was that they had stopped. She could hardly breathe. Only then did they look cautiously back to see if Kurt was following them. Neil took his glasses from the safety of his pocket and put them on.

Harriet felt sick, her legs like rubber. She slid down, before she fell down, onto a pile of snow, feeling the sudden hard jolt of stone as she reached the ground. Neil joined her, nursing a bruised fist and groaning that he was sure something was broken.

'I'm sorry,' Harriet said, her teeth chattering uncontrollably. 'You might have been killed.'

His breath was steadier than hers.

'Do you think—?' she began.

'No. I don't,' he said. 'I don't want you to think anymore. You're not a very safe person to be around.'

Gingerly, he hauled himself to his feet, trying to examine the seat of his pants, soaked in wet slush, rather than dusted with soft, powdery snow. He glanced down at her where Harriet sat, silently staring up at him.

'And, I take it, you *like* sitting in a pile of snow in a filthy doorway. See? You simply don't think of my health. C'mon. I'll catch my death if I stay here a minute longer.'

He took her hand and pulled her to her feet. His hair was covered in shards of ice, and he was frozen. For a moment, he held her to steady her and she didn't move, just rested her head against his shoulder and waited for what seemed a very long moment, knowing that what might happen next was something she wanted to happen, but only if it was what *he* wanted and not because she'd made it happen. And then, she was terribly afraid of finding out what that was, in case it wasn't what she wanted, so she pushed herself away and shivered. It was a matter of seconds.

'Here,' he said, in a voice that didn't sound anything like normal, 'give me that. It's getting crushed to death.' He took the satchel from her and stuffed it inside his parka. Then he took her hand and they half-ran and half-walked to the end of the street in search of a cab, before Kurt discovered that he was going to have the mother and father of all headaches and once again came in search of them. Speaking was out of the question. For a start they were too cold, but mostly because Harriet couldn't think of anything to say that made sense.

*

275

Harriet thought Martha's office even more impressive than her apartment. It was reached through a glass-panelled corridor, behind which an army of people were glued to screens, phones rammed to their ears. A young man in a grey suit, that looked like it had been created rather than made, led them to Martha's domain which lay at the end. Three sets of tall windows, which overlooked the city from the tenth floor of the twenty-four that made up this spiral in the sky, filled the room with light, even on a very gloomy day.

For a moment, Harriet wondered if indeed it was an office. Every surface was clear, a tall, sculpted glass vase, housing a single pale pink orchid, sat on a vast, chrome desk that could easily have passed as a dining table. Black leather chairs were scattered around the room, designed to make whoever sat in them, wonder why they even bothered with a bed. As she sank into one, Harriet certainly thought as much. But then, the narrow little couch in the room she'd occupied for the last month would have made a park bench seem right up there with a suite at the Ritz.

Martha had clearly arrived only moments before. A brisk-looking girl, with blonde hair swinging down her back, relieved her of a stack of files and stood aside as they came in. Having removed her black fitted jacket, Martha was now striding round on four-inch heels, a white shirt tucked into a pencil-slim skirt. All seemed at odds with the murky nature of the subject that had brought them together.

'Let me be clear,' Martha leaned her hands on the edge of the desk. 'You don't want his grandfather's identity to come out?' She looked at Harriet in disbelief. Harriet did not fail to catch the incredulous glance Martha exchanged with Neil. 'Is she *serious*?' Martha appealed to him. 'After all this?'

Neil spread his hands out in a helpless gesture. 'Don't look at me, I'm just the one he tried to knock into kingdom come. The one who got dragged through the snow, the one who—'

'Oh be quiet,' Martha snapped. 'Harriet?' Martha turned back to appeal directly to her, 'For heaven's sake. What else have we got? Why do you think I made you go to Bebe in the first place? No evidence against him, but I could not rule out that he might try and come after you again.'

'I know,' Harriet said meekly. 'I didn't realise. But I do know. I owe you a lot.'

Martha dropped her head on her chest. 'I have waited for a long time for concrete evidence. No-one talks in this town, but the reason he did all that stuff to you was to stop you scuppering his chances of running the country if this comes out.'

'Just the culture bit,' Harriet corrected flatly.

Martha snorted. 'You want to bet? What you had – and still have – is his whole future in your hands. He knows that. Of course you have. Listen. It's not – of course if isn't – illegal to have such a grandfather. He's broken no laws. But politically?' she began to count off on her fingers. 'Oh please. Who would want such a ghost haunting the government? Socially? In those circles? Kaput. The Bavarian princess hanging out for a wedding ring? Wouldn't be seen for dust, or the money for repairs to the schloss her father was banking on. Trust me. I know those people. Breeding matters. Harriet, we have nothing else. Beating women – which I personally think is by far his worst offence – is the weakest. Prosecution is not impossible, but realistically who will stand up and be counted? Gisela? Still in love with him. His ex? Not in a hundred years, not with what the Upper East Side in New York would have to say about Grandpa. Bebe? Second-hand testimony, that's all she's got. You? Yes, I know you would, but I bet you he's already got twelve people lined up to say they were with him when you were mugged. And now – when you're within a whisker of getting what you want – *Why?*'

'It's Natasha.' Harriet sounded as miserable as she felt. 'I'm totally torn. What happened to her was truly appalling, and all this prejudice isn't fair on her. But then I look at what she did to Elena. Kept her from finding Max, the last link to her mother. Claiming what was rightfully Elena's for herself and her daughter. And I can't blame her. To risk a future for someone she hardly knew? Would you? Martha?' She appealed to her, 'You didn't see the way Elena lived. I did. She was eccentric, I grant you. But she was bright as a button and very, very proud. She would have died rather than say she was stuck for money. She was practically living on the breadline, selling stuff to pay the bills. I could see that. Why do you think I waived commission when I sold anything for her? Why do you think I never asked her to repair my flat? Any other landlord would have been obliged to. But what was the point?

She had nothing. But I tell you, she would rather have had all that, than – all of this.'

She pushed herself out of the chair and promptly sat down again on the arm. 'Her health was failing,' she began, 'and in the end she could hardly get herself to the end of the street on her own, let alone to Berlin to find Max. That's all she ever wanted. And I know she tried. Derek Pottinger said she had asked them to help, but they got nowhere. And now we know why. Just before she died, he told me, she had made an appointment to see him. She wanted some advice but he didn't know what for. But I'm sure I do. And then she died before she could see him.

'And yes, I'm outraged – *furious* – at what they did to Elena, but,' she paused. 'Oh God. I can see that Natasha went through hell. Raped, starving, living in a bombed-out building, clearing rubble off the street to earn a living to feed her daughter. And then along comes Max looking for Elena – not her, mark you – and she grabbed what she could. Can I really, *really* blame her for doing what she did? Having it taken away by someone she hadn't seen since she was a small child? Hardly knew? Oh for God's sake, both of you, what would you have done?'

Martha sank back against the edge of her desk. Neil studied the ceiling.

'Okay,' Martha grumbled. 'I get it. So where do we go from here? And don't suggest we get him for fraudulent phone bills. Unless we're at rock bottom – we'll keep that one up our sleeves.'

'Negotiate,' Harriet said simply. 'Tell him, if he writes a letter to my solicitor in London, withdrawing all his accusations, compensates me for the financial fallout so I can at least get somewhere to live, and then if he puts a notice in the London papers that – oh, I don't know – something about new evidence that's come to light, he apologises unreservedly for causing me such misery, not a stain on my character, etc. and – oh yes – after that, an obscenely massive donation to Bebe's refuge and one to Roots in London, in honour of Elena, *then* I'll keep quiet. And – hang on – there was something else. Oh hell, what was it?'

She stopped and frowned. 'Sorry, just so tired. Oh that's right. If no-one will testify that he has a bad beating habit, then he has to agree to get psychiatric help for his violence. Otherwise he goes to jail. I'd add that he steps down from all public office but—'

'Oh, very good,' Martha said sarcastically. 'Thank God you're not a lawyer. That's not negotiating. It's called blackmail. Only a judge can decide what the sentence should be and based solely on the evidence available. And I can't do that. No matter what the justification, I have to deal with the law.'

'Oh,' Harriet fell backwards into the chair, her legs slumped over the arm. 'Then you tell me?'

A heavy silence fell, all three staring anywhere but at each other. Martha's phone rang.

'Is it on my screen?' she asked this unknown person. She swung her screen round for them to see. 'Come and look. We've traced his grandfather.'

They both got up and leaned over the screen to where Martha was pointing.

'Died nineteen seventy,' she said. 'Living in Argentina. Total drunk it seems. Killed in a bar room brawl. His wife died in Germany ten years later, and their two children, the legitimate ones that is, changed their names and both went to America. So there's another family nursing a big fat secret. Now, if the War Crimes Commission thought he was still alive – and he'd be over a hundred if he was – then yes, Natasha might be useful in helping to find him, but she wasn't married to him and never saw him again after the war finished.'

'DNA check?' Neil suggested.

'No point, unless Kurt tries to dispute it. Or you can find the other children to give a sample, but I think just looking at the photograph of him, no-one could possibly doubt where Kurt got his looks. And why would anyone claim such a connection? Hang on,' she held up a hand as Harriet tried to speak. 'Wait till I get to the end. So yes, you could publicly ruin him, and yes you would bring Natasha down with him. No, wait. Next – and again, this is tricky. There is not a scrap of evidence, beyond the letter Max left in that package you found today, that Elena could have legally laid claim to her share of Arcadia when he died. I've looked, it's a request to Natasha to meet his wishes if *it were possible*. She could – and probably would successfully – argue that she'd tried and failed.'

'I don't think she would,' Harriet pointed out. 'So that's that.'

She pushed herself upright, stretching her back. She felt exhausted.

'Not necessarily,' Martha rose to join her. 'You are perfectly entitled to all the stuff that Elena left you. The apartments in London, Elena's clothes, books. Sold now, but we can get you sizeable compensation – and trust me, I never do small – an acknowledgement from Natasha that you have been horribly maligned. I think that's a given.'

She pushed the screen away from her, looking questioningly at Harriet, who was staring fixedly out of the window. 'Your call,' Martha said.

Chapter Twenty-Six

The news came as Harriet sat on her hands in the corner, on the smooth wooden seat that ran the length of the windows in Martha's office, her back, aching and sore, the shock of the afternoon beginning to kick in. Suddenly she was no longer at the centre of this story; for that she felt both relieved and lost.

She felt like a patient with doctors standing around her bed discussing her condition without the smallest acknowledgement that she might actually want to have a say in the diagnosis and treatment.

In front of her, Martha was listening carefully to two colleagues whose names she couldn't recall, discussing the legality of blackmailing Kurt without Harriet's co-operation and without it actually looking like blackmail. It was obvious from the way they occasionally looked at her, to where she was sitting on her hands, that they had relegated her to the ranks of awkward customer and English to boot. Their efforts were now concentrated on pulling together enough evidence – to wit, Harriet's claims – to show Kurt was a real danger to both Natasha and Harriet, and securing an injunction against him to stop him going anywhere near them.

It was almost five in the afternoon and Harriet's brain was having difficulty in recalling which day it was, let alone helping her say anything that sounded thoughtful or considered.

Toto had been found in the homeless centre exactly where Bebe thought she would be and was already being ferried to Der Hafen. A doctor had pronounced Natasha exhausted, but had been summarily dispatched by her for suggesting that twenty-four hours' observation in hospital would be advisable. All Natasha wanted was for her and Toto to be taken back to her apartment near the Tiergarten, which she had not seen for the better part of five months. It would help her, she had insisted, more quickly reclaim what was left of her life, than being stared at by strangers.

Harriet wondered if she should just quietly leave. Earlier, a black lacquer tea tray had been brought in, accompanied by a plate, piled high with sandwiches, and on another, carefully arranged, small, sculptured cakes. Folded white linen napkins lay in a snowy pile. Except for the tea, the food had largely remained untouched. Unable to string more than two rational sentences together, Harriet fell back on considering how she could commandeer the miniature cakes to take back to the children at the refuge, along with the biscuits in their crisp little white wrappers.

Neil had arranged a later flight to Paris. Sylvia, it seemed, was already there. Waiting for him. She knew that he'd phoned her. Out of the corner of her eye she'd seen him, after a quiet word with Martha, when both had consulted their watches, slip quietly away into the corridor for privacy.

She tried not to mind that, either. That he hadn't consulted her. But then, another voice argued, why should he? This time last month, she hadn't known he even existed, that there was a man alive who would become – what was the word? She shook her head trying to think. Necessary. That was it. So *necessary* to her. Part of her – a rather silly part, she knew that's all it was, borne out of tiredness, of course it was – had thought he might not have gone to Paris. But going he was, to save his marriage. And who could argue with that?

'Harriet?' Martha made her jump. 'We'll need you here for a few more hours, until we get in to see a judge to issue an injunction on Kurt. We'll sort out a flight for tomorrow. You'll certainly be asked to return to Berlin for a further hearing, but that will be covered as well. Is that okay? And I think we can find somewhere more comfortable than Der Hafen for you to stay in.'

Harriet was about to insist Bebe's would be fine, when there was a flurry of activity. Two people came into the room and asked Martha to come outside. Through the glass screen, the looks on their faces made Harriet sit up. Martha's hand flew to her mouth. She saw Neil walk towards them. Instinctively she rose and waited.

'It's Kurt,' Martha said, quietly joining her. 'A plane crash. They don't think he'll survive. He was taking off from an airstrip. In his own plane. Someone said that he misjudged the take-off and hit the tops of some trees. There was a passenger. A woman.'

'Ilse,' Harriet said. 'His assistant. She was outside the refuge. Was she—'

Martha gave her head a brief shake.

Neil sat heavily down beside her. 'No. It wasn't Ilse. She seems to have told the police he'd left in a hurry, it was someone else.'

'No?' Harriet breathed. Her hand gripped Neil's arm. 'No. Surely not? Oh God.'

Chapter Twenty-Seven

Harriet felt sick. Gisela. Poor, poor lost Gisela. Neil had briefly gripped her arm when she gasped, her hand flying to her mouth, his expression telling its own story.

An eerie silence had now descended on the group of offices that made up Martha's kingdom, when only half an hour before, it had been enveloped in a low-level buzz; urgent, controlled, but focused.

Eyebrows had soared when the history of one of the most prominent men in Berlin had been revealed, and by an English woman, who looked like a good sleep and a haircut might help her credibility. Nevertheless, as Martha's client, she was being treated like porcelain, and she was grateful for that.

She shrewdly guessed it wasn't every day someone wandered so randomly into their lives with such a story. But even the dubious clout of being the one who'd brought such excitement didn't help much. Sitting, not knowing who to talk to, or whether she should talk at all, did nothing for her anxiety levels. This, she decided, must be like the moments when perfectly calm people gave up pretending they could manage, and sent out for industrial-sized vats of tranquilisers. The thought of Gisela made her shudder. And her poor mother – she could hardly bring herself to think of it – was probably, right at this minute, opening the door to a police officer to be told the crushing news.

All this must also, (she tried not to think of it), be costing a fortune. No matter what Neil said, any company able to afford this address, these surroundings, this terrifyingly clever staff, didn't pay its bills by working for nothing.

She tried to tell Martha, but was dismissed with, 'We're talking hefty compensation for you, don't worry, we won't be out of pocket. Natasha will be responsible, you mark my words. She'll want to help you. You'll see.'

'Even so,' Harriet insisted. 'You didn't have to help a total stranger. I'm afraid Bing rather foisted me on you.'

'No,' Martha shook her head vigorously. 'He'd do the same for me. We didn't make it as a couple, but we have a – what you call it?' She pressed the tips of her fingers together to demonstrate. 'A connection. That is it. A strong connection. That will never stop. He saved me from myself.'

'In what way?' Harriet asked cautiously. For a moment she thought Martha would ignore her question, which suddenly seemed quite intrusive. After all, she had only met her half a dozen times, liked her but didn't know her. Instead, Martha sat down next to her on the window sill.

'Okay,' she said. 'This is the deal. I had been seconded to a company in London for a year; he was an expert witness on some dispute on first editions of Pushkin – turned out, as he'd said, they were fake, so we won. I thought he was one of the smartest men I'd ever met. In my year as a student, I didn't really know anyone, apart from Neil – I shared a flat with his then girlfriend, we still send Christmas cards. But once I met Bing . . .' the sentence trailed off.

'My family, all my friends are here,' Martha said. 'So I had all the time in the world for him, but he knew when I got back to Berlin, I would be working these killer hours and he would have had to accept that. But how would he occupy himself? Shopping for me? Keeping house? Trying to get to know my friends and family when I was hardly ever there?'

She was sitting next to Harriet now, the nearest they'd ever come to having a conversation that was normal, one that made Martha sound human and not just a sophisticated legal machine with a designer wardrobe. For the first time, Harriet thought she could see what it was that Bing had fallen in love with, and tried not to be curious about this long ago girlfriend of Neil's, at the risk of sounding as though she had regressed to a twelve-year-old.

'And it was him, Bing, not me,' Martha confessed, 'who realised we were living in this bubble. Just the two of us. And the world hadn't intruded. He tried, he really did, we both did, but we didn't know each other. Not enough for marriage and all that stuff.

'So,' she shrugged. 'I came back. And after a while, it stopped hurting and then one morning, I woke and he wasn't the first person I thought about. And last year I met someone – it didn't last – but it made me see that Bing was recoverable from. And if,' she suddenly turned and looked directly at Harriet, 'I am ever asked to pass on a lesson from this, I would say, be careful about your feelings when you're out of your comfort zone. You are a strong woman, I think you would be like me, step out of the bubble, see it for what it is. Realise other people might be affected badly by decisions made inside the bubble. We understand each other? Yes?'

Harriet blinked. Martha's tone was unmistakeable. A gentle warning; not to back off, but advising her to take time to step back. To think. Martha could see the situation, knew the characters involved, in a way Harriet couldn't.

'I am,' Harriet said levelly, 'a world expert on living in nightmares, not bubbles.' She tried to keep her voice light, unconcerned. She probably failed, but so what? She knew, right then, with Martha looking at her with her head on one side, and seeing Neil coming to join them, just what she had to do. 'I just need to get back home, restart my life,' she said, knowing her voice could be heard. 'Not easy, but that's the plan.'

'And Kurt's grandfather?'

There was a long pause. Several people were looking in her direction. What was the point? How would it help? Her life, her past, her future were not all bound up in such a history in a way that Natasha's always would be. It was time to end this.

'What grandfather?' she looked up. 'I know nothing. None of my business. Not my story. And I'm not going to hurt Natasha any further. She's lost a grandson, her daughter and – if it matters at all – a cousin. I'd say if this gets out, then she's got enough to deal with without me adding to it.'

'That's your final decision?' Martha looked briefly towards her colleagues.

Almost to a man, they lowered the important-looking files they were clutching and waited.

'You said I would be compensated,' Harriet said. 'That's all I want. Just enough to get back on my feet and to pay you and Christopher Pottinger. I know Kurt isn't expected to live until the morning, but if you can find some way of letting Christopher know what's happened, he can have something published somewhere to say – well, whatever. But I also think for all our sakes, a little peace is now required.

'Gisela's mother. She will need support, I don't know what you can do, but the last thing Gisela said to me was she needed to get her mother out of that terrible flat. Maybe someone can find help for her. But me? I just want to go home. That's it.'

She sat down on the window sill, feeling overwhelmed and a little sick.

'Come with me?' Neil sat beside her. 'To the car. We can't talk here.'

It was unbearable. All she had to do was say, 'Don't go. I don't know what this is, but it's so important to me.' But she didn't. Martha was right. *So* right. It had been a moment, that's all, an episode outside her own reality. And his. But now the moment was gone.

She didn't know him. Not really. They'd never had a fight, they'd never made plans, gone on a date. And now, the background cast of characters were, one by one, falling away. The glue that had kept them together. And he didn't know her. The only fact that they knew for certain about one another was that she didn't take sugar in her coffee, and that he was married.

'No,' she tried to smile. She stood up and he stood with her. 'No,' she said. 'Just go. Get your plane. No,' she stepped back. If he touched her, she would be lost. If his marriage was dead, he would not be going to Paris, but he was.

'I *have* to go,' he said, trying to make her look at him. 'I have no idea what this is – between us – but a month ago, I was tearing my heart out over my marriage and now—'

'I know,' she said. 'Give it a chance. This . . .' she tried to find a way of describing the odd relationship they were caught up in, but failed, 'is just what Martha said.'

'Bugger Martha,' he muttered.

'No. She's right. It's been a bubble. A moment in both our lives. If you don't go to Paris, you will never be sure. And neither of us could live with that.'

'You don't know that,' he said stubbornly. 'Five minutes. Please. On the way to the car. I want to try and make you understand – I didn't want to mislead you. I tried to be honest—'

'No,' she said more loudly than she had intended. Several heads turned in their direction. 'No. Please. There is nothing more to say. I don't want to hear any more.'

And nor did she want to hear a word of how he was torn, that Sylvia deserved more, or that his marriage needed his attention. She could see it coming and she wasn't at all sure she could bear it.

'It's none of my business,' she said more quietly. 'Neil? Please. I will always, *always* be grateful to you. I will miss you, but I want – *need* – to go home. I need to be in my own life again. Like you do. Please. Go.'

She turned and looked out of the window. She had no idea if he was staring at his shoes or looking after her. Then, in the reflection, she saw him speak briefly to Martha, and Martha glance in her direction. She folded her arms and gazed out over Berlin. When she was quite sure he was in the car and on his way to the airport, she would tell Martha she needed time on her own, slip her parka on, pull her bag over her shoulder, take the elevator down to the ground floor and then walk out onto the street. She would make her way to Der Hafen, say goodbye to Bebe – she dreaded that – and tomorrow she would restart her life. She'd done it before, she could do it again.

*

Gregor, the young lawyer fielded by Martha to help Klara, was the first voice Harriet heard as she pushed open the kitchen door. 'Generally, if the accrued gains – that is the difference between the value of the assets of a spouse as of the *end* of the marriage and the value of the assets owned at the *beginning* of the marriage, of one spouse exceed the accrued gains of the other spouse, fifty per cent of the surplus is due to the other spouse as an equalization claim – sorry? Shall I go over that again?'

'Gregor,' Bebe's voice was weary, 'even if I understood one word of that, what possible assets has Klara got? If she had so much as a bagel to her name, do you think she'd be in here? Now let's get real.'

She glanced up as Harriet came in and mouthed, 'Okay? Talk later.'

Bebe's world had resumed. Harriet, surrounded by the best lawyers Berlin could produce, was, by Bebe's standards, doing okay. She had also dealt with Kurt, for which Bebe would thank her forever. But Klara, who didn't possess Harriet's fierce determination not to give in, and had two children to protect, needed her more.

Harriet quietly closed the door and went into the little room that had been her home for almost a month and began to pack her few belongings. Tomorrow she would see Natasha, say whatever needed to be said and then get the late afternoon flight to Heathrow. It was weird, she thought, that her feelings for Kurt were so torn.

A wicked man, a vain man, a man who hit and bruised his way through life, but then, look at why he'd done it?

She could never think of him with anything approaching forgiveness, but nor could she condemn him for something another generation had left him to deal with. She thought only of Elena and wondered what she would say.

'A plan,' she smiled to herself. She would say, 'always have a plan.' She glanced at the time on her phone and began to text Liz and then James. She would make a plan while she waited for Gregor to go, and then tell Bebe about Gisela.

Chapter Twenty-Eight

Harriet sat back against the back of the booth. James was ordering more wine, Big Jake had squashed himself in between Lizzie and Bing and was holding the floor with his account of spotting Vince, who had now ingratiated himself with a rich, twice divorced, American widow, who lived in expensive but doubtful style in Berkeley Square. Vince had described himself as her art advisor, although his duties appeared to be no such thing.

'You should see the big Nellie,' he chuckled. 'He carries her shopping, drives her around in her Bentley and prays to God no-one finds out her entire family have been told he's the new butler and to address him as Channing.'

Lizzie sat opposite, not saying much. Harriet knew that less than a week after her arrival home, Lizzie was waiting for a private moment to try and understand what the real problem was. Later, she would try and turn her mind to why she found it odd that Lizzie had arrived with Bing and had left with him. For now, she was too exhausted from watching so many dawns break, instead of sleeping; too wrung out to give it much thought.

'Did you ever find out why Gisela was with him?' James asked, putting a tray down in the centre of the table. 'I still can't get my head round what she was doing right under our noses.'

Harriet was sparing with the details. Let them believe it was the lure of a fortune tucked away, what harm could it do? The outcome had been the same, after all.

'I gather,' she said. 'She simply turned up at his office and, according to the dreadful Ilse, Kurt's PA, there had been no argument when he saw her, he didn't even try to make her go away. She just said he needed her and she wouldn't leave him. And then—' Harriet stopped. It seemed unreal. 'And then he had apparently smiled at her and said something like, "We'd better get going," and they left.'

*

The papers in Berlin had had a field day; the news channels had reported from outside Kurt's apartment on the Ku'damm, a helicopter had circled his vast home on the lake at Wannsee, experts positioned against a backdrop of the Bundesbank, which had so little to do with the story it was a nonsense. Their choice was justified by the financial implications for Arcadia of Kurt Weber's untimely death in a plane crash, alongside a woman they described as 'his long-term companion', and the astonishing fact that it looked like an elderly woman – and a frail one at that – now held the major stake in such a vast company.

Harriet had found Natasha in her drawing room overlooking the Tiergarten, sitting upright in an armchair. Her only nod to such a shattering experience was to use a footstool, to not argue when Toto fed her the daily diet of pills that was keeping her – in spite of all the doctors' predictions – alive.

She looked pale and utterly exhausted, with dark circles under her eyes. But her hair was in place and her wool dress neat. An abundance of rings and bracelets on her arms argued to the world that she could not be so frail that death was staring her in the face. So like Elena, Harriet thought, and just like Elena, determined to make her wishes felt.

Toto was in attendance and before she left, Natasha had said they had contacted Gisela's mother to offer her sanctuary.

'They did it for me,' Toto had said gruffly. 'Took me in. And if anyone needs a haven from this ghastly world, it is her.'

'But you don't know her,' Harriet had pointed out.

'They didn't know me,' Toto retorted. 'I came for four weeks and found security and loyalty because they didn't judge me on what I'd done, but what I meant to do. And it means something to Natasha, that even though Gisela had no reason to be loyal to him, for her own sad and damaged reasons, she loved him for better and usually worse. She stayed with him, no matter what he'd done or who he was related to.

'Not,' Toto said savagely, 'like his mother, who even now with her only son dead, has nothing to say. Gisela, God rest her soul, was misguided but loyal, and when he died, Natasha is grateful that he was with someone who loved him. We owe her that. Will you come back?' she abruptly changed the conversation. 'I know it would comfort Tash.'

'In a while,' Harriet promised. 'Once I've sorted out life in London.'

Then Harriet had left and walked back across the park, her coat wrapped tightly around her, but without, for once, noticing the cold, or even that a very watery sun was breaking through the grey clouds, as if trying to make her look up through the leafless trees and lift her spirits.

The depth of such understanding, such compassion for Gisela's mother from these quiet elderly women left her humbled. She wasn't sure she could be that generous. Later, she realised if Natasha was to be allowed to give free rein to her *mea culpa*, and bring some sort of peace and closure to her final days, it was no-one's business but hers how she did that.

If any good had come of this whole saga, at least Gisela's mother would find a haven in which to mourn her daughter, if not her daughter's dangerous lover. It was over. Nothing was perfect. No fairy-tale endings here.

Reality, she had lied to Martha, was her middle name. But really the truth was very different. Just how close had she come to living in a bubble? Now she was going home, knowing she had got what she came for and was able to restart her life.

She wanted none of the jewellery that Natasha tried to press on her, nor Elena's clothes and bags and shoes from a life when she was in her prime. It was a relief to know she would not be obliged to hear about them ever again. And Natasha had been left knowing that if her past was to be laid to rest, then it was entirely in her own hands. Harriet Flynn, jewellery trader, with a life waiting for her in London, wanted no part in it other than as a concerned onlooker.

It was a stance that Christopher Pottinger had been relieved to discover when he had asked Harriet to stop by his office. But she wouldn't. No more lawyers offices if, she inwardly shuddered, she could ever help it, again. Instead, she had said she was happy to meet him for a cup of tea one afternoon, where she assured him she was happy with the arrangements he had made to have a notice placed in the announcements section of a national newspaper, clearing Harriet's name. It read:

Ms Harriet Flynn, the London antique jewellery dealer at the centre of a widely reported court case brought last year by the late financier, Karl Weber, has generously and without reservation, accepted a full apology and undisclosed damages from his family in Berlin, for wrongfully contesting the will of their late relative, Mrs. Elena Banbury. Mrs Banbury, (née Guseva) of Denbigh Mansions in London, widow of the late Arthur Banbury, had named her neighbour and friend, Ms Flynn, as her sole heir. Lawyers acting on behalf of Mrs Natasha Weber, cousin to the late Mrs. Banbury, have now acknowledged that in every respect Ms Flynn is the rightful and legal heir to Mrs. Banbury's estate and now wish to thank her for the care she gave to Mrs. Banbury in the last years of her life.

The next day, The Standard had picked it up, followed by enquiries to Christopher from a couple of other tabloids who promptly lost interest in the entire story when he told them the 'market trader' had politely declined to be interviewed. She now regarded the matter as closed.

'I did my best, within the law,' he began, sitting stiffly upright in the chair opposite her. A waitress, with her hair tied in a ponytail, her skinny frame wrapped in a black apron, made him pause while she clattered cups and saucers and a white teapot in front of them.

'I'm sure you did,' Harriet agreed, beginning to pour for both of them, knowing that the truth was that he had been abruptly forced out of his comfort zone and pitched into a world that was beyond his reality or understanding. Poor Christopher.

'And I just wanted to say,' he paused as she indicated the sugar bowl. 'Just one lump, thank you. Waistline.' He gave a self-conscious smile. 'Noreen is a bit of a sergeant major at the moment on that subject and – well never mind. I just wanted to say – well – I admire your persistence. But we – that is I – well, as I said—'

'Christopher,' she stopped him gently. 'Really, it's all in the past. Now, tell me about the family.'

The look of pure relief that swept across his face was almost palpable.

'Well,' he stirred his tea. 'I've got big news of my own. I've decided not to renew the lease on the offices in Fenton Street.'

'Goodness,' she said, injecting as much surprise into her voice as this totally unsurprising announcement allowed. 'What brought that on?'

'Well,' he said. 'Noreen thought – and I agree – that it would be a great deal more conducive to family life if I were nearer home. I mean these days, with the Internet and communications being so sophisticated, it doesn't really matter where I am. And the time saved on commuting! And as she said, I can see more of the children, so I've transferred the company to Chislehurst. Of course, it means laying off some staff – well at least my secretary – so that will be a loss of course.'

'My word,' she said admiringly, but privately was thankful that he was married to someone as shrewd as Noreen, who quite clearly had realised these last few weeks that anything beyond the familiar and trusted that was his life with her, was far too stressful and she would have to defy both her parents-in-law and rescue their son from their ambitions. And a dreadful, tyrannical secretary.

'That is a big move. Well done you, for taking such a leap,' she finished. 'Very brave. Stay in touch won't you?'

She knew he wouldn't.

*

'And where does that leave you?' William now asked.

Harriet started, 'Sorry. Miles away. Leave me? In what way?'

'Compensation or what?' William asked.

'Okay,' Harriet assured him. 'I'm good. Martha emailed the statement she's worked out for Christopher from Kurt's lawyers, saying they were instructed by Natasha to apologise for the distress, blah blah. And I had accepted an undisclosed sum in compensation. Now,' she smiled around, 'I just want normality. I want this.'

Without warning, William leaned over and kissed her on the cheek. 'Welcome home,' he said. 'I've missed you. And I need to talk to you about James.'

Chapter Twenty-Nine

September never ceased to amaze Harriet. Nor how summer in London, when you least expected it, could be so hot. Almost as hot as her parents' house in Madrid, from where she had just returned. Her second extended visit in six months, this time because her mother's milestone birthday had to be celebrated and her brother and his brood had been over from Brooklyn for the occasion.

The first visit, when she'd only just returned from Berlin at the end of March, had seen her simply sleep. For hours and for days, watched over by her appalled parents, who were coming to terms with the fact that while they had been celebrating the arrival of another grandchild, and texting pictures back to her, their sane, level-headed daughter had been taking wholesale leave of her senses. They had not known whether to be horrified or proud. They settled for proud, but thought it prudent not to tell Harriet that sleep had bypassed them for several weeks after.

She'd loved this last visit; her whole family around her, including her parents' oldest friends and new ones they had made in their new home. But she needed to be in London, to get used to a new flat and a new job.

The flat was easy; it had seemed sensible to buy rather than rent, now that mortgage companies and banks weren't regarding her as someone with a nasty poverty habit and to be kept well away from. She found a place near her new office at Roots, where she was now working full time.

After a while, she found that she could walk past Raglan Parade without her heart flipping over at the history it held for her. When she occasionally saw a former colleague, who had once quickly shied away from her when they thought she was damaged goods, she even found it no trouble at all to simply wave a hand in greeting. Easier still to keep walking, rather than allow them the opportunity to delay her, merely to explain how they had always believed she was badly treated and wanted her to know that. Their problem, she decided, if they felt the need to unburden themselves, no longer hers.

The apartment, on a rather old but inviting square, a stone's throw from Victoria Station, had a small courtyard, with casement doors, two bedrooms and a large sitting room where the evening light flooded in, and for which Lizzie had plans – on the grounds that Harriet wouldn't have a clue. Harriet could only agree.

At night, she curled up on the sofa facing the window and went through the work that she always seemed to bring home with her. When it grew dark, she switched on a couple of lamps and closed her eyes to dream about – well all sorts of things. But even that was getting easier as well.

'This,' James had said with a groan of pleasure easing himself into a chair in the little yard, swinging his legs onto the wooden table, 'is bliss. And so handy on the way home.'

James had taken a job with an auction house and the anxiety of wondering how he was going to earn enough each week to pay the rent on his one-room flat in Shepherds Bush, let alone be able to afford to stay in London at all, had been lifted by the dual arrivals of a regular salary and his agreeing to live permanently with William in Clapham. The rows had subsided, which was a relief, although Harriet was still called on to mediate on a fairly regular basis. Lizzie said they might as well get married; it would at least give them something proper to argue about. After all, Mimi and Colin had surprised them all by slipping quietly away to make their unofficial union official and would soon be moving to Hastings, where they had bought a wonderfully light old house in full view of the sea, with a spare room for visitors, of which Big Jake was keen to be the first. Harriet promised that she would not be long in following.

'They never rowed though,' she pointed out to Lizzie when she heard the news. 'Colin and Mimi, I mean. James and William do nothing else.'

'But that's the point,' Lizzie said. 'Colin has stopped banging on about his book on all those old maps and Mimi loves having someone to look after. You see, marriage changes everyone. It's not easy to walk away. That's why I think James and William might be better off if they married too. Harriet? Are you okay?'

Ah, Lizzie. Harriet frowned. Bing had taken to finding his way to her flat in Shoreditch these last few months, more and more frequently, and often didn't find his way back to his place until a few days later. He also took great delight in trailing after Liz around the country, to fairs and markets where *The Real McCoy* was becoming a familiar sight, and Bing just as much. Lizzie had finally broken cover and told Harriet she was, if not serious about Bing, well on the way. Only Martha troubled her.

'Is he still in love with her?' Lizzie asked one night. 'Should I walk away? You like her, don't you? Is she really as smart as he says?'

'Doubt it, no, yes and yes,' Harriet said crisply. 'If they were meant to be together, they would be.' But in her next email to Martha she made no reference to Lizzie. Or Bing. Martha didn't mention him either. Or anyone really. And Harriet didn't ask.

Her new job helped the sleepless nights, and after a while she found, as Martha had predicted, that the dull ache that seemed to have taken up permanent residence in her chest, no longer immobilised her. Her first waking thought was no longer where he was, or what he was doing. But before she fell asleep, she would stare at the only photograph on her phone that she had of him, drinking coffee at a pavement café somewhere in Hackesche Höfe, a scarf loosely tied round his neck, and she recalled she had told him he might catch a chill. She remembered he had been complaining about a headache that hadn't actually started, but this sharp wind, he had claimed, might bring it on. And he'd mentioned that an exceptionally boring colleague's dinner party that night might have to be avoided, but a very nice place near there would be perfect for a quiet supper. Just the two of them, to see if the headache materialised.

She no longer found herself checking Sylvia's website, but a month after she had arrived home, she had sort of accidentally – okay, deliberately – read that she had won the artist of the year and had attended the ceremony where she had collected her prize, which ran into six figures, with her proud husband in attendance, currently Professor of Maths at Humboldt University.

The creeping paralysis, stopping her from starting the day at these times, was dealt with by concentrating on her new job at Roots. She didn't deal directly with those most in need of its services. The trustees had been able to create a new position of director of fundraising – all made possible by the hefty donation Natasha had given them – and she had been offered the role. She had put a presentation together, of media promotions, ideas for targeting news programmes, fundraising, fun runs and maybe an annual fair in the summer, where she might lure a celebrity or two to endorse their work. Not promising the moon, but a steady income for Roots to at least cover the rent on the office, staff wages and running costs. The Tamworths were beside themselves with delight.

Each morning, for the past three months, she had arrived at the office in Victoria, where, with her staff of two, she would gather for a daily progress briefing. And each Friday evening, she took both of them to the nearest wine bar before making her way home to her new apartment, making sure that every evening and spare moment was filled with friends.

At Christmas, she was going to go to Brooklyn, where another country, children and a chaotic but cheerful sister-in-law would make sure she had no time to think of anything beyond which child was wearing the right shoes and put to sleep in the right bed.

Her mother had been very worried by the sea change in Harriet's career, but in the face of such dogged determination was forced to retreat.

'Have you ever raised funds before?' she had asked. 'I don't think you can count selling raffle tickets for my bring-and-buy stall that time.'

'Very funny,' Harriet grinned. 'The thing is Ma, it's really weird, but I know now, I'd stopped caring about jewellery. A long time ago. I mean, I love it, but I began to want, really want, to do something that makes a difference, (in a much smaller way, of course), like Elena and Valentina did. You understand, don't you?'

'Totally,' Jane said. 'I'm very impressed.'

In a minute, they'd walk down to the bistro owned by their friends Jorge and Larea on the edge of the village, and have a farewell supper before Harriet flew back to London in the morning. She didn't say it out loud, but Jane wouldn't have cared if she'd just heard Harriet was going to run away with a circus, if she would, *could* be happy. And while Harriet might be cheerful, she was most certainly – as far as her mother was concerned – nowhere near that covetable zone that would bring her contentment. That Neil person was involved, she knew that. She also knew that since the age of seven, Harriet had been unbudgeable on anything, until she decided to talk. She would, Jane sighed, just have to be patient.

Instead she said briskly, 'Now buck up. Dad will be waiting. You might need a jacket, it's not that warm.'

*

'So,' James said after Lizzie and Bing had left. The remains of supper were piled in the kitchen, he'd topped up their glasses and announced that as William was away, he was staying – never one to a pass up a chance to simply walk to work rather than battle it out on the Northern Line from Clapham.

'What's the real problem eh?' Harriet had said very little throughout the evening, but she realised she had caught him several times looking at her with a thoughtful look on his face. Finally, he said, casually, 'Still married is he?'

Harriet's glass scraped on the table top as she replaced it clumsily. 'What do you mean? Who?'

'Oh dear,' he sighed. 'Are we going to play guessing games, or are you for once going to give me a direct answer? The maths genius? Oh stop it. You know it is. Lizzie is now so wrapped up with Mr Bingley, she's given up. But I notice these things. No that's a lie,' he corrected himself. 'William guessed. I promised I'd ask. So are they divorced?'

'No idea,' she sighed. 'Well, probably. Oh God. I don't think so. But it doesn't make a scrap of difference. He hasn't been in touch and I don't ask Martha when I email. Then, a couple of months ago, Peter Tamworth said the board at the school where he used to work, the comp up the road, asked him for recommendations for the post of head teacher, starting next year – he'd heard about Neil from Bing and thought he'd be perfect.'

'So how were you involved?'

'Bing didn't want to ring Martha to get his address because he doesn't want to deny his thing with Lizzie, so he asked me to ask her. I was so embarrassed, I just got Martha to forward his address directly to Peter. But I made it plain to her, she was to be the intermediary, not me.'

'Ah.'

'Well exactly,' she sniffed. 'And anyway, it might just have looked like a ruse to get in touch and he may not want to. And he hasn't. That was two months ago, and I know he must have been here or is going to be here to talk to them about it, but I haven't heard a word. I'm sure he thinks I'm just all about me, which is why he hasn't bothered.'

'C'mon,' James chided. He glanced at his phone as a text appeared. William. For once he would have to wait. 'No-one thinks that.'

'You'd be surprised,' she said bitterly. 'Take Dermot. Straight away I didn't even look at how I was behaving. I never stopped to ask if he wanted to marry me. I thought it was enough that I wanted to marry him. I must have suffocated him but I didn't mean to. I didn't think it through. And don't even get me started on Christopher Pottinger. So out of his depth, and I kept pushing him.

'And Elena. I never thought about what I was doing with her. Plenty of times I should have got other people involved when it was so obvious she was so lonely, stopped her being some kind of circus act round the stall.'

'Stop that,' he commanded severely. 'Complete rubbish. You gave her a new lease of life.'

'But it didn't look like it. So easily misinterpreted. I swear I didn't deliberately set out to exploit her, but I did. No, let me finish. I have to say this to someone. I couldn't sleep at night for a long while afterwards, not because I was penniless, which was bad enough, but because I couldn't work out what kind of person I'd become. I drive everyone away in the end because I use them. That's what I do.'

'For heaven's sake, Harriet, stop this,' James exclaimed. 'This is nonsense.'

'It isn't,' she insisted, a year's worth of worry and anxiety welling up in an unstoppable tide of recrimination and misery. 'I didn't even know I was doing it. Look at Martha. I never stopped to think the pressure I put her under to help me or Klara—'

'Klara?' he sounded bewildered. 'Who's she?'

'Just someone at the refuge,' she shook her head impatiently. 'She wanted her children back and I leaned on Martha to help her. Or rather, Gregor did.'

'I'm sorry I can't bear this. We'll come to him in a minute. But did he?'

'Yes, he got the children back into her sole custody, her house back and her dreadful husband isn't allowed anywhere near her. Martha was so busy, and I should have considered that, but I didn't. I had to ask her because it was my last chance to find Gisela. And I haven't got to how I used Bebe as well.'

'Bebe?' he yelped. 'Now you *are* being ridiculous. She loves you. She told me, when she was here at Easter. She said without you, Natasha might not have given the refuge all that dosh, so they gave her a pay rise and now she's renting her own flat in – yes, yes Neukölln. *Of course.* And she can go home at night. You *helped* her,' James finished.

'Bebe earned every last penny of all that,' Harriet reached for another tissue. 'All on her own. I didn't do a thing. I'm a terrible person, with no insights into my own behaviour and a shedload into other people's. Usually wrong, incidentally.

'All this stuff with Elena rebounded on me because I never thought about her, James. I used to avoid her. Doing her shopping or posting her letters was nothing. She deserved more. I should have actually *thought* about her, like a granddaughter would. The way she thought of me. And when she died, I should have refused the money, given it to charity or something, but I didn't. And let me tell you, no good comes from money you haven't earned.'

She began to cry. 'And then everyone kept asking me who she was and to my shame I didn't really know very much. Lorna Tamworth did though. Lorna's mother was interested.'

'Nosey,' James corrected.

'Whatever. And I just couldn't live with myself when I heard what she'd been through; I had to find some way of proving I wasn't a ghastly little opportunist. God knows why I went to Berlin, believe me it was nothing to do with finding out if Natasha was alive or dead. It was to help me, and no-one else. I had to do something. To finish her journey, if you like. But even that, he said, was ridiculous.'

'He? Who?'

'You know,' she nodded towards an invisible person.

'Ah.'

She nodded.

'Now hang on,' James interrupted, seeing her about to launch into another mournful condemnation of her entire life and times. 'Stop beating yourself up. Dermot was a grown man. No-one was holding a gun to his head. He was a shit. The only person who got hurt in the end was you. So draw a line under it. And as for Christopher, please, stop it. He's been saved from a life he didn't want in the first place, and he was useless. So he's got more than he deserved.

'And Elena. She got a lot out of you. She was a bright, intelligent woman, she needed another bright intelligent woman in her life. She could have gone to anyone in that Russian community if she was lonely, all kinds of people approached her, you know they did. She sent them away, not because you made her, but because she chose to send them away.'

'But Neil,' she said hardly listening. 'I did use him. He made it so easy and I was so lost and he came to the hospital when he didn't have to. I mean he came back again the night I was carted in there. And the next morning. He said it was to get out of the cold, but I knew – well not then, later – that he was concerned because he's a good man. He'd have done it for anyone.

'But he was there, when no-one else understood, and he made me laugh and in the end I didn't want to ask him about his divorce because I was afraid of the answer. He was married, unhappy, just wanting to do the right thing by his flake of a wife, but I didn't want to be part of it. And I was hurt that he went to Paris instead of ending it. It was all about me, *me me,*' she finished. She splashed more wine into her glass. 'He was honourable. I wasn't.'

'But he must have got something from you,' James objected.

'Oh he did,' she said wretchedly. 'A headache. Now I've got a permanent one.'

'Then don't you think,' he said handing her a fresh handkerchief, 'it's about time you told him?'

Chapter Thirty

James said he would call for her on the way home. Lizzie and Bing were having a joint dinner party. A sort of coming out, James had said.

Daisy, her new PA, was just going and Robert, who Harriet was supposed to be training in the ways of the media, was simply not up to dealing with closing up for the night, let alone, as she had asked him to do much earlier, contacting a busy news editor at the Mirror. In fact, Robert was fairly useless on so many levels, anyone else would have gently let him go. But Harriet didn't have the heart. It was only his earnest desire to help that made her give him chance after chance. It would have to stop, she knew that. But not tonight.

'Harriet,' Daisy put her head round the door of her office. 'Visitor.'

'Tell him I'll be there in a minute,' she called back.

'It's not James,' Daisy whispered. 'Says he thinks you might be expecting him.'

For a moment she stood very still. Then she turned to Robert. 'Robert,' she smiled at the hapless young man, 'off you go. I'll lock up. And you Daisy. See you in the morning.'

His back was turned to her, as he studied some leaflets on a side table next to Daisy's desk. He turned when he heard her come in.

'I was looking for someone,' he said with a cheerfulness that didn't sound like he was too bothered if he found them or not, 'who knows all about amber. Someone once said you have to be careful with it. I think rubbing it with a cloth was mentioned and a hair from my head—'

'Stop it,' she said. 'That is not funny.'

James chose that moment to arrive and looked uncertainly at her, noting her pale, shocked face. 'It's all right,' she said. 'I'll catch you up.'

James looked from one to the other, raised a slight quizzical eyebrow at her, mouthed an 'oh' as she just nodded, gave Neil the once over, introduced himself and said he'd be out of there in less than half a second. 'Don't,' he warned her in whisper as he passed her, 'fuck it up will you?'

She shut the door after James had gone and leaned against it.

'Why didn't you phone?' she asked, when she felt she could speak. 'To say you were dropping by.'

'Because I – couldn't remember your number.'

'Liar. Call yourself a maths teacher?'

'Could we talk somewhere else?' he asked.

'If you like. I'm just walking home.'

He watched as she locked up, set the alarm and pocketed the keys.

'Not far is it?' he enquired as they set off. 'Only I've got a very busy evening ahead planned.'

'I'd hate to detain you.' She looked coldly at him. 'We can talk here then.'

'Oh well,' he said. 'I suppose a street corner in Pimlico is better than nowhere. Not what I had in mind, of course.'

'Neil,' she said. 'Please get to the point. You know why I rang Martha. I'm just the go-between.'

'Well,' he took her arm and guided her out of the way of the steady stream of people walking past them. 'I'm taking a huge risk here,' he began. 'Apart from the fact that I might catch my death in this temperature.'

'Please stop that. It's September. And you must have noticed, it's also very hot.'

'Um – well – I could be about to make a complete fool of myself,' he studied a passing bus. 'But I wonder if you've thought about me at all?'

She studied her shoes. 'You know I have. I wouldn't have phoned if I hadn't. And I didn't want to if you must know, but Peter put me in a difficult position and I'd rather you didn't make this harder for me.'

'I would have thought my coming here would have made it easier, but then I never can tell what you might be thinking. Could you actually tell me in very simple terms because—'

'All right. *All right*,' she shouted. '*I'm* now going to make a complete fool of myself, but James said it won't be the worst thing I've ever done.'

'He sounds a sensible man.'

'Occasionally,' she agreed. 'But please don't interrupt because I might stop and I don't want to stop. I rang you because I don't stop thinking about you and I can't sleep properly and I've had to make huge decisions and you weren't there to tell me what to do. Actually that's not true. I knew what you'd tell me to do.'

'Sorry?' He blinked. 'Tell you what to do? When? You've never listened to anyone in your life but yourself, I distinctly recall suggesting—'

'Stop it,' she begged. 'You know exactly what I mean. I just wanted to hear you say it, and I just want to turn round and see you there. And to tell me to eat, or to take care. And to take more care of everyone around me. And, oh God, I can't bear it if you tell me I've got all that wrong. And I wish more than anything in the world that I'd handled this better, because I've rather stupidly become besotted with you and this must sound so stupid.'

'Actually,' he said in a voice that didn't sound like his at all, 'it doesn't sound stupid at all. Quite the most sane thing you've ever said, in fact.'

'Are you divorced?' she asked, staring along the street.

'Yes. Three months ago.'

'Why didn't you get in touch?'

'Because I had the rest of the semester to go at Humboldt. Because I knew I had to give my marriage a shot because you don't just walk away after seven years together without some kind of effort and you don't just wipe your hands and say right, that's done, and move on. Because Sylvia is a good person – nuts, I agree – but good. She is. She won't be alone for long, but I didn't want her to think even though I don't love her anymore, that it didn't mean anything at all.

'And,' he stopped as they reached a crossroads. 'This way is it? Thanks. I was a rotten husband in so many ways. And I didn't know how you would feel when you got back here, all your friends rallying round. Not needing me as much—'

'And if I hadn't called Martha?'

'You beat me to it. You don't think I could have come here and not tried to see you? Oh for God's sake,' he muttered. 'Come here.'

Then he wrapped his arms round her and just rocked her to and fro and said he'd be happy to do more than kiss her, except it didn't seem appropriate in the middle of the street in such hot weather. He wasn't that sort of person.

'And I didn't get in touch because as Martha said, I had to be sure this wasn't a bubble—'

'Bloody Martha,' she said happily. She pressed her forehead against his shoulder and thought it might be the best place to be for a very long time.

So he suggested that she showed him where she lived – which he seemed to know for some reason. Then he thought it would be a good idea if they had dinner, which was not, he admitted, as exciting as getting beaten up in Berlin or rescuing old ladies, and not exactly living against the wire, as she tended to. He thought it might help if he told her he had decided weeks ago that enough was enough and she had no say in the matter. He wasn't remotely interested, for once, in what she thought.

'Even though you're prone to getting into fights,' he said, as they reached her front door. 'And it would, of course, help if you tried to curb that side of your nature. But Natasha said – oh sorry forgot to mention – I had tea with her and Toto and I said I was pretty sure you could get to Berlin for her birthday next month—'

'You said *what*?'

'I said her birthday is next month. She's invited me, too. Remarkable woman. Still going, in spite of what that doctor keeps telling her. And Toto said I spent too much time analysing life instead of getting on with it, so I pretty much had to get on a plane. She terrifies me, that woman.'

Harriet started to shake with laughter, which turned to tears; it didn't seem to make much sense at all. Neil didn't seem bothered.

'By the way, what do you think about the job?' he eventually asked, when they hadn't made it to dinner and Harriet was ringing for pizza.

'It's got your name all over it,' she said.

'Do you want me to take it?'

'That's not the point,' she said quickly. 'I want what you want.'

He laughed. 'Then I will,' he said. 'And,' she felt him look over her shoulder, 'is that what I think it is?'

She turned and followed his gaze to a shelf lined with books, interspersed with photographs, some in silver frames, out of which the smiling faces of her parents and an array of nephews and nieces beamed. Other frames, made of wood and painted white or pale grey; several with decorative edges that Lizzie had thoughtfully filled with photographs of moments she had shared with Harriet. And in the centre, small and not noticed unless you were making a careful study of Harriet's private life, a miniature frame, pink translucent enamel, surrounded by pearls with a jaunty bow engraved on the top.

'That?' She reached out and straightened it up. 'Oh, it's just a memento of a journey I once made.'

Once it had housed a picture of a fair-haired young man in a white jacket, a flop of hair falling across his forehead, his expression calm, gentle. Now it was filled with an image of a young girl holding hands with a much smaller child, not more than a toddler. The older girl had a thick blonde fringe, a shapeless cotton summer dress that skimmed her knees, probably aged around fifteen, hand on hip, scowling on a day when the sun was shining.

Natasha had insisted she took it and Harriet had been glad to. She knew from Martha that rumours had swirled around about Kurt's true grandfather, and still did. You couldn't keep that kind of information quiet forever, but Natasha refused all requests for enlightenment by a stream of newspapers and magazines, and seemed not to care that she would take her secret to the grave. Since she said nothing, and those who had lived through the events of this last winter in Berlin had done the same, it could only ever remain conjecture.

Kurt's funeral, of course, was not as well attended as a man of his significance might have expected. But then, the circles he moved in tended not to take chances. Natasha had gone, mourned him publicly and grieved privately. Gisela's mother was still with them.

'It's odd,' Harriet said now. She ran her finger across the frame. 'At first I couldn't stop looking at it, but now it's just part of me, like the sofa over there.' She pointed to the Beidermeir couch placed against the wall.

'Do you think she'd be happy?' he asked, both his arms round her shoulders. 'Elena? That you took nothing, just that frame? Wouldn't she have wanted you to have more?'

'I think,' she said, turning to smile up at him, not needing dreams anymore, 'that she'd know I've now got everything I ever wanted.'

And it was, she told James the next day, when he refused to leave until she'd told him everything, so very true.

Later, as she walked home to meet Neil, she made a detour, as she knew one day she would.

'I'll be half an hour,' she told him when she phoned. 'Just got to go somewhere.'

'Take all the time you need,' he said. 'I'm getting to like this sofa.'

For a long time she had avoided Denbigh Mansions, partly because her route to work no longer took her past there, but mostly because it was the sense of loss, late in coming, that had been so hard to deal with, and she had feared it would haunt her, when she so wanted to remember it all with a sense of calm.

Her heart wasn't racing as she reached the corner of the road, but she knew she was holding her breath. The familiar sight of the line of red-bricked mansion blocks, lining either side of the road was as it had been when she last saw it almost a year before. She waited for a line of cars to pass before she crossed the street and stared up at Denbigh Mansions, once her home, now bathed in late evening sunlight, which cast long shadows onto the little Juliet balcony on the first floor that had been Elena's apartment.

Pots of jasmine now curled themselves along the freshly painted black rails. Long, straggling roses climbed up the drainpipe. The casement windows that had, that night, brought a shower of plaster and screwed-up pieces of card down onto her head, now pushed as far open as the mended and now sturdy hinges would allow.

But none of these she saw. Instead, the image of a tall, elderly woman rose up, her hair tucked carefully under the narrow brim of a straw hat, a bright flowered silk shirt tucked into a plain cotton skirt, leaning on an elegant silver-topped cane, smiled at her, raising a heavily ringed but fragile hand in greeting as she saw her.

Harriet almost raised her own in return, so wanting to talk to her, to tell her all that had happened, to ask if she was happy, to tell her that she would always have a plan. But after a moment she knew she already had the answers she needed. She smiled and turned away.

No need to look back.